D0119404

'…fresh and original. The writing is direct, assured and compelling.'
CWA Debut Dagger 2015 Judges

'An Engrossing read, well written… an engaging and important story.'
SI Leeds Literary Prize 2016 Judges

'I found it to be an accomplished debut, an honest and unsparing story, at times almost unbearably harrowing.'
Cath Staincliffe, CWA Short Story Dagger-winning author of *Witness*

'A powerful story, compassionately told.'
Ros Barber, Desmond Elliott Prize-winning author of *The Marlowe Papers*

'An authentic, courageous debut, told with unflinching honesty and exceptional insight.'
A. D. Garrett, author of the *Fennimore and Simms* series

'*Dark Chapter* is a must-read. It's gripping, compelling and all the more authentic for inhabiting both voices so completely. Stunning.'
Erin Kelly, author of *The Poison Tree*

'*Dark Chapter* had me gripped from page one and I was with its heroine, Vivian, every step of the way. The threat to her is conveyed with nerve-shredding tension, then with vivid horror. Extremely well written and inspired by real events, this is an impressive and powerful debut.'
Isabel Wolff, author of *Ghostwritten*

'This is a book about survival. *Dark Chapter* should be seen as a beacon of hope, as well as a tale of how sadistic and destructive male violence really is.'
Julie Bindel, feminist, journalist and political activist

'Gripping, intense and exhilarating. This book should find its way to the hands of every man who has ever downplayed the magnitude of such a matter.'
J. J. Bola, author of *No Place to Call Home*

'A tour de force not just of writing, but of the human spirit. A definitive novel about trauma after violence – and the ability to recover and to empathise. Both suspenseful and inspiring.'
Trina Vargo, founder of the US-Ireland Alliance and the George J. Mitchell Scholarship Program

'Winnie Li's novel, like those by Roxane Gay, Cara Hoffman, and Jessica Knoll, is an important addition to the literary landscape... a unique and unflinching story about sexual violence... It is not easy to read, nor could it have been easy to write, but every page proves how essential it is that none of us look away.'
Sarah Knight, bestselling author of
The Life-Changing Magic of Not Giving a F*ck

'*Dark Chapter* is equal parts terrifying and gripping, confronting and illuminating, shocking and insightful. It had me in a welter of emotions, I couldn't put it down – and it is also, above all, a brave and brilliant piece of writing.'
Bidisha, broadcaster and journalist

'Affecting and powerful, Winnie Li's work as both a writer and activist shows incredible depth and passion. An important story, beautiful and brutal in equal measure, which addresses a vital topic from a rarely told female perspective.'
Tiff Stevenson, award-winning comedian, actor, and writer

DARK CHAPTER

Winnie M Li

Legend 📖 Press
Independent Book Publisher

Legend Press Ltd, 107-111 Fleet Street, London, EC4A 2AB
info@legend-paperbooks.co.uk | www.legendpress.co.uk

Hardback ISBN 978-1-7850790-4-7
Paperback ISBN 978-1-7850790-6-1
Ebook ISBN 978-1-7850790-5-4
Set in Times. Printed in the United Kingdom by TJ International.
Cover design by Simon Levy www.simonlevyassociates.co.uk

Winnie M Li is a writer and producer, who has worked in the creative industries on three continents. A Harvard graduate, she has written for travel guide books, produced independent feature films, programmed for film festivals, and developed eco-tourism projects. After completing her MA with Distinction in Creative Writing at Goldsmiths, she now writes and speaks across a range of media, runs arts festivals, and is a PhD researcher in Media and Communications at the London School of Economics. She was Highly Commended for the CWA Debut Dagger 2015 and won 2nd place in the SI Leeds Literary Prize 2016. She lives in London yet is somewhat addicted to travel. *Dark Chapter* is her first novel.

Visit Winnie at
winniemli.com
or on Twitter
@winniemli

This is a work of fiction.

Although the novel was inspired by the author's own rape in similar circumstances, and while the two main characters are therefore loosely based on the author and her impressions of that rapist, this book is the product of the author's imagination. The specific details of the characters' lives independently of that crime are fictional.

Save for the supportive friends and advocates mentioned in the Acknowledgements, details of the friends and family members of the two main characters, in particular of all of Johnny's friends and family and their lives and deeds, are completely made up.

The trial never happened, because the real-life defendant pleaded guilty, and so it has been imagined. Any resemblance of any fictional character or organisation to real persons (living or dead) or organisations throughout the novel is coincidental.

For all the victims and all the survivors – and most of us, who are somewhere in between.

PROLOGUE

They say events like this change your life forever. That your life will never be the same as it was the day before it happened. Or even two hours before it happened, when I stood waiting for that bus out of Belfast, along the Falls Road to the west of the city.

Is it melodramatic to think of life like that? Of a clean split struck straight down the breadth of your existence, severing your first twenty-nine years from all the years that come after? I look across that gap now, an unexpected rift in the contour of my life, and I long to shout across that ravine to the younger me who stands on the opposite edge, oblivious to what lies ahead. She is a distant speck. She seems lost from my perspective, but in her mind she thinks she knows where she's going. There is a hiking guidebook in her hand and a path that she is following: it will lead here, up this slope, and then along the edge of a plateau to gain the higher ground merging with the hills above the city. She does not know who follows her. She is only thinking of the path ahead. But some things she cannot anticipate.

I stand now on this side of the ravine, desperate to warn my earlier self of the person trailing her, skulking from bush to tree in her wake. Stop! I want to shout. *It's not worth it! Just give up the trail and go home*. But she wouldn't listen anyway. She's too stubborn, too determined to hike this trail on a day this crisp and clear. And now, it's too late. She is in isolated country, and even if she were to turn back, she would inevitably encounter him, because he is behind her. Watching her.

By now, she has traversed the slope and found the trail that runs between a sunlit pasture and the steep incline of the glen. She pauses for a moment, breathing in the beauty of this green track, the tree branches arching over the path, the bright field that stretches to her left. She has escaped the city. This is where the countryside really begins. It seems like a little bit of heaven, for one last, peaceful moment. But she is perched on the edge, and to her right, the ground plunges sharply into the ravine.

The river below is a distant roar. The air up here smells of manure and sun and warm grass, and lazy insects drift in the filtered light beneath the trees. And then, glancing down the wooded chasm to her right, she sees a figure coming up the slope, trying to hide in the brush of the forest. Something skips unnaturally in the beat of her heart. Only then, does she realize she is being followed.

Now, years later, it is as if I am the one following my earlier self. Haunting her every step, like some guardian angel arrived too late. She parts the branches in front of her, and I do it too, invisibly. She quickens her pace to lengthen the distance between them, and I fall in step. She instinctively knows she must reach the open ground before he catches her, so she tries to cover the last few yards of the path as it clears a ridge. With an invisible hand, I want to hold back the little bastard, lock him into position like a rugby player, while shouting to her to keep on going, to reach the meadow and then abandon the trail, forget about the hike, just head straight to the busy road and go home. But I am powerless to stop it. Events must unfold as they already have.

The past is our past. So I am stranded here on this side of the ravine, watching as he catches up to her. I don't want to see the rest of it. I have replayed it enough times already. If I could just freeze it there – in that final moment, perched between the sunlit pasture and the plunging abyss – then everything would still be fine. Only then, it would not be my life. It would be someone else's pleasant stroll through the Irish countryside on a spring afternoon. But my journey turned out to be a little different.

PART ONE

She sits in the office, waiting for her psychologist to finish fiddling with a video camera. It is a small room, fairly cramped in an academic, state-funded way, and tall bookshelves yawn above her, filled with no-nonsense fare about trauma recovery, patient monitoring, cognitive behavior therapy methods. On the cork board to her right, Doctor Greene has pinned handwritten thank-you notes from past patients and one postcard image of a lone palm tree on a white sand beach.

She turns her gaze to the grey skies outside the window. South London in November. The arc of the London Eye visible in the distance, astride miles of council estate blocks that seem to run in an uninterrupted forest of concrete down Denmark Hill, past Elephant and Castle, all the way to the Thames.

Satisfied with the blinking red light on the video camera, Doctor Greene sits down, smooths her corn-blonde hair, faces her patient.

"So, talk me through it one more time. In as much detail as possible."

She tries not to sigh, she has been expecting this, but a note of exasperation escapes. "Really? One more time?"

"I know it's exhausting for you. But it's an essential part of the therapy. You can do it as slowly as you want."

"No emotion?"

"Focus just on the facts. The details. The emotions will be there, but that's fine."

Doctor Greene is patient, non-judgmental, and that's what she likes about her. That and her librarian sense of fashion and dowdy obsession with cats, so unexpected in a slim, blonde thirty-something. Normally she might feel intimidated, but here she only senses tacit support from the psychologist, a certain nerdish-ness, and a guarded dedication to understanding her patients.

She looks at the video camera, exhausted. The last thing she wants is to talk through it one more time. She has been talking through it for months now, to the police, to her doctors, to the Crisis Response Centre, to the Mental Health Board who assessed if she needed treatment, and now – multiple times – to her psychologist. Always slightly different versions. Some focusing more on the medical details: where she'd been hit, what she'd been forced to do. Some more on her attacker: what did he look like, how did he speak. But always the same scene rises to the surface: the bright spring morning, the sunlight filtering through the trees, the figure with the white jumper coming up the slope.

She could probably recite it in her sleep by now, and in fact, that's what her mind does every night these days, concocting myriad adaptations in her dreams. Sometimes the dreams are with people she once knew, forgotten faces of grown-up jocks from middle school. Sometimes it is in an imaginary place – a science-fiction landscape, half-absorbed from a film she's seen. But there is always the meeting point between forest and field, that liminal space hovering like some safe, illuminated refuge beyond the trees. Only it isn't safe, because the bright field had offered no refuge, and it continues to tease her in her sleep, gleaming on the edges of her consciousness.

The red light on the video camera blinks. The palm tree beckons from its rectangle of postcard.

She clears her throat and starts again.

An hour later, she walks down Denmark Hill towards Camberwell Green, in the last hour of daylight that afternoon. It is a familiar routine now. Tuesday afternoons: take the bus to Camberwell, have your session with Doctor Greene, maybe stop at the Chinese grocery store on the way back before catching the bus home.

She feels constantly drained of energy these days. A three-hour outing is the limit of her abilities. That weird, debilitating agoraphobia, which had plagued her in the weeks immediately after the incident, always threatens to come back. The sun can be too bright, the wind too sharp, the masses of people on the street too loud and incomprehensible. Why risk being outdoors?

There is always the safety of her apartment, her bedroom, her bed.

On this afternoon, her bed seems particularly welcoming as she draws away from the Maudsley Hospital, down the hill, into the real world.

Focus just on the facts. The emotions will be there, but that's fine.

But the thing is the emotions aren't there. For months now, she has felt stripped of any feeling whatsoever. Parties come and go, friends get engaged, her mother nags her on the phone – and she feels nothing. Just a strange sort of detachment from the world, a ghost floating through the land of the real people: observing, noting how the living live their lives and then drifting away. She can't even bring herself to feel sad or angry about her lack of feeling. There is just a blank void of sensation. No emotions, no reaction from this one. Noted.

She drifts into the Chinese grocery store. Wang's Supermarket. She can't read the labels on the products, or talk to the staff in Mandarin or Cantonese, but there is a certain comfort in being amid grocery store aisles that remind her of her childhood. Stacks of ramen packages for 30p each, glistening in their plastic wrappers and promising flavors of Curry Prawn, Spicy Beef, Imperial Chicken. Hefty cans of water chestnuts, straw mushrooms, lotus root. Ingredients she wouldn't think of buying a year ago, but which she had grown up on, stir-fried in her mother's wok or stewed in a winter broth.

Why she is buying them now, she has no idea. They aren't any easier to cook than a Tesco ready-meal. But she had come to Camberwell for her first assessment at the Maudsley Hospital, and the Wang's Supermarket had been right here on the high street, smelling just like the Chinese grocery store of her youth.

As she wanders the aisles, the store speakers play a Chinese-language song, one of those half-wailing renditions seemingly voiced by a suicidal middle-aged woman, singing about love and loss. It's something her mother might listen to, but it holds no meaning for her, other than an uncomfortable familiarity, just like anything Chinese that she encounters in her adult life.

She selects four ramen packets, a can of baby corn and a tall bottle of soy sauce. She pays for them with a five-pound note and steps out of that musty space onto the street, the Chinese soundtrack still ringing in her ears.

A group of youths push past, coming home from school in their uniforms. They are black, all five of them in their early teens, shouting loudly, and she pays them no heed. Drifts past them, oblivious.

At the bus stop, there is another group of teens. There are three of them, white, and they are looking at two girls on the sidewalk. Snickering, and making some comment she can't hear.

She brushes shoulders with one of them as she steps onto the bus. He turns and looks at her for a moment. She can't quite gauge what is in his look – adolescent lust or rage or maybe just annoyance. But his ice-blue eyes lance through her, almost recognizable, and her stomach turns. Sweat stands out on her forehead. Stumbling her way up the stairs, she sits down, tries to quell the rising nausea in her gut. She watches as the teenage boys continue down the street, knowing he is not the one, he is just some other teenage kid with a slight resemblance.

But the shame of it all. That even a passing encounter with a random schoolkid can cause this much disruption.

The nausea wells up, yet she controls it, keeps it at a manageable level. She will not be sick. Just haunted. She draws her knees to her chest and hugs them, curls up into a ball and looks out the window, as the bus draws away from the curb.

*

For a moment, he can't remember how he got home. Still in clothes from the night before, head pounding. Must've fallen asleep on the couch. Late morning, and the sun streams in through the window, too bright. Birds chirp somewhere.

Da is out, and his brother, too.

Then he remembers: just a few hours earlier, swaying in the dark street with Gerry and Donal, drinking a mouthful of cheap whiskey and then another. There'd been pills that night. And dope. He remembers wandering into a pub with the lads, getting chased out by the owner. Then hunkering down at Gerry's and watching porn.

He'd seen this one before. Where she bends over to blow your man and you can see everything, *everything*. That gaping pink hole between her legs, so alien and bizarre. Like some extra-terrestrial mouth out of a sci-fi film, only this one comes with tits, giant ones, enough to make you hard just thinking of them.

He thinks about them tits and already, with the sun streaming and the birds chirping, feels himself stir.

He reckons it's too early. Even though he's got the whole place to himself.

He looks round. Da and Michael are out for sure. But save it for later. Besides, he's got a smashing headache and happens to be starving. Fucking ravenous.

Still reeling, hungover, he staggers to the caravan's cramped kitchen. Pulls open the refrigerator, the cabinets, finds a quarter packet of biscuits.

Biscuits. Fucking biscuits for breakfast.

A half-drunk mug of water sits on the counter and he drinks that, scarfs down the biscuits, leans against the counter. Another search through the cabinets, but there's nothing, only a mouldy loaf of bread, expired six days ago.

His stomach gurgles, hungrier than before the biscuits.

Christ, how long did Da say he'd be gone for? Four days, was it?

He sits back down on the couch, cradles his head in his hands. Maybe them pills haven't worn off. Maybe he's still rolling and can go another few hours without eating. Wouldn't that be grand?

Oh Jaysus, it'd been a good night. The look on the pub owner's face, the three of them legging it out the back door, packets of crisps in their arms. The sting of the whiskey down his throat, the spin of the night air after he took them yokes.

He cracks a grin at the thought of it, wishes one of the lads was with him now. But he can't remember what came of them, or how he got back from Gerry's.

Silence. Sunlight. Then he hears a pebble crack against the outside of the caravan.

It's that little gimp from next door.

Sure enough, a toddler's voice cuts through the morning, the mam shouting something miserable at him from their caravan. Another pebble hits the wall.

He clenches his jaw, realises it's still aching from the night before.

Another pebble. *Plink.*

Annoyed, he bursts out of the caravan, the sunlight flashing into his eyes and he rounds on the toddler.

"Will you quit it?"

The toddler giggles and runs a few steps closer. Brown curls and stupid wide-set pale eyes that just laugh at him. Like he's playing a game or something.

He scowls at the kid again, raising a hand like to slap him, and this time the kid squeals and runs inside.

He snorts and squints against the too-bright sun. Warmer today than it has been. Ten caravans crouch in the April morning, brilliant white against the green and brown of the field, and the sky races along the horizon, crisp and clear with the springtime.

For a moment, his hangover fades and he smells the mown grass and turned-up earth. Nice smells, but cut by the diesel of some engine in the next field over. Sunlight on his eyelids and he can stay there for another minute or two, his eyes closed, just him and the field. Summer is coming, and with it, long bright days when you can go out wearing only a T-shirt and relaxed tourists make easy targets. Warm evenings, girls in thin dresses, girls who want to let you touch them.

A child's voice breaks his thoughts.

"Your da's gone down to Armagh."

He opens his eyes. "Yea, I know."

The toddler watches him from a few metres away, leaning against the corner of the caravan. Christ, you can't take a piss here without everyone knowing.

Speaking of, it's about time for a slash. He turns and heads away, to the edge of the field.

"Where you going?"

He don't answer. Just keeps walking away, feeling the kid's eyes on his back. Twenty metres out, he stands on the ridge of the plateau and undoes his flies for a piss.

The wind pushes clouds along the horizon, and he sees Belfast stretched before him, a cluster of grey and brown buildings rising up in the ugly knot of the city centre, before reaching the sea.

Between him and the city, the glen winds down below, under housing estates and patchy fields. The sound of the river, loud with spring rains, drifts up to where he stands, shaking his last drops of piss onto the ground.

He breathes in the morning air. Best fucking view in the world for a slash.

*

"The West Highland Way. That's the last one."

She pushes the pin into the map, stabbing the mountains somewhere north of Glasgow, and sits down, satisfied.

"Okay, so only five long-distance trails," Melissa says with a note of sarcasm.

"Five trails," she nods. "I can do that. Sometime in my life."

"So… you're still going to be hiking these when you're fifty?"

She laughs. God, fifty. "Hopefully by twenty-five I'll have done all of these. Maybe thirty?"

She is eighteen and sits on her bed in the dorm room. Melissa flops down next to her, unkempt hair sprawling on the dark-green bedspread. For a moment, they rest in silence on the bed, staring up at the map of Europe dotted with its colorful push-pins.

"Viv, that's nuts. You're gonna do these all on your own?"

She shrugs. "Haven't thought about it, but why not?"

After all, isn't that the whole point? Thoreau living in solitude, off in his cabin by Walden Pond. Walt Whitman waxing lyrical about leaves of grass, writing under a tree while his beard grew longer and shaggier with the passing seasons. Edward Abbey drifting down a vast canyon in the American Southwest, the rock walls rising on either side of him, just him and the canyon.

"You're completely nuts," Melissa says, shaking her head. "Meanwhile, I'd just be happy if I could get Danny Brookes to have coffee with me."

"Really? You're still into him?"

"Well, until someone better comes along to crush on."

She smiles to herself. At the moment, there is no one – not one boy on campus – who interests her. Maybe on the fringes of some crowd she has glimpsed a boy who looked thoughtful, different from the others. But boys in general, with their unfunny jokes, their swaggering need to be seen as confident in class… boys don't hold much interest for her at the moment.

Melissa is still gabbling on. "I caught Charlie Kim staring at me a few times in Econ."

"Would you be into him?"

"He's kind of interesting. I've never kissed an Asian guy before."

"Neither have I!"

They both break into giggles.

"But wouldn't your parents want you to?" Melissa asks.

"What, kiss an Asian guy? At the moment, I don't think my parents want me kissing any guy, to be honest."

"You're lucky." Melissa reaches out and strokes her friend's hair. "My mom keeps making these annoying comments. *Have you found a nice boy yet? Any special someone in your life?* I mean, we've only been in college four months!"

"I'm kinda glad my mom doesn't ask me things like that."

Another pause. It's Friday night and from outside in the hallway, they can hear other students getting ready to go out in search of the loudest, most alcohol-fueled party. The boys at the end of the hall are bellowing; the girl next door shouts at them to shut up. Someone on the floor has turned up their stereo and the sounds of Oasis drift through several walls.

"You have the most amazing hair," Melissa coos. She runs her fingers through Vivian's thick black mane.

"It's just my hair. It grows out of my head."

"Yeah, but see what grows out of my head?" Melissa gestures to her own limp brown hair. "If I had hair like this…" She trails off, but continues to stroke the long black strands.

"What?" she asks, curious. "What would you do if you had my hair?"

"I'd… I'd… I dunno, I'd come up with the most amazing kinds of hairstyles for it. I'd wear it different every day!"

"Too much trouble," she scoffs.

But Melissa jumps up, excited. "No, let's do it! Do you have any bobby pins and hairspray?" She looks around the room, but hardly any hair products or accessories sit on the dresser.

"Doesn't matter. I'll figure something out. Honestly, this'll be amazing." Melissa gets up on her knees and begins brushing her friend's hair. "You can wear it to the Sigma Chi party later tonight."

And for a moment, she likes the thought of that. No longer the unsure teenager who only started wearing contacts two years ago. And maybe she can meet a nice boy who isn't a braying jock. Someone who might make her heart skip a beat.

She winces a bit as Melissa pulls tightly at her scalp, too eager with her brushing. But she relaxes as the fingers work through her hair, sometimes plaiting, sometimes bunching the strands into elastics. She sits patiently and looks at the map on the opposite wall. The West Highland Way. The Camino de Santiago. The GR15. Trails that snake their way over hills and through valleys, somewhere on the other side of the world.

*

"Where'd you find this one?" Gerry's asking, as he cracks open another can of Carlsberg.

"In the park."

"What was she doing in the park?"

"I dunno, just going for a walk."

"Anyone see you?"

"No." There wasn't a soul around. He'd made sure of that.

"So why you afraid? Think she might blab?"

He shrugs. As much as saying yes.

"She was also a bit older," he finally ventures.

"How much older?"

And he can't remember. It was all such a blur. He knew she was older and he liked that about her. Knows he asked her how old she was, and she answered straight away. Didn't giggle the way some girls do. Only he can't remember what she said.

"I dunno. Twenty-something."

"Like twenty-one or twenty-eight?"

"Jaysus, Gerry, I don't remember! I was still rolling. She was older than she looked."

"And she looked like she was in control?"

"Well, yeah, sorta. In a strange way."

Even though he had to punch her a few times, squeeze her throat to get her to listen.

*

She is eight when she first sees the book at Barnes and Noble. In the Edgewood Hills Mall, New Jersey. *Legends and Folktales of Ireland*. On the cover, there's a circle of standing stones, a green hillside, a full moon. A path through the mist.

A lone traveler walks on that path, past the standing stones, under the moonlight.

"Mommy," she says. "Please, please can I get this book? It's only $2."

And of course, if it's a book and it's cheap, Mommy can't say no as easy. Books are good for you. They'll make you smart.

She smiles as she turns the book's pages, looking at the pictures before reading the stories. Imagine being that person on the cover, walking on that path. Somewhere in Ireland. On her own. The moonlight silver on the standing stones. Imagine that.

*

"Your brother, Michael... he'll be the death of me." Mam is crying, as usual, and he wants to slap her to shut up. The way Da does. "Just in and out of prison, all the time. And at his young age already. I get worried sick thinking about him."

He says nothing to Mam. She's always griping about Michael. Embarrassing, how much she whinges.

He looks out the window, to the fields outside the caravan. They picked a good spot this time, here in Cork. Not so many houses near. Not so many buffers staring at them. Lots of open space for him and the other Traveller kids to run around.

"I'm going out," he says. "Just for a bit. 'Fore it gets dark."

"Johnny, you be a good boy," Mam says and reaches to touch his face.

He jerks away from her. He's not a babby anymore. Doesn't need his mam touching him like that. What would the lads say?

*

In second grade, when she is six, a speech therapist comes to their class and talks to all the kids who speak funny. That includes her.

One by one, they go into another room and sit with the

29

speech lady. The speech lady has short hair and her name is Jason. It's funny that a woman has a man's name and wants to look like a man.

"And what's your name?"

"Vivian."

"What a lovely name."

The speech lady had her read out some sentences. Then she showed her a bunch of pictures and asked her to say what they were. Rabbit, Red, Lemon, Wheel, Giraffe, Snake.

Could she say the words real slow?

She says them again. Raaaaaa-bit. Rrrrr-ed. Leh-mon.

The speech lady nods.

"Very good," she says. "You're a very good reader."

The next time she sees the speech lady, Mommy is there with her. They ask Mommy to say some words, too. The same words. Rabbit, Red, Lemon.

"Ah," the speech lady says. "See, you get it from your mommy."

Mommy laughs. "Really?" she asks.

The speech lady says she needs to work on the letter R and the letter L. And maybe a little bit of S.

Right now, she is not saying her Rs the right way.

"It's because your mommy is from another country, so she says English words differently."

She never noticed she said things different from the others. Or her mommy.

"So every Tuesday, we'll meet, and we can play some games to work on your Rs and your Ls, and you can start to say those nice rounded Rs. How does that sound?"

She nods. She likes the sound of that, but she notices all the other kids who have to see the speech lady are either the slow kids (the ones in the lowest reading group), or Priya, who is Indian, or Mo, who gets made fun of because his older sister wears a scarf around her head.

It's a little embarrassing to be with the slow kids. But at least the speech lady is nice.

Every week, there is homework she has to do for speech. Funny things, like balancing a Life Saver on the tip of her tongue and curling it backwards five times. That's so her Rs don't sound so flat.

Or pressing her tongue against the back of her teeth and making the L sound. L–L–L.

Five months of R–R–R–R and L–L–L–L every Tuesday afternoon.

Her tongue gets tired, but she keeps trying. Currrrl it backward. Touch the roof of her mouth with the tip of her tongue.

And then, one day in spring, the speech lady tells her she doesn't have to see her anymore.

"Your Rs sound beautiful! You've done it!" She gives her a certificate with a ribbon on it, blue for first place, and a big R with a Rabbit that she can color in Red.

"Now say it for me again: Rachel the Rabbit is Red."

"Rachel the Rabbit is Red."

The speech lady claps. "You should be very proud of yourself." She gives her a hug.

She never sees the speech lady again. After that, no more Tuesday afternoon speech class with the slow kids and Priya and Mo. She's back with the rest of her class, and her Rs sound different now. Like someone else's Rs. Her tongue curls back automatically. It can no longer remember what it was like once to lie flat at the bottom of her mouth.

Currrrl back. From now on, only those beautiful rounded Rs, the way they're supposed to sound.

*

He is three and this is his earliest memory: music. Laughter. Heat coming from an open fire. At night, on a field. Looking up at the stars. Shiver with the cold. Breath puffing into the air. Playing hide-and-seek in the mud, between caravans. Giggling with his babby sister, Claire. Michael knocking him

31

over, then showing him how to punch. Granda tossing him into the air, his ring shining in the firelight. Snuggling up to Mam when the night gets too cold.

The smell of whiskey being passed around. Adults laughing. The fire dying down.

Later, inside, Da shouting and Mam shouting back. He hides under the table when this happens. Da hitting Mam, again and again. Da falling asleep. Mam still crying, huddled in a mound.

She looks up at him, face all dark and wet. He crawls round to her. "Come on, Johnny. Off to bed with you now."

*

Sunday mornings, and she's always sprawled on the kitchen floor, reading the newspaper. The floor tiles stick to her skin, especially in the summer since her mom never turns on the air conditioning to save money.

But she doesn't mind. The Sunday paper arrives as a thick brick of newsprint, all different sections folded into layers. She's twelve going on thirteen, and she can spend hours reading it, while Serena's busy practicing piano. Propped up on her elbows, her stomach pressed against the floor and legs swinging upward, she leafs through the big pages.

Mom walks around her and washes the breakfast dishes. Dad always reads the Business section, which is boring. For Current Events in class every Monday, she has to pick out an article from the front section and talk about it. Once, she cut out an article about how a dead woman was dragged from the Passaic River. "A woman's naked, beaten body was discovered." The boys giggled, and the teacher yelled at her for choosing such a violent story. Guess she was supposed to be reporting on peace talks or a Supreme Court case or something boring like that.

But it's the Travel section she reads cover to cover. Everything from vacation destinations to special cruise-ship deals in the Caribbean to train itineraries through the

Norwegian mountains. There are so many questions in her head: how do you fly to Turkey? What's the difference between all those Caribbean islands? How long does it take to walk the Appalachian Trail?

The newspaper covers North Jersey, and sometimes it talks about a museum exhibit or a play that's on. Then she'll look at the location of that museum or playhouse, unfold a map of New Jersey onto the floor, and try to find the town where it's located.

The map sucks her in, she could study it all morning. The paper's edges are frayed and fuzzy where the map is folded into rectangles, and she has to be careful not to tear the map apart. The towns are all squashed up next to each other, sometimes a river or a highway separating one from the next. She'll try to figure out how to drive from Edgewood to that museum or playhouse, following the familiar highways, tracing down this interstate or that to get to her destination.

She knows that really, they will never end up going to see this play or that museum exhibit. Her parents are too busy running the dry-cleaning shop, and they don't have the money for those kinds of trips. But if she did ask them, if they did say yes, she could tell them right away how to drive there. Knowing how to get there is close enough to actually going. There is some small satisfaction in that.

She will look at the map, noting where the parks are. The state parks spreading as giant green swathes on the map, and the regional parks, and the lakes and the rivers. Try to match what's on the map with what she can remember from drives with Mom and Dad. But the maps always extend farther than she knows. And the more she looks the more she sees how many towns there are in New Jersey, how many lakes, and how the interstates run past the borders of New Jersey into Pennsylvania, Delaware, New York. And that's just this one corner of the USA. She thinks of all the highways connecting all the states, all the different parks and lakes and townships, right across the continent. So many places, she'll never get to know them in her lifetime.

At night, she often has trouble falling asleep because she's thinking about these maps and the places beyond the borders. Imagine the possibilities, towns and hills and valleys waiting to be discovered. If you go all the way across the country, you'll get to places John Steinbeck wrote about. If you go halfway across, you'll hit Kansas, where the cyclone transported Dorothy to Oz. Even close by, in New York City, is where Holden Caulfield walked forty-one blocks to get home late at night.

So many places she can visit when she gets older. She lies there in her narrow bed, wedged between the piano and the corner of the room, and she imagines riding along those highways on the map. Roads leading everywhere and beyond. Sleep can come later; she's too busy imagining. She shoots down an interstate and a string of towns passes her by. She reaches the top of a ridge, like in those TV shows about pioneers, and a whole valley spreads open below her.

*

Him and Mam are going to the Garda station in Kilkenny, where it slopes up from the cathedral. Women shoppers are rushing past. A few old men hang around on benches.

Mam marches right up to the police station. She wanted to hold his hand, but he lurks behind, better for looking at people.

She pushes open the blue doors of the Garda station, and waits, impatient for him to follow.

Inside the lights are bright and it's nice and warm. But they don't feel welcome here. There's a counter and a few men behind it. Michael calls them pigs. They look at him and Mam grim-faced. Stiff and mean in their uniforms.

"Can I help you?" one of them asks. He looks around Da's age, dark hair with white streaks.

Mam pauses. Then finally speaks. "I, ehm... I'm here looking for me son. You have me son here." Her hands shake as she grips her red handkerchief.

The pig's face changes, not in a good way. He sorta grins, looking at the other two pigs, then back at Mam.

"And what makes you think that?"

"You... you found him in the sporting goods shop on Ormonde Street. His name is Michael Sweeney. He's fourteen years old, brown hair. About this high."

She gestures with her hand, above her head.

"Mi-chael Swee-ney," the police says, stretching the name out. He asks one of the others. "Tell me, sergeant, do we have any boy by that description in here?"

"Michael Sweeney," the other one says. "Let me think..."

He can tell they're making fun of Mam. It's just a game they're playing to wind her up. And it's working, Mam's fingers are twisting the handkerchief, twisting and twisting.

"Please, sir, just tell me if you have him."

"And would you happen to be Mrs Sweeney?"

"Yes, yes I am."

"And is this Michael Sweeney's younger brother here?" The pig turns and stares directly at him. He don't like the way he's being looked at.

"Yes, yes. My Johnny. He's only eight."

He looks back at the pig, tries to look cold and mean.

"Only eight?" The police nods at the others. "Tell me, Mrs Sweeney... Are you residents of Kilkenny?"

"I... we..." Mam stops, nervous. "We are staying here in Kilkenny at the moment."

"At the moment... and what do you mean by that?"

"We've been here a few weeks."

"And does that mean you'll be leaving Kilkenny soon?"

"Well, no, not sure. We don't know yet."

"Ah, so you move around, do you?"

"Well, yes, we do. That's how... that's how we like to live."

"How – we – like – to – live," the pig repeats Mam slowly. "And tell me one other thing, Mrs Sweeney... This way that you like to live... Does that also involve letting your son steal from honest, hard-working people? *Settled* people, as I once heard your kind say?"

He is talking straight at Mam now.

She don't know how to answer. He'll die of embarrassment if Mam starts crying again, right here in the police station.

"Answer me, you knacker! Do you think it's all right for your son to go around stealing from our businesses, because he's bored, unschooled, because you don't know how to discipline your twelve children and we have to suffer all the time from the likes of tinker scum like you?

Mam is trembling.

"Mrs Sweeney," the pig booms at her. "Do you think that's all right?"

Mam finally finds her voice, tries to control her breaths.

"No, no, of course not, no. No, it's not all right! And I don't want my son doing this, I just want him to be a good boy, and I don't know why he does it. I am sorry, and I really truly apologise."

Somehow, the way Mam is acting makes him sick. He wants to walk out of the station, forget she's here. Other people don't act like this in front of the pigs.

The pig snorts. "Apologise all you want. That's not going to help. It's us who have to deal with criminals like your son. He's been a terror to businesses since you got here. Stolen from other shops, lifted handbags off the street. We're glad we finally caught him."

Mam looks shocked, but he's known all along about Michael. Them nights when Michael came home breathless, a haul stuffed in a black bin liner. Purses with money in them, phones and fancy make-up and scarfs and all them things women carry around.

"It's dead easy," Michael told him. "Once you get the hang of it. Look for women with prams. They'll never be able to chase after you. Or older women. But if your one has a man with her, that's too risky"

If there were sweets or coins, Michael gave them to him. "Till you're able to pinch your own," he'd say with a wink.

Any money, Michael would stuff into his own pockets. He'd open up all the phones, take out the tiny cards and toss them with any credit cards. But everything else had a use: the phones, purses, key chains, scarfs, even the make-up. Michael would polish them up, put them back in a black bin-liner and knot it tight.

"What you doing with those?" he'd asked.

And Michael just winked at him. "I'll tell you when you're older."

He knows all this but of course hasn't told Da or Mam, and now Mam looks shocked and embarrassed here in the police station.

"Me Michael?" she asks, still about to cry. "He was always lively, but a criminal?"

"You need to open your eyes, Mrs Sweeney. Your son is more than just a lively boy He's a proper thief. We caught him trying to stuff two pairs of expensive trainers under his coat. Where's your son learned to do that?"

"Not from me! I take them to church. I teach them to be good."

"Yeah, well, it doesn't appear to be working. So maybe the best thing we can do for him is put him in a detention centre for a little spell."

Mam seems to be choking. He wants to keep on staring at her, but he ends up looking away. "Jail for me Michael? No, please, sir..." Mam is pleading now.

But the pig just looks down at her. "A detention centre is the best thing for your son, Mrs Sweeney."

"No, he'll die there. It'll be terrible."

"Oh, come off it. He's a little shite and needs to be taught a lesson."

"Oh, please just give us one more chance. Don't send him away this time. I'll teach him. I'll teach him to be better."

"You'll teach him? I think you had your chance, Mrs Sweeney. Maybe if you stopped moving around so much, got proper jobs, and sent your kids to school..."

He hates the policeman something deadly. Didn't like him to begin with, but right there, he fills up with hatred. Clenches his fists, the way Michael taught him.

"How... how long will you send him away for?"

"It's all up to the courts, this matter. We have witnesses, of course, but for something like this, a few months, maybe? It's better to get them disciplined early. Prevent anything worse happening later."

"Oh, please, believe me. He won't do anything like this ever again. I promise."

The pig only laughs. So do the other two behind the counter.

"Mrs Sweeney, you have no idea."

Mam is quiet then.

"The facility is north of Dublin. You'll be able to visit him once a week. So that might affect you moving around so much. But think of it this way, at least he'll be getting three square meals a day. Probably better than, ehm, what's at home."

He looks hard at Mam, and she goes cold then.

The pigs are grinning, nodding, shuffling papers on their desks.

"Come on now, Mrs Sweeney. I'll let you see your son for a bit. No use in crying over this one, he's gone down a bad path. We just have to see if we can get him off it."

The policeman moves to a door on their left. Unlocks it with a jangle of keys and looks impatiently at them. Mam makes for him to come along, and he does. But before going through, he shoots another look at the pig, a black, cold, hard glare. He wishes that pig would drop dead, right then and there.

*

She's working in her parents' shop, tagging the dry-cleaned clothes, stapling the papers through the plastic sheeting, when she hears the news.

It's April, she's thirteen, and she has to do two hours in the shop, before one hour of piano practice, and then her homework. Dad is in the back doing the accounts. Mom's been antsy all week. She knows the Ivy Leagues are mailing out their decision letters, so every day, she's out the door the moment the mailman drives away.

Already, Serena's been accepted into Yale, Princeton, Georgetown, Cornell, UPenn, and Rutgers (which was the safety school). She applied to ten schools in total, and the only big one left to hear from is Harvard.

Mom has been mentioning Harvard for as long as she can remember. Last summer, they went on a college campus tour for a week, driving around New England and visiting the major Ivies. It was the first time they'd gone on vacation in years. She liked walking through the college campuses, the wide green lawns, and the big ancient buildings with the Gothic arches and the vines crawling up the walls. Everything seemed so quiet and peaceful. So old. The tour guides told stories about the buildings, but part of her wanted to wander off on her own, among those stone columns and steps, and get away from the crowd of people.

Anyway, she can see why Serena wants to go to Harvard. They had some of the oldest buildings, right alongside a river, and after the tour, they bought sandwiches and sat on the grass by the water. The college buildings rose up along the river banks, towers with domes and clocks, and it seemed like a whole different world – an ancient, magical world – so different from here in New Jersey.

She looks up as the shop door pushes in, and Mom and Serena are practically running in, big smiles on their faces.

"She did it! She did it!" Mom screams.

Dad rushes up from the back, and Serena's jumping for joy. "I got into Harvard!"

"I knew you could do it!" Mom is shouting.

Dad gives Serena a big hug. "See, I don't know what you two were so worried about."

She feels the joy bubbling up inside of her, too, and she gives Serena a hug. Has it actually happened? Harvard? "That's so cool," she says.

Serena shrugs. "Well, I still have to decide where to go."

"Of course you're going to Harvard," Mom says, as if there's no question. "Now that you got in."

Just then, the shop door opens again and one of their regular customers, Mrs Weissman, walks in. Mrs Weissman is an older woman, sixties or so, with short hair dyed orange and wrinkled hands. Mom shares the good news with her. "Can you believe it? My eldest daughter, she's going to Harvard! She just found out."

Mrs Weissman claps in delight. "I always knew you were a smart cookie. Well, you must be so proud of her."

"I am, I am. I'm very proud of her," Mom says. Despite all the straight As, the piano competition trophies, the high test scores, Mom rarely says anything like this. These things are just expected. Mom turns from Serena and Mrs Weissman, and looks to her, smiling. "Now, I just have to make sure this one gets in, too."

*

He's nine and is going to school in Dublin for a few weeks now. Traveller kids mixed in with settled kids, though not really. There's a big stripe down the middle of the schoolyard. Travellers play on one side, buffers on the other.

Of course, after enough scraps, he ended up in the room for really bad boys on the first day, the ones the teachers don't bother teaching no more. There's a few things he can learn from these boys, even the buffers.

One of them, Joe, must be rich. He can tell by his clothes and shiny shoes. Joe's always too smart with the teachers. Never gives them what they want. Joe talks to the teachers like they're dirt, and they hate that.

He secretly loves it. Wishes he could speak to them the same way.

But he remembers what Mam says: "Don't be giving us Travellers a bad name when you're at school. Be respectful. Listen to the teachers."

But why listen to them? They're boring and they hate me anyways.

Joe asks him loads of questions: where is he from, how long they been in Dublin, what do Travellers eat. Joe says they're lucky they don't have to go church or talk to neighbours. It's the first time he hears a buffer call him lucky.

"You lads have it good. You can always feck off whenever you want."

But Joe is the best when it comes to girls. Always has something new to say.

"You have any sisters?" Joe asks him once, when they are hanging about on the street after school.

"Yea, I gots two. Claire and Bridget." He kind of spits their names out, the way he spit out that stuff the school nurse made him take.

"How old are they?"

"Claire's seven and a pain in me arse. Bridget's just a baby. Just started walking."

"Oh, so they're young. You haven't seen their titties yet 'cause they don't have 'em."

He swallows a laugh. "Why'd I want to see my sisters' titties? That's mad."

"Naw naw," Joe insists. "Titties are amazing. They're like milking a cow, except all soft and watery and nice to touch. Like a waterbed."

What the feck is a waterbed? But he don't ask this. He asks something else.

"You've milked a cow before?" City boy like Joe?

"Yeah, once. At me uncle's place in Wexford," Joe says, nodding. "But forget cows, it's about titties. They're bleeding amazing."

Titties. Amazing. He thinks of the magazines Michael brings home, he's seen a few of them stuffed under the bed. One of them fell open once and the big, stretched titties of a blonde woman gaped out at him. He didn't really get how a woman could walk around with things that big hanging off her neck, and not get dragged down to the ground.

"D'ya get hard thinking about titties?" Joe asks.

He snorts for an answer. He should say yes, but that first

41

blondie in the magazine sort of scared him. The look in her eyes was different from any way his mam or sisters or aunties would look.

"You know you're supposed to, or you're a poof," Joe says.

"I'm not a poof."

"Well, you should start thinking about titties more, because they're the bejesus."

He nods, like he's agreeing.

"You've touched 'em, yeah?"

He shudders thinking about it.

Joe snorts and laughs. "We're supposed to! You touch a girl's titties and then you'll get hard, I swear."

They've rounded a corner now, aren't nowhere near the school. Joe pulls him into an alley, and the cars whizz past.

"How'm I going to get to touch a girl's titties?" he asks. Claire is flat as a board, and Da would skin him alive if he ever tried to touch her.

Joe laughs. "That's why it's good to have older sisters."

Joe takes out a pack of cigarettes and turns it around in his palm. The shiny plastic wrapping on the box flashes at him. "Here, me sister Helen, she's sixteen. She's got a savage pair on her. You can come over to me place sometime and look at her if you want."

What? How? He imagines Joe's fancy home, shiny wood floors, a fridge full of Coca-Cola and ice cream. Him in there? Looking at a girl's titties? No way.

"You don't mean that," he says. They won't never let a pavee boy in there.

"I'll let you," Joe says.

He doesn't believe him.

"I swear. On me mother's fanny, I will," Joe insists. "But ye'll have to do something for me."

What could he do for this kid, who's got everything?

"What d'ya mean?"

"I'm going to ask you for something, and then if you do it, I'll let you into my house after school and I guarantee, I guarantee you'll get to see me sister's titties."

Gua-ran-tee. Joe says the word all posh and clear. He's heard that somewhere before. Some slick man saying something on the radio once.

"What d'ya want me to do?"

Joe shrugs and smiles. "Dunno. Lemme think about it."

"What?" He's never dealt with a buffer boy this slippery.

Joe puts up his hand, putting on a holy show. "Sweeney, me man, just you wait. I'll think of something. I will."

Joe claps a hand on his shoulder. "You're a good one for a pavee, you know?"

No one likes it when buffers use the word pavee. But he says nothing.

"Listen here, I gotta go. But this here is for you. Me mam gives me loads of these and I can't eat all of them."

Joe hands him a chocolate bar, a little warm from his pocket, but it's not been opened. A Lion bar, bright orange wrapper. He's never had one of them before.

He takes it and stuffs it in his pocket.

"Gotta make it home for tea," Joe says. "Me feckin family. Always going on about tea this, tea that. See you tomorrow. Don't forget."

Joe snorts, and is off, down the road.

He watches Joe dodge between cars. Watches and fingers the crinkly wrapper of the Lion bar. Then he rips it off, crams half the bar into his mouth, and starts walking back.

Them girls in the magazines at home. Have another peek, tonight.

Maybe they'll say something new to him.

Flip flip flip, go the girls and their titties.

*

She's never really understood boys, at least when it comes to the sexual part. Someone can seem like a great friend, someone to talk to about movies and politics, drink beer and joke with, and then, late at night, when you least expect it, they seem to want something else.

43

Deceptive isn't quite the right word. These boys are friends, after all. But sometimes a strange current seems to be running underneath it all, threatening to crack the surface, when the whole time she thought she was on solid ground.

There is that one night late in June in Cambridge, after the school year has officially ended. She is hanging out with other Harvard students who have just completed their first year, and are working campus-based jobs over the summer: community service projects, admin work for the summer school. In the haze of these sticky New England summers, the dorms, once loud with parties and gossip and awkward hook-ups, are largely empty. The handful of first-years left will gather to picnic along the Charles, eat microwaved dinners paired with illegally acquired beers.

She finds herself one night finishing off one of these dinners on the tiled floor of a dorm common room. She is with five other acquaintances she hardly knows. In the buzz of your first year at college, anyone can be your friend, another person to speak to and learn from. Two of these five are a couple, a red-headed girl from Illinois and a Latino boy from the Bronx, who sit with their feet touching as they perch on the window-sill of the room, overlooking the quiet expanse of Harvard Yard four floors below.

Then it's herself, a black boy from Texas, a Korean-American girl from California, and a white girl from Connecticut, who was in her Introduction to Anthropology class this past semester. They sit on the floor, swigging from bottles of alcoholic cider.

"Let's go to Herrell's!" the Korean-American girl suggests. "I want to try their latest flavors."

Herrell's. Ice cream. She isn't too excited by that for some reason. On a Wednesday night in Cambridge, when not everyone has fake IDs, there is surprisingly little to do.

But there is no urgent need to decide on any plan. The couple wander away, hand-in-hand, perhaps to some bedroom somewhere to touch more than each others' feet. The remaining four sit talking about their classes last semester, what they want to take in the fall, what extracurriculars they're involved in. She chats to Tom, the black boy, asking him about Texas and the long distances they have to drive in that part of the country.

A summer breeze blows in through the window and crickets chirp from the Yard down below.

"We're gonna start washing these dishes," the two other girls announce and they trundle off to the nearest bathroom.

After a while, they don't come back. She wonders where they went, but she and Tom are having an in-depth conversation about Fitzgerald and Hemingway at this point. He's a nice guy, with interesting things to say. But likes Hemingway, whom she hates.

They are alone, the two of them, and after a few minutes, Tom suggests giving her a back rub.

"Really?" she asks. She hadn't been expecting that.

"Yeah," he says. "I'd like to give you a back rub."

So she lets herself sit between his legs, not too close, her back to him, as he kneads her shoulders with his hands. She feels no electric pulse; this boy is not someone she would consider as more than a friend. It's just a platonic back rub.

"It might be better if you lie down on your stomach," he suggests.

Does she find this odd? She stretches out on the bed, fully aware she's never been given a back rub by a guy before, but there's a first time for everything. Back rubs happen between members of the opposite sex, and they mean nothing, right?

"Do you want to take off your shirt?" he asks.

"No, that's okay," she says. "I'll keep it on."

"Okay."

His hands, firm and masculine, work their way beneath her T-shirt, his fingers stretching the elastic straps of her bra, but still kneading the muscle underneath. To her, there is nothing romantic about this moment. Just a little unusual.

"I like your bra," he says.

"What's so nice about my bra?" she asks, realizing he can't actually see it through the T-shirt.

"It's cute," is all he says.

He continues in silence, and she can't say if she particularly enjoys it or not. It just feels different, having someone you don't know touch your back like that.

Eventually he stops. His hands stay resting on her back.

"Thanks," she says. There's a slight pause and she sits up.

They are sitting next to each other on the bed, and she wonders why the conversation has stopped. She has the feeling she's wandered into unknown territory. What previously was just a casual conversation has become some kind of ritual she doesn't quite understand. Unspoken codes and implicit silences. She wonders if she's supposed to do or say something.

But then, Tom leans in close to her, as if to kiss her. *Kiss her.* Surprised, she pulls back.

Tom sees the look on her face and starts to crack up. His face twists into a grin, as he shakes his head in disbelief.

"I'm sorry," she says, suddenly embarrassed. "I thought we were just hanging out."

Did he actually expect them to kiss? The thought comes as a complete shock to her. So this is how people hook up...

They both laugh awkwardly.

"Come on," he says, standing up. "Let's go find the others." And he pulls her to her feet and they wander out the dorm room, down the empty stairs, to the darkened, green pathways of Harvard Yard.

After that encounter, she realizes how naive she must have seemed.

But looking back on the incident, analyzing it in her rigorous academic manner, she could detect no trace of sexual frisson on her part. It was just a conversation with a random guy. How could she even imagine kissing someone she hardly knew?

She is glad she didn't kiss Tom that night. Why waste your first kiss on someone you didn't want in the first place?

But she is slowly becoming aware of some kind of unspoken language, barely audible, but most certainly there.

The way dogs can pick up on sounds beyond the human range of hearing. She wonders why she is so deaf to this language, and what is so wrong with her that she can't hear it. Maybe she should listen more closely next time.

*

He is eleven when his parents finally split. Michael isn't surprised at all, thinks it's better off this way, but then again, Michael is hardly around these days. He's in and out of that jail for kids half the time.

He's lonely without Michael. There's no one at home to really speak to. His sisters are up to their girly things, Da's out working and when he comes home, he's drunk and rowing with Mam. Which means they'll all get a lamping when he's done with Mam.

Lately, he's started spending time with the other boys in the Traveller sites. He don't have a very good mind for remembering faces and names. But everyone seems to remember him.

"You're the little scrapper. Mick Sweeney's young son, right?" And he's always a little proud to hear this. They all remember Michael, too. What he gets up to. "Here, when's your older brother coming back from inside?"

So he comes home one day. Dinner is quiet and dull, some beans on toast, swallowed down with that lemony squash that makes the back of his throat sting. Michael's been in jail for a month. Claire is washing up the dishes, and he hopes she don't use up all the water, to save having to go to the pump again.

And Da, instead of fucking off as usual, is hanging around. Seems kind of tense, and he and Mam are trading sideways looks all the time. Better than rowing, at least. When Claire's almost done with the washing up, Mam reaches a hand to her.

"Leave that, now, Claire darling. Come over here. We've something to tell you."

He gets excited at first. Maybe it's something like they're getting a new caravan, bigger, with doors that aren't half-

47

broken. But then, when he looks at Mam and Da's faces, he knows it won't be any good news. Been a long time since Mam ever seemed happy about anything.

"What is it?" Claire asks. She sits by Mam, who strokes her hair.

Mam is about to say something, but looks at Da instead. "Mick, are you starting?"

Da grumbles, but leans forward and clears his throat. "Look, children... It looks like your mam and me will be..."

He hesitates, Mam glares at him, and he continues.

"We'll be living in different places from now on."

Claire is shocked, and he is too, but he don't show it on his face. Claire starts to tremble and cry. He rolls his eyes. Girls. Always whinging.

"What do you mean?" Claire asks.

"Well, ehm..." Da begins. "Ehm, it means—"

"It means we are going to be living separate lives from each other," Mam cuts in.

The way she says it like that, so blunt, shocks everyone. Mam, who normally is so soft and sweet with Claire (but not with him), cutting it straight, the way she might slice through a hard loaf of bread.

"But, why?" Claire asks, her eyes all filling with tears.

Mam and Da look at each other again. Mam angry, Da looking kinda sorry.

Da for once seems unable to talk his way out of this one. "Your mam—" he starts, but Mam butts in.

"Your da needs to stop the drinking, else it won't be a good place for you all to live."

He sees a strange look on Da's face. A look he only saw once before when Da went to pick up Michael from the jail.

"So... so Da's leaving the rest of us then?" Claire asks. He can see, almost, a small gleam of hope in Claire's eyes. Like this is what she wanted all along. And if she did, he hates her for it. Claire with all her whinging and moaning. When she was younger, she used to cower in the corner and bawl whenever Da came home plastered. That's probably what caused it then. Mam, seeing how scared Claire was. That's what's making her send Da away.

"Ehm, not quite, darling," Mam is saying. "Da and your older brothers will be going away from us. You and Bridget and Sean will stay with me."

Silence then. So him and Da and Michael will be living as one family then. Who's gonna cook? And wash the clothes? He hopes it won't be him, but he's the youngest, and he can't imagine Da or Michael will want to do it.

Claire starts crying some more, and Bridget, who don't understand what's going on, starts crying too when she sees Claire like that. Mam seems flat and empty, like a balloon when you let the air out. Da turns to him.

"So, Johnny, what do you think of the new... arrangement?"

He looks up at his da. No whiskey on his breath for once.

"It's grand," he says. They won't have to deal with none of this crying from Mam or Claire no more.

Mam is looking at him like she's going to cry now, and he squirms and he don't want to be there.

"My wee babby," she says, and reaches out to draw him to her.

He wriggles out of her grasp. "I'm not your babby anymore, Mam," he says, keeping his voice hard. "You've got Bridget and Sean, and sure, Claire cries enough to be a babby."

Mam looks at him for a moment, blank, then turns her face away.

Da puts an arm on his shoulder. For once, his touch is soft. "Your mam was only trying to comfort you."

He grips Da's arm, harder. "I don't need no comforting. I'm grand."

Da gives him a strange look, turns back to look at Mam and Claire, both crying. A savage miserable scene, this. Him and Da and Michael will be glad to be rid of them all.

"When we splitting off?" he asks Da.

"Well, we'll wait until after your cousin's wedding. Michael'll be getting out before then, and we'll have a massive knees-up before we part ways."

He nods, his mouth firm, the way he's seen Da do.

"And where we going?"

Mam turns back to look at Da. Her eyes are red.

Da is tapping his fingers on his thighs. "I'm after going up to Belfast."

"Belfast?" he asks. He's been there once or twice, but can't remember much of it. They speak funny up there, he remembers Da complaining about paying in pounds. Wandering on empty streets. Walls painted all colourful with big pictures on them.

"We've some cousins up there," Da explains. "There's some good work up that way."

He likes the idea of somewhere new. None of these buffer lads calling him a knacker, throwing stones at him, shouting at him because of his brother. Maybe Michael won't be in and out of jail so much. Maybe there's more richer people up there to nick from.

Mam gets up, she's not as weepy anymore, and she gets down next to him. Hands on his shoulders, looking into his eyes. The tears have left some muck in the corner of her right eye.

"Ye can come down and see me whenever you want," she says.

"You're not coming up to Belfast to see us?" This comes out angrier than he wants.

Mam pauses. "I'll have Bridget and the babby and all. It won't be as easy."

He looks at her. Nods again.

Mam strokes her hand against his right cheek. "Be a good boy for me," she says. "Don't take after your brother so. Make me proud."

Before he can do anything, she swallows him in a hug. Arms clutching desperate at his back. "You'll promise that to your mam, will you?"

She says this into his neck, and he don't know what to say.

"You'll promise?"

He nods, hoping that's good enough. But she keeps clutching at him.

"Promise," he finally says. "I'll be good."

Mam releases him, still holding his arms, and looks at him through her tears. Searching and searching, almost hopeful. Her nose all red, and there's a start of a smile on her.

It makes him feel weird, so he pulls out of his mam's hug. He needs some fresh air.

Another push and he's out the front door of the caravan, running off into the field. It's raining, but feck it. Just keeps on running through the mud, the rain pelting onto his face, mixing with the tears he don't want no one to see.

*

She is standing in the train station in Oberstdorf, on the western edge of Bavaria, in Germany. She is nineteen years old, and has been hired to work as a writer for an American travel guidebook. Daunted at first, because she only started to learn German in college five months ago. But four weeks into her trip, and she's doing just fine.

It's a budget guidebook, so they only give her the equivalent of $45 a day to live on. Which means only staying in youth hostels, or *Jugendherberge*. She's become quite adept at finding the local *Jugendherberge* wherever she arrives. Find a map of the town, orient yourself, start walking. At least five miles of walking, in a new town, each day.

She's learned to keep a compass in her back pocket. The compass has a mirror with a vertical line down it for orienteering, but the mirror is also useful if she wants to check how she looks. Not that she's grown particularly vain, but it helps to be reminded that she looks decent.

Here in Germany, she's had more attention than she's used to getting. Nothing overly lewd. Once in a kebab shop, the Turkish guys gave her a free kebab and winked at her. Another time on a train, the ticket controller spent an inordinate amount of time explaining to her which connections she needed to make. This was all in German, and at the very end, he said in heavily accented English: "I hope we meet again."

She's pretty sure they won't. But it's interesting, perhaps eye-opening, how men react to her: a young, obviously foreign woman traveling on her own, with long dark hair and dark eyes.

It *is* lonely, this work. Constantly on the go, constantly updating information, and even if she has a friendly conversation with someone, makes a friend, what can she do? Her itinerary requires her to move on the next day. Every Sunday night she finds a phone booth and calls her editor and then her mom. At least she has that for regular social contact.

Still, the thrill of the job can't be beat. To see new places everyday, be able to wander in and out of old cathedrals, describe baroque squares and explore hiking trails. This is what she always wanted, all those years growing up in the American suburbs.

Earlier that evening, she'd somehow ended up in a pleasant conversation with three Germans, just standing right there on a country road. The Allgäu Alps rose up huge and real right in front of them, laced with snow at the summits, exactly the way they'd looked in the photographs. The Germans were on vacation here in Oberstdorf. They came here every summer and told her about the best trails to hike. An entire twenty minute conversation – in German! She came away from that secretly delighted at her language skills.

But now, at the Oberstdorf train station, she realizes she's spent too long talking to the Germans. The last bus to the youth hostel left thirteen minutes ago and it isn't within walking distance. It's up on the mountainside, in another village called Kornau.

Her delight gives way to worry. She needs to get to the hostel somehow. She steps out of the train station and cranes her neck, to see if she can spot the village on the mountainside, but it's getting dark. The mountains cast long shadows across the valley. Storm clouds have been building up all evening, and now it starts to rain.

There's a taxi pulled up at the train station, and she asks in German how much it would cost to get to Kornau.

"Fourteen marks," the man replies. The equivalent of seven dollars. She can't spend that.

She turns away from the taxi driver, and starts to panic. It's getting dark, it's raining, and the youth hostel seems unreachable. She could find a hotel somewhere in town, but at this late hour, it'd probably be impossible. Not to mention, beyond her budget. *How could I be that stupid, missing the last bus?*

At that moment, she sees someone else get in the taxi, and it pulls away. Unsure of what to do, she hesitates on the sidewalk. She resists the urge to cry and realizes how tired she is from walking the entire day.

In front of her, there's a parked car and the window rolls down. A man leans out.

"Brauchst du Hilfe?" Do you need help?

She sizes him up, unsure of how much information to reveal. The man seems fairly young, clean-shaven. Blond and blue-eyed like everyone else here. But at this point, she's grateful just to have someone ask if she's okay.

"I, um, I missed the last bus to the youth hostel," she replies in German.

"You can wait for a cab?" he suggests, gesturing to the empty taxi rank.

"I don't have enough money," she admits. *At least now he won't try to rob me.*

He pauses for a moment. "I can drive you there, if you're okay with that."

She can't believe her luck. *Or is it luck? Can she trust this man?*

"Are you sure? It's kind of far." She explains it's in another village.

He nods. It's not a problem for him to drive her.

"Um... *ein Moment, bitte.*"

What have they always said since childhood? Don't get into cars with strangers. But what if you're in a foreign country, you're low on money, and you have no other way to get to the youth hostel?

She looks around her. There's no one to be seen. She peers through the window into the back seat. There are children's toys there, a rattle, a few stuffed animals, and even a child's car seat. He's a father. He's safe enough.

She nods. Okay, he can drive her. He gets out and puts her backpack in the car's trunk. She wonders if that was wise to let him do that, but to request otherwise would seem rude.

They both get into the front seat, and drive off into the lowering evening. Raindrops speckle the windshield, and he turns on the wipers.

"*Bist du Chinesich?*" he asks.

"*Ich bin Amerikanerin,*" she explains and continues in German. "My parents are Chinese."

Conversation is stilted. It's obvious he wants to speak more in depth, but it's also obvious her German has limitations. Gone is the confidence she had speaking to the German tourists on the open road, standing in full view of the mountains. Now she's strapped in by the seatbelt, and she peers through the misted space cleared by the windshield wipers, out into the evening.

They drive for ten minutes through the darkening landscape, the car climbing along empty roads, up the mountainside.

Oberstdorf appears below them, a cluster of lights at the bottom of the valley.

She asks him what his job is and he explains, but the German is too dense, she can't understand what he's saying. Sounds like something mechanical. Or scientific.

"Are you traveling on your own?" he asks.

"No," she replies. "I'm going to meet a friend at the youth hostel."

That's what the guidebook editors told her to always say, as a woman traveling on her own. The precautions she needs to take: make up an imaginary friend, put your backpack in the empty seat across from you, don't hitchhike.

She checks her map against the road signs they pass, gives a few directions. He follows along, offering no objections.

Then they pass a sign. She could swear it indicated a turn-off for Kornau. It's pitch black now, and she strains her eyes in the gloom ahead for the next turn-off.

They keep on driving. Another sign rears up in the headlights, then passes behind them, but there's no mention of Kornau.

Apprehension lodges in her throat. Do I say something? Does he know where he's going? Maybe wait till they pass one more sign...

"Hey," she cuts in. "I think we might have passed the turn-off we need."

He looks at her. "Oh really?"

"Yeah," she insists. Up ahead, there's a fork in the road with a more detailed sign. "Can you stop there so we can check that?"

He looks at her with what seems like a certain amusement. "Sure, no problem."

He pulls over in front of the sign, and she gets out, consults the place names and cross-references them on her map. Yes, they did need to turn back there.

She gets back in and indicates where they are on the map, where they need to go. She's aware of him looking at her this whole time. He's not looking at the map.

This makes her feel uncomfortable, but she plows ahead, no-nonsense, masking her anxiety.

"So is that okay? We just need to go back and make that other turning."

He nods and grins at her. Why isn't he starting the car?

His right-hand fingers the keys in the ignition. Then he turns and asks her something. "*Wollen Sie heute Abend mit mir schlafen?*"

She translates it in her mind almost instantaneously: do you want to sleep with me tonight? Her heart nearly stops. Stay calm. Did he really just ask that? What should she say? What the hell has she just gotten herself into?

"*Nein,*" she says rather adamantly. God, if only her German were better. "*Ich habe keine Freizeit.*"

I have no free time. That's the best she can do in German.

"I have to meet my friend at the youth hostel."

He nods. *"Aber ich werde dir Geld geben..."*

Yes, but I'll give you money...

Outrage floods her, and fear, but she has to calculate the best approach.

"No," she repeats in German. "I told you, I don't have any free time. I really have to be at the youth hostel now, my friend is waiting for me."

He's still looking at her.

She shifts her gaze out the windshield, her jaw set, looking determined. Just act decisive, like you know what you're doing. Inside, she's livid, her mind racing through her options. She could just get out of the car now and walk away, but her backpack is in the trunk.

The rain smatters the windshield, the downpour heavy now.

Finally, he turns away. "Okay." He turns on the ignition, and wheels the car back onto the road, heading in the direction they just came.

She is on tenterhooks as the car continues through the dark and the rain. Expecting the guy to do something violent any moment. She could attack him from where she's sitting, she could grab the wheel and try to steer the car in a certain direction, but what would that do? She could open the door and roll out of the car while it's still moving...

No, she's best off sitting here, strapped in, waiting to see what he'll do, a prisoner of his good or bad intentions.

But he's driving in the right direction, rain beating against the car in the summer squall, and minutes later, he's turning onto the Kornau road, as directed. And then, miraculously, they're pulling up to the youth hostel, an immaculate-looking white building rearing up in the darkness.

She's never been so relieved to see a youth hostel.

Another minute and he's opening the trunk of the car, handing her the backpack. She straps it on in the rain, nods, and thanks him. For what? For driving her here and not violently raping her? For letting her live?

She doesn't dwell on the possibilities. Just get inside the youth hostel and don't look back. The man seems awkward now with his advance rebuffed. He holds his hand out to say goodbye. "Enjoy the rest of your trip." She shakes it.

She doesn't even wait to see him drive off. She pushes in through the front doors of the hostel, it's bright and warm inside. She hopes they haven't closed the reception yet. She edges up to the desk, her hair wet with rain, the backpack straps digging into her shoulders. Rings the bell and waits impatiently for someone to come. Still not quite believing that she's safe, she's out of the car, she'll never have to see that man again. Her heartbeat is starting to slow down.

Someone steps behind the desk. "Got caught in the rain?"

She looks at whoever said that. It's a young man grinning at her, blue eyes, blond hair. A German version of Leonardo DiCaprio. *This* is the guy who works here? To go from that potential horror show inside the man's car to this...

"Yes." She shrugs, and flashes a smile in return. She replies in German. "I got a little delayed. But I have a reservation for tonight."

"I know," he answers. "We've been waiting for you." His eyes smile at her.

"So I can still check in then?"

"Absolutely."

She looks around the reception area, musing an unfamiliar, reckless thought at the back of her mind. "Do you guys sell any beer here? Because I could definitely use a drink."

The young man leans in conspiratorially. "We're not supposed to sell any, but I can give you some from my stash."

"Yeah?" And something, the adrenaline from before, or the thrill of having escaped, fear reshaping into something else, something shifts in her, makes her bolder than she'd normally be. She looks at him, peering straight into his blue eyes.

His eyes don't look away. And she thinks, What is there to lose? By tomorrow, I'll be in another town.

"Thanks," she says. "But I kind of don't want to drink it on my own."

*

In Belfast, he starts to envy Michael and the older lads because they can get these skanky girls. You know, the ones who wear bright lipstick and tight clothes and stand in that way which shows off their tits, making you all hard if you look at them long enough.

But they'll laugh in his face if he ever had a go at them. One of them did that to him once, when he chatted her up in the back room of Flanagan's.

"What, is your little brother trying it on with me?" the beour asked Michael. Her big hoop earrings dangled above her tits.

Gerry and Donal and everyone laughed at him, and he wanted to grab Michael's pint and ram it into his face, broken glass and all.

"How old are you?" she asked. She was wearing black make-up around her eyes and her top was low-cut. He kept trying not to look down there.

"How old you think I am?"

But Michael and the rest of them only laughed. Her, too.

"Dunno, sixteen?"

Truth was, he was thirteen when that happened. Michael bought him another pint and said he'd teach him in time, how to get your way with them beours. Or with anyone, really.

First rule is always act like you're older, and everyone will believe it. Part of the beauty of being a Traveller is that no one really knows where you're from. They can't place you, can't tag a name to a face or an age to a name. You're invisible, you can be whoever you want.

You chat them up with your jokes and your charm. Then you're gone. With their purse. And maybe their phone.

He learns to use this to his advantage. He listens in on settled people's conversations, picks up names of places and cars and shiny objects that they're proud of. Tries inserting these names into his own blather somewhere down the line. You can never hear too much.

"Mallorca... now there's a gorgeous place. The beaches, the food, the mountains. Could live there all summer."

"Oh absolutely. I much prefer Mallorca to Ibiza."

A group of posh 20-somethings are saying this, outside a wine bar near Victoria Square one June evening. The men wear blue shirts, fancy leather belts, and wankery shoes. The women have on dresses that wrap around their tits and hips. Earrings and bracelets that sparkle when they move, designer handbags with posh logos.

He is hovering nearby, sketching out the best handbag to lift. Not the red one – your one's not letting go of hers. And not the big brown bag, looks too heavy. But there's your last woman: the drunk blonde one. She's plastered, leaning against the wall, staggering around. Her handbag is white, and it sits open on the ground, almost teasing him.

Always go for the drunkest, most desperate one. Another rule of thumb that Michael and the lads live by.

As she gets drunker and drunker, she leans in closer to the men, her handbag a foot behind her on the pavement. A foot away, then a foot and a half.

He tries to imagine what's inside – a purse with 100 quid? 200? A phone. An iPod full of whiney music. Some credit cards he can never use. Lipstick he can give to some girl he's trying to sweeten up.

Don't imagine. Just do it.

He clenches his jaw, scans the group one more time. Her back is still turned, they're raising their glasses for another fucking toast. Surging in his blood – he breathes in, feeling that familiar rush.

Now.

He races forward – five leaps to the bag, grabs it, turns back to the shadows, breathing fast.

Not fast enough.

His shoulder is clamped by a hand, he's snapped back.

"Oi, what you doing?" one of the men shouts.

The drunk woman screams. "My bag!"

Legs are straining to bolt, but one of the men in the group

– square-jawed, dark hair, like some fucking superhero – holds him back and raises a fist to punch him. He ducks, elbows Square-Jaw in the gut, tries to run off again. He is still clutching the bag when the phone goes off, confusing him for a moment. The ring tone is some awful dance tune he remembers from the clubs.

The men are still at him. The other one – shorter, freckled with sandy hair, grabs him now, and holds him in place while Square-Jaw readies a superhero fist to knock him into place.

This one's gonna hurt.

The blow snaps his head back, and he feels his right eyeball shoved into its socket, the cheekbone throbbing. He drops the bag. The phone stops ringing its hellish dance anthem.

Pain lights up everything he sees, a giant flashing strobe on acid.

But he is used to this. Not nearly as bad as Da. On impact, Freckled Man lets go and he stumbles forward once, twice, still reaching for the bag.

"Someone call the police!" The blonde one screeches.

Square-Jaw tries to belt him again, but he headbutts him. Ouch.

"He's right there!" one of the women shouts.

Time to go.

Don't look back, don't let them see your face.

Head still reeling from the punch, he races off into the shadows, turns right, and skitters around the corner, blood pumping in his ears, heart thumping in his throat.

"Fuckin knacker!" he hears a man shout.

Still running at full speed, though he doubts they're behind him. He is always fast on his feet, has never been caught before. He knows when to run and when to hide.

He keeps running. Just a bit more now, slowing down now to catch his breath, getting ready to melt into the shadows. He slips into the dark by the waterfront.

Under the cover of a bridge, he finally rests, his breath returning to normal. He leans forward, hands on his knees. It's quiet here by the river, none of the buzz of the high street.

Blood's not surging anymore. Now, he begins to really feel the pain, flooding his head, his face. He knows he'll have a black eye.

Jaysus, what a waste. Nothing to show for it neither.

He'll get the full clatter from his da about this. And the lads.

He starts to make his way along the water. There's street lamps here and there with strong yellow light, the rest of the pavement's in shadow. Somewhere from the wall by the river, he hears a girl's laugh and a man's voice, lower, saying something he can't make out, something manly and romantic that'll make her giggle some more and rest her hand on his chest, allow him to cup her tits.

Some eejits are always lucky. Never him.

"A group of five? Never take on five."

Michael says this as he dabs a hot damp cloth on his face. He flinches at the pain.

"Your one was so langers, she wouldn't of noticed her bag missing."

"Yeah, well, her man noticed. Noticed enough to lamp you right in your gorgeous mug."

Michael wrings the cloth out again and leans over with it.

He turns away. "Enough. Fucking hurts."

Michael snorts. "Don't be going all soft now. Next thing I know you'll be growing a pussy and wanting to live in Dublin with Mam."

He don't say nothing.

Michael tosses the cloth into the sink and hands over his can of Carlsberg. "Here. Have some of this. I can send you over to Old Thomas to take care of the pain, but then everyone'll know you had a clatter."

He gulps down the lager. Warm and tasteless, but better than nothing. He hopes a buzz will come, ease off the pain.

"Da's gonna be asking about that when he comes back, you know." Michael gestures to the black eye.

"I'll just tell him I got in another scrap."

"With who?"

He shrugs. "Dunno."

Michael starts up with his preacher tone again. "Not with buffers. We don't want to be stirring up trouble with them. And you know we don't fight with ourselves." Christ, he's worse than the Pope sometimes.

"Ok, then. I got in a fight with some tourists."

"Better. But you know what he'll say: 'You get in a fight, you better be giving out the black eyes, not getting them.'" Michael does a good impression of Da with his drunken slur and his awkward gestures, and he's forced to laugh. Which makes the pain in his left eye flare up again.

Flinching, he sets the Carlsberg down on the table. "Guess I got some room for improvement, then."

Michael grins. "You could say that, yeah."

He gets up and moves to the caravan window, looks out the small square pane into the night. Nothing except the sound of the wind. No cars on the road.

"Hey, you think I need to worry about the police?"

Michael thinks for a moment, then shrugs. "Peelers? Nah."

"Really?"

"You didn't take nothing from them, right? And they were out drinking. They won't bother to do a report. Why ruin a good night?"

He starts to laugh.

"What're you laughing at?" Michael asks.

"These posh people. They make it too easy. I reckon I even made their night more exciting. Think of how easy I made it for them to shag the ladies tonight, them being the big heroes and all. They should fucking pay me for that kind of foreplay."

They both break out in laughter.

"The day they pay a Traveller for robbing them is the day we got it sorted," Michael says.

"I'll drink to that." He raises the can of Carlsberg, holds it to his lips, but it's empty. Foam slides slowly into his mouth, tasting like metal.

He keeps his eyes shut, keeps the can to his lips, and swallows the foam. And as he does, he thinks: Mallorca... now there's a gorgeous place.

Outside, the wind whistles against the caravan sidings.

*

One year later, he's in Dublin.

The first girl he has is a skinny brown-haired girl he finds wandering home after a birthday party. He is fourteen, and he's been kissing girls for two years now. He reckons she's about the same age. A settled girl, somewhere near a housing estate in West Dublin. It's not too late, early summer evening, and she's walking on her own.

He sees her, long hair and narrow legs, arms stuffed into her jacket pockets. From that distance, can't tell if she's pretty, but it don't really matter. Just some girl to practice on. All them tricks the lads told him would work.

He moves in her direction. Trying to look aimless, casual, like he just happens to be there.

"Hiya," he says, when he's close enough.

She stops short, turns around. Mainly she looks bored, and a little sad. Her hair is brown and lank, but her eyes are pretty enough.

"Hi," she says. Not particularly warm. But he'll change that.

"Where you coming from?"

She don't answer right away, looks unsure.

"My friend's party."

"What's your friend's name?"

"Niamh."

"And what's your name?"

"Sarah."

"Sarah..." he says, as if breathing in a rich perfume, the way he's seen Michael say the name of a girl when he tries to chat her up. This gets a faint smile out of her.

"Sarah, I'm Donal."

"Hi, Donal."

They stand there in the late evening sun, casting two long shadows.

"Sarah, why'd you leave the party?"

She shrugs and looks down at her feet, balancing on the outside edges of her trainers. "They weren't being very nice. Started leaving me out of the talk. Niamh kept going on about her boyfriend, and the other girls too."

"And you – you don't have a boyfriend?"

She shakes her head, keeps her eyes down as if too embarrassed.

Bingo. All easy from here on in.

"Well, hey, Sarah, you know I'm always looking for a party. But I'm glad you left, because I'd rather be here with you."

She looks up. He can tell she don't quite believe him, but she likes what he says.

Sarah blushes, looks down, and starts walking away.

"Where you going?"

"I should get home." But this time, a little coy. Like she wants to be followed.

Which he does.

"Oh, come on, don't go just yet. We've only just met."

That line he's heard Michael say loads of times to other girls. Most of the time it's worked.

It works on Sarah. She slows her steps and looks at him curious.

He cracks a smile.

"Come on, Sarah, come with me. Let me show you something."

She pauses, liking the attention. "No, I should go."

He grabs her hand – playful, as if drawing her somewhere. "It's only just over here."

He don't actually know the area too well, is making things up as he goes along. But he can remember there's a stand of trees clumped somewhere beyond those buildings.

All it takes is a nice quiet place. Make sure there's no one else around. This is what Donal and Michael have told him. That's how easy it is to get off with girls.

He looks around – the neighbourhood is completely empty. Families gathered in their homes, watching telly or eating dinner. But there's no one else out on the streets. Safe enough.

She is startled at first when he grabs her hand, but lets him guide her. She is even smiling.

"Where you taking me?" It comes out in almost a giggle.

"Oh, you'll see."

He blathers on as they head towards the trees. A bunch of lies really, but he knows she believes him. He's just moved with his family here. He grew up in County Tyrone. His da's a doctor. He has three sisters. Does she like living here?

"It's all right. Never been anywhere else."

"Where've you been on holiday?"

"London once. Spain another time. But always with my family, so it's not much fun."

He's been to London three times. He has an uncle who lives in France and another one in New York.

"Wow, New York."

New York is amazing, the skyscrapers, the crowds of people, the Statue of Liberty.

"Have you been up the Statue of Liberty?" she asks, her eyes wide.

"I have, yeah. It's gorgeous, the sun shining on the water, and you can see all of New York."

What's the name of that main bit in New York? Manhattan.

"Manhattan, now there's a grand place to live."

"Wow," she says. He can tell she's impressed. No longer so scared.

He still has her by the hand, and now they're just a few yards from the clump of trees. Not sure what to do once they get there, but he'll figure something out.

"Just this way here."

He steps high over a fallen tree, pushes his way under a screen of wire-mesh fence that's been knocked over.

She stops. "What's in there?"

"Don't worry, it's safe."

He tugs on her hand, and she leans down to hunch under

the wire-mesh. He holds up the screen for her, glancing at her tits. Nothing hardly. Might as well be a cardboard box.

But he can still feel the blood stirring in his veins. She's here, trapped on this side of the fence. And there's no one else around.

She brushes dirt off her jacket and looks up. He is staring at her.

"Sarah," he says.

"What?" she giggles back, a little uncomfortable.

He don't answer, but leans in against the fence, partly to block any escape.

"What'd you want to show me?" she asks, looking around at the trees, the scuffed-up ground.

"Well, I kinda lied."

She's nervous again, and he can see it, almost enjoys it.

"Why'd you bring me here?" A note of alarm in her voice.

"I just wanted to do this."

And he leans in and kisses her.

She pulls back for a moment, staring at him. He kisses her again; this time she don't try to squirm out of his grip. She tries to settle into the kiss.

The thing you need to remember is: all girls secretly want to be kissed by a boy. You just need to make sure you're that boy. Michael and Donal have told him this over and over.

And after you kiss them long enough, you can do other things with them.

Her mouth tastes of Tango and Doritos, and after long enough, he releases her. She looks a little shocked, but flushed.

"You like that, Sarah?"

She don't say nothing, but don't seem upset either.

"Ever been kissed before?"

She shakes her head, a little embarrassed.

"It's my first time, too." And he leans in and kisses her again.

Now that was another lie. He's kissed a few Traveller girls, but by now he knows it's always easier to go for the settled girls. Less risk of their parents finding out and chasing you down.

And no matter what, the older girls are always the best at kissing. They know how to twist their tongues around his, sexy and sometimes forceful, which always gets him hard. The younger, shyer ones just kind of freeze up and don't do anything with their tongues. Like this one here.

He has Sarah by the shoulders now and her Dorito-flavoured mouth is boring him, so he tries to slip one of his hands up her jacket. She flinches and pulls back; his left hand is still gripping her shoulder.

"Didn't you like that?"

"I... I don't know." She is like one of those rabbits on the lawn outside the caravans – frozen, waiting to be pegged with a stone.

"Let me kiss you again."

Without waiting for her reply, he leans in again, one hand behind her head. Presses his body up against her tits, but there's just that cardboard-box flatness, and he don't know what to do.

She wrests her mouth away from his.

"Please, I want to go home. I want to stop."

But it's way too late for that.

He's pulling at her jacket zipper now, twitchy, trying to get his hand on her tits. She tries pushing his hand away, but she's panicking, like that rabbit already pegged through the head, brainless, and his cock is jerking to attention, pushing him on.

The jacket undone, he can feel her breast now through her shirt. A slight bump and the nub of her nipple, but it's enough to get him harder.

And from here just move your hand lower...

"Please stop." She's practically crying now, her voice all crumpled and whiney and the sound of her begging makes him even harder. Girls, so predictable. They want to be kissed, but then they say they don't want to do anything else.

"Please don't." She starts to sob, an awful wheezing sound, and he can't risk her making noise like this, so he slaps her across the face, once, hard.

"Shut the fuck up, bitch."

She goes silent.

Enough of that now. He's crossed over, and he's going to get his way this time.

*

At twenty-three, she is hiking on her own in the Beara Peninsula in Southwest Ireland. The landscape here never fails to intrigue her. The rocky hillsides, interspersed with scrubby vegetation; the cottages and villages that are like mere specks on the great, contoured hide of a beast, rippling with ridges and valleys and streams.

She's been living in Cork for a year now, studying for a Master's in Irish Literature, while on a prestigious scholarship. She now lives in the center of town, after answering a flatshare ad a few months ago to live with an eighteen-year-old boy, in a rickety addition built on the roof of a popular pub. It's right in the nightlife district, and on weekends, the air is loud with people, streaming out drunk after all the clubs have closed at 2am.

In the summer, she often sits on the edge of their roof terrace and looks into the alleyway below. Late at night, there are inevitably men urinating against the wall, hidden at street level in the dark shadows and swaying, but still visible to her. There is something amusing about it, the men relieving themselves with drunken abandon, completely unaware of someone directly above them, watching.

Once in a while, she'll see a couple going at it in the shadows. Heavy kissing and groping, accompanied by the occasional moan. The woman with her back braced against the wall, the man pressed against her, hands reaching frantically up shirts or skirts. She'll feel guilty looking down on them, and partly disgusted, that people could act like that, in public. But also intrigued. She'll watch for a minute or more, then turn away, disturbed.

In the morning, when she walks past that alleyway on weekends, it will stink of urine. Occasionally she'll see a used condom, kicked against the wall, in an attempt to hide its existence.

The boy she lives with does not bother her. He lives his own life, has his own friends, his posters of Tupac that he collects, and a girlfriend, Emer, whom he's been dating for four years.

"Emer's pregnant, like," Jamie announced one day, when they both happened to be in the flat at the same time.

"What?" she asked, unable to keep the shock out of her voice. This eighteen-year-old boy – a father? "How do you feel about being a dad?"

"Oh, it's grand, like."

Their other friends are already parents at the age of seventeen, eighteen. They'll inherit their baby clothes. Emer can get good money from the government as a single mum. They'll be grand.

She can't understand that simple, happy acceptance of their future lives. Parents at the age of eighteen. And looking forward to it.

So it's about time for her to get away from the city – the stinking alleyways and beer-sodden evenings and teenage parents – and spend a night in the countryside on her own.

She's chosen the Beara Peninsula, because she read about an intriguing hike in her Lonely Planet guidebook. A trail leading from the small town of Glengarriff, through a nature reserve, and then into the Coomarkane Valley, the upper part of which remains entirely uninhabited. And at the end of that empty valley, there are two lakes bearing impossible names: Lough Derreenadavodia and Lough Eekenohoolikeaghaun.

What would it be like to follow a trail to such fantastically named lakes?

So late September and she's taken a bus out here on her own, determined to walk the trail outlined in her map and guidebook. Her hiking shoes make their way nimbly over stone and dirt, as the footpath snakes along the slope of a hill. To her left below her, there's a ruined cottage or two, roof fallen in, trees growing in corners where children used to play. She knows now that Ireland is full of these ruined cottages, spotting the countryside in these out-of-the-way places.

She read that two centuries ago, Ireland used to be more heavily populated with over 8 million people living off the land. But that was before the potato famine and the mass exodus of Irish off this island to America, Canada, Australia, New Zealand. And of course, England.

She herself is thinking of moving to London after this. The past year, she's visited the city a handful of times on those spectacularly cheap Ryanair flights. Even a few days spent there are a heady thrill. So much theatre and shopping, so many museums, the throngs of people in Trafalgar Square and Covent Garden and along the Thames. She could even be entertained by sitting in a McDonald's on Oxford Street: eating fries and watching the whole stream of humanity move past, black and white and Asian and Middle Eastern faces. Tourists, commuters, schoolkids, homeless people, and her. An anonymous face, observing it all.

After Cork, the multiracial world of London is always a relief. There's no one staring at her, commenting on her excellent command of English, men remarking on her 'exotic looks' and then asking for her number, as if that's supposed to charm her somehow. She chafes at the thought of being judged merely by her appearance.

She has tried dating a few Irish men, but with little luck. Nothing's lasted longer than a few weeks. This is unexpected compared to the steadiness of Hendrick, whom she dated in the last two years of college. Loyal, attentive Hendrick who gave her this very Lonely Planet guidebook. She broke up with Hendrick a year ago when she arrived in Ireland, knowing the country would somehow make less of an impression on her if her thoughts were constantly tied to a man who lived elsewhere. And at first, being single, she was pleasantly surprised by all the looks she drew in Ireland, the men who chatted her up in bars. But each of these guys, in their own way, turned out to be a disappointment, an unexpected source of pain. The men who stopped calling her after she didn't sleep with them on the second date. She wonders if they were expecting something more sexual, something promised by her 'Oriental' looks.

Dating is a minefield. Too much potential for hurt, too much unpredictability.

And so she's glad to be free of all that for a day or two, in this valley where she hasn't encountered a single other human since she left the hostel this morning. To have all of humanity behind her, and just a trail ahead of her, waiting to be explored.

Now, the trail comes down the slope of the hillside and empties into the green bowl of this valley. She looks at her map again. The Coomarkane Valley ends with those two fantastic lakes: Derreenadavodia and Eekenohoolikeaghaun. They are as wild and remote and breathtaking as their names.

The valley gathers together at its head here, cradling the two lakes, while rocky cliffs clad in grass and heather rise up, forming the sides of the green bowl. Grass edges along the lakes, which sparkle blue and silver in the sun. When the wind blows, she can see it passing over the grass, then ruffling the surface of the lakes, an unspoken presence that quickly vanishes. She watches, mesmerized for a few minutes, while the shadows of clouds and the gleam of sunlight pass in turn over the grass, the water, the cliffs.

There is not another soul, not even a stray handful of grazing sheep.

She finds herself grinning, not quite believing her luck. To find a place this beautiful and abandoned, and to have it all to herself. She breaks out in a laugh, delighted.

She wants to rush forward into those green fields, but the trail has disintegrated and the grass is too wild to run through. Carefully, her eyes pick out a faint animal track, and she follows this toward the lakes. She wonders who was the last person to ever come to this valley.

The track leads down to the stream, which pours out of the lower lake. A flood of water runs rag-tag between scattered stones, so she has to pick her way across, leaping from one stone to another above the rushing water.

She does this too quickly and jumps onto a loose stone that skids through the water, before grinding to a halt against other rocks. A fall would have twisted her ankle, but she manages to stay on top, tensing her body.

Not a good idea to get injured out here.

Another hop and a jump and she's made it to the other side of the stream.

She looks back at it. Nothing to be scared of really, a shallow slide of water, but it's funny how scared you can get by the smallest of details once you're out on your own.

She passes a sheep's carcass embedded in the grass, as she starts to edge around the first of the lakes. Taking more care this time. It's fairly easy at first, but a number of smaller streams flow down the walls of the valley and feed the lake. As the walls become cliffs, the streams become more vertical, until she finds herself practically having to jump across waterfalls that splatter into the lake.

She can't see how deep the lake is, but she can hardly swim. Never had much of a chance to learn in childhood. Which makes jumping across slippery rocks hardly the safest thing to be doing alone.

After enough clambering past waterfalls, she reaches the far end of the lower lake, and she realizes this is where she should stop. The terrain is simply too rugged from here, and she doubts how much can be gained from struggling on any further. Even so, she looks longingly at the stretch of lush terrain between this and the upper lake, the wind blowing the grass from green to silver and back, the verdant slope of the valley rising up from the far side of the upper lake.

There's always a farther place to go. Somewhere else to explore.

But no, she'll stay here, have a snack, enjoy the view, congratulate herself on how far she got, and then head back. She checks her watch. 4:15. She's aiming to catch the 6pm bus from Glengarriff to Cork, and even that'll be a stretch.

It's 5:30 and she's hot-footing it back past the ruined buildings, down the road through the village.

As she walks, she realizes this will probably be the final time she'll be in this valley. What are the chances that she'll come here again, to this remote corner in the far southwest of Ireland?

No, in a few months she'll be moving on. She's decided that already. Rent may be cheap in Cork at 60 euros week, but it lacks the vibrancy and drive of London. From volunteering at the Cork Film Festival, she made a few contacts in London's film industry. One director had handed her a card and said to call, if she was ever in town.

A few months later, she was having lunch with the lady in Soho House.

"After I finish my degree," she ventured, "I'd be interested in moving to London and trying to work in film or television."

The director said she would ask a few producers she knew. Maybe one of them needed an assistant.

Something about that sounds exciting, a possible trail that could lead somewhere new.

But for all her visions of living in that heady metropolis, she'll need to get to Cork first. And right now, she checks her watch and realizes she has 20 minutes to catch the last bus. Only the bus stop is over 2km away. It's virtually impossible to get there in time, unless she can manage to catch a lift.

In this remote valley, that seems highly unlikely.

She continues along the road at a fast pace, knowing that without a passing car, she is doomed to spend another night in this small forgotten town, on her own.

Her adrenaline picks up, while she curses herself for not leaving the valley earlier. But no, it was worth it just to see those two lakes.

Just then, she hears a car driving up the road, out of the village and back toward civilization.

Please be someone normal. Please be someone normal.

As it approaches, she can make out a gold-colored sedan.

She'll always remember her scare in Germany when she backpacked for the travel guidebook. Hitchhiking isn't a thing she wants to do, but sometimes time and geography and transportation schedules conspire to make you a bit more desperate.

The sedan approaches, coursing its way past the sprinkling of cottages.

Now or never, she thinks, and sticks out her arm to flag it down.

The car slows and stops.

A window is rolled down, and she is relieved to see a young mother with one girl next to her in the passenger seat, and two younger girls in the back.

"Do you need help?" the mother asks.

"Yes, I'm trying to catch the 6pm bus in Glengarriff. Is there any chance you can drop me off on your way out?"

The mother hesitates, glances at her daughters in the back. "Sure, no problem." Her voice takes on a sharper tone. "Annie, Deirdre, make room for this young lady."

"Oh wow, thank you so much. You're a real lifesaver."

She says this as the two younger girls shift over on the car seat, and she buckles herself in, her backpack nestled on her lap.

She's aware of how broad and foreign her American accent must sound. She also realizes she's covered in mud from her hike and apologizes for this. The mother says not to worry. "Hello." She smiles at the two girls next to her.

But they just stare at her with wide eyes, half-disbelieving.

I must look like some swamp monster to them, stumbling out from the middle of nowhere.

She wonders if they've ever seen an Asian woman before, living as they do in this remote rural valley in Ireland.

The young mother is kind enough. "Where are you from?" she asks.

"America," she answers. "New Jersey, near New York."

She asks the mother if they've visited the States, but they haven't. England is the farthest they've been.

"Are you traveling through?" the mother asks her.

"Mmm, sorta," she answers. She explains she's studying in Cork for the year, but had read about this walk and wanted to hike to see the two lakes in this valley. "Have you been there?" she asks.

"Not really," the mother answers. "No one really goes there."

And she wonders – to have a magnificent sight like that, right where you live, and to never see it. How strange it must seem to them, that people from as far as America would come here, to this forgotten valley to practically hike in their backyard.

The girls are still staring at her wide-eyed, but the car's reached the main road now, and approaches the centre of Glengarriff. It's really just a collection of pubs, a post office, church, school, hotels in the off-season, and one shop. And the bus stop.

"I'll let you off here now," the mother says, as they reach the Bus Éireann sign.

"Thank you so much, I really appreciate it."

"Not a problem." The mother nods at her, a close-lipped smile. "All the best, and safe travels."

"You too." She turns to grin at the girls in the back. "Bye now."

They nod, still staring, and the youngest girl offers a shy, wordless wave. She waves back and the car drives off.

All quiet on the streets of Glengarriff. She walks towards the bus stop, where there's no one else waiting. She checks the bus schedule, and then her watch.

5:58pm. Plenty of time to spare.

*

It is Halloween, she is twenty-five, and at 3:05 in the morning, she's drunk at a costume party in the center of London. Fancy dress, as they say here in England.

Her own dress isn't all that fancy.

She just put on a cheongsam which she had bought on her last trip to Taiwan, banded her hair up in a bun, pierced it with a few chopsticks, wore a redder shade of lipstick, and there you go – I'm your stereotypical Chinese woman.

Easy enough. Resort to the stereotype when it works for you.

This particular Halloween party is always a good one – the annual party thrown by this ex-pat American couple, the party everyone always wants to go to. The barricade of alcohol stacked up on the kitchen counter, the canapés, the live DJ, a pulsating mix of energetic, attractive 20-somethings from all over.

She had started talking to this rather cute English guy, Alex, who works for Morgan Stanley but is currently dressed as a vampire. They were talking by the cheeseboard, hungrily picking at the last of the canapés in a late-night case of the munchies. She'd had a lot to drink, smoked the odd joint that was passed her way. By now, the chopsticks have come out of her hair, stashed back into her purse, and her black hair falls loose, past her shoulders.

Most people are piling into cabs and heading up to an after-party, somewhere in West Hampstead. But it's too far north for her, and she knows it'll be more of the same, only with more drugs as the night stretches onwards. No, she's ready to head home.

She stumbles into the spare room with all the coats, fumbles around in that giant slippery pile looking for her secondhand trench coat.

On her way towards the exit, a hand reaches out for her arm. It's Alex.

"Hey, we're heading back to ours in a cab. You live south, right? Wanna come with?"

He's with his friend, flatmate, whatever. Tim. Who's dressed as a pirate, although his eyepatch is gone. Pirate-Tim has been wearing eyeliner, which is now smudged.

"Which way you headed?" she asks. A cab ride sounds nice. No waiting in the cold for a night bus, no sharing a seat with an unknown drunkard.

"Clapham. We can drop you off on the way, or you're welcome to come back to ours and have a drink."

She understands the suggestion. She'll consider it. This guy is cute, though he works in finance, like everyone else in London. Most people, for whatever reason, finds it 'so cool' that she works in television. They probably wouldn't find her salary so cool.

"We have some good charlie back at ours," he adds, as an extra incentive.

She's not sure she finds this an incentive.

They find their way into a black cab, and as if by unspoken arrangement, Tim gets into the front seat, and she and Alex end up in the back. As they drive past Trafalgar Square, Alex's hand finds its way to the small of her back, his fingers gently curving around her waist.

This doesn't surprise her in the least. She's still considering it. She is drunk. He is cute. And clearly interested.

He sidles in closer to her.

"Oh, can you make sure to go over Vauxhall Bridge?" she shouts up to the driver. "I'll probably get off there."

"Sure you don't want to come back with us?" Alex asks, his face close to hers now. His other hand reaches to brush a lock of her hair from the side of her face.

She lets him do it.

"Come on, it'll be fun. We'll have a few drinks, snort some lines."

The coke doesn't interest her in the least, but before she can say anything, he leans in for the kiss.

She kisses him back – this is where it was always headed, after all. She closes her eyes, lets his tongue find hers. He's not a bad kisser, but she is very aware that his mouth tastes like those cubes of cheese stacked up on the cheeseboard at the party. He draws himself closer, moans a bit. One hand slides down her shoulder, grazes her breast, cups it through the embroidered material of her cheongsam.

She opens one of her eyes, peers out to see where the cab is headed. Down Millbank – good.

He presses closer, and she can feel his erection against her side.

God, this guy tastes like cheese. She realizes how hungry she is, and already knows what his place will be like. There's probably no food in the fridge, and all he'll want to do is snort coke and get in her pants.

She doesn't have sex with people on the same night she meets them. Having to negotiate this is always a hassle.

Somewhere around the Tate Britain, Alex finally releases

her from the kiss and catches his breath. His hand is still around her waist.

"So you'll come back to ours, yeah?"

His lips graze hers again, his tongue reaches in for another kiss.

Halfway across Vauxhall Bridge, she pulls back. No, that's enough.

"Can you pull over at the end of the bridge?" she asks the driver.

"You're not coming?" Alex asks, surprised.

"Sorry, I don't really... do cocaine," she says.

The taxi slows at the curb, and she opens the door. "I, uh, it was nice meeting you," she says, one hand on the door handle, the other on his arm.

The late October night blasts into the cab.

"Are you sure?" Alex insists.

"Pretty sure," she answers. And then she's shut the door in his startled face, the cold night air drawing goosebumps on her skin, and all she has to do is cross the bridge and be home.

A smile cracks across her face. There is something liberating about just being able to walk out of the cab like that. What had he expected her to do? Go home with him, snort cocaine, have sex with him out of gratitude for the coke? Not so appealing, really.

She thinks of how many other women he's tried this on, wonders if this deflated his ego just a little bit.

Let it be deflated, she's happy to sleep in her own bed tonight. And yet, as she crosses the deserted bridge under the waxing moon, a certain sadness undercuts her triumph. As if everything has to end like that – a drunken proposition, a sleazy promise of cocaine, a hand cupping her breast, and an inebriated kiss with a virtual stranger. These kinds of hook-ups are a dime a dozen in London.

She doesn't really like them, she doesn't see the point of them, and yet, nothing else seems possible in this city. The road is entirely free of cars, when she crosses it at 3:30 in the morning. The Thames laps its shivering waters alongside the city banks, and her high heels echo against the indifferent pavement.

*

Where they've settled in Belfast – him and Michael and Da – is this halting site high up on a hill on the very edge of the city, practically out in the countryside. Actually fuck, it is countryside. Not much to do for your average fifteen-year-old. There's cows and sheep and all their shite just outside, stinking up the place if the wind isn't blowing the right way. Fields all around them, but if you look straight ahead facing in one direction, you can see all of Belfast and the sea. All them Republicans and Loyalists and fuck-off murals and the Pakis and the Chinkies and the tourists and whatever else you find in this city.

Belfast is a different enough place from down south, that's for sure.

But there's a place where you can hide from it all. It's just down below. Literally right below his feet if he's standing at the edge of the field looking at the city. A steep slope right under him, and gurgling away at the bottom, a smallish river and a bunch of trees surrounding it where you can hide. They call it the Glen. He likes the wilder part, where there's hardly anyone ever around, just the trees and the stream and you feeling all closed in. Private. No one around to fucking bother you.

But if you follow the river down a bit, the valley widens up, there's less trees and more open grass and people going for walks. And that's where you can also find some kind of trouble, some distraction, if you're bored. People passing by to look at, and you can just lie real quiet among the trees, and wait, and wait for someone to come along.

*

Past 9:30 on a Wednesday night, and she's still in the office.
She is twenty-nine, and her life has become an endless

torrent of work. All interesting projects – ongoing television productions, new ideas to pitch and develop, evenings spent at screenings or in post-production houses or at industry drinks events. But she doesn't have much time to herself, after this ongoing trawl of energy spent on her job. Weekends she often has to work, read scripts, watch other productions to be informed.

Even yesterday afternoon, she had had a meeting with her boss and told her how stressed she was feeling over the amount of work she had.

"There's just so much to do, I don't even know how I'm going to get it all done."

Erika, her boss, had been understanding. After seeing Vivian's to-do list, she said she'd take on a few of those items, reassign others to their assistant. "Just get through these, go away, have a good trip, and hopefully things will calm down in a few weeks."

They've been hoping that for months now but in reality it's never-ending. Besides, busy means good in the world of television. If you're not busy, you're not producing anything. Work brings in more work; business leads to more business. That's the goal, isn't it?

She looks out the window, acknowledging that it's already dark outside. Everyone else has gone home hours ago, but she has that usual pre-trip crunch: emails to send, budgets to update, pitches to finalize, that final giant wrap-up email to her boss.

The office phone rings.

She frowns, looks at the time, and knows it can only be one person: her mom.

Great. It's gonna be another hour before I get out of here.

With a sigh, she picks up the phone. "Eagle Entertainment," she says in her professional voice.

"Hey, Eagle Entertainment," her mom says, trying to be light. "You sound very busy."

"Hi Mom. Yeah, I um… I'm trying to get a lot done at work tonight. I'm going away for something tomorrow."

"Well, that's good. It's good to work hard. I just wanted to see how you are, since it's been so long."

It hasn't been that long, really. Maybe two weeks since they last spoke.

"Yeah, I'm sorry. I've just been running around a lot and haven't had time to call."

"Well, you want to do a good job at work," Mom reminds her.

She sighs at the familiar statement. Words she's heard countless times before. Most parents would tell their kid to go home if they spoke to them in the office this late.

"What's this trip, then?"

"Oh, it's just this reunion to celebrate the tenth anniversary of the peace process in Northern Ireland." She says it as if it's something casual. When really it seems odd to her that they should be inviting *her* to such a momentous event, just because she happened to study in Ireland years ago.

"They're inviting all the former Mitchell Scholars," she explains to her mom. "Remember that woman Barbara, who runs the US-Ireland Alliance in DC? She's organizing the whole thing."

"Oh, so you're flying to Dublin?"

"No, Belfast. Northern Ireland. The peace process was for the North."

"Oh right… Is it for work?"

"Yes and no. I've scheduled in a few meetings with potential work contacts while I'm there."

The events are all day and evening Thursday and Friday. Saturday she's free. Sunday night, she's been invited to the red-carpet premiere of a film she helped develop the script for. So she's booked her flight to come back to London on Sunday midday. Get back, rest up, and get ready for this premiere.

She doesn't really want to go to the reunion, which consists of the usual schmoozing events, cocktail parties, dinners. She seems to be always doing this. If she can just make it to Saturday – then she'll be able to go on a hike she's been planning.

On the far corner of her desk sits her Lonely Planet

guidebook, which she brought into work as some kind of veiled incentive to get through her to-do list. The book has listed an 11-mile hike on the outskirts of Belfast. Start in some place called Glen Forest Park, and work your way up north, over hills with fine views of the city, to finish in Cave Hill. She imagines herself on her own, atop these hills and looking out at the city below her, and that will be worth it.

Get to Saturday, and you'll be okay.

"I'm coming back on Sunday, and then we have the red-carpet premiere of a film that night."

"Oh, that's exciting," Mom says. "So how are things with you otherwise?"

"Other than busy with work, not much really." Of course, her social life is always busy. Six years living in London and you collect a lot of friends – there's always birthday parties, flat-warming parties, leaving parties, and lately, a lot of engagement parties. She wonders if her mom realizes what her life, day-to-day, is actually like, who her friends are, how she spends her free time, what she'd like to do if she had more time.

"Oh, I was hoping maybe you've been busy because…"

And she knows what her mom is about to say, and a note of annoyance creeps into her voice. "Because?"

Mom's voice is mischievous and inquisitive at the same time. "Because maybe you've met someone?"

"No," she answers firmly. "I haven't. I told you. Please stop asking me about that, and if there's any news to report, I'll tell you."

Yes, six years in London and dating is more confusing than ever. There appear to be men aplenty in this city, but guys will offer any number of excuses for not really embarking on a relationship – *I'm not over my ex yet, it's not a really good time for me right now, I recently realized I've been in love with someone else my whole life.* Etc., etc. The flush of a night spent with someone inevitably turns to misread signals, unanswered text messages, a temporarily broken heart. Retreat, refresh, reboot, get back out there. Absolute minefield.

She doesn't say anything else on the phone, but her mom

continues on the same topic. "Oh, I don't really understand it. Your sister was already married at twenty-seven."

Her gaze wanders over to the Lonely Planet guidebook again, and she feels a familiar twinge of longing for the cover image: a solo hiker on a promontory, while green-and-grey cliffs fall away to the frothing ocean below.

Just get through to Saturday.

Her computer screen says 9:56 now.

She looks down at her to-do list.

"Mom, I have to get back to my work."

*

This is what they call a forest?

Well, maybe for West Belfast. There's trash scattered over the ground: plastic soda bottles, fish-and-chip papers, squashed cardboard boxes, crushed beer cans.

Hm, not quite pristine wilderness here.

She tries to ignore it.

It'll get better, the deeper I go into the park.

Glen Forest Park. The 11-mile Belfast Hills Walk that's described in her guidebook. She is impatient to skip through the uninspired urban part of the trail. But still, even being among this sorry version of nature is refreshing in some way. She breathes in the smell of the trees, a grin breaking across her face when she passes under a patch of sunlight.

Her watch says just after 1pm, so she has the whole afternoon ahead of her. The weather is balmy for April, perhaps the first time this year that she's been able to go on a hike. All the weight of London and the whirl of the past two days, the small talk she made at the tenth-anniversary celebration, the shaking of hands with Belfast politicians who were somehow instrumental in the peace process, slides away, forgotten. And there is just herself, and the trees, and the trail.

She consults her book where the page for the Belfast Hills has been dog-eared: *Well-surfaced paths lead away from the visitor centre into young, mixed woodland.*

The place isn't entirely deserted. For a Saturday afternoon this warm, there are enough locals walking around, enjoying the weather. She passes a father and his two young kids.

They smile and nod at her, and she smiles back.

There's something about being out of the city. Everyone's immediately friendlier, as if to acknowledge their mutual enjoyment of nature.

Don't cross the mini-suspension bridge but keep on the left of the river for 1km before crossing a bridge.

Following the directions, she stays on the path until it reaches a fork. She takes the left path, perhaps because it is empty of people. She has the path to herself for a few blissful minutes. Then two young men come toward her, drinking cans of Tennent's. They pass her, chatting to each other, then continue down the path, ignoring her.

A stream gurgles to her left. She steps off the paved path for a second, to pause on the stream's bank, watching the water slide over pebbles in the sunlight. An early swarm of mayflies dances above the water, and small white flowers star the grass of the opposite bank.

She smiles again, appreciating this, then continues back onto the path.

Climb steadily through improving woodland rich in ferns to a bridge carrying the A501 road.

Right, no sign of that bridge yet, but the woodland is definitely improving. Ferns nod at the foot of the trees.

A father, wearing a green-striped Celtic shirt, and his two sons and one daughter come towards her. They are all ginger-haired, the kids young and ruddy-faced. One of the sons has a Jack Russell terrier on a lead, and the father smiles as they approach.

"Hello," she says to them.

"Hello," they say back.

They pass her, and then they are gone.

*

He's down among the settled people now. Definitely still feeling them yokes from last night. But nothing better to do, so here you are down the glen.

He's skulking. He's seeing what he can see.

But not much here, really.

Everyone's old and ugly. Or has screaming kids.

Not even that many women. Here's a couple going for a walk, but she's probably someone's nan, she's that old. Minging anyway.

A man and his dog. A man and his wife and a dog. A man and his kids and a dog.

Boring.

A beour there, but she's with two lads. Two big lads who'd kick the shite out of him. They're laughing and carrying a crate of beers – ha ha, all the fun these buffers have. He hates them all. He has a closer a look and her tits jiggle in her tight pink T-shirt and his hard-on does a little jig jiggle too and… well, they're gone now, away off in that direction.

What to do. What to do.

Stand on the edge of the lawn here, where the grass meets the trees, and no one will look at you much. See, all too bothered with their own perfect settled lives. Walk the dog. Play with the kids. Breathe the fresh air. Ignore that pavee standing right there. He means no harm.

Heh.

Look who comes down the path. A man and his sons. A couple and their dog. And what's this… what's this…?

What's this girl coming down the path. On her own.

A woman. Alone.

Take a few steps closer, squint your eyes. See what you can see.

She's a beour, ain't she? Different. Dressed different. Blue shirt, long sleeves, everything all covered up, too bad. But see the outline of her tits, her slim frame. She's tiny, thin waist and all. And long black hair. Nice long black hair.

She's a Chink.

And not a bad-looking one.

Never expected to see that here, all on her own.

Imagine that long black hair, bunched in your fist...

Anyone with her? No, she's coming closer. Walking faster than the others, this one. Like she has somewhere to go.

Book in her hand?

Ha, no, she stopped. Bending down to put the book in her backpack. What's in there? How much money? Where's this beour from?

Not from here.

Let's find out.

*

She steps out of the shade of the tree canopy, as the tarmac path continues onto open ground. Here the park widens a bit – a green lawn under the sunlight. The sun warms her face, and she wants to stop and soak it in, but she is self-conscious, with all these people passing by.

Here there's more people ambling about. A couple pushing their baby in a pram, while another kid toddles at their feet. A woman walking two dogs: a big Alsatian and a Labrador, both of them straining at their leads when a man walks his cocker spaniel past.

The tarmac path skirts the wide green lawn and halfway across, she spots a lone figure standing there.

It's a young man, or a boy, and he looks out of place because... why? Because of what he's wearing. A bright white zip-up jumper, slim jeans. Almost what he would wear to go out at night, not for a walk in the park. Everyone else is wearing T-shirts and sweatpants, but not this one.

He's just standing there, not moving. Hands in pockets, a swatch of white against the green of the lawn.

Strange, she thinks. And keeps on walking.

The trail beckons, the bridge that she needs to pass under, and then the upper part of the glen.

But he moves now, the young man in white. A few steps. He's definitely heading toward her.

Why me?

That's the last thing I need, right now. I just want to continue on the trail.

*

Getting closer to her now, and he can see her better. Yeah, she's a beour. Black hair and tan skin and eyes a bit slanty like all them Chinks. How old?

Who cares? She's still slim. None of these fat-arses waddling around Glengoland.

She won't like 'Hello,' not this one. Seems too set on wherever she's going.

Something more. Almost in front of her. Turn on the Sweeney charm.

What to say to her? She had a book, like she was looking at it.

Here. Now.

Act innocent, act stupid.

"Hiya, I... I think I'm lost. I don't know where I'm going."

Done now. It's begun.

See what she says.

*

What?

She's stumped for a moment. Is he talking to me?

But there's no one else it could be. No one else next to her, or behind her.

After a split second, she regains her composure, ever the helpful, well-traveled professional, even if this situation seems a bit odd.

"Um, where are you trying to get to?"

The boy – and it really is a boy, younger than he seemed from a distance – seems to waver on his feet, uncertain. He's just a kid, almost scrawny, ginger-brown hair, freckles. He's kinda out of it. She wonders if he's sober.

"I'm lost. I… I don't know where I am."

Maybe he had a big night out, but it's past 1pm. How'd he end up in this park?

"Listen," she says, attempting to mask her annoyance. Really, the last thing she needs when she's setting off on a hike. "Where are you trying to go?"

He holds a hand up to his head, like he's confused.

"I'm just… I'm just trying to get to Andersonstown," he mumbles, blue eyes not quite focusing. "Can you tell me where's Andersonstown?"

Andersonstown. She remembers it from the map. She passed through it on the bus over here. At least she can answer that much.

But, really. Of all the people, I'm obviously not from here. Why ask me?

"For Andersonstown, I think you just want to walk down the glen that way." She points helpfully to make it clear. "And you'll hit a busy road, and you can take a bus from there."

She looks at him, cool and neutral.

Firm, informative, hope that did the job. Now please let me continue in peace.

*

American, is she? And with a voice low like a man.

Didn't expect that to come out of her, did we?

Ah well, don't make her less of a beour, not really. Just an odd one.

Up close, he inspects her face. She's pretty. Nice lips. And no, don't look at her tits, not this early. Eyes on her face.

But beour beour beour beour… he feels it twitch, knowing how close she is.

All you have to do is reach out and…

But no, there's people close by. Fucking settled people with their dogs and kids and watch watching. See, see the pavee talk to the Chink.

But American. Not Irish. Not from here.

All on her own.

And talking to him. Actually answering his questions, not the way all them other buffers pretend he don't exist.

Maybe he's onto something here.

*

Why's he still standing there? I gave him the directions, told him where to go.

She turns away, heads down the tarmac. A definite signal that the conversation's over.

There's something weird about this kid.

But now, he's walking alongside her, like they're friends or something. Almost like he's chatting her up, but that's impossible, he's so young.

"How old are you?"

She frowns, but tries to stay lighthearted, conversational, yet firmly in control. "How old do you think I am?"

"*How old do you think I am?*" he mimics her.

Is this kid for real?

"How old are you?" she shoots back at him.

"I'm thirty-one."

Gimme a fucking break.

"No, you aren't," she tells him, irritated.

"No, you're right. I'm not thirty-one."

"How old are you?"

"I'm twenty."

She gives him a cynical look.

"Okay okay, I'm not. I'm twenty-three."

He grins at her, and her annoyance grows. She keeps on walking.

"Where you from?" he asks.

"New Jersey," she answers tersely, still walking. "Where you from?"

Don't give this kid an inch. Everything he asks you, you ask him right back.

But to be honest, she's just doesn't want to talk to him at all.

"Ah, I know New Jersey. I've been to New Jersey."

She almost stops, hearing that. "Really? No, you haven't."

"Yeah, I have."

"Where in New Jersey have you been?" Even more cynical now.

"I've been to Morristown."

She wasn't expecting that. Morristown is one random place to be bringing up, an unspectacular suburban town like all the suburban towns that make up New Jersey. Not that many people would have heard of it.

"Huh," she says aloud, almost conceding her surprise on that one. "Where are *you* from?" Pressing her point.

He shrugs. "I'm from here and there. All over, really. I'm in Armagh a lot. Sometimes I'm in Dublin."

She realizes then that it's true, he doesn't have a Belfast accent. So maybe he is from Dublin. Maybe there is something to him being lost.

Whatever the case, she doesn't want to be talking to him any longer.

*

See that, see that?

You mention Uncle Bernie's Morristown and she goes all 'Okay, maybe this boy's not so bad after all.'

Pat you on the back there, boy.

But Jaysus is this beour a tough one. So American and direct. The other girls giggle but she shoots it right back.

Makes it all the more interesting. How we going to crack this chestnut?

He shifts a look around, buffers still on the go. Here's two of them, man and wife, united in fat-arsed matrimony. They walk past him and the beour, but take no notice.

Too many people. Wait and see where she goes.

"So what you doing here?" he asks her.

"I'm just going on a walk."

"Where you going?"

"Up to the Belfast Hills and around." She gestures, pointing up the glen.

Lookee here. His territory.

Keep talking to this one. Keep her friendly.

"Why you going there?"

She shrugs. "Just wanted to have a look around."

Fuck me. What beour goes walking around on her own, just like that? She after something else?

He peers closer at her, but can't read her face. Maybe. Beour on her own. In the woods. Maybe.

"You know, I been other places. Not just Morristown."

"Like where?"

Up ahead is the bridge with the Glen Road. Other side, there's less people. Other side, you're almost there.

*

Ten minutes of talking to this kid and she's had enough.

He's not even making any sense, nothing interesting. He's just ruining the walk for her.

They pass under the bridge, the one the guidebook mentioned. She feels a chill, walking in the shade, under the rumble of the road. Their voices echo momentarily in the darkened space, bouncing off the metal underside of the bridge.

"Ah, I'm just, you know... kidding," he says.

Well, it's not funny. How do I get him to go away?

They emerge from the underpass, and she's surprised to see how deserted the park is here. The path deteriorates, a scraggle of cleared ground stringing its way between scrubby forest. It climbs up a steep slope to the right, until it's on the same level as the street they just passed under. She sees a thin grey man, walking his thin grey dog. He's heading towards them.

"Hey, listen," she says to the kid. "It was nice talking to you, but I have to call a friend now."

The kid still hangs about, uncomprehending. Or refusing to.

"So, um, I'm gonna go now and make this call." She gestures to a boulder on the side of the road, where she'll sit.

"Oh, so you want me to go then?" the boy asks.

"Yeah, if that's okay." Really, just get the hint now.

At this point, the man with the dog passes by them, and she nods to him. The man nods back.

"Oh, okay then," the kid says. He shrugs and wanders off down the path, up the glen somewhere, and she's glad to be rid of him.

She doesn't wait to see where he goes, she wants to appear busy as soon as possible. So she sits on the boulder and flicks through her phone. Calls Julia.

But the call doesn't go through. There's not enough signal in this remote place, surrounded by trees with the walls of the glen on either side. She frowns, wonders if that's a problem.

No, she's just overreacting.

Yet for some reason, she tries to call again, and speaks aloud, into the unconnected phone.

"Hey, Julia. It's me, Vivian, just saying hi. It's a little after 1:30 and I'm in the middle of a hike here in Belfast, but I'll be back in London tomorrow. So, uh, speak to you later."

She finishes the pretend call.

A car drives past her on the road, and she sits for a moment longer, thinking.

The kid is nowhere to be seen. Then again, other people are nowhere to be seen. The road is silent now. And it's just herself and the trail ahead, picking its way through the forest.

At last. She's all on her own.

*

Heh, knew it was gonna happen. Beour acts all nice and friendly, but sooner or later she's gonna stick her nose in the air and say fuck off.

'Oh really, could you just go now?'

Fuck her. We'll see about that.

No one just tells me to go away.

But yeah, hide, just for now. Crouch among the trees and wait. You know where she's going anyway. Up the hills. You'll be following her the whole time.

He peers from behind a tree, sees her, slim and dark, sitting on that rock. Phone to her ear.

Not one of them fancy iPhones, but still a good phone.

But that's not what you're after, is it?

*

Not a soul around and finally you have the whole forest to yourself. Let's get this hike started.

She consults her guidebook again.

The path is now unsurfaced as it passes through surprisingly beautiful woodland, seemingly miles away from its setting in Belfast's western suburbs.

Not much of a path, really. As she continues walking, the glen becomes narrower, more thickly forested, and the sides of the glen steeper and higher. Yet the stream, which runs in between, is now wide and shallow, ambling its way around sandbars and overgrown banks. The guidebook describes a wooden footbridge, but she sees only a ruined post or two, standing mid-stream. She paces up and down the bank, examining closely. There's no obvious way across.

The water's shallow enough that she could try splashing through, but then she thinks about tromping around in wet feet for the rest of the five-hour hike. She has a spare pair of socks with her, but wet shoes... Best to avoid wet shoes.

She'll have to go across barefoot.

Irked to be wasting so much time on this, she lowers herself down a steep bank to reach the gravelled foreshore of the stream. Another moment, and she bends over to undo her shoes and socks.

"Hullo," someone says above her. "I know how to get across there. It's dead easy."

That smart-ass kid again. What the fuck is he doing here? It's like he's just popped out from behind a tree, his white jumper dancing around on the bank above her.

Annoyance takes over, and perhaps a little bit of discomfort. Something tugging inside her. She pushes that away. Focuses on the trail.

"Oh, is it?" she asks, challenging. Back to the usual tit for tat.

"Yea," he says. "You just go there, there, and there."

He points it out as he speaks – low stepping stones where someone could potentially jump across, but it wouldn't be easy. She also notices he doesn't pronounce his th's: dere, dere, and dere.

"Well," she says, "I've already taken off my socks and shoes, so I'll just wade across."

The kid scrambles down the bank so he's on the same level as her now.

He grins and seems to do a jig in front of her.

What is this kid's problem?

He bounds across the stream, jumping across the stones he pointed out, his feet still dry.

"Very nice," she says, begrudgingly. "I'll take the long route."

But wait a second, didn't he say he was lost before? This kid seems to know the terrain pretty well.

She wades across, the cool water lapping at her ankles, and she'd find this relaxing, if it weren't for this kid watching her.

Once she rejoins him on the far side, she sits on another rock to mop her feet dry and put on her socks and shoes.

As she does this, she notices him looking at her bare legs. He's only a kid…

But at the pit of her stomach, a small lump of unease starts to swell.

*

Hah – did you see the look on her face just then?

Bet she didn't expect to see me again. Your friendly local pavee boy, here to show you the way.

94

This beour... who takes off her shoes to cross a little stream like that? Scared of the water, is she?

She'll be scared of more, once I'm done with her.

See, now, who's in charge? Who knows how to get across the stream?

Nice legs, though. Nice and smooth. What'll it be like to stroke them legs, push them apart, reach inside...

Look look, but not too obvious. See, she sees you looking at her.

She's a tough one. Won't wilt.

Say something. Her shoes are back on, she's raring to leave.

"See, my way was easier."

"Good for you," she says back. "I just didn't want to get my feet wet."

Go on. Be cheeky. Just the two of us standing here next to the stream. No one else around.

"Maybe we can walk together."

*

I did not sign up for this. A Saturday afternoon hike on my own. Not with some annoying kid as company.

"Look, that's very nice of you, but I kind of want to do this hike on my own."

Silence from the kid for a moment. He nods and keeps on staring at her with those pale blue eyes.

"You sure? I can show you the way."

Ten minutes ago you were lost, and now you offer to show me around? Fucking dodgy kid.

"No thanks, I sort of want to be on my own."

He shrugs. They're both standing on the sandy bank of the stream and she turns to go.

Only, there's no obvious path from here. Up the slope, apparently. That's what the guidebook said.

She doesn't want this kid behind her. She turns back, trying to make it obvious that she wants him to go first, but not as her guide.

"Ladies first," he insists, and gestures for her to go ahead.

She wants to roll her eyes at this, but shoots him a peeved look instead. "Fine."

How fucking ridiculous. Just get away from him.

To start up the slope, she parts the bushes in front of her. Her silver watch glints on her left wrist and she catches him looking at it.

That lump of unease pulses again.

But she heads up the slope. There's nowhere else to go. No proper path, so tromp through the underbrush and get away from this kid as fast you can.

*

Here we go, true colours being shown. Fucking Chinky bitch is making it clear now.

Well, it's not exactly your choice, now is it, bitch?

Teach her a lesson.

Sketched that nice watch she had, there's rich takings here. That watch, that phone, those legs, that pussy.

All up for grabs. No one ever comes up this way, not this far up the glen, so she's all yours.

Let her go ahead. Right now, she don't know you're following her. So stay low and creep up.

It's now or not never with this beour.

Throbbing harder harder, getting this close.

This is always the best part. You work yourself up, right before you strike. Almost like you can't bear it no more.

Creep creep.

Now.

*

Something, something is making her walk faster than she normally would. It's not an easy stroll, this part of the trail. She's crashing through the bushes uphill, ferns crushed underfoot, and brambles catching at her hair. But she just wants to get away, as far as she can and as quickly as she can.

The sooner she can get to the open hills the better.

So up, up the slope, there's no other way. She's lost the path, if there ever was one.

What did the guidebook say? Something about the path climbing high above the stream, and a lookout over a ravine.

Her quads are working hard on an incline this steep, heart beating faster, and getting slightly out of breath, but she's almost there, just a few more steps, and yes... she's here at the top. Pause, catch your breath. Look around.

No sign of him, is there?

No, just silence. The calm and quiet at the top of this slope. The edge of a plateau. Unexpectedly beautiful.

And breathe. A deep, relaxing breath.

This is what she came on this hike for. A place removed, away from the press of the city. Filtered green sunlight beneath the canopy. Cows grazing in the field before her. The hum of insects, the smell of manure, the distant tinkle of the stream below. She smiles, almost wants to laugh. She's free of him, and of the city.

Here's the path again. Starts striding with new energy along it: fields to her left, steep slope of the glen to her right. Up ahead, she can see a clearing in the tree canopy. That must be where the path emerges from the forest, onto open ground. The Belfast Hills. Almost there.

She's looking around with anticipation, and delight at her new surroundings. Path, fields, trees, ravine, and...

What's that flash of white down below on the slope?

She stops short and looks closer.

That's him. That's the boy, in his glaring white jumper. Climbing up the slope, and trying to hide behind this bush, and then behind that tree.

Trying to hide, but she can see him.

She can see him.

He's following her; there can be no mistake.

Her heart seems to hesitate before its next beat.

But beat it does.

And then she has one thought, and one thought only.

Run.

*

Bitch started running.

Musta seen me. So now run, run after her. Chasing, chasing, hound on the hares, or you and the lads closing in on the Maguire boys. You know what's next – you know what's next. That tingling sensation, the familiar rush.

She's yours anyway, no matter how hard she runs. No one to help her around here.

Up the slope now, onto the path, and feet pound pound pounding after her.

See her run. Nice long black hair streaming behind, and that backpack jumping. Run and grab it. Almost.

Shite now, she's reached the end of the trees already. Get her, get her while she's just there. Before she gets any farther.

Out of breath, but you're almost there. Yoke still pounding in your head.

Out of the trees now, out of the trees. And sunlight sunlight, catch your breath, onto the field now, and there she is. There she is.

She's turning to you. She's turning…

*

Made it out of the woods, now get your breath back.

But what is this place?

Sort of a no man's land. No one around. Uneven hummocks, scraps of tarmac, piles of garbage, and just sort of a waste land.

Where is anyone?

She can hear a busy road on the other side of the field. But she can't see it. Should she head there anyway, just to get rid of this kid?

But there's no time to decide.

A flurry in the bushes, and here he is. Out of breath. Something different in his eyes.

She turns to face him, finally confrontational. All manners gone. Annoyance has given way to anger now, uncertainty to fear. Her voice is steel, trying to hide the panic that now engulfs her, renders her nauseous.

"What do you want?"

*

You know what I want.

But don't say it yet. See if you can get closer.

"I… I'm just looking to get back to Andersonstown."

This bitch is angry now. Probably used that line one time too many. But step closer, get within striking distance.

"Look, I already told you how to get there. Go back down that way, walk down to the bottom of the glen, and you can catch a bus."

She's a bossy one, trying to be all in charge. But she's scared. You can smell it.

Ask her. Now.

"Do you like to have sex outdoors?"

*

It strikes her then, a silent blow, like the bottom of her stomach falling out, and she knows she's in trouble now.

Do you like to have sex outdoors?

But he's so young, I don't get it.

"No," she snaps back quickly. "And certainly not with you."

Dread, disgust, some survival instinct immediately turns her away from him, towards the busy road. Get the fuck out of here.

But nothing has prepared her for what happens next.

"Stay right there, bitch!" the boy screams.

His friendly act has been dropped, he's suddenly feral,

menacing, an angry fire alight in his pale blue eyes, and he holds out a threatening arm towards her.

"Don't move. I just wanna lick your pussy."

What kind of twisted... Is he for real?

Instinctively, she rears up, muscles tensing. Knowing that he'll want more.

What do I do?

Get to the road.

"Don't you fucking move! I have a knife!"

He's holding his left hand taut behind him, and she's peering around, trying to see if he actually has a knife.

"I have a knife! I'm gonna slit your throat open! I'm gonna stab you!"

Does he have one? Is this kid serious?

It's almost as if he's play-acting, as if he's flipped a switch.

And yet her heart shudders at breakneck speed now, the fear and adrenaline surge in her blood.

Can I take this kid on? Can I overpower him? Or do I just run, head straight to the busy road?

She's ready to start sprinting, but she knows her backpack will slow her down. Can she outrun him?

He moves closer, breathing hard and tense, and she's still thinking: run or fight... What do I do?

Then, from somewhere in the near distance, closer than the road, they hear a motor.

The boy's eyes move warily toward the noise, and she sees this.

Is there someone nearby?

"Help!" she screams. "Help!" Louder.

Then, he is on her in a flash.

Fucking bitch, shut up don't even fucking think about it. If one of them from the halting site find us... don't you fucking ruin it now, you filthy bitch. Get over here.

He grabs her forearm with surprising strength, shoving her toward the cover of the trees.

"Help!"

Struggle away, get free, but he grabs again. She tries to wrench his hand from her forearm.

"Help!"

"Shut up, you say another word I'll slice your throat open."

Clamp your hand over her mouth before she says anything again – drag her over to the bushes before they see us.

Get away, just get away from this kid. Get his hand off my mouth.

She skids on the loose pebbles, pulling herself away from him, then is pulled back towards the trees, the pebbles rattle underfoot.

Then she slips
    Hits the ground
    Is down.

Get on top of her, get your hands round her throat. Hold that fucking bitch down – hold her down and make her listen.

"Don't you fucking scream or I'll kill you!"

Shit. I'm down. I'm right on the edge, before it drops into the ravine.

The backpack is stuck, digging into me. One water bottle tumbles out, falls down the slope. But he's grabbing for me...

Put out a hand to stop him. He grabs the two fingers of my left hand, bends them back – the pain, what *is* this kid? Blue eyes burning into mine.

Punch her in the head, good and hard so she listens. All Da's punches, the famous Mick Sweeney. Like he did to Mam, like he does to you. Now do it to her. Teach her that lesson. Get her to fucking listen.

"Don't you scream again!"

He just fucking punched me… fuck that hurts, never been punched before.

Yeah, that's it, see her flinch. So close, so close to that nice soft pussy. Punch her, punch her again. Get your hands round her throat. Squeeze squeeze squeeze the fucking bitch.
   "I'll stab you!"

He's on top of me… Choking me… Can't fucking breathe… Eyes darting around… Where is his knife?
   Still can't breathe… Just want air.

Squeeze squeeze her tight. Can't shout now, can you, bitch?
   Now get that fucking rock…
   "I'll bash your head in!"

His fingers digging into my throat… No air.

Raise a rock and smash it in her face if you have to.

Gasping but no air… All closed off… Need to breathe…

Make her listen, the fucking bitch.

Not the rock… Not my head…

Iron rod now, can't wait to ram it in.

Can't breathe… This kid is going to kill me…

Never been this hard before.

I need to breathe…

Girl's never fought back like this one. "Just let me lick your fucking pussy."

Just… Whatever you do, don't kill me… Give up… Not worth it… Need air.

"Just let me lick your fucking pussy."

Do whatever you want.

"Just let me—"

Just let me… Ow, fucking pain. Mud. Bruises. How do I get out of this alive? Just let me breathe.

*

Oxygen rushing back into your lungs… but what happens now and what do you do to get out of this alive… you have no idea what this kid is or what he can do – oh, bitch, now you're mine… now's the best part, blood racing and dick pumping, getting ready for the plunge – if he gets my underwear down… no… bargain with him, offer something else think… think… "Let me give you a blow job"… start with that see if you can get him off – happy days, bitch is getting the idea now, get your lips round that, start sucking – this is disgusting… wish I could get him off with just a few licks but I'm not that good – get your tongue, lick my cock… nice… that's it, yeah, now – but don't stop there – "I wanna lick your pussy. I wanna lick your pussy" – if he gets my underwear down you know what'll happen… just no, don't – "BITCH!" – fuck, he fucking punched me again… get him away, get him away from that, get him to think you're cool with this… oh gross, he's actually licking me, what the fuck is going on, we're in the middle of the woods – yeah yeah, so this is what Chinky box tastes like, get her wet so she wants it, she wants you to slam it into her… you can't wait any longer… "Yeah, I'm gonna fuck you now, I'm gonna fuck you now" – I can't believe this is happening… this is disgusting… underwear down, all the way down, pinned down onto the mud, he's actually inside of me, that disgusting, kid's prick is inside of me but I can hardly feel it, just do whatever the fuck he wants and you can get this over with – yeah, now that's the business, slide into this bitch, "Nice tight Asian pussy" – did he just fucking say that... this isn't actually happening – pump, pump away and get your fill of that nice, tight Asian pussy, yeah now that's it – lying on the ground, pebbles in my back and looking up at the trees... he's not paying attention anymore, maybe you can grab a rock and smash his head in... but what would that do, he's already inside you, it's too late and he'll just get violent again... just let him finish, just get it over with – now another position, bitch, "I want you to go on top" – okay I'm on top, look him in the eye, you're not scared, you're not scared, you're not going to fight him again, you just want him to fucking finish – see, see she's a horny bitch and she wants me, knew it, knew, and I'm fucking her so hard and fucking grab her titties – did he just rip my bra... fuck you my favorite bra... but just get him to come and it'll be done... talk dirty to him, talk dirty and he'll think you want this and then it'll be over... "I bet you can go all night"... did I just fucking say that... I can't believe I did that – oh yeah, see, told you she wants it, bitch was dirty all along... "I want to fuck you doggy-style. I want to fuck you doggy-style" – what kind of a twisted fuck is he... on my hands and knees now, pebbles cutting into my skin – and slam hard... harder into her from behind... shite you fell out, get it back in... "I want you to get on your back"... shite position, can't get inside her proper... what is wrong with this bitch... what else what else what else do you see in the pornos... cock getting hard just thinking about it... "I want to fuck you up the ass! I want to fuck you up the ass!" – no no no no not anal, I've never done anal and this is going to fucking hurt – yeah yeah, now where's the fucking hole, where is it, just ram it in – kid keeps falling out, can't even get it inside me – there it is and slam! slam! slam it home... no, it fell out again – when is this ever going to be over – back on top and yeah this is kind of boring now, isn't it... why aren't I coming... why aren't I coming – is this kid almost finished… he's looking bored, not even dangerous anymore… just be done, just be done, just – "Do you want to go home now?"

And what does that mean? Where is home? Go our separate ways or back to my hotel room? What does it matter? He's suggesting we stop… we stop… we stop.
"Yeah, let's do that."
And finally, finally he's out of me and we're just sitting there. In the mud.

What did that bitch to do to me? Why can't I come? Done with it now. Done with it. It's over. What just happened? Did it really happen? Why didn't I come? Why didn't I come? Why didn't… Oh, who fucking cares, you got inside her and that's what counts.

*

She's sitting by the side of the trail and has pulled her clothes back on. The ripped black bra covered again now by the blue hiking shirt. Her hiking pants are scuffed with mud, hiding the bruises and scratches. She's drawn into herself, like a snail pulled into its shell, tight, vigilant, protected.
He's still there.
He has his clothes on, too, and he's blabbering on about something, anything. None of it seems to make any sense.
"I come back and forth between here and Armagh…"
She doesn't care. Why is he saying this? She grits her teeth and wishes he'll go away soon.
"Where'd you say you were from again?"
"New Jersey." Her voice is monotone. All emotion drained.
"Oh right. And what was your name?"
She hesitates. She should give him a false name. Can't remember if he asked her before, in the park, only an hour or so ago, even though it now seems a lifetime ago.
She'll just have to guess.

"Jenny."

He nods. Either that was the same name, or he couldn't remember himself.

Part of her wants to laugh and cry at the same time. This whole situation is a woeful parody of a one-night stand. *Oh, that was really good. What was your name again?*

"And what was yours?" she asks him.

"Frankie," he answers.

She doesn't believe him. But then again, she doesn't care. Just wants him to leave.

And then he stops being so conversational and chatty. He takes on that menacing air – the tone he had before, when he confronted her in the field.

He leans in close, ice-blue eyes alight and fierce, and points back down the trail, where she came from.

"I want you to go down the road that way there."

But she's not scared of him anymore. What's he going to do to her? Rape her?

Sorry, kid, you already played that card.

She shrugs. If she's walking away, it's not back down the way she came. Hikers don't backtrack. And there's no way she's turning her back on him. Who knows what he'd do? Push her down the slope? Slam her head in with a rock? She's not taking any more chances.

"I don't really feel like it," she says.

He seems a bit surprised by her disobedience, unsure what to do.

He tries it again. Menacing blue eyes glaring at her, finger pointing down the trail.

"You need to go back that way."

She wants to laugh in his face, but knows that wouldn't be wise. She looks at him, not giving anything away. "I will in a bit. I just want to rest for now."

She senses the danger has passed. He's now just a confused kid playing at being an adult, and it's all rather pathetic.

She wants him to leave first. To stall for time, she fishes the remaining water bottle from her backpack – the other one she distinctly remembers falling out of her pack's side pocket during the scuffle. It fell down the steep slope and she imagines it nestled somewhere among the ferns and undergrowth: a gleam of clear plastic among the tangled vegetation, never to be found again.

She takes a few sips, offers the bottle to him.

"Do you want some water?"

But he waves her away.

She'll stall for longer. She takes out an apple from her pack and starts eating it.

He continues to stand around. Why is he still here? She'll wait as long as it takes for him to go away. Her heart is still beating hard. Beneath it all, a concentrated knot of fury is forming, hard and compact, like a stone at the bottom of a lake. Yet above the lake, a mist of apparent calm hangs over her.

"How old did you say you were?" she asks. Forcing her voice to sound casual and conversational.

"Eighteen."

She distinctly remembers that was different from what he said in the park.

"No, you're not," she jokes and affords a laugh, half-sarcastic, half-I-don't-give-a-fuck.

"How old do you think I am?" he asks.

"Seventeen," she says. She has no idea, but at least flatter him.

"I'm sixteen."

She wants to vomit. She just had sex with a sixteen-year-old. Uncomfortable, mud-covered sex that she didn't ask for.

"Listen," he says. "Sorry. I do this all the time."

Does what? Attacks random strangers in the park? Has sex with older women? Did he just say sorry?

She doesn't say anything. Let him ramble, let him say something they can later track him down with.

"I've raped girls three or four times in these woods before. I've raped prostitutes in Dublin."

Is this kid for real?

"Have you?" she says. But it's not an invitation to hear more. More of a challenge, as if to openly doubt him.

"I have, yeah," he rambles on. "I do this all the time."

"Don't worry," she says. "I'm not going to tell anyone."

She wonders how genuine that sounded. She just wants to put him at ease, have him think this was casual – a tumble in the proverbial hay. Anything to keep him from becoming violent again, doing something worse.

He's still talking. "I know these woods really well..."

Just. Go. Away.

"I come here all the time. Have girls here all the time."

Good for you. Now get the fuck out of here.

But she just repeats what she said before. "I won't tell anyone."

He stands around for a bit longer. She concentrates on eating her apple.

He kicks at a rock, turns it over with his white trainers, which are now scuffed with mud. Takes out his iPod and unwinds the headphone cords from around them. Winds them back.

She continues to chew her apple.

"I... I guess I'll go now," he says.

She looks at him, briefly, and doesn't say anything.

And he doesn't look at her either.

"Sorry," he mumbles. "Sorry." He tucks his head down, shoulders hunched up around his neck, and he hunkers down the path – the way he had told her to go, the way she had come from.

A skitter among the dirt and leaves, a flash of white among the green, and he's gone.

She waits to make sure he doesn't come back.

Checks her watch. 2:35. How much time has passed?

Waits for another minute, peers down the path, but doesn't see him. He's not coming back.

And then... exhale.

And let yourself cry finally. The tears come down, warm and confused and unsure of what the fuck just happened. Did she just have sex with a strange kid in the park? How the hell did that happen?

What about her hike? And why shouldn't she just continue? She thinks about it, still crying. She still has enough time to cover the what… nine miles left in the trail? Nine miles. Think about it. Stretching all the way along this ridge, above the city, all the way to Cave Hill in North Belfast. Clean air and an unobstructed view and the springtime afternoon. Just get away from this surreal nightmare which happened here, in this place where the trail has been scuffed up and the rocks overturned and the branches snapped. She closes her eyes and envisions the trail stretching away to the horizon: the escape she'd always wanted, when she first set out on the path this morning.

But that stone at the bottom of the lake is there. The quietly growing fury, expanding like an unspoken tumor, impossible to remove.

In her rational mind, she knows she should get medical attention.

As much as she wants to, she can't escape what's just happened. This is the reality of her afternoon, forced upon her. Brutal and unasked-for.

Here, this is what you have to deal with now.

So she stands up.

She doesn't move away immediately. She peers over the edge of the slope, trying to gauge how steep the fall is. Not because she wants to throw herself over it in grief, but more out of curiosity: how close *had* she been to the edge during their scuffle? And if she had fallen over, what would have happened? Perhaps she is half-looking for that lost water bottle, so out of place with its manufactured plastic curves among the undergrowth. But she sees nothing – only an unbroken monolithic slope of tangled weeds and vegetation. Nothing to indicate the awkward struggle which took place at the top of the slope minutes before, right where she is standing now.

The apple is finished now and the core rests in her hand. She weighs it in her right palm, a strange hulk reduced down to a skeletal pile of seeds and browning flesh.

She takes a step back, winds her right arm back like a baseball outfielder and throws the apple core as hard as she can, over the edge, down the slope, into the ravine. It lands somewhere unseen, a gentle crash in the underbrush and then no more, another intruder swallowed by the immense forest.

And then, without further hesitation, she shoulders her backpack and walks away from the scene of what just happened.

Up the path, towards the field, to where she can hear a busy road.

PART
TWO

He comes down the path, heart still knocking ba doom ba doom from them yokes and fucking that beour. Did that just happen?

Down the path he wants to grin, got his hole after all, but why ain't he grinning? Something's not right.

Trees and sun swirl together, the ground below trips him up. He slows down. Puts his hand on a tree to steady, looks down at the sleeve of his jumper – it's streaked with mud. Fuck. It's his best one, the white one he saves for wearing out at the clubs.

His trainers are scuffed, too, mud all round the edges.

Let's get that off. Don't want no one looking at him suspicious.

Bottom of the slope, back in the river. Water washing the mud from his trainers.

Fuck. Feet are wet now.

Fuckin eejit.

Get your head on straight.

Wet feet, head's in a state, what do we do?

Sit down. Right on the ground, damp soaking through the jeans onto his arse, but who gives a fuck. Catch your breath. Think think think.

She wanted it, right? 'Course she wanted it. Women always do.

Then it flashes through his head again.

The woman shouting for help, the sun bright in his eyes. Grabbing, her throat so soft like he could squeeze, squeeze the living breath right from her.

Maybe she didn't want it so much.

His cock is still kind of hard. What'd she say?

'Don't worry, I won't tell anyone about it.'

But he can't shake it – this dark clawing at the back of his mind. Like ticks burrowing inside your skin and eating their way out. He starts scratching. Suddenly, everything's itchy. His arms, his legs, his neck, his dick. Jaysus, just get the fuck away from here.

He jumps up, stares towards the path along the ridge and thinks he hears sirens, maybe. No, he's imagining things.

It's just the wind in the trees, the clattering river.

He's got to go. He's got to hide.

The dark clawing, his cock still throbbing and angry. His head pounding and his heart, too.

Don't go to the caravan, she's gone that way. The other direction, then. At the bend in the road, he nearly smashes into a fat woman and her man, out on a stroll in shell suits. They look at him, he tears away, wants to burst into a run.

Don't run. Don't make them suspicious.

Head down, get yourself up the road into town.

If only he could fly, legs leaping into the air, wings pumping, away from Belfast and the whole fucking mess of forest and town and hills, till they are specks – tiny little specks on the great broad land below him.

*

She's cleared the woods now, the tangled undergrowth, the path with upturned stones, and she's heading across the field. The field she never managed to cross the first time she got there.

If she were following the trail she'd keep to the right, alongside the glen, but she makes a definite turn left. Straight towards the busy road.

Out of the shade of the trees, bright, disorienting light floods her vision. It's still only mid-afternoon, though it feels as if she's lived an entire day in the past half hour. The green grass of the field pulses in front of her. She wobbles, she's exhausted, she's tempted to sit down. But no, reach the busy road first. Get some distance between you and that place.

Somehow, in her mind, she equates the busy road with safety. Anonymity. Drivers and passengers cruising past in enclosed vehicles and moving on to far-off places.

Between her and the road, a clutch of trailer-vans occupies the green field. There's even a few people out. A woman, hanging up laundry on a clothesline. A toddler stumbling by her feet. A man with dark hair shoveling something into a bucket. She hadn't been expecting this; she hadn't been expecting people so soon. She's almost tempted to turn back to the trail. Who lives in these trailers? Is it safe to approach them for help? Can she trust them?

They stop and look at her, but she keeps stumbling past, very aware of their eyes on her. She skirts around, keeping a healthy distance from them. Knows she sticks out, knows they probably don't want her here. She's trespassing in their backyards, isn't she? And yet, part of her still wants to run up to them, plead with that woman for help. Tell her what's happened. Say it. Say the words out loud.

Help. I need your help.

I've just been...

I've just been raped.

Is that the word? Has that really just happened to her? He was just a kid.

She keeps on walking. She instinctively doesn't feel welcome here among the trailer-vans. Doesn't think they want this sobbing, foreign woman thrusting her problems upon them.

Tears are drowning her eyes, and she puts her head down and keeps walking forward to the busy road.

Everything is so bright in the sun. She needs to go somewhere and rest, but she doesn't know this terrain, not even the name of the road. She's somewhere in West Belfast, somewhere near Glen Forest Park. Her breath jerks in uneven gasps. Her mind spins with half-formed thoughts, flitting and ducking: what should she do? What should she do next?

She needs a plan.

You're a producer. You're a backpacker. You can handle this. Form a plan of action. Control your sobs. Control your sobs. Control your breathing. Just walk. Just get to the busy road. Call Barbara. Just get to the busy road.

She leaves the people and the trailer-vans behind to her right. Twenty, thirty feet more until she reaches the road.

But she doesn't want to wait that long. She needs to speak to someone now, or she'll never tell anyone. She needs to put it into words to confirm them, confirm to herself what just happened.

She stops and gets her phone out of her backpack. Grateful he never took it from her, never even tried to take that or her iPod or her wallet. Relieved when she sees three bars of reception at the top of the screen.

Barbara. Call Barbara. Who is still in Belfast.

She calls Barbara. Barbara is surprised to hear from her.

"Hey, how's it going?"

She attempts to be chatty. Doesn't want to freak Barbara out right away. "Barbara, how are you... what are you up to right now?"

"Oh, I'm just finalizing some of the press releases for the event last night. Making sure our publicist is on track, stuff like that."

There's a pause. She can't break it.

"How... how are you?" Barbara asks.

She hesitates. "I'm... I'm not doing that good. Actually, I... I think I need your help."

Get it out.

"I... I think I've just been raped."

There. She said it. She crumples into tears, but she's passed on the burden to someone else. She doesn't have to deal with this on her own anymore.

There's a pause, then Barbara leaps into action: fast, decisive, efficient.

"Oh my God. Where are you? Is he nearby? Who was it? Are you safe now?"

A flood of questions – logistical, practical – and that's what she needs to pull her out of this mess. A safety rope, thrown down, and all she has to do is hold on and follow instructions. She grabs onto the questions, tries to answer them even as her answers dissolve into sobs.

"Yes, yes, I'm safe now. I don't know where I am."

And again, more tears. But she has to be practical. She controls her sobs, gets her breath in order. Tries to tell her as much as she knows.

"I went hiking... I went hiking, and this kid just came up to me. I'm in Glen Forest Park, or somewhere just near it. I'm not in the park anymore. I'm by a busy road. I don't know the name of the road. It's surrounded by fields, it's got to be the only road in the area."

Barbara's voice is firm.

"I'm going to call the police, Viv. Stay on the line, don't go anywhere. I'll be right here, but I'm going to call the police."

She tunes out, doesn't want to hear Barbara on the phone reporting a rape. Too many exacting details.

But two, three, four more steps... And finally, at last, she's at the road. Not really busy. In fact, it's empty at the moment, the macadam stretches in a great grey band across the fields to the horizon. But it's calm and safe. Nothing can happen to her here, in plain view of the cars that might be driving by.

She crosses the macadam, an invisible border separating her from that place behind her. There's a mound of green grass, waist-high, and she collapses upon it.

Just wait. Now, she can just wait.

Barbara's speaking to her again. "Hang on. Stay right there. The police are going to come find you, and I'm coming, too, but the police need to speak to you to get more details on where you are."

There's a beep on her phone. Call waiting. Must be the police.

How does call waiting work again? Which button does she press?

And then she's speaking to the police. It's a male voice, the

Belfast accent heavy and hard to understand but at least he's friendly. Where is she?

She describes again. Glen Forest Park. She took the bus west, past Andersonstown, along the Falls Road. Walked up the glen...

"We'll get there as fast as we can," the policeman says. "It may take a while, but we'll get there. We do apologize, but please just be patient and wait there."

She'll wait here all day if she has to. She doesn't have the energy to go anywhere else, or even to get up again.

She takes another sip of water and fixes her gaze downward. At the ground. The sun is too bright. She can't look up. Just look at the ground and wait. And wait.

Cars race past her on the busy road. Do they see her, this girl sitting by the side of the road, looking down? What do they think she's doing there? She doesn't want them to stop, doesn't want them to ask if she needs help, if she's okay.

She's not okay. She's just been raped.

Yes, she can use that word now. Has used that word now. Will use that word again in the future.

Rape rape rape rape rape. She's just been raped.

Never thought she'd use that word, ever. That it would apply to her in her lifetime.

Of course, she'd heard that word before. Had on some level, like all women, always carried that fear that comes with the meaning of that word.

Other women had been raped. Women in news stories. Nameless friends of friends of friends. But not her. Not her. It wasn't something that could happen to her.

But now it has.

Now she's been...

Raped.

The word itself is the worst. This label slapped on her like some cheap and tawdry fly-poster that can't be ripped off. A hot iron-brand, stamped painfully into her flesh, burning burning burning burning. Permanent.

Raped.

This afternoon. In this place. With the sun so bright, still so bright, forcing her gaze down to the ground.

The wail of police sirens. She looks up.

The police have arrived. One car, two. Yellow-and-white vans with sides checked blue, sailing onto the scene. Blue lights at the top of the vans, flickering in the sunlight.

They get out. Two women, two men. They are here. Casting lean shadows on the ground like sheriffs in a western.

Are you Vivian?

She nods.

One woman squats down next to her, looks into her eyes.

Are you okay? Can we help you up?

She squints against the sun. Nods.

And one of them leans down, offers her his hand, which she takes, and pulls her onto her feet.

The policewoman speaks with a thick Belfast accent she can't understand.

Authoritative questions twisted around words, the vowels all distorted. "Can you describe what he looked like? How tall was he? What colour were his eyes?"

His eyes were blue. Ice-blue. That detail she can't forget.

Other things, height, build, age... These facts swim around in a viscous mire, difficult to grab. She guesses, admits she's not good with estimating distances, heights of people.

Freckles, ginger-brown hair.

Not huge. Medium to slim build.

And age? And age.

She has no idea how old he was. He told her so many different versions. Realistically, how old could he be?

Sixteen? Seventeen?

He said he was sixteen, and again, she wants to vomit. She just had muddy, unasked-for sex with a sixteen-year-old.

She's sitting in the police van and they are asking her

119

these questions. One policewoman is filling in a form on a clipboard. Outside the sunlight is still blinding, but Barbara has arrived, and sits next to her in the shaded interior of the police van, holding her hand.

She's spitting out details, trying to provide as much information as she can. She's an open collection of facts, exposing everything she can for the police to sift through. Here, take whatever you need: descriptions, estimations. No emotions, no human feeling.

Did he say where he was from?

He said a bunch of things. None of which might be true. He said he was back and forth between Dublin and here. But that he went to Armagh a lot. He said he'd raped girls in these woods lots of times before.

Did he have a Dublin accent?

No, it didn't sound very Dublin.

So it was more of a Belfast accent?

Well, no, not quite. The accent wasn't from here.

So it wasn't a Belfast accent?

I don't think so, no.

Was it an Armagh accent then? Or more like an Omagh accent?

What? I…I'm not sure.

Barbara pipes up. "For Chrissakes, you can't expect her to know the difference between these kinds of accents!"

She's grateful for that.

Listen, all I know is that he didn't really have a Northern accent. Didn't twist his vowels the way you do.

That's the best she can do.

The policewoman nods. Scrawls something on the form.

Okay, would you be able to come with us now to the scene of the crime? To explain what happened where?

The scene of the crime. That place in the woods, along the trail, before you reach the field.

Yes, she can go. Doesn't really have a choice now, does she?

That place in the woods. She'll go back if she has to.

So she ducks down as she gets out of the police van, and

shields her eyes as she steps out. Back once more into the bright sunlight.

As she walks back across the field with the police, she notices the people standing outside the trailer-vans again. There are more of them now. Not just the woman and the toddler and the dark-haired man. But a few more women, an older man. All standing outside, staring.

They stare at the police entourage. This criminal investigation tromping right through their backyard.

Right through their backyard and toward the woods.

This is where he confronted me.

She points this out to the police. Tries to explain what happened. She was walking, he came out of the woods.

Then over here, he became... what's the right word... threatening.

Then over here, he grabbed me, dragged me towards the woods.

And then right here, in this spot.

You can see where the stones are upturned, the mud scuffed up.

The police take out the familiar tape – the kind you always see on television shows – POLICE BARRIER. They cordon off the area.

The bright, fluorescent tape stretching around thin tree trunks, blocking any further passage along the trail.

Over here, this is where he was choking me and I was lying on my back, before any of my clothes had come off.

Over here, he had me in this position.

And then over here, in this position.

And on and on.

This where he... where he wanted doggy-style.

And over here where he, um, wanted anal.

The police nod, understanding. Barbara isn't with her, she was asked to stay in the vans. She's glad of that.

"We'll be bringing dogs out now," the policewoman says. "To see if they can pick up a scent."

Police dogs. She imagines a whole horde of them, sniffing their way down the trail. Barking and sniffing, straining at their leashes. Because up ahead runs a solitary figure. Frantic, desperate, out of breath. That pathetic, miserable, scumbag boy with a pack of dogs and the police on his heel.

Could they still catch a scent even now?

She glances at her watch.

It's not even 4pm. Another hour that lasted forever. How time slows down now.

She's suddenly tired. Can she go?

Yes, we'll take you back to our special Rape Crisis Unit on Ladakh Street.

Isn't Ladakh in India? Tibet? She nods. Tibet, wherever. As long as she can sit down.

She turns to go.

"Oh."

One more thing.

"One of my water bottles came out of my bag during the struggle and it fell down the slope. You might find it down there."

She gestures to the weeds and undergrowth carpeting the steep side of the glen.

The police mumble something generic. They'll have a look. Maybe they'll find it.

Maybe it's not important to them.

She turns away, and the lost water bottle, undrunk, nestles in the undergrowth of her mind.

She looks back to where she needs to walk. Back across the field, past the people who stand outside their trailer-vans, staring. And she wonders what they're thinking.

*

All the way into town he's walked now. No buses, no money for it anyway. Walking fucking miles through Andersonstown, then down the Falls to the city centre, and here he is on Castle Street, people out doing the weekend shopping. Kids who won't stop whinging, pulling at their parents. "Mummy, I want this, I want that…" Oh, fucking shut it.

Never comes into town during the day, but here he is. City Hall looming up, never seen a building that fucking big before, back when he first saw it.

He shouldn't be here, should he, right the fuck next to City Hall after what he's just done.

But what has he done? Nothing bad, right, no, nothing out of the ordinary. Not me.

No, no it's good. You're fine. Look at all these people, in their faces. Anyone suspect? No, you're just some kid.

You just blend in. You're nobody.

*

In the police van, on the way to the Rape Crisis Centre, the rage sets in.

"That little fucker, I'm going snap his neck in two," she seethes to Barbara.

She sees his face before her, the ice-blue eyes, the cheeky expression. She wants to throw a solid square punch right into that freckled smirk. Split his face open.

She's never punched anyone before, never felt the urge. But now she feels it. Something vital and relentless, implacable.

How the fuck did this just happen? It's about to be Saturday evening and right now she is muddy, scratched up, confused, exhausted, because some scumbag teenage boy has just shoved his penis inside her when all she wanted to do was go for a hike.

How dare he?

And now she's in a police car, heading somewhere unknown. All her plans have been ruined, shredded, and a new terrain has suddenly opened up. Unexpected, unwanted.

And something tells her: this is only the beginning.

Inside the Rape Crisis Centre on Ladakh Street.

The lights are dim, the furniture in earth tones, muted. She's sitting on a soft brown couch and it feels like the lobby of a spa. Racks with women's magazines. Dried grass arranged artfully in vases. She half-expects someone to bring her a glass of cucumber water.

But no. They're not offering her anything to eat or drink. They can't until they've examined her body for evidence.

Oh, she says. I already ate an apple and had some water.

That's okay, they say. But best not to have anything else until after the forensic exam.

She wonders about what the exam will be like, but there's no time, they're asking her question upon question. Tells us what happened again. In as much detail as you can possibly remember. Even the tiniest detail could help us find him.

So she tells them. From the very beginning. That morning, when she set out from the bed and breakfast near the university. The bus she took after she had bought supplies for the hike. During the bus ride, she texted a few acquaintances to try and make plans for that evening in Belfast.

She got off the bus and started walking through the park. She passed a few people, and then she saw him, standing right there in a bright white jumper against the green. And he approached her.

When she's finished, the policewoman, Detective Joanna Peters, thanks her. "You've done very well. You've given us a lot of information we can work with."

Yes, information. That's what she is. A database of facts for you to download.

They have a map. Can she point out where these things happened? Where he approached her first, the second time, and the final time? Where he dragged her into the bushes?

The map is a blow-up of the area around Glen Forest Park. She's good with maps, but this map isn't great. Though the streets are clear, the park itself is patchy, a mess of green and tree-icons, with no trails marked out. And no topographic markings. The river is just a thin blue line.

She gets annoyed. Either with the failure of her map-reading skills or the vagueness of the map itself. Or both.

"This map isn't detailed enough," she says, frustrated. "Can you get me a map with topo lines on it?"

She's practically demanding it. A map! With topo lines! How difficult can that be?

The police hesitate. They'll try. She knows they must think she's crazy.

But what they don't understand is the topography of the place is key. The hollow of the glen itself and the rise of the land, steeply, along the slope up to the level plateau.

Without that topography, she can't retrace what happened.

This map depicts everything as if it were a level playing field. Flat, undynamic, static. But in reality, there are bends and dips in the land, ridges and valleys. Places for people to hide, places for people to lose themselves and never be found.

*

Not in the city centre no more, with the straight streets and the glassy shops and the loud families and the big old City Hall. Naw, he followed the river, started walking along it. Grey warehouses and bridges with cars going over them. Grey water trickling past.

Walking. Walking. Most of the time forget what he's walking from.

Then it might break through to him. The woman, her long dark hair, scrabbling with her in the mud, her soft throat under his fingers, flashes of sun through the trees.

But it's all right. She was fine with it. She weren't angry toward the end.

She wanted it. Like all them bitches.

No just keep walking. Don't let it catch up to you.

Keep walking.

*

The forensic exam. This is something she'd never thought she'd be part of in her lifetime.

These are things you see on television, in oppressively lit movies set in chilly Scandinavia. These are not events meant for her to experience.

Yet here she is, in the exam room. Bright fluorescent lights and grey-green walls.

The examining doctor is a warm, maternal woman by the name of Bernadette Phelan. Late-fifties or early-sixties, with soft padded hands and a gentle way of speaking.

"First, I need to ask you to comb your hair very slowly with this comb."

Doctor Phelan presents her with a plain straight plastic comb, the kind they used to give out in school. She is to comb this very thoroughly through her hair, over a piece of stiff grey paper, which will catch any dirt or other bits of potential evidence.

She stares at the comb. She hasn't combed her hair with this kind of comb since third grade. Slowly, painfully she draws the comb through her thick hair, which is matted, tangled with who knows what she picked up while forced down onto the forest floor. The fine comb-teeth snag on her hair, rip out a few strands, shaking loose dirt and mud. She does it again and again, showering crumbs of mud onto the paper.

Doctor Phelan promptly curls up the paper and tips any evidence into a labeled bag.

"Next we need to take swabs from you, so we can get samples of any genetic material he may have left on your body."

They've taken notes on where she said he touched her. So they swab her neck (when he started to choke her), her hands and wrists (when he pulled her into the woods). Her lips, her fingertips, and her mouth. They swab her mouth thoroughly, cotton buds going in and out.

And now she can finally have a sip of water.

There will be more swabs later.

"But for now, the photographer will need to take pictures of you. We need this as evidence, to document the injuries you've sustained."

The doctor apologizes the photographer is male. He was the only one available just now. Will she be okay with that?

She nods. She doesn't have much choice.

Stand on this piece of paper. There's a white backdrop behind her, blank and clinical.

Bright flashbulbs flare into her face and she's momentarily blind. Again and again. A few shots from the front. Now turn around. Now to the side. And the other side.

Now, very carefully, take off your clothes. Slowly, so we can catch any evidence on that paper beneath your feet.

She takes off the long-sleeved blue hiking shirt. It's difficult getting it over her head, there's something like whiplash setting in her neck, her back, stiffening up her body. But she has to do it on her own. No one can help her and risk accidentally getting their genetic material on her while they're collecting evidence. Eventually, she gets the shirt off, drops it on another piece of thick grey paper.

She is photographed with her shirt off, showing the torn bra. Looking straight ahead, face neutral, tired, wishing she weren't here.

It's rare she's ever taken a photograph and not tried to smile. Isn't that what you're supposed to do for photographs? Say cheese? She's been saying cheese since her first kindergarten photograph at the age of five.

But she's definitely not smiling now.

She looks straight ahead, eyes dull and blank, staring at the wall and nothing more. Perhaps she should be holding up a sign with a long number in front of her. Like a Holocaust victim. Like an arrested criminal. Awaiting whatever lies ahead.

*

"Gerry," he says, shivering on the doorstep. "Gerry, I think I done something."

Later that evening. It's dark, finally. Somehow he's found

his way over to Gerry's neighbourhood, then his street, then his house, wondering if he was back yet from his job at the building site. Peeped through the window, and there he was, feet up, watching telly. None of Gerry's family was around. Safe enough. He knocked on the window.

"Jaysus, you look a wreck," Gerry says, pushing the door open.

He looks around. No one else here. Steps inside, where it's warm and bright and smells like cheap air freshener and cigarette smoke and old fry-ups all mixed together.

"What happened to you?" Gerry's got a tin of Carlsberg and a bag of salt-and-vinegar crisps. Which he starts to chomp down on. That yoke's worn off, finally. He just knows he's been walking all afternoon, all over Belfast, and now he's cold and hungry and his feet are still wet.

He says nothing, so Gerry points to the mud on his jumper. "Look at the state of you."

"I think I done something, I'm not sure what," he repeats, between crisps.

Gerry looks at him funny. "Well, start from the beginning."

He sits down on the couch. It creaks.

"There was a girl…"

Gerry laughs. "That's how it always starts."

"No, well, it didn't go the same way." He can't put this into words. What was so strange about it? About her?

"This one was different."

Gerry snorts. "What d'ya mean?"

He and the lads have always thought there are three types of girls: our girls, the settled girls, and the tourists.

Our girls: the ones you grow up with, in the caravans next door, their virginity watched over by angry mothers and placid images of Mary, even though our girls may show their navels, wear tight shorts and thick makeup, you don't touch our girls. Not until marriage. Or at least that's what Michael's always told him.

Settled girls: fair game. You need to be smart about them, though. Only go for one when you're in a place for a few days, or about to leave – and then, scram. Clear out of there. You never know when settled girls will blow the whistle, scream for their da because they regret shifting some tinker, and then the last thing you want is the peelers after you. Peelers always hate us.

Tourist girls: now there's your golden ticket. They're here on holidays, spending money like fools, like they have too much of it and don't know what to do with it. Out for a laugh, a bit of craic. Make sure they're drunk, give them a bit of the Irish charm, a wink or two, and they're yours.

'Tourist girls – they'll lie down in nettles for it,' Donal used to say.

And it was true. How lucky had the lads been these past few summers? Michael – he'd struck gold with all those hen parties over from England. Ridiculous girls with too much make-up on, gabbling like a flock of eejits, yours for the price of a Bacardi Breezer or two.

And somewhere down the line, if they protest, try to get out of it, it won't matter. Too late for them. You'll still get what you want. And in the end, they'll never call the peelers, Michael says. They don't want to ruin their holiday. They'll leave town in a couple of days, fly back to their posh life in Manchester or Liverpool or wherever, and you never have to worry about them again. End of. Easy takings.

"Tourist?" Gerry asks him, pulling him back to the here and now.

"Yeah, of course." But he can't remember what it was about her that made her so different. Everything was mixed up, them yokes still floating him high and his head pounding when he shouted at her, pushed his hand up her shirt.

"This one was Chinese."

"Chinese?"

"Yeah, like, long black hair and all that."

"Sexy." Gerry nodded approvingly. "Like your one in the porno?"

He nods back, swallows a swig of beer. Yeah, but not quite.

She peels her clothes off, one by one, in order to be photographed. FLASH FLASH FLASH. Now the trousers, down to her torn bra and underwear. She turns around, to the side, the other side. So they can get the best shots of her bruises and cuts. FLASH FLASH FLASH.

"Get a close-up of the right foot."

She looks down. Her right foot is covered in dried mud and there are scratches and scrapes all along it.

They don't ask her to remove her underwear. Not in front of the male photographer.

Eventually, he leaves. Then they ask her.

She pulls her underwear to the floor. It's cold in the examination room, and she stands there for a moment, naked, on top of the collecting paper.

She looks down at her body and only then notices all the bruises and scratches and surface cuts. There's a giant bruise on her right thigh. A chain of them all down her right calf. A big scratch on her abdomen. Her arms, both left and right, are covered in bruises. Both knees are mottled brown and blue, almost unrecognizable.

It's as if she's looking at someone else's body. She can't register these injuries as her own. She can hardly feel them.

Her underwear and all the clothes are taken away for evidence. The paper she stood on is taken away for evidence. They need to swab her some more for evidence. Her breasts, the finger-shaped bruises on her arms and legs where he grabbed her – these places are swabbed by Doctor Phelan, all for evidence.

They give her a thin paper gown to wear. It does little to insulate her from the cold of the room.

And now, she is sitting on the examining table.

She remembers how traumatizing pap smears have been for her in the past. The metal stirrups. The dreaded speculum. Every time she had one scheduled, she dreaded it for days, cried whenever she had to open her legs for the speculum.

The notion of inserting anything cold and metallic and mechanical in there now, after what she's just gone through... She instinctively flinches.

Doctor Phelan unloads the metal stirrups from the corners of the examining table.

The nausea builds to a breaking point.

"Wait," she says.

She knows she can't get out of this. She knows this is a necessary part of the process, that inexorable process which was set in motion hours ago when she decided to phone for help. But to have to be subjected to *this*, the burrowing and the mechanical scraping inside the most vulnerable part of her body...

She tries to calm herself down. "Can I... can I ask for my friend to come and sit here so she can hold my hand?"

That's the best she can hope for in this situation.

"Yes, of course, love," Dr Phelan replies.

So Barbara comes and sits down next to her. "You squeeze as hard as you need to, sweetie," she says reassuringly.

And she squeezes. Harder than she could ever imagine squeezing in her life.

In that place in the forest, with the boy, she was numb, devoid of any feeling or sensation because there was so much adrenaline, so much confusion and fear about what was happening.

But here, in the cold, silent examination room, she feels everything.

The speculum slides in, forcing a wider space open between her legs, and she shuts her eyes and silently, she cries.

*

"Never had a Chinese girl myself. What are they like?"

Gerry's saying this as he munches on crisps, but he's in no mood for joking. He can remember, in flashes, her small soft tits, the softer pussy, but there's no pleasure no more. Instead there's that something clawing at the back of his mind, jabbing into his memories, flapping and blocking out the light.

"Come off it, Gerry. She was fine, I guess. But something's not right."

Gerry shrugs. "She's Chinese, don't worry. She'll just go quiet. When's a Chink ever raised the alarm on anyone?"

"No, but, she weren't just Chinese, she was American, too."

Gerry stops, puts down the beer. He's got a funny look on his face, like he's trying to imagine this one who's Chinese but also American.

"American?"

"American. It was like… she knew what she wanted. She had this deep voice, spoke straight at you. She didn't cry, she didn't beg, she didn't giggle. None of that."

"Where'd you find this one?"

"In the park."

"What was she doing in the park?"

"I dunno, just going for a walk."

"Anyone see you?"

"No." There wasn't a soul around. He'd made sure of that.

"So what's wrong? Think she might blab?"

"She was a bit older," he adds.

"How much older?"

And he can't remember. It was all a blur, seems like forever ago now. He knew she was older and he liked that about her. Knows he asked her how old she was, and she answered straight away, no hesitating the way the other girls do. Only he can't remember what she said.

"I dunno. Twenty-something."

"Like twenty-one or twenty-eight?"

"Jaysus, Gerry, I can't remember! I was still rolling. She was older than she looked."

"And she looked like she was in control?"

"Well, yeah, sorta. In a strange way." Even though he had to punch her a few times, choke her to get her to listen.

Gerry don't say nothing. The Carlsberg is empty. He goes over to the fridge for another. There's only one left, so he sets the tin halfway across the table, so they can share it. Cracks it open and the foam fizzes out, down the side of the tin.

"You nick anything from her?"

"No." This time he's ashamed. He'd had her down on the ground, doing everything he wanted, and he forgot to take her purse. Remembers now that silver watch on her left wrist, flashing like a fish just out of reach, when she bent the branches away. And he regrets not ripping that off, too, claiming it his own.

"You didn't even try?" Gerry looks at him like he's mad.

"I forgot." Everything had been so confusing.

Gerry shakes his head. "Well, I reckon that makes it safer. Less likely she'll tell anyone. If you'd taken her purse, an American like that might've gone to the peelers. How'd you end it? When you were done with her."

"It was strange, like. She took out this apple and just sat there and started eating it."

Gerry starts to laugh.

"I told her I wanted her to go down the path, but she was having none of it. Just sat there eating this apple."

"You said she didn't cry?"

"No, didn't cry, didn't seem angry. Just sat there."

"Did she say anything?"

"Not much." Then he remembers. "She did say something, she said, 'Don't worry, I won't tell anyone.'"

That don't sit right. Why'd she say that?

Gerry seems cagey, too.

"And you don't trust her?"

He hesitates, then shakes his head. "I don't know." And why trust her? Or anyone else?

Gerry sucks in his breath, studies one of the beer coasters. "I don't know, boy. You may just be fine. She may just get on her plane tomorrow and be off and you'll never have to worry about it."

He nods, unsure.

"I'd say, sit tight for now. See if anyone blabs in the next few days."

"And if she does?"

"Then I think you need to run."

But where to? Back down to Dublin? He's been walking around town forever, and he's suddenly so tired, fucking knackered from the past day. And where's Michael and where's Da? And how's he even going to get down to Dublin with no money?

Gerry puts a hand on his shoulder. "Jaysus, lad, you're about to burst. I didn't mean to upset you there. It's just a girl, don't worry. My guess is, she won't make a peep. And you'll be just fine. Just fine."

Gerry looks around and starts to guide him out the door.

"Listen, me mam and some of me brothers and sisters are asleep. So you go on home, go home and get some rest and you'll be better in the morning."

"I'm shattered."

"Yeah, I'll bet you are. Got your hole with a rich Chinese girl in the park. That's quite the feat. I bet she secretly loved it."

He grins and claps him into a brotherly hug.

"Fuck, you musta loved it. I bet it was worth it, and you came in pints."

Gerry sends him out the door, waving him off, and he steps into the night, saying nothing.

'Cause that's one thing he can't admit to Gerry. He didn't come. For all the different positions he tried, the soft tits, the tight pussy and silky black hair, and her muddy fingers on his cock, he didn't come. He didn't come.

*

Pain twists her into a fierce knot down there. She wants to squeeze it away, but she can't squeeze. She has to let this thing violate her.

Another eternity of scraping inside of her and finally, finally, the speculum is slid out.

She collapses into a wordless surrender of tears. Relieved it's over.

"Very good, you've been very good," Doctor Phelan says. "I know that must have been very difficult for you."

She breathes a sigh of relief.

"And I am very sorry," Doctor Phelan starts to say. "But because of what happened to you during the assault, we are also going to have to gather evidence using an anal probe."

An anal probe. No, not this.

The fear and nausea swell up anew. The tears are never-ending. This is never-ending.

She can't do this.

She just wants to erase everything's that's happened to her in the last six hours and start over again. Saturday morning in Belfast and she wakes up and decides not to go hiking. She can stay in the city centre. She can just go shopping or go to a museum. She doesn't have to hike. She never had to hike. She never had to set foot inside that park.

The forensic exam is finally over, and the doctor is once again explaining things slowly to her.

This forensic exam was designed to gather evidence for the police. She still has to be seen medically by a doctor at a hospital now, to make sure she's okay. She is given a letter explaining her situation, instructed to hand this over to the next doctor.

At the hospital, they'll be able to conduct tests for sexually transmitted diseases. There's something called post-exposure prophylaxis which is very effective against HIV, but it needs to be administered within seventy-two hours of exposure. Does she need the morning-after pill? Probably not, if you said he never came.

She takes the Levonelle with her anyway, a small lavender box, with a soft feminine name.

Barbara is pushy on her behalf. And the other injuries? But what about the bruises? And her whiplash? And the fact she was punched in the head?

The doctor at the hospital will take care of all that.

Barbara has called ahead and found out the best hospital in Belfast is the Royal Victoria. A police escort can take her to the A&E unit. They'll explain everything upon arrival, and make sure she is seen straight away.

But first, before she goes, she can finally shower.

With her clothes taken away as evidence, she'll have to change into something else. A policeman has already gone to her bed and breakfast, spoken to the management, and managed to pack up all her things and brought them here. She is suddenly reminded of that bed and breakfast, the bed she'll never sleep in now, with the sunlight slanting across the duvet.

She can't sleep alone tonight. She knows that much. Barbara says of course, she can stay with her in her hotel room.

So her suitcase is here now, and she rummages through it for something suitable to change into. There's business attire from what seems like someone else's life: a fashionable blazer with an embroidered pattern, a black pencil skirt, a pair of heels, the black cocktail dress she wore a few nights ago. None of these.

She finds a pair of jeans and a long-sleeved shirt. A clean bra and underwear. Socks and her other pair of casual shoes.

She is given a bar of soap, a packet of shampoo, and a towel.

Doctor Phelan is saying goodbye to her now, but she doesn't want her to go. She has a question. One that she almost feels embarrassed asking, but it's nagging at the back of her mind.

"What if… what if there's some dirt that got up there inside me, during the incident? How can I wash that out?"

So much mud. There was so much mud in the scuffle.

The doctor nods, puts two soft hands on her arm. "That is something your body will eventually just flush out on its own."

She didn't know the body could do that. But it's comforting to know: the dirt will just flush out on its own.

"You've been very brave," the doctor says. "And I know you'll be very brave in the future. But I'm afraid I must go now."

She's clinging onto Doctor Phelan like a toddler around her mother's legs. Knows she'll miss this warm, maternal, knowing presence who has made the past few hellish hours that tiny bit more tolerable.

"I'm needed to examine another victim," she explains.

Have there been a lot? Is she always very busy?

"You're the third rape victim I've seen today. And it isn't even nighttime yet."

She nods, and the doctor leaves.

In the shower, all she can think of are the doctor's parting words. Three cases so far today. And more to come.

She turns the water temperature up, feels the hot stream of water against her skin, and watches as the dirt and the mud and the filth wash from her body and swirl down the drain.

*

On one of the high streets, he skulks his way into a shop. He's left Gerry's. Didn't want to go home yet, so he walked even more, and now he's on the other side of town. Proddy part of town, apparently, but who cares. The main thing is, they don't recognise him here.

It's been dark for hours, but his feet are freezing and still wet. Fucking lakes in his trainers. He's probably left a trail of water leading right to this shop.

His head's stopped spinning and pounding so much. Those crisps at Gerry's didn't help, though. Again, he's fucking ravenous.

The store is brightly lit, a small television blaring away near the ceiling, and rows and rows of shiny packages: crisps, chocolate bars, pasta and curry sauces in jars. Behind the glass, a fortress of fizzy drinks and lagers. But no, he's got nothing in his pocket, he'll have to do it the usual way.

Fast hands and the usual Sweeney charm.

He edges up to the row of chocolate bars. What'll it be, Snickers? Mars?

He looks over to the till, where the shopkeeper sits bored, eyes raised to the telly. Middle-aged, balding, one of them Pakis, may or may not be trouble. Up north, you're always finding Pakis behind the tills. Don't happen much down south.

The evening news comes on and the Paki perks up.

"Over the past few days, politicians have been celebrating

the 10th anniversary of the Good Friday Accord, with famous lawmakers coming from Dublin, London, Derry and Belfast to commemorate the long and arduous process of arriving at the agreement ten years ago…"

The shop door opens with the ring of a bell, and a man and woman come in. The man's wallet bulges from the right back pocket of his jeans. She is laughing about something.

They aren't here to linger. They pick up some ready-meals from the fridge, a bottle of red wine from the shelf.

"Really, it was a tough but vital struggle we had, months and months of debating and arguing. But we should be proud of what we accomplished ten years ago – to have all of these parties in the same room, agreeing on the same thing, the future of Northern Ireland."

Some grey-haired politician on the news. Suit and glasses and posh accent.

The couple move to the till, and the shopkeeper starts to ring them up.

He's about to stuff a few Lion bars into his pockets, but freezes when he hears the next news story on the television.

"The PSNI are appealing to anyone who may have information about a violent assault and rape on a foreign woman which happened this afternoon in Glen Forest Park in West Belfast…"

That fucking bitch.

He can't believe it. The adrenaline shoots up in his veins. He starts to sweat. He can't even move. She said she wouldn't tell anyone.

The shopkeeper is done ringing up; the man takes out his wallet to pay.

Come on now. What is wrong with him? He's been nicking chocolate bars his whole life. This is the easiest thing in the world for him. Just take the fucking bars and stuff them into your pocket.

"The woman was going for a walk on her own when she was attacked by a teenage boy, dragged into the bushes, and raped…"

How could the news have gone out so fast? What did the bitch do, call the peelers the moment he turned his back?

And he freezes... he freezes. He's never frozen in his life before, he's always been fast on his feet. He always knows when to bolt.

But running draws attention. Just stay. In one place.

The couple are almost done paying.

"The boy is described as fifteen to eighteen years of age, medium height, slim build, with blue eyes and ginger-brown hair..."

Take the Lion bars, stuff them in your pocket.

They turn around, finished at the till, and at the very last moment, he somehow jolts from where he's frozen, nudges two bars into his pocket unseen.

He turns his back to the till, head tucked down, ready to head out immediately. Now, go, before the couple have left.

"The suspect was last seen wearing a white jumper and jeans..."

The couple brush past him on their way out. Your man whistles, all happy and jaunty, and swings the plastic bag. By accident swings it into him, and the wine bottle knocks into his legs, he flinches, brushes against the shelf, a shower of crisp packets falls down.

"Sorry, boy," your man says. "All my fault." He kneels to pick up the fallen crisp packets and glances at his white jumper.

Be cool. Stay calm.

The Sweeney charm.

"That's all right, sir, no offence taken," he says, grinning, chest puffed out like the posh people. "You got yourself a nice little meal there?" He gestures to the carrier bag.

"Oh, aye aye," your man replies, placing the last of the crisp packets back. "We've had a long day out, we're knackered."

"You're telling me." He nods, mimicking the man.

There's a police drawing of the rapist up on screen.

"Again, if you know anything about the whereabouts of this assailant, please do contact the PSNI at the number shown..."

"Hey," the man says, grinning, gesturing to the telly. "That could be you."

He turns around and glances at the screen briefly. Grin pasted across his face. "Oh ha, yeah! It could be! In fact, it is me." And he plays at being menacing, lowering his eyebrows down, and the man laughs along with him. "That's the spitting image of me there."

"Away on down to the peelers with you!" your man jokes.

"I will, I will. I'm heading there now!"

More laughing. Isn't this funny? Joking around with proddys.

"Well, you have a nice relaxing evening there with your lady." He claps your man on the shoulder.

Your man laughs and nods at him, your one glares at him and they both breeze out the shop.

The bell rings into silence, and he's still standing there in the middle of the aisle. Two Lion bars jammed into his jeans pocket. Frozen to the spot like an eejit.

"Can I help you?" the Paki behind the till asks, his voice all funny and singsong the way they speak.

"No, sir," he says, turning back for a moment. "I'm grand."

He's still listening to the television, though he has his back turned to it.

"The victim is described as a slim Chinese woman in her mid- to late-twenties with long black hair. She was wearing a blue shirt and grey trousers when she was attacked. She is now being looked after by the police."

Fuck. She's with the peelers.

He raises his voice to the Paki behind the till. "Sorry, sir, I don't think I've found what I'm looking for. Catch you another day."

The Paki nods the slightest of nods, his eyes wandering back to the telly. He's too far away to see the look on that brown face, but he knows to get the fuck out of there.

So he pushes through the shop door, bell ringing in his ear, and the night air blasts his face, suddenly chilly.

Worst fucking time for his feet to freeze up. 'Cause right now, what he needs to do is fly.

*

The A&E unit of the Royal Victoria Hospital. She waits in a room with Barbara. At first they didn't want her bringing company, but she needs Barbara's efficiency and pushiness at her side. Because she can hardly do her own thinking now. She's a shell of whom she once was, hollowed out and thinned out and devoid of any sense.

The receptionist had looked from her to Barbara. "Oh, are you needed to translate?"

"My English is fine," she told the woman curtly. Chastened, the receptionist showed them to their private waiting room.

The police escort had explained her situation to the receptionist, ensured that she wouldn't have to wait in the general reception. The thought of waiting there, surrounded by all the other random patients who washed up to the A&E unit on a Saturday night... She knows she couldn't handle it. She feels vulnerable, skinned, and exposed, a collection of nerves and muscle and bone that can barely function together.

As they wait, she listens as Barbara explains how the Royal Victoria, during the Troubles, was known for servicing victims from both communities, Catholic and Protestant, without bias. She imagines what the hospital must have been like in those days: men and women beaten and blown-up, victims of indiscriminate bombings, trails of blood on the floor. She flinches. At the moment, she can't cope with the thought of any more violence.

Eventually, a nurse comes in. She has spiked blonde hair and a sharp, slanted Belfast accent. The nurse takes her temperature and blood pressure, height and weight.

She wonders if the nurse has been told about her case. This must have been passed on by the receptionists, *This here girl, the foreign one. Be gentle to her now. She's had a tough time.*

But the nurse hardly acts as if she knows. Just makes the standard measurements and goes about her business.

"Our Sexual Heath Clinic is unfortunately closed for the weekend," the nurse says. "So any kind of testing for sexually

141

transmitted diseases, you'll have to do when you're back in London on Monday."

Barbara is incredulous. "Wait, you're telling me she needs to wait until Monday? Seriously?"

The nurse is firm. The Sexual Health Clinic is simply not open. No one is around who can do those tests.

"So you mean to tell me that if a girl gets raped on Friday evening, she still has to wait until Monday to be tested for sexually transmitted diseases?"

The nurse nods. Yes, that's what happens.

She exchanges glances with Barbara. Not much they can do about this.

"Very well, then. The doctor will be in shortly to see you."

Five more minutes of waiting. Then the doctor comes in.

He's a serious man, younger than she expected, spectacled with sandy-colored hair. If he knows anything of her situation, if he's at all aware of the fact she's just been raped, he makes no mention of it.

"I can see you have some heavy bruising," he says, examining her neck and shoulders.

His hands are tentative on her shoulders.

"These bruises should heal in a few more days."

He shines a bright light into her eyes, down her throat, tests her reflexes.

"All right then." He draws himself up with an air of authority. "The bruises will heal within a week, and other than that, you just need to rest and recover."

But Barbara won't let him go that easily. "But what about her whiplash? And a possible head injury, you know she was punched in the head, right?"

"I'll have the nurse give her something for that."

And then he's gone.

She and Barbara are momentarily confused. "Was that it?" she asks. "Was that the doctor's whole visit?"

"You're kidding me," Barbara says in disbelief.

Five minutes. He was there for five minutes and then he was gone. As if he didn't want to be there. As if dealing with a rape victim was that uncomfortable, he'd rather be seeing someone else, some drunkard, some car accident victim or a thug who had gotten into a fight. Anyone instead of a rape victim: this frail, shocked woman whose very presence, whose very vulnerability was something he'd rather ignore.

In another minute, the nurse shows up again, and they flood her with questions.

"The doctor's very busy. It's a Saturday night in Belfast."

What about her head? She may have gotten a concussion during the attack.

"If the doctor didn't think you needed to be treated, then you don't."

Can't you give her something to ease her whiplash?

The nurse steps away for a moment and comes back with a blister pack. Big pink round pills encased in white plastic.

Ibuprofen. They're giving her ibuprofen. She could have just gotten this from any corner shop.

Can't they give her anything stronger?

"If she's going on a flight tomorrow, she shouldn't take anything stronger."

You can see she's quite upset. Isn't there anything they can give to calm her down?

The nurse pauses and attempts to be more sympathetic. "Listen, I know you've had a rough day of it. Really rough day. You must be very tired. Maybe just go home and take a nice long hot shower, rotate your neck a bit in the warm water. And then, just, take it easy. Drink loads of tea. Spend time with your friends. Maybe have a wee glass of wine or two."

The nurse puts an awkward hand on her arm, the hot pink nail polish ludicrous against her bruises. "You take care there."

And then she leaves. The fluorescent lights buzz above the blue walls of the examination room, and there's nothing more to say.

*

143

He's home, or near enough. It's past midnight and he's dead tired. Walked all the way from East Belfast where he was in the Paki's shop, to here – up the Falls, past the cemeteries, past Andersonstown. It's too dark to go through the park and somehow he knew to steer clear.

If she already blabbed to the peelers, who knows what's going on there?

No, he's taking the long way up the road, walking past houses and fields and more fields. Where no one drives this time of night.

Maybe Da or Michael will be back, but he doubts it. Bastards couldn't give a fuck about him anyway.

Except for Gerry, he hasn't spoken with anyone real today. Just random buffers – the Paki, your man in the shop.

Oh, and the woman.

That bitch.

Just couldn't keep her mouth shut, could she?

He'll figure how to deal with this in the morning. Too fucking tired and hungry now.

The moon is half tonight, and there's a silver glow on everything. The road, the street signs. Even when he holds his hands out, he can almost make out his fingers in the moonlight.

Here on the fringes of the city, it's all quiet. Back in town, he passed pubs with loud music and chat spilling out. Buffers all carrying on with their perfect happy fucking lives.

Saturday night, and he's walking home alone by the light of the moon.

What a loser.

His feet have frozen to ice blocks inside his trainers. He's got blisters. He don't care.

He breathes harder, as the road slopes up to the halting site. This is the best bit: the lights of the city are behind him, the fields spread as far as you can see.

He can smell the shite of cows and sheep nearby, but he don't mind.

He stops for a moment to breathe it in. The fields, the moon, the dark hills.

But he just wants to go home, lie down, and sleep.

Not far now. Not far to the caravan.

*

Barbara's hotel room. It's a cozy, boutique place, away from the main tourist drag of the Europa Hotel. Again, she's grateful for that.

She's taken her bath, picked her way through some bland room service dinner, and is in bed, trying to distract herself by reading the newspaper. *Political Leaders Commemorate Good Friday Accord, 10 Years On. Titanic Studios Welcomes New Hollywood Production.*

Her whiplash has worsened – her neck and shoulders have stiffened to the point where they refuse to move.

Barbara called reception and asked if they could borrow a hot-water bottle, but they only have the large glass bottles that their posh spring water comes in.

So she fills that with hot water, and it's almost comical. Pressing a hard glass bottle against her stiff neck and shoulders, trying to wring some comfort out of that. How fitting for Belfast. But it does help, in some minuscule way.

While she was in the bath, Barbara made phone calls for her.

"Do you want me to call your parents?" she had asked.

No, no. Definitely not.

"Call my sister and my boss," she had said. "You can call them from my phone." Her boss is in London, her sister in California.

"Tell my sister not to tell Mom and Dad." Serena, the lawyer, will understand. But her parents won't be able to handle the news. And she is in no state to handle their reaction right now.

And her boss? Erika will be expecting her to show up at the red carpet tomorrow – be her usual practical self, outgoing, networking, dressed to the nines. Somehow she knows she can trust Barbara to speak with a calm voice, convey the facts, suggest the best plan of action.

"Tell Erika I'll still be coming to the premiere. I just…"

I just won't be the same person she knew when I left the office on Wednesday.

I am not the same person.

I am different.

I am now a rape victim.

She still can't quite bring herself to use those words. I was raped. I have been raped.

She flicks off the light now and settles awkwardly under the duvet, the whiplash wracking her body. That word continues to echo in her mind. Was raped. Have been raped. Am raped.

A nightmarish conjugation through all the many tenses, without knowing where this verb will take her. What happens in future tense?

I will be raped. I shall be raped.

If only she'd had that kind of premonition that morning when she stepped out on the trail. But the thought had never crossed her mind.

And even then, was it too late?

Why didn't she run faster? Or fight harder? Or realize, just a moment earlier, what she was walking into?

"You didn't have any choice," Barbara had reiterated to her. And the policewoman, Detective Joanna Peters, had as well. You did what you had to do.

Then why does she feel like she should have, could have, done something else? At what moment could she have stopped, thrown her backpack onto the ground, and made a beeline for the road, just run like hell over the field, to safety. What would have happened then?

A million scenarios could have played out differently.

In a parallel universe, she was never raped. She never met the boy. She finished the hike, triumphant, in the late afternoon, took the bus back to her bed and breakfast and would be out with her friends right now at a pub.

In a parallel universe, she did throw down her backpack and she did reach the road. And even though she no longer had her wallet or her phone or her guidebook, she still was able to walk, still was able to find her way back to the B&B and all she had to do was cancel her credit cards, get a new phone. But she was safe. She would be cozied up at the B&B, after a pint or two to take the edge off her strange encounter. But she would remain unraped.

The parallel universes splinter into a shower of countless possibilities and what-might-have-beens, as she drifts off to sleep, stiff muscles stiffening further, exhaustion quickly bearing her away from consciousness.

That night, she dreams she is running.

Straight across a bright field. As fast as she can toward a busy road. Legs pumping, heart racing, lungs drawing air in and out.

She is running away from something, but cannot see it in her dream. In front of her, other creatures reach out to grab her.

They have haunted faces.

Ice-blue eyes boring into hers.

Skeleton fingers wrap themselves around her throat, burying into her neck. She can hardly breathe. Her mind goes blurry.

She's thirsty, so thirsty.

She just needs to drink. And somewhere nearby, she knows there's a bottle of water, unopened, gleaming somewhere in the undergrowth. If only she can find it.

But she can't move. She struggles, trying to pull these hands from her throat. In the dream, she knows she still hasn't been raped. Still has time to get out of there, reach the busy road.

But she can't. She's pinned down, she's choking, and the skeleton fingers close in, relentless and final, sealing her air passage shut forever.

She wakes up. She's drenched in sweat, and a wall of pain has entombed her back and shoulders. She can't move. Her heart hammers in her chest.

Her throat is dry.

She is surrounded by darkness, in some unfamiliar place, and for several moments, she can't remember where she is.

Then she remembers.

The trail, the forest, the field, the boy.

This hotel in a quiet part of Belfast. And in the bed next to hers, Barbara sleeps away soundly.

She needs something to drink and turns her head, slightly, to the nightstand on her left. Her sore muscles, almost paralyzed, refuse at first, but she glimpses the glass bottle of water standing next to the clock radio.

The digital blue numbers glow 2:04am.

She waits a few minutes, somehow needing to gather all her strength just to pick up that bottle. Her body has never been this disobedient before; it's like pushing against a block of stiffening molasses just to get any of her muscles to move.

She grits her teeth, wrenches herself to the left, and then, in a flash of pain, she has the bottle in her hands.

Even swallowing hurts. She feels around her throat. Knows there will be bruises.

She looks up at the unyielding dark ceiling above her. She should go back to sleep, but she doesn't want to return to those dreams.

A tear escapes the corner of her eye and runs a wet trail down the slope of her left temple. Her shoulders are too stiff, she doesn't bother to wipe the tear away.

How did she get here? How did she possibly get here?

*

Sunday morning.

He wakes up to someone rapping on the caravan door. He's having the creepiest fucking dream – some faceless woman screaming and clawing at him, wailing right in his face – when he hears it.

Rap rap rap.

First he thinks it's that muppet from next door, but the rapping's too heavy to come from a little kid.

Leave him alone. He just wants to sleep this off.

Rap rap rap.

They're not going away. He sits up.

Shite, maybe it's the peelers already. Could they have found him that fast?

A cold feeling slices through him. It freezes him to the spot, twists his insides until they want to burst. Maybe it's called fear.

He bunches up tighter into a ball, wishing he were invisible. Go away. I'm not here.

Whoever it is, they don't say nothing. The rapping stops after a while and he hears footsteps moving away from the caravan.

Another five seconds, and he creeps silently to the window and looks out. It's Gerry, standing with his back to him, looking at the field and the other caravans. Another bright day, not as sunny as the day before, clouds and shadows here and there.

He's about to call out to Gerry, when the Callahan woman from next door comes by. The last thing he needs.

"Morning, Gerry, how are ya?"

"I'm grand, Nora. You?"

She don't answer his question, just nods. "What brings you here?"

"Ah, just happened to be in the neighbourhood, wanted to see if the lads were in." Gerry jerks a thumb back to the caravan.

"I saw Johnny here yesterday, but not his brother for a while. Nor Mick neither."

"Oh, is that right?" Gerry feigns. "Guess they went away then."

Nora shrugs. "You know how them Sweeneys are. Here one minute, gone the next. And that young one, with no one round to feed him."

"Ah, Johnny's practically all grown up. Bet he can take care of himself now."

That's me boy, Gerry. Put her straight.

149

"Well, I try to do what I can. Make up for his da being away all the time."

Gerry coughs. "And your own man, Brian? Can't recall seeing him around here recently…"

She stops smiling. "Now that's different. Me Brian's away earning good, honest money, bringing it back to me, not scrounging around like them Sweeneys here."

Gerry holds his hand out. "Nora, I was just having a laugh…"

But she's angry now. "For sure you were. You want to know where your friends are? Ask them peelers who were here yesterday."

She spits this out fierce, goes to leave, but Gerry's onto her like a starving cat on a field mouse.

"Peelers? Here?"

Nora turns around, still fuming.

"They speak to anyone here?"

"Not to none of us, no. But they come marching out across that side of the field into the woods, and then for the rest of the afternoon, they were all over that area – see, where they've set up the police tapes." She points to the far edge of the field.

He squints in that direction.

How could he be that blind, not seeing nothing? There's the flash of bright yellow police tape, he can just make it out. But he stays where he is behind the door, straining to hear what else Nora says.

Gerry's playing it cool. "Jaysus, what do you think it was about?"

Nora shrugs. "Can't say. They didn't come over. Spoke to none of us, as usual. But about a half hour before, I saw a young girl come out of those woods. Couldn't really see her. She had a backpack on and long black hair, that's about it."

Gerry's nodding. "And then?"

"Then that same girl come back with the police and they went into that area and that's when they started setting up the tapes and all, bringing over dogs."

"Dogs?" He bolts up, alarmed.

"Yeah, those kinds of sniffer dogs, but I couldn't see very well what they were doing."

"The dogs ever come over this way?"

"No, not this way."

"And what happened to the girl?"

"She went back with the police, into their van, and drove off."

"Jaysus," Gerry says. "What do you think it was?"

"Can't say. Poor little girl. Maybe got roughed up by someone? Hope she's all right."

"Aye, I hope so, too," Gerry plays along. The two of them stand there, looking out, faces soaking in the morning sun.

"So... what do you reckon you'll tell the peelers if they come asking?" Gerry ventures.

"Just what I told you," Nora says. "Nothing else to say."

Gerry grins, and circles Nora around her shoulders with a bear hug. "You're grand, Nora," he says. "Your man Brian don't know what he's got."

"Ah well, that's how it goes, I suppose," she says, and pauses a moment. "You want a cuppa tea or something?"

"Nah, thanks, Nora, I better be going. But, uh, if you see either of the lads, can you tell them I'm looking for them?"

Nora nods and walks off. Gerry stands for a minute longer, watching to make sure she's back inside.

"Gerry!" he hisses, pushing the door an inch open.

Gerry slips inside the caravan. Door closed, his head pushed down close, whispering quickly to him.

"You feckin eejit, why'd you come back to the caravan?"

"You told me to come home and sleep!"

"Aye, well, I reckon you should scram. There's peelers just over the other side of the field there. Vans, lights flashing and everything."

"Fuck! Fuck fuck fuck fuck fuck. That fucking bitch!"

"She pulled a fast one on you. Looks like she called the peelers right after you left."

He don't understand. He can see her sitting right there by the side of the trail, eating her apple.

Don't worry, I won't tell anyone.

He's gets up and starts pacing around. Kicks in one of the kitchen cabinets. Heart beating, head filling with anger. They have dogs after him. Fucking dogs.

"Whoa whoa whoa, there – take a deep breath." Gerry puts up both arms to calm him down. "Whatever she said to you, she's done something else. And you need to figure out how to get out of this."

He tries to calm down, taking deep breaths.

Gerry keeps on talking. "Because if the peelers figure out who you are, it's open season on the pavee boy."

Open season. He don't like the sound of that.

He sits down, puts his head in his hands. That pounding headache is coming back and there's that dark clawing at the back of his mind, scraping away, trying to remind him of something he wants to forget.

Gerry stands up.

"Let's get that white jumper off you," he says quickly. "Take that with us and bin it. You need to grab a change of clothes and get the fuck out of here."

"Where we going?"

"I'll take you to mine, you can lay low there till we sort something out. Let's hope my mam won't pick up on anything for a while."

"Where the fuck is Michael?" he shouts. He's raging at Michael and Da for being fuck-all there for him. Where's his own family when he needs them?

"Yeah, where the fuck is Michael? Don't worry, I'll find him. I'll track him down."

He's peeling off the white jumper, rummaging around for another shirt, another jumper, clean socks and pants.

"Put on another pair of trousers, too," Gerry says. "You've got dirt all over this pair."

Gerry finds carrier bags in the kitchen cabinets, stuffs the soiled clothes in one of them.

"Where'd you say you have family? Other than Armagh and Dublin?"

"Ah, I dunno… everyone moves around. Cork? Kilkenny? Wicklow? Michael and Da have all their numbers."

"We'll sort something out."

He's put on a T-shirt and grey hoodie, his other pair of jeans. Gerry bends down and scrubs some of the dirt off his trainers. Stands back and looks at him.

"Put on a cap," he says.

He finds a New York Yankees cap an uncle once gave him.

"Michael have any aftershave? If they've dogs on your scent, you'll be wanting to cover that up."

He rifles through Michael's stuff and finds a posh-looking bottle called Hugo Boss, something his brother must have pinched from somewhere. He splashes it on, sneezes. Ain't this stuff supposed to make you feel older, manlier? He just feels out of place, a toddler play-acting. If the dogs won't pick up on him wearing this, for sure everyone else will.

"Good. Perfect," Gerry approves. "You're a whole new person. Now let's get you the fuck out of here."

He crouches down low beside the door and Gerry peeks out the far window.

"What d'ya see?" he asks.

"Three, four police vans. Parked by the road. Peelers going back and forth with dogs from there to the woods."

The dark clawing has scraped its way to the front of his mind, but he pushes it back. Not now.

"Any way to avoid them?"

"Yeah, they're all busy over there by the woods. Just be fast about it and walk away. Not too fast. Don't want to be attracting any attention."

At least the front door is on the opposite side of the caravan, facing away from where all the peelers are. He looks around one more time at the inside of the caravan. "Wait, hold on a second."

He runs back to his and Michael's room and grabs something. His granda's ring, the one Mam gave him years ago when he died. He stuffs it in his pocket.

"Forget something?" Gerry asks.

"Ah, nothing important. Let's just go."

Another deep breath, and Gerry pushes open the caravan door.

Outside, it's colder than he expected, and the chill hits him to the bone, despite the bright sunlight. The brim of the Yankees cap shields his eyes from the sun. He can hear the beep and chatter of police radios. The bark of a dog.

He hesitates, but Gerry nudges him forward, his hand on his shoulder.

"Just keep on going. Don't look back."

They walk quickly across the field, away from the peelers, away from that place where the woods meet the open ground. Along the ridge to the north, with the glen and the soft roar of the river below on their right.

Before they disappear behind a rise in the ground, he turns around one last time and looks back. At the huddle of white caravans on the bright green field. He squints against the sun and he can make out two figures standing near Da's caravan. Nora is looking away, towards the police, but her little kid runs a few steps after them and raises a hand to wave at him and Gerry.

He almost wants to wave back, but he won't.

*

Sunday morning and she's with the police again, in the Rape Crime Unit Centre, to give her official statement. Last night was just for the forensic exam.

"This should take about three hours, but it's important that you're as thorough as possible," Detective Peters says, looking at her watch. "So if we finish at noon and your flight is at 1:20, you should be able to make it. The City Airport is just down the road."

It's as if she's in a new job, one that she never applied for. A whole new set of tasks and responsibilities. Just do as you're told.

"Tell me about what happened yesterday, starting with what you did that morning."

"I checked into a bed and breakfast, after a few days at the Europa Hotel for a conference. I had always planned to go for a hike that day…"

The morning sun slants through the wooden slats of the Venetian blinds. She tells her story. Again. Detaching herself from the detail. Watching the dust motes dance in the light.

*

He spends most of Sunday holed up in Gerry's bedroom. Gerry's family don't live in a caravan anymore. They've moved into a proper house, which feels weird. Too many straight lines and too much furniture. It's even got stairs.

In the hallway, Gerry tries to keep it smooth with his mam.

"You know the young Sweeney boy, right? He's not too well and is staying over here for a bit. His da and his brother aren't around."

His mam mumbles something.

"No need to send for Old Thomas or anyone. He's just needing a bit of company with everyone else gone."

Another mumble.

Gerry pokes his head into his room.

"You after any breakfast? Me mam is doing a big fry-up, but it'll be with all me brothers and sisters."

Not all, just five of them. At the table, it's Gerry, then his sisters Grace and Fiona, his brothers Eamon and Darragh, and his youngest sister Oona, who's just three. Mrs Donohue bustles between the hob and the table, frying up eggs and rashers, unloading them onto plates.

He's forgotten what it's like to be part of a big family. Everyone talking all over each other, all at the same time. The last time his whole family was together was… four year ago? In Dublin?

"D'ya have any sisters?" Fiona or maybe it's Grace asks him.

"I do, yeah." He's shoveling rashers into his mouth as fast as he can, but still manages to talk. "I've a sister, Claire,

155

that's… twelve now? And a younger one, Bridget, that's eight."

"How comes we never seen them around?"

"Oh, they're down in Dublin with me mam. They don't come up here."

"Johnny, when's the last time you seen your mam?" Mrs Donohue asks as she's clattering away at the hob. All mothers always ask the same thing.

"Oh, a while ago. Longer than a while, really."

"How comes your parents don't live together?" Eamon or Darragh asks.

Jaysus, this is worse than the nosy child counsellor grilling you at school.

"And you've a brother, Michael, too, yeah?" Fiona or Grace says. He can tell from the way she says his brother's name that she's got a sweet spot for him. He wonders if Michael's ever shifted her. She's not bad. A little skinny, but kind of pretty.

"Yeah, me brother Michael, yeah."

There's a noise at the door and in walks Gerry's younger brother, Liam. He's about nine or ten.

"Liam Donohue, where've you been?" Mrs Donohue asks.

Liam's out of breath and grabs Eamon's glass of orange squash, swallows half of it in one go.

"Sorry, Mam," Liam says, as he reaches for a rasher. "It's mad, like. D'ya hear about what happened up near those quarries by the Glen?"

"What happened?"

The whole table pipes up except him. He wants to sink into the fancy tiled floor and disappear. There it is again, that stupid dark clawing, front and centre of his brain.

"Apparently this foreign girl was, uh, raped around there." Liam casts a glance at his mam when he says 'raped'. He can't help smirking when he says the word.

There are squeals and squawks from around the table.

"That's horrible!" Grace or Fiona says.

"Do they know who done it?"

Liam's shaking his head, chewing on more rashers. "No, not a clue. But there were peelers poking all around the Traveller site there."

Gerry looks at him, looks away.

"They started asking the Traveller families some questions."

"Ah, they're always after us Travellers," Gerry grumbles. "Any crime happens, they get on to us straight away like we automatically done it."

"Hey, isn't that where you and your family live?" Grace or Fiona says this, the one who likes Michael.

He can feel sweat standing out on his neck. Get a fucking grip. He swallows the toast he's chewing, but it's dry and almost won't go down.

"Yeah, we're in that same halting spot, right above the Glen."

"Didn't you see nothing, all those peelers poking around?"

"I saw something this morning when I left. Didn't know what the Jaysus it was about, though."

"That's just terrible, terrible," Mrs Donohue says, shaking her head. She's at the kitchen table now, unloading the last of the fried eggs. It's gone within seconds. "Terrible for someone to do that to a girl."

"Yeah, what happened to the girl?" Grace or Fiona (the other one) asks.

Liam shrugs. "No one knows. They say she was Chinese."

That starts a murmur around the table.

"Wonder what she was doing in that part of town," one of Gerry's sisters says.

"Well, I hope they catch him, whoever's done it," Mrs Donohue says. "Terrible thing to do."

She starts to collect some of the dirty dishes. Grace/Fiona gets up and starts filling the kettle from the tap.

He eyes the tap. None of this hauling yourself outside to pump water.

"Johnny." Mrs Donohue turns to him. "Would you like a cuppa tea?"

157

He looks at her. Of course he wants some tea. But he also wants to get out of this kitchen as fast as he can.

"I'm not feeling so good," he mumbles.

"Oh, that's right, love," she says. "You go on to Gerry's room and get some rest."

Inside, behind the closed door, Gerry turns to him.

"You just lie low here. Don't say nothing to me brothers and sisters, and I'm gonna make sure they don't bother you none."

Gerry starts to put on his jacket.

"Where you going?"

"To the shop and the pub, see what I can find out. And I'm gonna look for Michael. I haven't a clue where he is. And we need him here. Now."

*

They're at the George Best City Airport, where she's supposed to check in for her flight at 1:20.

But the police report took longer than expected, and they didn't arrive here until around 12:45. Didn't get to the actual check-in counter until 12:52.

The woman at the counter says it's too late for her to get on the flight.

She shakes her head sternly. "The sign here says check-in closes strictly thirty minutes before take-off."

Barbara is arguing with her. "You have no idea what she's just been through. She has to get on this flight."

"I don't care what she's just been through. She's too late and I can't compromise our security measures just because of one passenger who couldn't get here on time."

Security measures.

She doesn't say anything herself. Somehow, she seems robbed of her voice. She's been talking for the past three, four hours for the police report, and she doesn't have the energy to argue with this horrible woman.

But she needs to get away from this place. And she can't miss that premiere in London. The airline woman is still adamant. "I can't help you. If she can't follow the rules, I can't do anything for her."

"This isn't about following rules," Barbara says, her voice raised. "This is about showing a little compassion."

She puts her hand on Barbara's arm. "I *have* to get on that flight. I have to get to London this afternoon."

"Well, you're not getting to London on our flight, because it's closed," the woman announces with finality. "We have another flight in three hours."

And then... just like that... she cracks. An unfamiliar anxiety takes over, and she starts to cry, her face screwing up, tears and snot welling up in an instant. She can't miss that premiere, she's worked years on this film, this is the company's first big red carpet in Leicester Square. If that scumbag kid somehow makes her miss it...

Just get me out of this fucking city.

"I have to get out of Belfast," she sobs. The woman stares at her, dumbfounded.

She doesn't care.

The woman stammers, but doesn't back down. "It's too late now anyway," she says, pointing to the clock. It's past 1pm, and they'll never get her onto the flight.

"It's okay, it's okay, sweetie," Barbara says, enveloping her in a hug. "We'll find another flight for you."

The woman packs up the check-in desk. Head down. Removes the sign for the upcoming flight

"I hope you feel good about yourself," Barbara says as a parting shot at the woman.

The woman says nothing. Then pauses and says, "If you had just come ten minutes earlier."

Ten minutes earlier, she was still giving her police statement in the Rape Crime Unit. If she had only set out on the trail ten minutes earlier, maybe she wouldn't have encountered the boy. How different our lives would be if we went about doing everything ten minutes earlier. To think that ten minutes separated us from crashing into that near-fatal car accident, or meeting the love of our life, or encountering our rapist?

Or was life really that arbitrary? She thinks that is the only way she can really accept what happened because it was so random. Ten minutes earlier and she wouldn't have been raped. Ten minutes earlier and she'd be on that flight.

Barbara has instructed her to sit down on a bench, while she goes about buying her a ticket onto the next flight bound for London.

She sits there in a daze and watches people checking in, rushing off to the gates. Families saying goodbye to one another, parents seeing off their grown children who live in London. The occasional businessman, leaving a bit earlier on a Sunday, to get plenty of rest in London and start fresh on Monday morning.

And her. Her. Recent rape victim. On her way back home to attend the red carpet premiere of the film she worked on.

Barbara's back. She looks flushed, but positive.

"I got you onto a 2:30 flight to London, which will get you into Gatwick at 3:45. Is that okay?"

She manages a grateful smile. "That's perfect. Thanks so much."

Barbara hands her the ticket. "Here, let's get you checked in so you don't miss this one. I bought you a business-class ticket, thought it'd make you a bit more comfortable."

"How much do I—?"

"No, no, I'll take care of it. There's no way in hell I'd have you pay for this."

So she says goodbye to Barbara. She has no idea how she's going to get through the rest of it – whatever that entails – with no Barbara by her side. She can't even think about what is yet to come. Previously, she's always been able to imagine the life ahead of her, but now, everything ahead is just opaque, a dark forest with no obvious path.

She makes her way through security, to the business-class lounge. Helps herself to a can of Sprite and nibbles at a sandwich. The same tastelessness as before.

She sits in the row of seats closest to the windows. For a few minutes, she watches the runway, as planes maneuver themselves along the tarmac, lining up against the grey-blue background of the harbor.

The business lounge is nearly empty. A couple of middle-aged businessmen sit behind her to the left, another in an armchair. Save for the woman at the service desk, she's the only woman there.

Her logical mind takes over again. She needs to think of what to do. Her next step. She should alert her friends in London about what's happened. So she composes a few texts.

Hi there, just to let you know, something really bad happened to me and I was raped yesterday. Flying back to London and will be home soon. So please don't ask me how my weekend in Belfast went.

She sends this to her two flatmates, José and Natalia.

She then amends the text slightly and arranges with Jacob, one of her gay best friends, for him to meet her at Gatwick.

Then she calls another gay friend, Stefan, the one who was going to be her date to the film premiere tonight. She tries explaining what happened, but there isn't a good connection and he can't hear what she's saying. She makes plans to meet at Leicester Square at 6:45 that evening. He'll be wearing black-tie, as requested.

She gets a text from her boss, Erika, asking if she's okay. Their assistant, Becca, has arranged for a cab to pick her up at home and take her to Leicester Square.

Another text, from her sister, Serena.

I'm so so sorry to hear about what happened. What can I do? Can you talk tonight?

She sighs, wants to put the phone away. Wants just to drift into oblivion and keep on drifting away and not have to come back to the reality of her life now.

Did she really just break down crying in the airport? What functional adult does that when they've missed their flight?

But she's not a functional adult, that much she knows. Yesterday, she morphed into this helpless shell of an adult, and now she has to pretend like she knows what she's doing. When really, she has no idea.

She's full of shame and disgust at herself. For what she has become.

The lady behind the service counter makes an announcement.

Will all passengers for Flight 5230 to London Gatwick make their way to the boarding gate.

In the business-class queue to board, she's looking out the window, doesn't want to make eye contact with anyone.

One of the flight attendants comes up to her, a pretty woman with a high ginger ponytail.

"Are you Vivian Tan?"

"Yes, that's me."

"So sorry to bother you, but there's a police detective on the phone for you."

What now? If they try and stop me from getting on this flight...

She obliges and follows the flight attendant to a beige phone set in the wall behind the desk.

It's a man on the phone. A strong Belfast accent, like all the other police.

"Hello, I'm Detective Thomas Morrison. I don't think we've had the chance to meet yet, but I'll be in charge of handling the case to find your assailant."

"Hi," she says tentatively. "How are you?"

"I'm okay, I hope you are, too. Or as best as you can be." He has a kind voice at least.

"Listen, there's just one more thing we wanted to ask you. We forgot to ask if you would leave behind your watch. We just think it might be useful for the investigation."

"My watch?" She looks at it. The thin silver band around her left wrist, and she remembers how the boy eyed it, the second time he approached her in the forest.

"Yes, you said he was looking at your watch, before he

attacked you. And we thought there might be some kind of genetic evidence we could find on it."

"But he didn't take it, obviously. It's still with me."

"Well, we don't want to leave any stone unturned. If there's any chance we can get his fingerprints from it, that would be very helpful."

She distinctly remembers he never touched her watch. But if it'll somehow help the investigation, she'll surrender this too. Who needs to keep track of time anymore?

"Just wrap it up in some paper and leave it with the airline staff, we'll come pick it up shortly."

She hangs up the beige phone. It seems like a rather crude way to be collecting criminal evidence, but she does as instructed. Hands the paper-wrapped bundle to the flight attendant.

The rest of the passengers have already boarded, and the ginger flight attendant smiles at her kindly, leads her outside to the plane.

She climbs up the stairs. The wind nips at her jacket, and before she steps inside the warmth of the plane, she glances around briefly at the broad tarmac, the bright sky, the grey waters of the cold harbor.

Belfast. Not a moment too soon to be leaving.

The police, or perhaps Barbara, must have informed the airline staff about her situation, because they are acting uncommonly kind to her.

"If you need anything, anything at all, don't hesitate to let me know," the ginger-ponytailed flight attendant says to her, smiling. "I'll be right here."

She's been given the first row of the plane all to herself, and she's thankful she won't have to pass anyone else, interact with anyone on this flight. The plane gathers speed for the take-off and lifts itself at a sharp angle, banking to the right as it circles over the harbor.

Instinctively, she looks down at the city, tries to map her recognition of Belfast onto what she sees below. City Hall is visible and Victoria Square, and she can just about make out the Europa Hotel. Further north, set amidst green lawns, there's the grey hulk of the Stormont, not so imposing when seen in miniature.

She glimpses Cavehill, with Belfast Castle upon it, and her eye tries to trace an invisible line along the ridge of hills. She looks southward, all the way to where a wooded glen creeps up against a plateau of pastures and quarries. To a place where the forest meets a field.

But the plane dips and swings away to the north, abruptly changing her field of vision. She pulls her eyes away from the window, back into the mundane, artificially lit interior of the plane.

Why look over there? What can be gained from recognizing that place from the air?

And the weight of the past 24 hours comes shuddering down around her. She begins to cry again, tries her best to stifle her sobs, and just weeps silently into the hood of her jacket.

Tears come pouring down her face. She must look pathetic to everyone else on the plane, but she can't help it. She uses up her tissues, searches about for more.

Wordlessly, the flight attendant hands her some tissues, smiles and nods.

She smiles back, and glances out the window. They've cleared Northern Ireland. Grey-blue waters drift below, glimpsed momentarily in the sunlight before the clouds close over.

*

That afternoon, all he does is lie in bed. Gerry has some porn mags, but he won't look at them. Don't want to be reminded of the fucking nightmare he had last night.

Downstairs, he can hear the television chattering away and Gerry's brothers and sisters laughing at it. He'll not be going down there, not with all their questions.

The light changes with the day going by, and end of the afternoon, Gerry comes back. He's carrying a bundle of chips wrapped up, still warm, and a tin of lager.

"Here, got you something to eat."

The warm, greasy smell of chips drifts up as he unwraps the bundle, making his mouth water.

"What'd you find out?"

Gerry's pacing back and forth now. It's making him nervous, and he wishes he'd just come out and say it. "You're in pretty deep. Deeper than I thought."

"What d'ya mean?"

"It's all over the news. Every Traveller I spoke to knows the peelers been poking round your home. The Glen this, the Glen that."

"How much they know?"

"Just that it's a Chinese girl who's been raped near there, and it's a teenage boy that done it."

"Anyone know who?"

"Listen, they all know I'm friends with you. No one's mentioned your name. Or Michael. But they're not gonna tell me if they suspect."

"The Travellers wouldn't say nothing, would they?"

Gerry shrugs. Steals a chip from his bundle. "Wouldn't think so, but you don't know who to trust these days."

"And the buffers?"

Gerry pauses. "I spoke to some settled folk I know. Some of the girls, some of the shopkeepers."

"What they think?"

"The girls are all freaked out. It's like they don't want to talk about it, not to me. Just keep saying how horrible it is. The shopkeepers, they're saying other stuff. Like they have a few ideas who it could be."

"What's that mean?"

Gerry's shaking his head. "They're saying stuff like they know a few lads who fit the description. They got their eye on one or two kids."

"You think anyone's gonna blab?"

Gerry looks at him like he's stupid. "Oh, I dunno. Maybe them shopkeepers you've been stealing from? The buffer boys you get in scraps with? You've been in Belfast long enough for people to know who you are."

Nothing to say there. He looks down at the greasy pile of chips in his lap.

Gerry's still pacing. "Have you had other girls in the Glen?"

"One or two."

"How recent? Were they tourists or from Belfast?"

"Jaysus, I can't remember. They were from Belfast, I think. What's it matter? They didn't blab."

"Well, they might now, now that your Chinky has gone to the peelers."

"Fuck," he says. "This is shite."

Gerry sits himself down on the bed next to him. Grabs a few more chips.

"So, I still can't find Michael."

"What? Oh, come off it."

"He's not answering his phone, no one knows where he's gone."

"Well, that's fucking grand. Me own brother, leaving me in the lurch like this."

"Maybe he's shacked up with some sweet beour, or maybe he found some work. I haven't a clue. So..." Gerry pauses, clears his throat. "I had to call your da."

Anger flares up and he punches Gerry in the shoulder.

"You didn't. You fucking didn't."

Gerry puts up his hands. "I had to, I had to. You've no one else to help you out here."

"What the fuck d'ya mean? What about you, Gerry?"

"Listen, I'm trying. I'm doing all I can. We just need to get you out of here. Over the border and holed up with your own folk somewhere safe. But I need your da or Michael to help me. Can't do it on our own."

"Aw, that's the last fucking thing I need! Me own da on me case about this." He crumples the greasy chip-paper into a ball, throws it hard as he can at the wall. It bounces and rolls into the corner, wilting where it stops.

A fierce beating from Da is what he'll get now. He's filled with the old hatred.

"It's better than the peelers," Gerry says. "It's that or fucking jail for you."

But there has to be some other way. Da or jail. How did his life get squeezed down to one or the other?

Two days ago he was fine. And now what are his chances?

He stands up. "I can't fucking believe it!" he seethes. He thrashes his fists above his head, wants to punch through the wall. But Gerry gets a hold of him, wrestles him back onto the bed.

"Shh... shhh, would you? Me family's outside. If they hear you shouting, they're gonna start suspecting. Am I right?"

He growls, low and angry like a dog on a tight chain. No other way to let it out, so he's punching the bed, then kicking at the ball of greasy chip-paper, wishing it were Da, just asking to have his teeth smashed in. Da and the fucking peelers. Lamp their faces in.

Eventually, he stops, gets his breath back.

"How much you tell me da then?"

"Not too much. Reckon he figured enough out. He's coming back tomorrow."

Gerry kicks his shoes off, leans back on the bed. "I started just by asking if he knew where Michael was. I says Johnny was after asking for him, since Michael weren't around."

He groans. No way Da would believe that.

"So then he figured something was up. He says, 'So what's Johnny done this time?' And I says, 'Don't think he's done nothing. But the peelers are poking around the halting site and asking all sorts to the Travellers there, so Johnny's staying with us for a bit.'"

He nods. Maybe it's not so bad then.

"But listen," Gerry says, quieter. "After your da gets here tomorrow night, you should be staying with him again."

Fucking hell. Is he being kicked out?

"Not 'cause I don't want to help you. I'm doing all I can. But me family are gonna start asking questions, bound to. And you never know what kind of rumours are gonna spring up."

"Your brothers and sisters gonna rat me out, Gerry?"

"No, of course. They don't suspect nothing. But what I'm saying is, I don't want peelers come knocking at our door. That's the last thing me family needs right now."

He stares at Gerry. He *is* getting kicked out. So much for pavee loyalty, bastards.

Gerry's still trying to explain, all apologies and shame. "We've done well to get this house, we don't want to be getting on bad terms with the council."

"Oh, so you're cosying up to them now?"

"That's not what I said, Johnny. We just don't want to give them any reasons to take this house away from us."

"Jaysus, they're not going to take a house away from a Traveller family, Gerry! They're well on their way to turning you into buffers, they're not gonna stop now."

Gerry's eyes harden. "We're not buffers just 'cause we live in a house."

"Well, you're not acting like Travellers now, are you? Turning me loose when the peelers are after me."

"Oh, fucking stop with the drama, Johnny. Am I not the one helping you here? Getting you your breakfast and tea, tossing away your evidence and all."

"Yeah. Yeah, and what did you do with me things? You after handing them over to the peelers?"

"Aw come off it! Threw them into a skip the other side of town, I did. They're never going to find them there. And this is me fucking thanks."

The blood is pulsing in his head and he stops. Knows he's being an arse to Gerry, but who else can he get angry with? He just wishes everything could get rewound, back two days. He wouldn't of gone out and roughed up that Chinese girl. Would've just gone home and had a wank.

"Fuck, listen, Gerry. I'm sorry, yeah? I don't know what the fuck I'm doing."

Gerry nudges him in the shoulder.

"Yeah, well, that's kinda obvious."

They both laugh a bit.

"Jaysus, what am I gonna do?"

Gerry sighs, picks up the chip paper. "Listen, me mam's trying to get all us to church tonight, but you're best off laying low in here. Don't want people seeing you out and about."

Church. Jaysus. When's the last time he'd been to church?

"So I'll just remind her you're poorly and she'll, uh… she'll just pray for you." Gerry winks at him. "Gotta go down now, you just take care of yourself in here, all right?"

"Yeah, I'll be fine." He nods and watches as Gerry leaves, closing the door behind him.

But he's not fine. He knows that much. The sun's set by now, and in the gloom, the dark clawing returns. He thinks of the woman sitting by the side of the trail, eating her apple.

Don't worry, I won't tell anyone.

But you did, you fucking lied. You went straight to the peelers and told them. He wishes she were in front of him all over again. And then he would rape her hard, rape her until he came, pull her black hair and bite into her neck and grab her tits. And then he would squeeze her throat until she stopped breathing, and toss her over into the ravine. He should've done that. He should've done that.

But he didn't, and now look where he is.

*

Three hours later, she's in her flat in London, attempting to get ready for the film premiere. Jacob is with her. He'd met her at the airport as requested, asked no questions, just hugged her tight and chatted along pleasantly on the train back, without expecting her to say much.

Now they stand in her bedroom, looking at the dress she's borrowed for the premiere. Five days earlier, a designer had lent it to her, and it hangs in its plastic sheeting – a delicate, white, Grecian gown.

169

Again, she wants to cry. This time, because the gown is so beautiful, yet she knows she'll never do it justice. Before yesterday, she could have pulled it off. But now she can't enjoy anything. Beauty and luxury are wasted on her.

"We'll make it work," Jacob says, clapping his hands.

She has twenty minutes before the cab arrives. Twenty minutes to go from rape victim to red-carpet guest.

She knows this is an unnecessary amount of stress she could do without. But she's not backing out. Refuses to let that kid take this from her.

There's no time to shower, so with a quiet, joyless desperation, she finds her strapless white bra and steps into the gown as Jacob zips her in. And then... her hair. Her goddamn hair.

"Just wear it down," Jacob says.

But no, it's Grecian-style, she has to wear her hair up. Only, with the whiplash, it's virtually impossible to lift her hands up and twist her hair, so she talks Jacob through it.

"Just pull it back, twist it around and secure it with the elastic."

"Isn't this going to hurt if I pull your hair like this?"

"Don't worry about it, just get the elastic in." She doesn't exactly feel pain the same way these days.

The hair is up. Sort of. She instructs Jacob to slide in a few bobby pins. She looks in the mirror. Good enough.

And now make-up. After a half-hearted attempt at eyeliner, eye shadow and mascara, she examines the bruises on her throat. They're fairly dark, so she dabs concealer on, up and down her neck. Does that really cover up the bruises? Not really.

Thankfully the gown is long, so she needn't worry about the bruises on her legs. Her arms are another matter. She and Jacob sit on the bed and for a few minutes, they both work at applying concealer onto the bruises.

It's semi-successful. But at this point, she doesn't have any more time. The cab is down there waiting for her.

She finds the white handbag she borrowed from the

designer and instructs Jacob with what to put in it: some cash, credit cards, chapstick. And her camera. Does she really want to bring her camera?

Under any other circumstances, of course she would. The red-carpet premiere of a film she'd worked on for almost two years. Of course, she'd want to capture this in photographs.

But that's all changed. She doesn't really care anymore. The film premiere has become secondary in her life, just an obstacle standing between her and a chance to rest. Yet in a previous life – her life before yesterday – it would have been a time to celebrate. So play that role for the next six hours. Smile. Look nice. Engage people in conversation. Act as if you're proud to be here.

She steps into her silver heels and Jacob hands her the clutch, pearly white with rhinestones.

He nods approvingly. "I have to say, I'm impressed with how quickly you were able to transform."

She smiles. "See, I can do it when I have to."

But there is no joy in this, no excitement. Only a sense of anxiety.

Jacob walks her out to the black cab. She gets inside, the driver already knows where to take her, and she watches silently as the Thames, the Houses of Parliament, the London Eye move past her window.

When she steps out of the cab, straight into Leicester Square, there's a huge crowd gathered for the premiere, hoping to see the A-listers.

In the midst of this jostling crowd, she feels ridiculous in her long white gown and silver heels. The people around her start to stare. I am no one. Stop looking at me.

She keeps her eyes down, fishes out her phone and calls Stefan.

A few seconds later, he comes striding by, looking every bit the part – tall, dark, and handsome, in his dinner suit. He leads her to the entrance of the red carpet.

He asks how she is and she mumbles something, but the

crowd is all around, shouting and straining. She shows her invite to the security man at the barriers and he waves them through. Now they're on the red carpet.

Anxiety and nausea build up inside her. All she wants is somewhere quiet and safe and peaceful, but that's exactly the opposite of where she is right now. They can hardly move down the red carpet; there's a hold-up because the press are photographing the stars at the far end.

So they have to stand here, in full view of the crowds on either side of the carpet.

Stefan looks at her. "Are you okay?"

She nods, but it couldn't be farther from the truth. She still hasn't told Stefan what happened in Belfast, but now is not the right time. Not on the red carpet. Everyone staring at them must be thinking: who are these glamorous people who got invited to attend the premiere and why aren't they smiling?

They should be smiling. She should be smiling.

She turns the corners of her mouth upwards, and that's the best she can do. But she can't look at anyone or she'll start crying, so she just looks ahead.

She interlaces her arm with Stefan's to steady herself. She won't last much longer on these heels with the crowds shouting and the confusion and the nausea.

They slowly inch forward along the red carpet. There's someone announcing something, and camera crews, bulbs flashing.

Please don't turn the camera this way, please don't. We're nobodies, we're not anyone you want to photograph. We're not here.

They're almost at the end of the carpet, just another few yards before they can escape into the theatre.

Nisha, their publicist, is in front of her.

"Darling, you look fabulous. Where is the dress from?"

She forces a smile. Racks her brain for the name of the designer and fishes it out from oblivion, somehow.

"Absolutely gorgeous. Can we get a few shots of you two on the red carpet?"

Really? It's not necessary… we're not famous.

"Oh, come on, don't be silly. We'd love to. No harm in taking them."

And then she and Stefan are thrust in front of all the sponsor logos, and the photographer is crouching down, ready to take the photo.

"Looking beautiful. Smile!"

And all she can think of is the bruises… her bruises… are they visible? And somehow, she forces her mouth into a smile, show those teeth, look happy, look proud. FLASH FLASH FLASH. Who are all these people? FLASH FLASH FLASH. The world lights up white-hot around her and she can hardly see.

She has no idea how she'll ever make it through the night.

*

That night, he sleeps in Gerry's bed. Gerry's snoring next to him, but it's ages before he gets to sleep. Still thinking about the shite he's gotten himself into.

What if he tells Da the whole truth?

Everything. Not just the pills and the stealing. But all the girls he'd roughed up before, in Dublin and in the Glen and wherever else.

But that'll just make Da angrier, the lamping harder.

No, just some of the truth. Enough for Da to help him out. But will Da even give a toss?

He thinks of how Da always frowned at the porno mags Michael brought home. But look at all the children he had with Mam, and now she's down in Dublin. So Da must want to shoot a load out every now and then.

Da must get it somehow.

Next to him, Gerry mumbles and turns over, lost in whatever dreams he's got going on.

Lucky eejit, with his house with running water and a big shiny telly and his mam cooking breakfast for him and his proper job. Not like anyone would ever hire him or Michael, the bad-news Sweeneys.

Maybe he can just bust out of here now. He's seen Gerry's wallet, in the pocket of his jeans on the floor. There must be other cash stashed away somewhere in the kitchen. Oh, Mrs Donohue, where do you keep your life savings? I'll just be helping myself to that there, thank you very much for the breakfast and prayers, too, Mrs Donohue.

How much does he need to get down south? Bus ticket must be what, £10?

There must be enough he can scrape together here. Walk to the bus station in the dead of night, catch the early one down to Dublin. The more he thinks about it the more excited he gets. Dodging the law, skulking around, and making his own way. That's what real Travellers do anyway, right? None of this Council housing and paying the bills and following the rules.

"Christ, Johnny, can you stop shaking your fucking leg?"

His leg's been shaking away a mile a minute. He stifles a laugh. Didn't even notice that.

"Fucking wait till morning," Gerry says, and slumps back to sleep.

That's right, that's right. Fucking wait till morning.

He sighs and turns over, his back to Gerry. Now just face the wall in the dark and wait.

*

Monday morning. She wakes up to her phone ringing.

She's on the couch, in her pajamas, where she collapsed after the premiere. The tealights are on the coffee table, the flat white discs of wax burned through.

Next to them, her phone shudders, but as she reaches her arm out, the whiplash becomes unbearable. She winces, brings the phone closer.

She doesn't recognize this number.

A flash of frenzied possibilities through her mind: what if it's a journalist? What if it's him?

But what if it's important?

The phone keeps ringing. She grits her teeth.

"Hello?"

"Oh hi, I'm Sergeant Nick Somers, I'm with the Sapphire Unit of the Metropolitan Police. Sorry to contact you so early in the morning, but the Police Service of Northern Ireland passed me your number."

Of course, the police have followed her here to London.

They need to take more photographs of her bruises. Now that a few days have passed, the bruises will have darkened and will be easier to photograph. Sergeant Somers can come pick her up, take her to the police station in Walworth. How about noon?

She thinks for a moment. She needs to visit a sexual health clinic this morning.

They agree on 1pm. Can she bring a friend?

She hangs up and buries herself back under the duvet. The last thing she wants to do is leave the house. But she can do this. More photographs. That's all it is. More photographs.

Her flatmate José wanders into the kitchen. It's the first time she's seen him since she came back. He looks over at her, and it's obvious he doesn't know what to say. But he tries his best.

"How are you holding up?"

"All right," she says. "Well, obviously not great, but yeah, I'm back. I'm here."

They chat for a few more minutes, avoiding a direct discussion of the rape. Her flight back yesterday, the premiere, his weekend.

"Is there... Is there anything I can do for you?" José asks.

"Actually, yes. Would you be able to come with me to the police station this afternoon?"

"Sure, no problem." José nods. But she can tell he is hesitant.

Hesitant. Just like Stefan was last night, when she finally explained what happened. Everyone seems to be hesitant around her these days. Except the police. They, at least, seem to know what they're doing. No hesitation on their end.

At Walworth Police Station, Sergeant Somers ushers her into the photography studio.

It is a drab, empty room, largely dark, except for the broad, curved expanse of the white backdrop. A fairly elaborate camera is set up, complete with flash apparatus.

Sergeant Somers has stepped out of the room. A friendly female photographer is there.

Would she mind taking off her clothes? Let's see how those bruises have come up.

And my, they are looking lovely and dark. Purple and blue against the sallow of her skin. More fierce than before, more damning.

Would she mind standing this way? And this way?

FLASH FLASH FLASH FLASH

No more photographs, she thinks. Please, just let me be invisible.

And now she can put her clothes back on. That's lovely, she's been a good sport. You take care now.

She files back into the police car, Sergeant Somers chatting away, José sitting awkwardly in silence. For some reason, he had felt it necessary to wear a suit jacket and tie for their trip to the police station. She doesn't mind that, but she wishes José were just able to say something, anything to try and participate in the conversation.

Somers at least keeps up a steady stream of helpful advice. Has she been seen by a medical doctor? Has she done all the necessary tests for STDs? If she hasn't, she should call The Haven. They're a center for excellence in the treatment of sexual assault victims, sort of a one-stop shop.

Yes, she left a message for them this morning. Hasn't heard back.

He's sure they'll call back. Has she received post-exposure prophylaxis yet?

And then she remembers what Doctor Phelan had mentioned to her that night. PEP. Very effective against HIV, but it needs to be administered within 72 hours of exposure. How long has it been?

She checks her watch, tries to calculate the number of hours, but numbers aren't easy for her these days. The panic sets in again.

This PEP, she asks the police officer, how can she get a hold of it?

Oh, The Haven will be able to sort her out.

Okay, because 72 hours is running out.

As if she needed another reason to be stressed. She imagines a clock ticking backwards, like in one of those films about a pandemic gone wrong, a disease infecting the world. What if she's been infected? What if this is the lasting gift from the boy who raped her?

As Somers drops them off, she remembers the handwritten note that Doctor Phelan gave her to show at her medical exam. *This woman is the victim of a sexual assault and I have performed the forensic exam. Please see that she is tested and treated for STIs, including PEP.*

How could she have forgotten that note when she visited the Royal Victoria Hospital on Saturday night? Or the sexual health clinic this morning? How could she have forgotten a note that important?

Perhaps she really is going crazy. Her brain seems to have developed large holes through which basic information and key facts drain out. She worries about this. If she can't rely on herself, who *can* she rely on?

*

Da's fist hits him square in the jaw. Not as fierce as he'd expected. Da must be getting old or something.

But the pain is still there, his good old friend. Ringing away in his head. Hi, welcome back, pain.

Thump! Another proper one, right hook, on the side of his skull.

Nice one, Da.

Some other voice is saying: Johnny, you just gonna lie here like an eejit?

But there's nothing to be done. No way to escape Da's fists this time around.

Now the stomach, Da! Punch me in the gut to finish me off. He can predict the old man so easily. Right here!

But Da gives up. The coward.

Da leans over, hands on his knees, trying to catch his breath. Is that it?

From where he is on the ground, he reaches up and kicks Da in the chest.

Da looks at him. There's the Mick I know. Da charges straight at him, and he squares up, fists at the ready. But he's no match for the famous Mick Sweeney. BOOM. Right there, in the gut, just as he'd predicted.

He's knocked flat on his back. Da finishes him off with a half-arsed kick in his ribs.

He's lying on the ground, and Da holds his foot right above his balls.

"I should stomp these right off you, boy."

He bursts out laughing. Fuck, his ribs hurt.

Da isn't smiling. "What's so funny, you pathetic gobshite?"

Go ahead. Stomp off his balls. No more Sweeney men after this. Sorry, Mick, end of the line. Happened when you knocked your son's clackers off. He almost shrieks with laughter.

Da kicks him again in the side. "Shut up, you eejit. Nothing's funny here."

Oh, but it is. Fucking hilarious.

Da gets down and clamps his bloody hand over his mouth. "Shut up. Or I'll turn you into the peelers myself."

Now he shuts up.

A few minutes' silence. Da stretches his arms, sits down on the ratty couch and glares him an eyeful.

He props himself up on his elbows, winces, looks around. Da sure chose a scenic spot. They're in some dingy garage, some part of town he hardly knows. Smells of diesel and he wants to gag. Must be where Da collects his shite bits of scrap metal and stores them.

He tries to get up, is knocked back down by the pain. Da's over now, pulling him up by the arm, flings him onto the couch, sits next to him.

"Why the fuck d'ya do it?" he asks.

"Do what?"

Da smacks him on the left side of the face. "None of that, you gobshite. Why'd you rough up the girl?"

He wants to laugh. "'Cause she was a beour and she was on her own."

"Oh, that's it? That's all the reason you need?"

He shrugs.

Da keeps at him. "That won't be enough for the courts when you tell them."

"Who says I'm going to court?"

"*I* says you're going to the peelers." Da says this cold and quiet, slips it in like a knife, not the messy raging he's used to.

He laughs again. "I'm not going to the fucking peelers."

Da headbutts him this time. BANG! Forehead against forehead. Clamps his hand over his mouth again. "Listen to me. You turn yourself in. There's no other way around it. Do you hear me? There's been some calls made. People knocking on our door."

He jerks his face free of Da's hand.

"You're having a laugh," he says. "Who's been calling?"

"I'm not laughing, Johnny. We're in West Belfast. It's not just about them peelers. You think the buffers around us don't know every inch of their neighbourhood, after all they been through these years?"

He fishes around in his mouth. Feels like one of his teeth got knocked loose, but he can't tell, his whole jaw is so swollen and numb. His fingers are covered in blood and spit.

"Rape is fucking serious. How do you think your mother will feel when she finds out?"

"A whole lot you care about Mam, all the times you beat her."

Another smack on his head. But he knew that one was coming.

"That's what you want me to do? You just want me to turn myself in? Yes, Mr Proddy Officer, please arrest me. All us Traveller boys are scum."

"That's what they're all thinking now, thanks to you. Just listen to the news."

"Fuck 'em." He spits out the blood that's been pooling in his mouth. It smacks onto the concrete in a dark red glob.

They sit there another moment.

"Did you really do it?" Da asks him.

"I fucked her." By now, he wishes he hadn't. The thrill's worn off from that memory.

"That wasn't what I was asking," Da says. "Did you rape her?"

He shrugs. "What difference does it make? We had sex, she seemed to like it."

Da fixes him with a look. "The peelers say she had a load of bruises on her."

"Maybe she liked it rough."

For a split second, it looks like Da will lamp him again. But he don't. "If you think she wanted it, then maybe you have a case. You should turn yourself in, you won't look as guilty."

"Of course, she fucking wanted it."

"Because you're such a casanova, you little shite?" Now it's Da's turn to laugh.

"She said she wouldn't tell anyone."

"Really?" Da cocks a curious eyebrow at him. "Maybe you should learn to control your women better."

Right now, this very moment, he hates Da more than anyone else in the world. Wishes he would drop dead, sitting right there, right next to him on this manky couch.

Instead, Da stands up. Turns to him. Still that preachy voice. "Do you know how long you can go to prison for, on rape?"

"What? Two, three years?"

Da snorts. "Up to ten years, Johnny. Maybe even longer. You're only fifteen, you'll be a grown man when you come out."

Ten years? Fucking impossible. Something twists his insides and he jumps off the couch, grabs at Da.

"Fuck off, Da, I'm not going to prison. I didn't do nothing wrong!"

Da pushes him up against the wall, his hands boring into his shoulders. "Well, all of Belfast thinks you have. So you better explain yourself."

Ten years, he thinks. Ten fucking years shut inside with metal bars all around. He can't. He'd rather die.

He starts to cry. Is this really happening? The fucking embarrassment of tears and snot, just like his mam always cried, just like Claire and the babby and the young stupid girls he roughed up. He's not crying. He can't cry. Not like them.

Da slaps him hard across the face.

"Stop sniveling and explain yourself."

What is there to explain?

"Listen, I was high, I didn't know what was going on, she seemed to want it. I didn't do nothing wrong. There was no one around and no one saw us."

"Did you hit her?"

"Yeah, of course. Only a bit."

Ten years. An entire fucking lifetime.

"Da, you've got to get me out of here."

Da is thinking. Never Da's best thing, but he can see the gears turning inside, all slow and rusty. Turn turn turn. Come on, Da, help me out here.

"Gerry says I just need to get over the border. Get me down to Mam and I can hide out at hers. Or maybe one of your sisters in Galway."

Don't fail me now, Da.

"If you can get me over the border, I swear, I won't bother you no more. I'll be good, I'll take care of myself."

But Da's shaking his head. Lets go of him and holds his hands up as if he's done.

"No, Johnny, I've had enough. You turn yourself in."

The shock of it all. His own miserable Da, handing him over to the peelers.

Then he lets it loose. Screaming, shouting, raging, fists, nails, teeth, kicking everything, everything, everything you can throw at it until he feels Da's hands on him again. Only this time, instead of punching, Da's holding him down, clamping him. He strains to bust free, but Da headbutts him again. Kicks him in the groin, pushes him up against the wall so his nose is inches from a rusty steel panel.

Da's elbow digs into his back, that stupid thick voice in his ear.

"You listen to me, Johnny. It's too late. You made your own bed. It's time you lie in it."

"Where's Michael? Where the fuck is Michael?" Wouldn't rat him out like his own Da.

"Stop fucking thinking about Michael. This is about you. You run, you look guilty. You turn yourself in, you stand a better chance."

"I didn't do nothing wrong."

Da spins him around. Looks at him dead-on. "You so sure about that?"

"Yeah."

"Then you tell that to the police. See if they believe you."

Da turns and walks away, to the other side of the garage.

He can feel the tears running down his own face. He wants to split out of that stinking garage and keep running, as far as he can go. But he's tired, so tired, and his ribs, his head, his legs are aching wherever Da's clattered him. All he can do is slide down the wall and collapse on the ground. His head in his arms, crying, knackered. All he wants to do is sleep.

*

Monday afternoon, she sits in front of her computer. She feels unmoored, like she's been set adrift on a grey horizon-less lake with no oars, and the shore of normal life is drifting further and further away. Just this flat, grey expanse and no one else in sight.

Natalia is still at work, José has gone out for a bit. She

knows they're freaked out about the whole situation, but what can she do? She can't un-rape herself. Every time she steps out the door, she has to pretend like everything is normal. Here, inside the flat, at least she doesn't have to pretend. She can just stretch herself out on the grey surface of that lake and float.

The flat boasts floor-to-ceiling windows overlooking the Thames – a luxury that the three of them have been willing to pay for, the added sense of calm that comes with the river view. Now, she is grateful for this view, as she is for all the small things that have made her past two days a little easier: the kindness of the police, friends she can rely on, a boss who understands.

At their Ikea worktable, she goes through her work emails half-heartedly. They've piled up as usual, and she knows her mind is in no shape to deal with the finer points of a television distribution contract.

She starts typing a response to her contact at the distributor:
Dear Geoff,

I'm sorry, but over the weekend I was assaulted and raped. Could you please handle this with my colleague Becca for the time being?

She hits Send, wonders if she should have sugar-coated that response. But why? It's the truth. It wasn't an accident. Someone raped her.

She's done with work emails for now. They're just giving her more of a headache.

Barbara and the police in Northern Ireland had mentioned something about the press picking up the story. So, out of curiosity, even though she knows she might regret this, she types into Google: *Rape Glen West Belfast.*

BBC News. *The Belfast Telegraph. The Irish News.* UTV. Reuters.

She is surprised to see the amount of coverage online.
Chinese Tourist Raped in West Belfast
Foreign Woman Sexually Assaulted in Park
Sex Attack on Chinese Student

She registers a bemused sort of detachment when reading these headlines. Chinese tourist? Is that how the media portrays her?

Police are still searching for the teenage boy who is alleged to have raped a Chinese tourist in Glen Forest Park in West Belfast on Saturday afternoon...

Why are they making such a big deal about her being Chinese?

On the BBC website, there's a photograph of the entrance to the park. A twinge of nausea as she recalls that entrance, caught in the bright afternoon sunlight, as she walked through the gateway to start her hike.

On another website, a photograph shows the familiar yellow tapes of the police barrier, cordoning off a section of forest. The queasiness rises again and she clicks out of that webpage.

But still that detached curiosity in her wants to know more, that computer-part of her brain that just wants to eat up more facts, register more statistics, more news reports.

A wave of violence swept West Belfast with several unrelated incidents marking an unusually eventful weekend. In Glen Forest Park, a foreign woman was dragged into the bushes and raped by a teenage boy. On the Ardoyne Road, three men were arrested after a car chase and a shooting. In Crumlin, another man was stabbed in an attempted robbery.

What in hell possessed her to ever visit Belfast?

Scanning a UTV article, she discovers something unsettling.

This attack happened four years ago to the day that the body of sixteen-year-old Josephine McCrory was found in a nearby part of Glen Forest Park. McCrory had gone missing after a night out, and her body was discovered two days later. She had been sexually assaulted and had died of severe head wounds.

Her throat closes up.

If she could cry, she would cry now. But all her tears have been spent.

A separate case entirely, yet to think that a girl's body had been unceremoniously dumped, not far from the place where she herself was raped. Bodies forced upon the ground, dirt caught up in hair, open wounds exposed to the mud and rocks.

She shivers, and perhaps feels an odd sense of communion with the spirits of the bruised and the raped and the female. If she could speak to Josephine McCrory's spirit, what would she say? Why did you die and why did I live? Why did your rapist kill you, and yet mine did not? If we can call this living, the emotionless existence she now leads.

On the website for Radio Ulster, she notices that a morning chat show earlier that day had addressed the topic of her rape. She clicks on a link, and the slant of Belfast accents streams out at her.

"...Well, shocking news over the weekend about that tourist woman who was raped in Glen Forest Park."

"Yes, can you believe it? It's horrible, truly horrible."

"Of course, as you may know, it's not the first time that park has been associated with criminal activity..."

They mention Josephine McCrory and welcome callers who might live in the area and have any thoughts or comments about the crime.

A man calls in, the tone of his voice angry. "That park... it needs to be cleaned up! You see the young lads there day and night, carrying on, drinking beer and doing drugs, and this that and the other. Something like this was bound to happen..."

The radio host's voice takes on a somber tone. "And now, we have a very special caller. We have here on the line, Anne McCrory, the mother of Josephine McCrory. Of course we can't begin to imagine what grief you've gone through since the loss of your daughter. But tell us, if you can, what thoughts are going through your head now, with this latest news of the tourist who was attacked?"

There's a pause, the sound of a throat being cleared, and she strains to understand the thin voice coming down the line. She imagines a woman with a prematurely wrinkled face, hands folded over a cup of tea. The words come slowly, gnarled up in a thick working-class accent, almost too difficult to decipher.

"Just… shocking. Absolutely shocking. It brings it all right back…"

The radio host says more sympathetic platitudes and Anne McCrory recounts briefly the incident of her daughter. Josephine hadn't told her where she'd be going, just out. She didn't say she was going anywhere near that park. Maybe they had brought her there afterward. Not a day goes by where she doesn't think about her Josie. The assailants were never caught.

"And what do you make of this latest incident?"

Anne McCrory sighs. "Well, my heart goes out to that wee Chinese girl. I'm sorry she had to see this side of Belfast. That poor girl, her life is now ruined."

She pauses as she hears this. She knows she should feel pulled in by this woman's sympathizing and, yet this woman doesn't know her.

Wee Chinese girl. She wants to laugh at that.

Is that what they all imagine when they hear the news? Broken English and a Chinese accent? A helpless girl cowering in the mud?

And how dare they pronounce that her life is ruined? A mute outrage burns quietly inside her.

The conversation with Anne McCrory has ended and the radio host announces another special guest: George Powers, the Lord Mayor of Belfast, is on the line. He speaks with the smooth confidence of a politician, the shallow glossing-over of facts with a veneer of calm control.

"We are trying very hard to curb the crime rates in Belfast. There has been definite improvement over the years, but every now and then an unfortunate incident like this happens."

The radio host slings a few difficult questions at him. The elections are coming up. The rapist is still at large. How safe *are* the streets of Belfast?

More smooth glossing-over from George Powers. "Belfast is still a safe city. Let the PSNI do their work—"

"And do you have any news of the young girl? Is she all right?"

"I've heard from sources that she is back home and recovering. I have made a few attempts to get in contact with her, and I will be speaking to her later today."

Does he even have any clue where I am?

She switches off the radio stream. As far as she's concerned, the Lord Mayor of Belfast will be making no attempt to comfort her. But it certainly sounded noble on public radio.

She exits the Radio Ulster website, and looks out at the undulating surface of the Thames. All those people in Belfast, generating headlines and sound bites from her plight. Did they have any idea she might be listening to them from her flat in London?

Or in their minds, is she just a nameless face? A Chinese girl who became a statistic? Devoid of identity, of individuality. An empty vessel on which they can project their preconceived notions of 'rape victim'.

And yet, ironically, she feels that these days, she has become that empty vessel. Hollow, lacking in spirit and substance. Maybe she will float on the surface of this grey lake forever. Maybe she will never locate her moorings again.

*

When he wakes up later that day, he ain't in that garage no more. Thank fuck. The diesel fumes were enough to drown him. Maybe that's why he blacked out.

He's lying on a flimsy fold-out cot in a shed somewhere, one of those cheapo extensions someone builds to the back of a house. Uncle Rory's house.

It's raining, a bunch of raindrops pattering the glass above him. Grey daylight. Pain all over his body.

Uncle Rory's right in front of him, holding a cup of tea.

"Afternoon," he says.

"Where's me da?"

"He went out. Had to look after a few jobs. Reckoned you'd need to rest up here a bit."

Fuck you, Da. His skull aches and he rests his head back on the pillow, looks up at the raindrops hitting the roof.

"You got yourself in some deep water there, boy."

You got yourself a sharp brain there, Uncle Rory.

Rory hands over that mug of cold tea, and he gulps it down. Somewhere he hears young kids chattering and smells dinner cooking. His stomach kicks up another fuss.

"D'ya got anything to eat?"

A few minutes later, his Auntie Theresa comes in with a bowl of steaming food, passes it to Rory. He wonders if he should say something. But when her eyes meet his, her mouth draws in tight, her glance hardens, and she turns back into the house.

So much for a warm welcome.

He don't care. He's shoveling the stew down this throat so quickly it don't have time to burn him. Fuck Aunt Theresa and that stick up her arse. Rory's mumbling some boring shite about his sons gone over to England, and little Janey getting married…

He's finished the stew. Licked the spoon clean and all.

"D'ya know where Michael is?"

Rory stops his blathering. "Your older brother was never the easiest to pin down, boy."

"That's for sure."

"But look, we've put the call-out for him. He knows what's happened. Knows you'll want to see him before you turn yourself in."

At those words, his insides churn up again.

Turn yourself in. So it's been decided then, has it?

Rory mutters something about a hot shower, he'll just be a minute getting him a towel, and then steps out.

He sits there waiting like an eejit, the raindrops pattering away. A dog noses its way into the room. Don't growl or bite, just comes snuffling his muzzle at him.

He puts his hand out, strokes the dog. The dog don't move away. Eventually, it sits down, puts its head in his lap.

A smile creeps across his face. For once, here's someone friendly. Here's someone don't care what he done.

Monday evening she speaks to her sister again. Serena's arranged with her law firm to take a few days off. Air fares were surprisingly cheap from San Francisco, and she's booked a flight that will get her to London on Thursday morning. Will that work for her? She can stay until Tuesday.

Should be fine. It's not like she has anything else planned except for doctor's appointments and phone calls with the police.

She fingers through her diary. Before, she had never been able to function without it. Each year, always a hard cover diary, week-to-view in A5, generally meticulous. Trips away are labeled weeks in advance in capital letters. PARIS. BERLIN. She looks at the box she drew around this past weekend: BELFAST, and then on Sunday night, PREMIERE.

Guess not everything goes according to plan.

Flipping through the upcoming pages, she sees social appointments and film screenings pencilled weeks in advance. Someone's birthday. Someone else's engagement party. Lunch with that person. Potential coffee with this person.

She takes a pen and draws a huge diagonal line through the next few weeks. See all these plans? You can forget all of them now.

In an alternate universe, some unraped version of her is probably going ahead with all of this. Ambitious, sociable, steaming ahead with the energy she once had.

But in this version of reality, her life is a blank slate.

From now on, her life exists only inside this apartment. Minus a few timid forays into the outside world for groceries and doctor appointments. From busy working professional to social recluse in a matter of days. Amazing how quickly we can transform.

She imagines she should tell her friends what happened. No point in making up excuses for being antisocial. If her life has transformed this drastically, then people need to know about it.

She opens up her Gmail account and hits Compose.

Dear Friends,

I am sorry to be the bearer of bad news, but this past weekend, something very serious happened to me. While walking through a park in West Belfast in the middle of the afternoon, I was followed by a stranger, who then assaulted and raped me.

Words have never been a problem for her, and these words come out almost mechanically, as if issuing from some highly rational internal dictation machine. Yes, dear friends, I shall tell you the tale… I shall not be dramatic or overly emotional.

For her, it is important to convey the facts in a straightforward manner, while also indicating that any help or support would be very much appreciated. She has a feeling of standing on the rim of a bottomless canyon, and the only way she can hope to get across is with the help of friends.

So she writes a few brief paragraphs, earnest and somber in tone. And now who to send it to?

Some names are obvious – her closest friends from university, her closest friends here in London. But who else?

Gradually, working her way through her contact list, she selects about twenty names. Some in London, others in New York, San Francisco, Chicago. Barbara, of course, and Serena, Melissa, Jen, her current flatmates, ex-flatmates she grew close to, her boyfriend from college. Twenty people she feels she can be completely upfront and vulnerable with.

Vulnerable. Now that's a new feeling for her.

She scans the email one more time and hits Send.

It's done, it's out there, she can't take it back. She shuts down her computer, looks at her diary one more time. Empty for the foreseeable future, and then some.

It's time for bed. She wonders if she'll manage to sleep tonight.

Tuesday, all he does is watch telly with Kevo and Martin. Can't leave Rory's house.

That's right, Da, let the bruises from the lamping heal up before you turn me in to the peelers. Wouldn't want them thinking you're an abusive parent or nothing.

On the telly, there's people looking to buy a new home and some geezer showing them around. "Oh, this flat is modern and visionary... Just near the Titanic Quarter is an up-and-coming area of Belfast... In five years, the property value will sky-rocket."

Imagine saving up your whole life so you can trap yourself within four walls. What the fuck is wrong with these people.

Around lunchtime, the news comes up on the BBC. Bright red background, chirpy newsreaders he wants to punch in the face. And then, right there... his news.

"Police are in their fourth day of searching for an alleged rapist who is believed to be responsible for the brutal assault on an American tourist in Glen Forest Park in West Belfast on Saturday."

He sees the park come up on screen. The yellow police tape marking off that bit of woods and field. Dogs sniffing round.

Gotta sniff harder, dogs.

If they just swung their camera round, they'd catch the caravans on screen. His home. The thought of his caravan – the one he shared with Da and Michael – tugs some strange feeling inside him. He can never go back there. Not in the same way. No more brilliant view of the whole world, as he takes a piss in the open air. No, now he's got to pretend he's not here, skulk out under Auntie Theresa's miserable roof.

"A number of witnesses have come forward and thanks to their evidence, PSNI are saying they have identified a potential suspect, and are investigating his whereabouts."

Kevo looks over at him, but he sets his jaw, refuses to think ahead. To what'll happen after he goes to the peelers. Another roof, more walls, and the metallic sound of a gate sliding shut.

No, fuck that. He shivers and scratches at his bruises some more.

Now what's this? Fucking Gerry Adams is on screen. Talking to the camera.

"We are shocked and saddened to hear about the tragic assault on the American woman in our district of Belfast. No woman should ever suffer an assault like that, and certainly no foreigner when she's visiting our neighborhood. As a show of support, we will be organising a candlelit vigil for her this weekend in Glen Forest Park. Come and join us at 2pm this Saturday, to show our solidarity, as she struggles to find justice in this difficult time."

Oh, come off it.

Kevo raises his eyebrows, but says nothing. Gerry Adams. Now that's serious.

"For fuck's sake, Kevo! Gerry Adams is always banging on about something or the other."

He turns the telly off and throws the remote into the sofa cushions.

As if that woman deserves a candle and vigils. She was well up for it.

Don't worry, I won't tell anyone.

Lying bitch.

And where's the candlelight vigil for him?

They just want to see him skewered alive, is what they want. Well, they can go fuck themselves, too.

He leaves Kevo in the room and steps into the shed out back. Where's that dog? He wishes it were here, so he could sit and stroke its furry belly. But Martin's just taken him out for a walk, so he'll have to wait for them to come back.

Even the fucking dog gets to go out. Even the fucking dog.

*

The Haven never called back and now, Tuesday afternoon at 1pm, she's starting to worry. If she counts back 72 hours from the time of the attack – When was it? 2pm on Saturday? – The deadline is 2pm today.

She continues waiting for The Haven to call, but they don't.

By 3pm, she realizes she'll have to take matters into her own hands. How firm is the 72 hour deadline? Surely, if PEP is administered within 75 hours, it can still have some effect against HIV, right?

She has no idea about these things and no one to ask. She tries ringing the sexual health clinic she visited yesterday, but the workers there don't seem familiar with PEP. They put her on hold, pass her around to a colleague or two, and she explains for the third time, that she was raped on Saturday, visited the clinic yesterday, but forgot to ask about PEP. Is that a drug they administer?

Finally, a staff member explains that is a facility they don't have, but another sexual health clinic might. Perhaps the Lilly Clinic at St. Thomas' Hospital. She presses on. Do they have the phone number for that one?

No, they don't.

She does a search online for sexual health clinics. There are ones specifically for the LGBT community, walk-ins, ones for male patients only.

For rape victims, the trail constantly leads back to The Haven. But she's called again and again, and only received voicemail.

A relentless ache is building up inside her head.

Part of her considers calling off the search, this seemingly futile race against the clock, and crawling back under the duvet. Accept whatever Fate has meted out to her. If the boy gave her HIV, so be it.

But that helplessness is only a passing fantasy. She knows in her heart, she doesn't give up that easily.

Another call, another explanation of her situation, and this time, she's reached the Lilly Clinic.

Yes, the nurse says. We do administer PEP, but the clinic will soon be closing for the day.

How soon?

If you can get here by 4:30, I can make sure you'll get the PEP today.

She looks at her watch. It's 4:05 and the clinic is in Waterloo and she's in Vauxhall. She can do this. Go to the bus stop, pray you don't have to wait too long.

She throws on jeans, a shirt, pulls on a sweater.

Stepping out of her apartment building, the familiar nausea hits her. The threat of being out in the open, away from the safety of her flat. The wide sky threatens to engulf her. So much air and light all around her and she feels very vulnerable, exposed. Anything could go wrong.

Just get to the hospital. Just get to the hospital. You can breathe easy once you're there.

At the Lilly Clinic, the nurse was true to her word. After only ten minutes of waiting, she was ushered to an examination room, where she explained what had happened to her.

Again, she was asked to lie down on the examination table, put her feet in the stirrups. The third time she's had to make way for a speculum since Saturday.

At the end of the appointment, she was finally handed her medication. One large bottle full of PEP pills, a bottle of loperamide and another of domperidone for the side effects.

Now, she sits in her lounge and stares at the PEP. They are giant peach-colored pills, bigger than any pills she's swallowed before in her life.

One lies in the palm of her hand and she stares at it. How is she supposed to get that down her throat?

But she doesn't have much time to waste. 76 hours have passed since the attack. If she doesn't take the PEP now, it may be too late.

So she takes a swig of water and attempts to swallow.

Her gag reflex kicks in. The pill's too big, and she almost spit it out of her mouth.

She tries again. She gags again.

And again.

On the fourth attempt, she gets the pill down, and she can feel it poking into the walls of her esophagus, stuck. Another gulp of water. She massages her throat, right where the kid had squeezed his fingers. There's a strange tenderness in her throat there, and this pill forcing its way down is hardly comfortable.

But it's down, it's in her system. Let the PEP do its work.

She tries to distract herself, starts to flick aimlessly through a magazine.

Within twenty minutes, the side effects kick in. A sudden urge to vomit seizes her, and she runs to the bathroom, kneels on the floor, and hovers over the pool of water, waiting as the tell-tale saliva collects in her mouth.

If she vomits now, she'll have to take another pill all over again. So she prays she won't. She's meant to take them strictly every twelve hours. For four weeks. Two pills a day, and if she finds herself running to the toilet every time... this will be unbearable.

But so what? This is the price you have to pay if you want to ensure you don't get HIV from your rapist.

This Faustian pact. She realizes this with bleak resignation, as she continues to stare, nauseated, into the unruffled water of the toilet.

*

He's still in front of the telly when Da stumbles in. Fairly sober for once. He's carrying a load of bags. Fucking Christmas, is it?

First time he's seen Da since yesterday's lamping, and they look at each other for a moment, before Da sidles off.

"Rory, I got these for your troubles." Da hands the bags over. Rory has a look inside.

"Chrissakes, Mick, d'ya buy the whole shop out?"

Da shrugs. "I figure one final night." They both turn toward him. "Johnny, uh, we're arranging a bit of a knees-up for you."

Before you turn me in. So big of you.

Rory and Da both come at him, hugs and pats on the back.

"Tomorrow night we'll have it. Gerry and your lads all been invited. Want to give you a proper send-off."

"And Michael?" he asks.

Rory and Da exchange glances. Da nods. "Michael will come. I'm sure of that."

"Just you rest up now," Da says, hand on his shoulder. "Keep yourself warm and cosy. Inside the house, like."

Rage pulses through him again, and he pushes Da's hand off his shoulder. "What, d'ya tell the peelers to come straight here and get me already?"

Da looks back at him, suddenly cold. Rory's lost his stupid smile.

"Haven't told the peelers nothing, Johnny. Just calm yourself down now."

He glares something hateful at Da, grabs a beer, and sinks back onto the sofa.

*

From the moment she sent that email, the responses flood in. Some are immediate, fellow women expressing shock and compassion, often anger at the rapist. Others are more measured: *If there's anything at all you need... I don't really know what to say...*

Words can be clichéd, but she knows they aren't insincere. At times like these, clichés are all people can rely on.

That week, her meals are cooked by friends who come over, preparing their best homemade dishes as an act of support. Honey-roasted salmon. Stir-fry chicken and peppers. Pasta with spinach in an aglio olio sauce.

She can't go out. The thought of venturing to a restaurant, with all its clattering silverware, strangers conversing, glances of men she doesn't know... It's enough to make her shudder and turn further inwards. Why ever go out again? No, just stay inside. Watch the sky brightening from dawn to day and deepening into night, from safe behind her floor-to-ceiling windows, while she sits in her pajamas on the couch.

With her friends, she is grateful for the company, but she is also aware that each visit uses up her short supply of energy. They come, they cook dinner, they want to know how she is doing, and most importantly, how did it happen? Was it someone you knew? Wasn't there anyone else near by? Will they catch him?

It's almost as if she's on autopilot. A prerecorded answering service, dutifully satisfying their curiosity.

"I was just going for a walk in this park, and this kid came up and started talking to me…"

She sees the look on their faces, their disgust at the boy. But she has decided not to sugar-coat the truth from the friends who ask for it. What happened happened. Women get raped, and friends, too.

Most importantly, she doesn't cry. She never cries.

Tears are only a distraction from the conveying of information. And by now, that same story told over and over again, has lost its emotional vitality. The prerecorded answering service has kicked in.

Her friends must find it strange, this lack of tears. That something this horrible could be told in such a matter-of-fact voice.

But they have no idea how far she is now from the person they knew a week ago. They just see her, hear her voice. But the real Vivian checked out days ago, and she doesn't know when she'll return.

*

He's thinking what it'll be like inside. Every time Michael spoke about it, it didn't sound too bad. Other lads can be gobshites, but some can be all right. Food's awful but you won't go hungry. Some pervs might try it on with you, but you just lamp them good.

But to have everything closed in around him. A tiny cell, guards staring at you everywhere you go, no fresh air, no sky. He's never thought about it like that. Until now.

Can't go wandering around no more, peering at people, vanishing again.

Everyone tells you what to do, every hour of the day.

That's what gets him. Being pegged. Slotted in. Just one of the others.

*

Wednesday morning, she goes to the office. Tries to ignore the agoraphobia that sets in every time she leaves her flat.

She's aware of a tug-of-war taking place inside of her. The previous her is still churning somewhere inside, trying to reclaim her life.

Don't waste your day! Get back to your job! There are so many emails to answer!

Establish normality, she thinks. Let's try that.

She takes the Tube to Old Street, walks the familiar route from the grimy tiled tunnels onto the streets. This must be what it's like for ghosts, returning to the scene of their previous lives.

Her colleagues were not expecting her. By now, she is accustomed to people not knowing what to say. Erika, her boss, isn't in.

"Hey, Vivian." Simon looks appropriately downcast.

Becca stands up when she walks in. "How is everything?"

She shrugs. "Yeah, I'm good," she lies.

Was that a lie? All things considered, she's good. She's safe. She has a nice apartment to sleep in and friends who come over and cook her dinner. Her medical needs are being taken care of, the police are following her case. Things could be worse.

Maisie, their American intern is in that day. Round-faced and eager, she is a nineteen-year-old college student on a semester abroad, interning at their production company for two days a week. Maisie seems pleased but surprised to see her in the office.

"Hey, so how'd your trip to Belfast go?"

Apparently no one's told Maisie the news.

She looks around. Simon and Becca are working with their heads down, hunched over their keyboards. She takes Maisie into the meeting room to break the news to her.

"Did Becca or Simon tell you what happened to me?" she asks

"No," Maisie says, her round eyes getting rounder. "Are you... okay?"

"No. Actually, I'm not."

And so, once again, she explains what happened to her, leaving the details out. She feels bad puncturing Maisie's college-age innocence. But as the shock registers on Maisie's face, she hears her own voice unexpectedly crack, and she deftly wipes a tear from her left eye.

She doesn't cry when she tells her friends, yet she can't hold it together when she tells the office intern. She is angry and ashamed at herself.

Maisie goes to give her a hug. "Is there anything I can do for you?"

But there isn't. There simply isn't.

In front of her work computer, she's plowing through her emails.

"Maybe you don't need to be so explicit about what happened to you," Erika had mentioned. Conscious of her previous mistake in her email to the distributor, she just decides to hand everything over to Becca without comment.

Due to unforeseen circumstances, I will be out of the office for some time, so please speak to my colleague Becca (CC'd here) regarding this and any other matters.

How lightly we can skim the surface of disaster with professional lingo.

She hits Control-C to copy that generic response and then, paste paste paste pastes it into one email after another.

There is something liberating about it, freeing herself of all these emails. Severing the cords to any responsibility she once had, until she is detached, undone, alone.

*

It's the big piss-up that night. His big piss-up. There's tins of lager and drams of whisky passed about. Someone's even gone and bought a big fuck-off ham they carve away at now and then. The little ones are running around, thinking it's Christmas, and the dog is wandering around and barking, nuzzling its nose into his hand.

Gerry and Donal and Kevo and Martin are all red-faced and happy. Uncle Rory is clapping everyone on the shoulder cracking his shite jokes. Da's working his way around the room, slurping whiskey out of his flask, nodding to this person and the other.

But Da's steering well clear of him.

He trains his eyes on Da, and reaches for a fresh tin of beer.

"Johnny." Gerry and Donal are next to him now.

"How's things?" Gerry says. Donal silent as usual, his big Adam's apple bobbing up and down in that thick neck of his.

He starts to laugh. "What kind of shite question is that, Gerry? I'm off to prison tomorrow, how d'ya think I am?"

Gerry cuts across him, looks at the spread, the stacks of lager. "Least they're making an effort here. Sending you off in style."

"Well, that's just the thing, right? Sending me off. 'Little Johnny's going to spend the rest of his life behind bars, so let's raise a fucking glass to that!'"

Some of the other men are looking over, but he don't care.

"So yeah, let's toast!" he shouts out.

Da steps up. Oh, right into the trap, Da. He's got his arm raised, holding up the flask as usual.

"That's right, Johnny. Let's have a toast for you."

And next thing, Da is going round, handing out whiskey glasses and shot glasses and plastic cups, pouring out the bottle of Paddy, until everyone in the fucking room has something.

Da forces a glass into his hand, "An extra bit for you, boy."

He don't say nothing, just glares back.

"And now," Da starts to say, and he stands up on a chair.

"Ah, Mick, get down from there." Uncle Rory taps him on the shoulder, but Da pushes him off.

"No, no, it's me own son's toast. I'm preaching this one from above."

200

Da staggers a bit on the chair seat, but manages to stay upright. He's still glaring, shooting hatred and embarrassment at Da. "Fifteen years ago, when me boy Johnny was born, I says to me woman, Bridge, at the time... now, there's a scrapper. Never saw a happier or a scrappier babby."

Aw, fuck off, Da. Before I knock the chair from under you.

"...There's a lad with the fighting Sweeney spirit."

The others laugh.

Just laugh me off to prison, you gobshites.

"...Well, he's grown up now, me Johnny. And even if we don't know what'll happen to him after this, we do know..." Da stops for a moment, clears his throat. "We do know that he'll always be one of us. He'll always be a Sweeney."

The others mumble, "*Sláinte.*"

"And we do know that whatever happens to him... we'll always love him, our Johnny."

Everyone nods. He narrows his eyes at Da. The whole fucking act not lost on him.

"So here's to me Johnny." Da raises his flask, and the others follow, glasses and cups in the air. "May the road rise up for you, boy."

"May the road rise up," they all say.

Loud cheers and someone's clapping him on the back, another person folding him into a hug. The party's gone up a notch in energy, people speaking louder, laughing more, but Da's words have gone through him, all sly and twisting.

That's right, Da. Beat the shite out of me, and the next day, toast to me like you've been the best fucking father ever.

Gerry and Donal are nodding at him. "It was a good toast, so it was."

He wants to punch them, too, pretending that Da's so fucking wonderful.

"Where's Michael?" he asks, and that shuts them up.

They look at each other, shrugging.

"I spoke to him this morning," Gerry says. "He said he'd be by tonight."

He throws his glass against the wall. Everyone stops

talking. Shattered glass and whiskey spread across the floor. That'll please Auntie Theresa.

"Johnny," Uncle Rory steps up, but he brushes him off.

"So I don't get to see me own fucking brother before I get packed off to jail?"

"Johnny," Da says. His voice is sharp again now, none of that sappy shite. There's the real Da. Knew it wouldn't take much for him to come out.

"What, you tell him not to come, Da?"

"None of that, Johnny." Da holds out his arm. "What Michael decides to do is his own choice."

"Oh, but I don't get a choice, do I?"

"Can't we just a have a nice bit of craic for once?" Da's holding him by his shoulders, but he wrestles free.

"Before you ship me off, eh?"

Go on, let's test Da. Would Mick Sweeney dare belt his own son at a cosy little gathering like this?

"Come on, Da. Be honest, you always wanted me out of the way, anyway. You can rest easy now, once I'm in prison."

"That's not fair, Johnny."

"Oh, and I'm sure you're all thrilled to see the back of me." He turns to all the others. "Uncle Rory, can't wait to get me out of your perfect little house."

"Johnny, you should watch your mouth," Da says, trying to lay a hand on him again. "Maybe you've had too much to drink."

"That's a clever one, coming from you."

Da draws back, and he sees it now, the dark look gathering. Just a little more now.

"If this weren't your last night here, Johnny…" Da warns.

"If this weren't, then what? You'd lamp me in the face, like all them other times?"

He steps up to Da, pushes him in the chest.

Gerry's trying to step between the two of them now, but he's having none of it.

"That's right, Da. Show 'em what you're really made of. The famous Mick Sweeney!"

He's shouting this in Da's face now.

"I'm warning you, boy."

But fuck warnings. It's too far gone for that.

"No wonder Mam left you, you gobshite. Made all our lives hell."

Da slaps him hard across the face. Not the famous Mick Sweeney right hook, but a broad, loud slap, the way he'd slap a woman.

He stands still for a moment, burning with anger.

The dog jumps in, snapping at Da, angling for a bite, and Da kicks the dog. He lunges straight at Da and there's a shout as Gerry, Rory and half the lads try to break them up. He can't get to Da, a wall of arms holds him back, he hears Da raging when a sharp whistle pierces the air. A familiar whistle.

He turns around. Michael is standing right there, far end of the room, a wide grin on his face.

"Michael!" he shouts, a million miles from Da. Suddenly no more arms pin him down and he runs over to his brother.

"Looks like you got the party started without me," Michael says, and it's like the room relaxes into a laugh.

Michael grips him by the shoulders, looks him up and down.

"I been hearing all about you," he says. "Sounds like you pulled off a mean feat on Saturday."

They both laugh, and in another moment, Gerry and Donal are with them, Uncle Rory and the cousins crowding round.

"Good to have you with us, Michael. We were getting scared you wouldn't show."

But Michael only laughs harder at this. "Me? Not show? It's me little brother's piss-up. Wouldn't miss it for the world."

Michael crushes him in a hug, and over his shoulder, he catches a glimpse of Da, on his own on the other side of the room. Da looks straight at him, sips from his flask, and turns away.

Three hours later, and it's just him and Michael sitting in the shed, nursing the last of the lager.

Da's passed out on the couch, Uncle Rory and the lads have gone to bed. Gerry and Donal left, in search of a bar or a club. Michael said he'd join them some other time. "But tonight, I have some catching up to do with Johnny here."

He smiled with pride when he heard that.

Now he's told Michael the full story, from beginning to end, and every detail he can remember. Fuck, Michael's the first person who asked to hear the whole thing.

Michael's taking it all in. He's not sure if he's proud or ashamed or what. When he finishes, Michael stays silent, just nodding.

"So?" he asks Michael.

A pause. Then Michael breaks out in the familiar grin. "You tell me. Do you want to go to jail?"

"Fuck no," he says. What kind of stupid question is that? "But Da's given me no choice, says I have to go."

"Fuck Da. If you're old enough to shag that foreign beour, you're old enough to make your own decisions."

He likes the sound of that. A moment as this passes between him and Michael.

"What do you want to do?"

He laughs. "I want to get the fuck out of here, is what I want to do."

"Then do it," Michael says.

"What, just like that?" What about Da snoring on the couch and Rory and the lads and the fucking news reports with the peelers...

"Catch the early bus down to Dublin. You'll get there before noon, even. Go to Claire, she'll help you out. Whatever, just get to Dublin and vanish."

A flash of excitement pulses through him – to escape, just like that. Get away from all this shite in Belfast, these Travellers and their tiny little caravans. Just him and the buzz of Dublin with no adults to scream at him. May the road rise up before him.

Michael's grinning. "Not too bad, eh? Master of your own game."

"What'll I do for money?" he asks.

Michael digs around in his jeans pockets, finds a fiver and a twenty-euro note. Then takes his trainer off and pulls out another twenty.

"This should get you started."

"Good man, you are."

"Ah, I wouldn't see me little brother behind bars. The rest of them are cowards for caving into the peelers just like that. Da, especially."

They both look over at Da, who's sprawled on the couch, snoring away to high heaven.

"The fucking loser," Michael says. "That's the difference between us and him. Poor eejit's probably only ever shagged his own wife."

A pause, as he tucks away the cash. He hopes Michael won't ask him no more questions about the woman. She was a poor choice in the end. Shoulda picked someone meeker, but how was he to know?

"So, if the peelers catch you…" Michael starts to say.

He's sick of advice, but Michael's is always worth hearing.

"If they catch you, what do you say?"

"That… I was confused."

"Confused?"

"Well, I didn't know what I was doing."

"'Cause you were on drugs?"

"Well, that, maybe. But she said she wouldn't tell anyone. She said she wanted it."

Michael smiles. "Did she say that really?"

He shrugs. "How they gonna know?"

"Clever lad. They won't. It's your word against hers. Most girls don't bother to say nothing at all."

"Well, not this one."

Michael pats him on the shoulders. "Just tell them it was a roll in the hay, she wanted it at the time, but regretted it after, and that's why she reported it. Happens all the time."

"Will they believe it?"

"Who cares what they believe. Do you believe it?"

He don't say nothing. The woman screaming for help in the bright sun, the feel of her soft throat under his fingers. She kicked up more of a struggle than the other girls.

He can see Michael studying him closely. "You have to believe it, for it to work. You're a good-looking lad, Johnny. She was an older woman out on her own. She was just waiting for you to find her somewhere quiet."

He nods. He'll make himself believe it.

"Fucking bitch. Taking it from me gladly and then calling the police after."

"That's right. That's what all the buffer bitches are like. Want a bit of rough like us, then they feel ashamed of it later. Like we're anything to be ashamed of."

"Fuck them," he says. And that's it. Decision made.

"'Consensual' is the word they're after," Michael adds. "And don't ever use that word, 'rape'. Makes you guilty the minute you say it."

Con-sen-sual. Try to remember that.

"Now pack your bag and get some sleep. Travel light, one change of clothes. Nothing to draw attention."

That's all he has, after all. One change of clothes, his phone, and Granda's ring. And the money and the iPod.

"I'll wake you up in a few hours. You want to be on the road before it gets light."

He looks out the window. It's still dark. A few more hours in this shitehole with Da's snoring and the peelers hovering round, and then he'll be gone. Just like that.

*

Her flatmates, José and Natalia, tiptoe around her during the day.

They ask if she wants anything from the shop, and she lists mundane groceries: orange juice, yogurt, bananas. They're fine with the stream of friends who come to cook her meals, with her sister visiting for a few days.

They're fine with her sleeping in the lounge at night.

206

Since she got back, she hasn't slept in her own room. There's something too dark and enclosed about her bedroom, with the door shut and the walls pressing in. Close her eyes at night and she could suffocate to death.

In the lounge, with the warm glow of the city lights along the Thames, there's at least a possibility of escape. She is reminded there's another world out there, even though she's no longer part of it. She wedges Natalia's blow-up mattress into the far end of the lounge, overlooking the water, and she attempts to sleep there, snuggled under a duvet.

But most of the time, she doesn't sleep.

Her insomnia becomes imperative now. The only way to keep her from dreaming. The images that encroach into her waking life and can morph into something worse at night. A bright field seen through the trees. The glimpse of a white jumper moving up a slope. The presence of someone behind her.

These stream through her mind on an endless loop and she can do nothing to stop them, except try and avoid sleep altogether.

In the grey dawn, in the dead of night, she'll wake up fitfully on that mattress, next to the window overlooking the Thames. It will seem like the mattress is a life raft and she is floating on that grey, flat water, unsure of what the day will bring.

As a child, she would have loved that sense of adventure, the make-believe of drifting on a raft to unknown shores. But now, as an adult, this is a journey she wishes she'd never started.

*

"Johnny, time to wake up." Michael's whispering this to him, shaking him gentle in the dark, before dawn.

He moans, starts to say something, but Michael clamps his hand over his mouth. Eyes blazing at him to keep quiet. He wakes up then for sure. Michael mouths 'Da,' and they both look at the couch.

Da isn't out cold anymore. He's tossing and turning like he might wake any moment.

Johnny's bag is on the floor, the small ratty hold-all he packed Sunday morning in the caravan. Michael picks this up, motions for him to take his shoes and jacket.

His shoes in his hand, they tiptoe toward the door. At the foot of the couch, he stops for a moment, staring at Da. Knows this is risky, he should get going. But there's something about the sight of him like this – the mouth wide open, the eyes closed in their wrinkly pouches, the hair greying and thinning. Maybe this is the last he'll ever see of the useless bastard. He almost feels sorry for Da. That he'll wake up from his hangover, and his grand plan to turn his own son into the police will be ruined. The look on Da's face, and the anger.

He smiles at the thought. Almost in response, Da stirs.

Michael tugs at his hand, jerks his head at the door.

Yeah yeah. He knows. One last look back at Da, and he's off.

But in the silence, there's a tap tap tap and that dog comes out of the dark, nosing for him. Not now.

Does it know he's going? It comes up to him, whining deep in its throat and sniffing at his hand. The tail's wagging and it's looking at him like it wants to play.

Come on, doggy, shut up.

He kneels and gently strokes the dog on the muzzle.

Be a good dog and don't bark and wake the whole fucking house up.

Da mumbles something in his sleep and they both look over at the couch. He turns over and goes back into a snore.

He strokes the dog. It finally sits on his haunches, tail still going, and he leans in, peers into those big eyes.

Michael taps him on the shoulder again, stares at him like he's crazy.

He gets up.

The dog starts to get up, too, but he motions at it to stay down. If it barks, they'll have to leg it out the door.

But the dog stays, a quiet whine in its throat, those doggy eyes staring at him all sad and miserable.

He backs off, silently, looking back at the dog. One step now, another, and Michael holds the door open for him. He steps backward out of it, into the sharp nighttime air.

For a moment, it's just the two of them, breaths puffing, praying the dog won't bark. Still probably sitting there all obedient behind the door, waiting for him. He feels a twinge of sadness, wishes he could take it along. But now's not the time.

Michael looks at him and nods. Not another moment as they both stride into the dark, the sleeping house behind them, the morning still to come. The air is sharp and cold, and he's fully awake now, raring to go.

Just get yourself to the bus station and be off.

The Europa Bus Centre right fuck in the middle of Belfast. Right next to the Europa Hotel, with its tourists and businessmen snoozing away in their giant soft beds, this early in the morning.

They get there, and the place is closed like a tomb. Everything shuttered down, not even a cleaner man sweeping away.

Michael looks at some signboards. "Looks like the first bus to Dublin's at 6." He checks the clock on the wall. They've an hour to go.

There's a dosser asleep on one bench, and Michael steers them away from him.

"Don't want to be near that eejit. The security'll come poking at him in the morning, and you don't want them to see you."

They hunker down behind a corner. He shivers as his breath steams in the air.

"Here, I brought you this." Michael hands him a bundle wrapped in kitchen towel. It's a hunk of last night's ham, squashed between two pieces of bread. "Best I could do," he says.

"It's grand." He takes a bite or two, then wonders if he should save it for later.

They sit down on benches opposite each other. He can feel the cold metal through his jeans.

"You remember Mam's address in Dublin, right?" Michael asks.

"Clones Terrace, Traheen."

"56 Clones Terrace. You got that? You need to remember all of it."

"56 Clones Terrace. 56 Clones Terrace," he mutters it over and over.

"You get to Dublin, you figure out how to get there. Mam and Claire will take care of you."

He hopes.

"D'ya think Mam knows?" he asks.

"Dunno," Michael says. "It's not like her and Da ever speak no more. And I'm sure Da's in no rush for her to find out. Gives her another reason to shout at him."

They grin at that.

"But news travels fast. Maybe she knows already. Maybe."

He don't like the thought of that. Mam with her prayers and rosary beads finding out what he done. He don't give a fuck, really, but think of all the praying she'll want to do for him.

Hail Mary, Mother of God, pray for us sinners…

He snorts. Surprised he even knows the words.

"What is it?" Michael asks.

"Nothing," he says. "Just imagine how many Hail Mary's she'll be after saying for me."

"Ah, she'll be at it all morning."

"And she'll make Claire and Bridget do it too."

They both break into laughter. The three of them on their knees muttering away and looking up at the smiling Virgin.

He wonders. How many Hail Mary's make up for your son being a rapist?

But no, we don't like that word. Use it and you're automatically guilty.

He turns to Michael. "What time's it?"

Quarter past five. Still not light yet. The homeless man is

an unmoving shape on the far bench, and the station is quiet as death. He wonders if Da's still asleep back at Rory's. He waits.

Just before 6am, the Golden Express Service 1X is ready to go to Dublin. Engine on, chugging in the morning air, and a bunch of sleepy punters ready to roll on down to the Big Smoke. One black fella, two Chinese, a handful of normal guys. One old lady. Jaysus, cream of the crop right here.

Michael pushes him to get on early, so not so many can see his face as he steps in.

"Go on," Michael says. "Let me know when you get to Dublin."

He nods. He'll get Mam or Claire to do that.

"Don't you worry about Da," Michael adds. "I'll take care of him somehow."

They pause for a second, and Michael reaches out for one last hug. "Get over here, you muppet. You take care of yourself. You stay low to the ground, stay in the shadows, and they won't find you."

He wants to say something, but his throat is swollen and he don't want Michael to see him sob like a babby. "Okay," he finally says.

"You be a good Sweeney, keep us proud." Michael clasps his forehead to his, then claps him on the back and sends him off.

His pulls his baseball cap on as he shuffles to the bus. He won't turn back to look at Michael. He's second in the queue to buy his ticket, right after the black fella.

He steps up into the bus, face hardly lifted.

"Single to Dublin," he tells the driver.

"Dublin City Centre or Dublin Airport?" your man asks, then has a look at him and his ratty hold-all, and already knows the answer.

No, won't be flying off to them sunny skies and warm beaches of Ibiza, not me. Just fucking grey old Dublin. 56 Clones Terrace, Traheen.

He takes a seat toward the back, against a window.

Hunkered low, he don't like being this far back, with only one exit at the front. But in just two, three hours, he'll be free, across the border.

The two Chinese men get on and he pulls his cap lower over his face. Them Chinks would probably hate him now, what he done to that girl. But they don't know him. Can't tell him apart from any other boy on the street.

That's right. Just melt into the crowd and be gone.

The bus driver leans out the door to see if anyone else is around.

No one, just Michael lurking nearby. Just go, just fucking drive.

Door shuts, bus backs out of that dingy garage.

He catches sight of Michael as the bus turns away, and they wave a hand at each other through the streaked glass. Michael nods at him and grins.

He sinks down in his seat, watches as the Europa Hotel and all the grey old buildings of Belfast fall away behind him.

*

On Thursday morning, The Haven finally calls back.

"We were sorry to hear what happened to you. That's a terrible thing for anyone to go through. Is there anything we can do?"

She's at a loss for words. Maybe it's the woman's overly English wording, but aren't they supposed to know what to do for rape victims? Aren't *they* the experts?

The woman explains that they normally offer all the forensic services and medical support for victims from the moment they report the assault. But having spoken to the Sapphire Unit, it appears she's already been seen to in Belfast.

It almost sounds like they don't want to help her.

"So, are you saying there isn't anything you can do for me now?"

"Well, not at this stage. We do offer counselling sessions for victims."

Angry, she confronts the woman about the PEP. "I never heard back from you within 72 hours of the assault, so I had to figure out how to get PEP some other way."

"Oh, that's good, we're glad you managed to get it."

"But did you not get the message I left you on Monday?"

She wants to ask: why did you take this long to call back?

"We aren't fully staffed here at The Haven, so we weren't able to listen to your message until this morning."

She knows it's pathetic, but she lets it slide. She doesn't have the energy to fight every battle. She asks about their counselling services.

They offer her eight free sessions. She can start as early as this afternoon, if she likes.

She books in a session at 3pm with Ellen. The call finishes.

She looks at her watch. Her sister is arriving in a few hours.

As she sits on the couch, she realizes she can feel anger at least. This must be a good thing. She's not totally dead to the world.

Her sister, Serena, has made the journey from Heathrow to her flat before, but she emailed the directions again yesterday.

Somewhere at the back of her mind, she's aware of how big a trip Serena has made. Seven-hour drive from Eastern California to San Francisco International. Eleven-hour flight to London.

And then, immigration, baggage reclaim, one hour on the Tube to Vauxhall. It's not an insignificant journey.

A little after 12:30, the intercom buzzes.

Three minutes later, she's opening the door to let Serena in, and there is her older sister, wire-rimmed glasses, hair in a ponytail, backpack and suitcase. Looking student-y and unglamorous at the age of thirty-four.

They hug briefly – they've never been much of a hugging family. She leads her down the hallway to the kitchen.

"How are you?" Serena asks. There's a note of concern that she's not used to hearing in her sister's voice.

213

She shrugs. Flicks on the kettle to make tea.

"As good as you can imagine."

Serena's still standing, goes over to her backpack, digs out a plastic sleeve full of papers and hands it over.

"Here, I printed these out for you."

She leafs through the print-outs. Internet pages of RASASC, Rape Crisis Centre, Samaritans, various helplines for victims of crime.

"I also emailed some of them to you as links."

She nods. She remembers looking at some of these webpages, but the thought of dialing up a number and having to explain (to a stranger) what happened (once more) is less than appealing. It would take too much energy, and she hardly has enough energy to get off the couch.

"Yeah, I looked at some of those."

"Have you called them yet?"

"I haven't gotten around to it, no."

"Do you want me to call them for you?"

"Maybe." She leaves it at that. She really just wants to drink Earl Grey tea and crawl back under the duvet.

World, please go away. Let's just take a break from each other, okay?

Serena's still standing and seems a little confused.

"So what do you have to do today?"

A plan? A schedule? Ah yes, I once used to schedule my days out.

"I have some counselling appointment at this place called The Haven at 3. Then I have to go into town and do some errands I've been putting off. I guess we can walk around Hyde Park a bit, if you want."

"Is there anything you want me to do for you?"

"You can just… come along with me to these things. I don't really like being on my own at the moment."

Serena nods. It's an odd confession to make.

Yes, I'm a freak. Your younger sister is a freak now.

The kettle flicks off. The water's boiled.

"Do you want some tea?"

*

Only an hour or so on the bus, and it's been sliding in and out of towns that all look the same. High street, church, post office, pubs – all empty this early in the morning.

Except some of these towns have Union Jacks all over the place. Literally, every single fucking lamp post and flagpole.

Glad they're so proud to be British, but honestly what difference does it make? Her Majesty's done fuck-all for me, so stop flying this shite in our faces.

No, he's glad to be leaving Belfast, he'll be better off in Dublin. Disappear into the crowd there. You're just another pavee boy, not worth nothing.

The bus comes to a stop in a bigger town, right by a shiny new bus station, by the side of a river.

They pull into one of the bays, the engine shuts off.

"Newry," the driver shouts. "Last stop before the Republic. We'll be here ten minutes." Then steps out for a smoke.

He'd fucking kill for a smoke now. Something to calm him down. He looks down and he's shaking his knee like crazy. No, just stay put. Almost over the border now.

He pulls himself deeper into the seat and closes his eyes.

Musta only fallen asleep for a few minutes, but they're still parked and people are buying tickets at the front of the bus. Guess everyone wants to get out of this town.

Come on, just sell the last fucking ticket and let's get going.

He's fiddling with his iPod, trying to find something he hasn't heard a hundred times when he clocks a car driving across the bridge, straight towards them.

Driving fast, like someone desperate to make the bus.

The last two people are on the steps now, about to buy their tickets, but he wishes they'd shut the doors already.

That manky blue car looks familiar.

And then he realises. Uncle Rory's car.

They've fucking followed him here. Not just Uncle Rory. Da's gotta be in there.

215

His insides turn to water. Get the fuck out of here.

He looks around, frantic, but there's no other exit, just the front door of the bus. The windows are too small to climb out.

At the front, the driver's done selling the last tickets.

Shut the fucking door, start the engine!

He'd run right up there now and beg the driver, but no, has to keep his head down, stay in the shadows.

Now the door slides shut and the engine starts up.

He looks out the window again. The blue car's stopped, the door opens, and yes, there's Da. Stepping out, breaking into a run at the bus. Uncle Rory's running, too, a pace behind Da.

He flattens himself onto the seat. Praying that the bus will just take off now, the driver won't notice, but now he hears voices shouting, the door opening again.

Da's voice, all apologies, the way he does the holy show for buffers.

"…Looking for me boy," he hears Da say. "…He's run off again. He can't take care of himself…"

Aw, fuck off now, Da.

From where he is, he scans the floor of the bus. Get down, hide yourself under the seat, maybe they won't find you.

Da's still mumbling. "It'll just be a minute…"

He hears slow footsteps coming down the aisle, pausing at each seat. "So sorry, just looking for me boy."

The floor of the bus is cold and smells like puke, the bottom of the seats torn open.

"Are youse almost finished?" the driver calls out. "I've got a schedule I gotta keep to here."

Turn around, Da, and head out. You don't see me here.

But he sees Da's boots coming closer, coming closer, just one row of seats away.

I'm not here. I'm invisible.

A sudden swish and he's grabbed by the collar, jerked back hard. Slammed up against a seat and Da's eyes boring into his, furious and silent.

"Nice try, Johnny."

*

At The Haven near King's College Hospital in Camberwell, she sits with her sister in a small waiting room. It's in one of those row cottages that cluster up and down English streets, with crooked doors that don't quite open or close properly.

The walls are painted a pale pink, the furniture nondescript. She's staring at six-month-old women's magazines, thumbed through repeatedly by strangers. All rape victims or their companions who waited here nervously before her.

"Vivian Tan?"

She looks up and sees a short, middle-aged woman, with curly grey hair and a tired demeanor.

"I'm Ellen."

Ellen is uninspiring. If your counsellor seems tired before you even begin the session, what hope do you have? Still, she follows her down a short-ceilinged corridor to a small, bare room.

The door closes and she's aware of a clock ticking very loudly in the room. Tick tick tick. That'll get old fast. On the walls, there's nothing but a framed image of a vase of flowers. At the window, vertical blinds dissect a view of the adjoining, sunny garden into stripes.

"Please, be seated."

A box of tissues sits on the table between them.

Ellen has a notebook out and a pen in her hand. She's still not smiling.

She wonders how many notes Ellen will write in the next hour.

"So, Vivian. Tell me what happened."

She knits her brow, reluctant to start the whole story again.

But the clock ticks, and she knows she somehow has to get through the next sixty minutes in this tiny room. No point in putting the thing off.

She begins: "So, I was in Belfast last week."

*

The whole drive back to Belfast, Da is in a black mood. Uncle Rory drives, his thick head nodding, pretending he don't hear nothing, but he knows he's listening in. Thinking how much better his own sons are than Mick Sweeney's no-good boys.

Fuck you, Uncle Rory.

Da's hand is on the back of his neck the entire fucking time, like a vise.

"Budge off, Da." He squirms. "I won't try to bolt."

"Ain't trusting you no more, Johnny." Da won't even look at him, keeps his eyes out the window. "Throw a party for you last night and this is what you do."

Outside, the same old towns and hills roll past in reverse. Eventually, Da's hand relaxes on his neck, but it's still there. It still won't move.

"They're gonna put you in handcuffs, they're gonna read some things to you." Da is saying this to him now as they sit parked on the street outside Willowfield Police Station. The car door's locked.

He wonders what the handcuffs will feel like round his wrists. Wishes he could ask Michael.

"You don't say nothing, just nod and say you understand. I'll be there, but they ask you anything, don't say nothing. And don't fight."

Outside the window, police are going back and forth between the station and their cars. One or two look over at them.

"Then they'll have us call a solicitor. He'll be there to help us. So don't say nothing about what happened with the woman in the park, till that solicitor shows. You got that?"

He looks back at Da. Nods.

"I'm warning you, Johnny. This is important. All this affects what'll happen to you."

Like you fucking care what happens to me, Da.

"Sure, Da. Got it. Happy now?"

"Right, let's go on then."

Uncle Rory reaches out an awkward arm. "You take care of yourself, Johnny. When you get out, I'll take you over to England, have you meet some of your cousins there."

He don't give a fuck about his ten thousand cousins who are in England, rattling around in caravans over there. There's only one person he gives a fuck about right now.

"Before we go in, can we call Michael?"

Da looks at him strange.

But there's Mick Sweeney, taking his phone out, pressing a button, handing it over.

It rings.

Come on, pick up, pick up, Michael.

What'll he say? Yeah, Da nabbed me in the end, but tell me what do I do when I'm inside…

Da looks away, a vein in his temple pulsing.

But there's nothing.

Michael probably saw a call from Da, didn't want to answer.

Something crumples inside him. He hands the phone back, not a word.

"Let's go then," Da says. And opens his car door.

He gets out, and him and Da stand there on the street, looking at the police station. A great fucking barricade all round the building, with barbed wire curling round the top.

The sky is darker now, and he feels the first drops of rain coming on. Thick, fat drops on the back of his neck. The concrete steps lead up to the police station entrance. Nowhere else to go but inside.

*

"She said, 'We're here to provide a space for you to talk about your feelings.'"

Serena smirks. "What does that even mean?"

"Beats me. If I want to talk about my feelings, I'll do it with my friends. Not to some random awkward woman I don't even know."

"Hm, well, maybe it'll get better."

"Maybe." But she's not hopeful.

They're sitting that afternoon in Hyde Park, in a soft hollow below a slope. There's still a crispness in the air, but clumps of wilting daffodils dot the grass. She's spread out her jacket on the ground, past where the shadows of the trees end. They seem strangely protected in the cup of the earth, green grass around them, sun on their faces.

She closes her eyes, soaks in the sunlight, hears the bark of dogs and the chatter of passersby she can't see.

"Are you okay?" Serena asks after a few minutes.

"Not really." She skims the palm of her hand over the top of the grass. "So, what'd you tell Mom and Dad when you said you were coming over here?"

"I didn't. I said I had a business trip to somewhere else. New York, I think."

"Oh, that's smart."

She realizes she hasn't spoken to their mom in over a week. Can't even begin to fathom how she'll handle that conversation without mentioning the attack.

"Did Mom ask about me?" she asks Serena.

"Yeah, she did, I told her you were really busy after your trip, but would get in touch when you were free."

That's all true enough, in its own weird way.

"When you do eventually talk to her, just keep it brief, try to sound normal," Serena says. "But I think it's really important that Mom and Dad don't find out."

She doesn't need to ask why. She agrees. She starts to pluck off the tips of the grass blades and curls them up into balls.

"Just… I think they'll freak out. I know they'll freak out. They'll come running to me because I'm a lawyer, but I don't even know how to handle this."

"They'll want me to move back to New Jersey."

"Would you want that?"

"Are you frickin' kidding me?"

She imagines, for a moment, moving into that old bedroom in the suburbs, the one she worked so hard to escape. What would she do with her time? No friends in Edgewood anymore, no job, not even a car. Stuck with her bickering parents, working in their shop again, pretending to be friendly to the same old customers. Neighbors who have never traveled, never left their dead-end street in suburbia.

No, anything but moving back in with her parents. She'd rather handle everything on her own here in London. Single, with not much money, living with two flatmates, sleeping on that blow-up mattress overlooking the Thames. This is the closest thing to home for her.

What they don't bother to discuss is how their parents would actually react. Mom would burst into tears in an instant, her voice growing shrill and strained. *I told you to always be careful! I told you not to go hiking on your own!* And Dad. Dad would just clam up, grow silent and angry, and later blame Mom for encouraging her daughters to be so reckless and independent.

"Yeah, don't worry," she tells Serena. "I'll keep it from them."

Not that it was ever in question.

The sun has clouded over, and it's become chilly. She shivers and puts on her jacket.

She feels guilty, somehow, keeping a secret this big and momentous. This deliberate act of deception, children concealing the truth from their parents. But there is so much they already don't know about her adult life. This is just one more thing.

*

There's a drawing of him on the wall behind the peelers' counter. Don't quite look like him. They got his hair right and his freckles, but the eyes are like some mental version of him, like he's been locked up in a crazy house his whole life.

YOUTH, 14–18 YEARS OF AGE
WANTED FOR ALLEGED RAPE

He wants to point to it and say: "Your artist is shite."

221

But Da's doing all the talking, the peelers nodding all-important. Like when he went with Mam to the station in Kilkenny, Michael's first arrest. The peelers looked at them like they were scum. They're looking the same way at him now.

"Johnny, is that your name?" the fat one says to him.

He nods.

"Right, it's good that you've come here of your own accord. Let me just show you into a room now, while I make a few phone calls."

Da looks at him.

"Come on, over this way," the peeler says. His two chins wobble. Opens up a door and waits for him to go on over like a dog.

One look back at Da.

"I'll be right here. Go on now, Johnny."

He steps into a small, bare room. Behind him, a click as the door is locked.

"On the afternoon of Saturday, April 12th, were you in the area of Glen Forest Park in West Belfast?"

It's the man in charge asking him this, some man named Morrison. Wearing a suit, youngish, don't even look like a peeler.

He don't answer right away, but Da is back, sitting next to him, and glares at him fierce.

"Yeah."

"And did you meet a woman named Vivian Tan, who was on her own in the park?"

Was that her name? First time he's heard it. Bitch even lied about her name.

"I met a woman. She didn't say what was her name."

"But you interacted with a woman, an American woman, who was in the park on her own. Is that correct?"

"Yeah."

"And you understand why you are wanted for questioning in relation to an incident that took place involving this woman, correct?"

What the fuck does that mean? Too many words coming out of this peeler's mouth all at once.

"I know that you're looking for me."

The peeler nods. "Okay then, Johnny."

*

That evening, she's at a dinner party. Stefan's invited her and Serena over to his flat in Covent Garden, and Magda, another friend of his, is there.

She's met Magda before, a thin, nervous Czech woman, who seems perpetually worried about any number of things. Tonight, Magda is rambling on about her latest disappointments in dating.

"He didn't even call back, he just decided that's the end of it, we don't need to be in touch anymore!"

Listening to this, she's silently toying with her uneaten lamb, twiddling her fork around the gristle and the fat.

Serena isn't saying much either.

"Well, you know, just forget about him," Stefan says.

"I mean, how much more of this do I have to put up with?" Magda asks.

The old her would have agreed. Chatted along. But now she's amazed at how self-absorbed Magda sounds.

She stays quiet. Slices another roasted rosemary potato, chews and swallows it.

Just then her phone rings.

"Sorry." She goes over to her bag, rifles around for the phone.

The number's been blocked, and with that now-familiar wave of nausea, she knows it must be the police. Their numbers are always blocked, every time they call.

"Hello?"

"Oh hi, Vivian, it's Thomas Morrison with the PSNI. Is this a good time to talk?"

She looks around. "Hold on a second."

She slips down the hallway, pauses in front of a framed print of a Francis Bacon painting. *Head IV*, according to the words on the matting. "Yes, I can talk now."

"Ah, so I have some good news," Thomas says, trying to sound cheerful.

Good news from the police. A bit ironic, really. "What is it?"

"He's been found, and he's been arrested."

The nausea turns into something else – a dour, ghostly version of relief, grinning like a medieval grotesque.

"Really?"

"Aye, that's right. So you can rest safe now. He hasn't said much yet, but I just wanted to let you know we've found him."

"Thanks, Thomas."

The detective mumbles a few other things. The community's organized a candlelight vigil in her honor, which will take place Saturday in the park. So people in Belfast are thinking of her. Everyone's relieved the boy's been found.

But it all seems so surreal. His arrest is a minor victory in what feels like a doomed war. What is she supposed to do? Run delighted into the next room, announce the good news, jump for joy?

And this community vigil... complete strangers sending their well wishes, but what good will that do her? She never wanted any of this. She cannot feel joy. Nor gratitude. It feels wrong to even smile.

So she stays in the hallway a moment longer, hesitating. She hears the murmur of mundane conversation from the lounge, and she can glimpse the outline of her reflection in the glass, a pale shadow layered over the Francis Bacon portrait. The painting is a face with no eyes, just a mouth, gaping wide open and hungry, the head itself vanishing into thin air.

She stares and stares. And she expects her own face to vanish too.

*

At the sight of the handcuffs, he wants to retch.

Do anything, get out of there, push your way out of that room and out the front door, run free, anywhere, down the street.

But Da's standing right there. And he knows he can't bolt, he can't retch. He just has to do what he's told.

He holds his wrists out like a coward.

The handcuffs snap round them, cold and hard. The metal scrapes his skin.

"John Michael Sweeney, you are hereby arrested for the assault and rape of Vivian Tan on 12th of April of this year. You do not have to say anything. But it may harm your defence if you do not mention when questioned something which you later rely on in court. Anything you do say may be given in evidence. Do you understand?"

Not really no, but that don't matter. Like they fucking care.

And the dark clawing takes over now, he can't breathe, he can't think or speak. He can only let himself be clawed apart, here in this small bare room.

PART THREE

I know what you're gonna say. That I was bound to do something like that sometime. You don't know when – what day or what bitch or what you do to her. But sometime, one of these times, it'll come and get you. And you'll regret it.

Do I regret it? Regret's one of them words they're always trying to hammer into you from the outside. Another trick to make you feel bad about yourself, because you're a tinker and you're dirt. Only, regret don't mean nothing to me.

They ask all the time, 'Do you regret what you did to that woman?' How about all them other girls? And all them purses and phones I grabbed, am I supposed to feel bad about them too? Am I supposed to feel bad about my whole life? And why should I, just cause they don't understand what my life is about and don't really care neither. Not till your life interferes with one of theirs.

But if I hadn't messed with her, if she hadn't said nothing to the peelers, I'd be just fine. Cruising along, just this pavee in the shadows, and no one paying no attention to me.

So yeah, thinking back, should I have picked some other beour? Yeah. Someone younger. Someone who didn't blab. Other boys never get caught, still wandering free as they please. But me? One bad choice, Johnny, and your life is fucked.

Unless it was always fucked from the beginning. So let's just pretend this pavee boy's not really there, hey.

Truth is, I'm not there. Not until some beour decides to moan about something I done. Then they think I'm something to be fixed. But I was there all along. They just didn't see me.

*

She's used to it by now, the look on peoples' faces when she tells them what happened. She's used to telling it the right way, the safe way. Because the truth is, they don't *really* want to know all the different positions he made her use. And that's maybe a little too private for her to reveal.

But even the censored version makes them flinch.

There's no point, in them knowing every single gory detail. That knowledge is for you alone. And the police. And your therapist.

But friends... in some weird way, they need to be protected. Otherwise, it might freak them out too much, shatter their safe middle-class lives.

The truth for you is different. Everything has changed.

So she gives them the safe version of what happened. When some friends ask for more details, she'll answer dutifully. Others say, "I'm sure you don't want to talk about it," as if that's their excuse for not asking questions.

But how could she not want to talk about it? How could she possibly ignore the enormity of what happened to her on that Saturday afternoon?

To do that would be lying on a colossal scale.

And that's a kind of deception she can't pull off.

*

"Johnny, let's take it step by step. Tell me where you were on Saturday, what you were doing. Let's start with the morning, shall we?"

He's sitting in that same small room, only more cramped than before, because this Detective Morrison is asking him stuff, along with another peeler, and then Uncle Rory. They wouldn't let Da sit in on this part, something about him being too close. So it's fucking Uncle Rory, and next to him is his solicitor, Mr McLuhan. McLuhan's all wiry specs and gray suit and shiny watch, the kind of buffer he'd try to snatch a wallet from, if he saw him alone on the street.

But now McLuhan's on his side. He'd said: "I'm only here to help you. Try to get you the best deal so you don't have to stay in custody for very long. But I need you to cooperate with me and tell me what you know."

So he did. Told him a version of the whole story, all with nice frills and ribbons this time, and now he's here telling the same story again to Detective Morrison.

Morrison's youngish. Brown suit, round face. Looks like he'd be a dopey young da on a telly advert, but here he is asking him questions with a face that means business, and the other peeler scrawling it all down, even though it's all being recorded on some machine. Morrison writes something now and then, but it's not like he can read it. Sweeneys aren't known for their learning.

There's a cup of water next to him on the metal table, but if he wants to drink, he has to ask someone to hold it up to his mouth and let him go glug glug glug. Pure class, huh?

"Take your time," Morrison says. "Take as much time as you need."

"I woke up in the caravan that morning."

"Which caravan is that?"

Jaysus, this is gonna be a while.

*

The other stories trickle in, unexpected. And after a while, no longer so unexpected. Because this is how frequently it happens, how often individual lives are blighted by rape. And she's only realizing this now.

A friend's friend.

An aunt.

A sister.

A classmate.

A woman was camping with her friend. She went to use the bathroom at the campsite, and two men were lying in wait to see who would come by. They attacked her right there.

231

A woman decided to go on a personal holiday volunteering in El Salvador for an NGO. On the last night, she went to a bar on her own, and somehow, two beers showed up at her table. The next morning, she woke up on a dirty mattress in a room she did not recognize. She knew she'd been raped; she hurt down there. But all she wanted was to get back to the hotel, catch her flight, and go home, go somewhere safe. Besides, the police in El Salvador weren't going to be able to find anyone. Rape happens all too often. It's hardly news.

A woman who had drunk too much was helped home from a party by a male friend. Who then raped her once he got into her house. He left her in shock, half-naked on her couch, at 4am. She called the police later in the morning, but she couldn't handle the officers crawling through her house, searching through her knickers. It felt like too much of a violation, after what had just happened.

There will be violation upon violation. This much she has come to realize in these past few weeks.

*

Not nearly as fun as watching it on telly, this ain't.

On telly, the criminal would be some big tattooed hard-man, head shaved and all, and he'd flip the table, and him and the detective would stare daggers at each other. Here, it's everyone crowding round him, waiting for him to answer the dullest questions ever.

"The caravan you live in with your da and Michael, where is it?"

"It's up by the road there, the one just above the Glen. You can see the waterfall and all."

"Okay good, Johnny."

Scratch scratch goes the peeler's pen.

"And what time did you wake up that morning?"

He shrugs. No clocks at home and no watch.

"Can you try guessing at all?"

Who the fuck pays attention to the time so much?

232

"I just woke up, is all."

"Was it... 9 maybe? Or 11? Try and remember, Johnny."

"I dunno. I don't look at the time."

The peeler stops, clears his throat, looks at McLuhan.

"If my client can't remember, I don't think it's fair to push him to name a time."

"Fair enough," Morrison says. "Well, do you think it was before or after midday?"

"Before, probably." Seemed like morning to him, the way the air was.

"And what did you do when you woke up?"

"Hung around the caravan a bit."

"Did you speak to anyone else?"

"Naw, me da and Michael weren't around."

"And where were they, if they weren't around?"

He pulls a smirk and wants to laugh, but a look from McLuhan reminds him sharp.

"Me da was prolly out on a job. Michael... I dunno."

"But they weren't at home, so you were just in the caravan on your own, correct?"

"Yeah."

"And did you speak to anyone else up at the halting site?"

"There's this woman next door. Nora Callahan. She's got a little kid, too. I was with them some. Had some food with them."

"She cooked you a meal, did she?"

"Yeah, that's right."

"Does she often do that, cook you food?"

Shrugs again. "Yeah, now and then. If me da's away and no food around."

"Did you speak to her about anything?"

"About some stuff. But can't remember what."

"Can you try and remember?"

"Not really, no. Just like... where was me da, where was Michael. What her man's been up to."

Another pause. Morrison clears his throat. "Right. So can

you tell me how you were feeling when you woke up that morning?"

"Hungry."

"Okay and anything else?"

Pause and look at McLuhan, who nods. They spoke about this. It's okay to say.

"I was… I was still feeling sorta high."

"High?" Morrison looks up like this is something important. "Had you been on drugs the night before?"

"Yeah."

The other peeler starts scribbling now like he's hearing the Word of God, but Morrison just nods.

"What drugs had you taken?"

"Some yokes. Ecstasy."

"Pills? How many had you taken?"

"Not sure. Two, maybe three."

"And anything else?"

"Some dope. I smoked some with my friends."

"When you say dope, you mean marijuana, correct?"

Seriously, how much do you gotta spell out for these peelers…

"Johnny, please answer him," McLuhan says. Fuck him.

"Yes, officer, I mean marijuana."

"How much did you have?"

"I dunno, we passed two joints around. Shared it between three of us."

"So you were still feeling the effects of this when you woke up on Saturday morning, correct?"

"Guess you could say so."

"Can you describe *how* you were feeling the effects of the drugs?"

"I guess I was feeling like I had a headache. And you know, everything all still, like when you're stoned. You can't remember things clear, 'cause you're sorta dizzy."

Maybe they're gonna stop asking him these shite questions now that he's admitted he don't remember nothing.

"So, Johnny, I'm glad you've told me that. But I'm still

going to have to ask you to remember things as best as you can. You've been arrested for a very serious offence, the most serious crime, short of killing another person. So it would be in your interest to tell me as much as you remember, so you can convince us that you haven't committed this crime. Do you understand?"

"Yes, my client understands completely."

Thanks, McLuhan, take the fucking words out of me mouth like I'm an eejit.

"So what did you do after you had something to eat with Nora Callahan."

"I hung around the halting site some more."

"Doing what?"

"Dunno. Just... whatever. There's not much to do up there. Thought about ringing me friends."

"But you didn't ring them."

"I mean, I maybe tried but no one picked up."

"And these friends are the same ones as Friday night?"

"That's right. Gerry and Donal."

Morrison asks for their full names, writes them down.

"So what did you do when you couldn't get through to them on the phone?"

"I dunno. I guess I decided to go on down the Glen to hang out at the park there."

"And what time did you go down to the park?"

"Dunno. Afternoon. Like I said, I don't have no watch or clock."

"Yes, of course, Johnny. And why did you decide to go to the park?"

"There's people there. More things to see."

"And what did you see when you were down there?"

"Just, normal people, you know what I mean? People walking their dogs, people going for walks. That sorta thing."

"Did you speak to any of these people?"

"No one, no."

"Except for the woman?"

"Yeah yeah, except for her."

She gets care packages from her friends in the US.

The first is from her friend Melissa. When the box arrives, she pulls back the cardboard flaps to find packets of jelly beans, pretzels, and lavender-scented bath crystals, boxes of macaroni and cheese, and a small plush pig.

The trappings of American middle-class comfort, nicely shipped to London via the US Postal Service.

Other packages arrive: organic soaps, exquisitely designed stationery, a Beanie Baby. All with a heartfelt notecard, a handwritten message inside: *I am so, so sorry to hear what happened...*

These small trinkets of love and friendship, which she displays on her nightstand and along her window sill.

After four weeks, she feels brave enough to stop sleeping on the air mattress in the lounge. She moves back into her bedroom, with the door that closes shut and seals her between those four walls each night. She reminds herself that it's just eight hours of darkness before the sun rises at 5:30 the next morning. Just eight hours that she needs to get through with the unknown blackness pressing up against the window, the city lights piercing through like small beacons across a dark sea.

If you were to ask her what she does with her time every day, she wouldn't be able to answer.

Sleep until ten or eleven in the morning. Then write down her dreams in detail, eat some food, take that horrific PEP pill, and then... what does she do inside the confines of her flat all day?

Just a few weeks ago, she'd get bored, even having to spend a few hours on her own inside.

But time runs on a different scale for her now. It is not something that can be filled with activities, made productive. It is just nothingness, a bland series of days and weeks, a lifetime of undefined joylessness stretching in front of her.

That is her future. And her present. Her past is no longer hers. It belonged to a different Vivian.

"And when did you see Ms Tan?"

"I dunno. I was just hanging around and we started talking, like."

"Who started the conversation? Was it you or was it her?"

Pause. How to swing this.

McLuhan speaks before he can get a word out. "Just to reiterate, my client was on drugs at the time, so he may not remember exact details like this."

"Yes, I understand, counsellor."

"I can't really remember."

"What did you talk about? Did someone ask the other one a question?"

"It mighta been. I think she asked me. She was asking me for some directions, like. Had this book and was sort of lost."

Just twist the truth a bit. No one's gonna know and makes more sense for her to be asking the directions. Tourist and all.

"What specifically did she ask you?"

"Well, like, she had this trail she wanted to follow and she wanted to know if she was going the right way."

"So she spoke to you first?"

"Yeah, that's it."

"And what did you tell her?"

"Just that she was going the right way. She wanted to get to the hills, like. And I says, yeah I know that area well."

"And then what happened from there?"

"Well, then, she says: "Really you know that area well? Like she wanted to continue chatting, you know what I mean?"

It's happening easy now, let the Sweeney charm flow. He remembers what Michael said, your story's as good as hers. So make it real, live it. Believe it.

Morrison nods. "Yes, please continue."

"So I keep on chatting to her. Just about the area and all."

"And why did you continue talking to her?"

"Didn't have nothing better to do. And besides, she seemed to fancy me. And she was a bit of a beour."

Morrison raises an eyebrow. "A beour?"

"A good-looking girl, if you know what I mean."

"So you found her attractive, and it seemed like you two were getting on well."

"Yeah yeah, I'd say."

*

I am so sorry to hear about what happened to you.

A friend has written this in an email. Jemima. A skinny, gawky, intelligent English girl whom she befriended working on a television project years ago. They didn't have that much in common, but for whatever reason, they've remained acquaintances since then.

Jemima's invited her to some drinks she is organizing in Soho.

And, as with everyone else, she's sent an email back with the truth. She's not quite up for socializing these days. Because of this thing that's happened...

Jemima writes back with two, carefully crafted paragraphs.

You may want to get in touch with a friend of mine, Annabelle, who was raped some years back by a work colleague. She said it was all right for me to tell you about her experience.

Annabelle had decided not to pursue a legal case. He was wealthy, from a well-connected family, she wouldn't have a good chance in court. She had to quit her job. It took her a long time to recover.

But she is now happily married and has a kid. I thought you might like to know that. That it's possible to move on and put your life back together.

On a distant plane, she is heartened by Annabelle's story. So it can happen, it's not completely hopeless. Lives can change for the better after something like this.

But if only she could know how. Fast-forward to that time when life will have improved. Only, there is no clear twelve-step process to guide you. This is where you start to improvise, blindly.

She does not end up reaching out to Annabelle. Somehow it seems like too much of an imposition. And how would she word her email?

Jemima may have told you about me. I'm her friend who was recently raped.

And then what?

*

"And what made you think that this woman fancied you, or at least wanted to keep talking to you?"

Lean back now and grin. Well, don't lay it on too thick. But remember it like that. Those first few moments, meeting a beour who fancies you. The flashing smile, the eyes flirting, the flick of the hair, the tits heaving when she laughs.

"Well, she smiled. And she kept chatting to me."

"And what did you two talk about?"

"Loads of things."

"Such as?"

"Herself and her life and me, I spoke about me family a bit. But I can't remember much, the whole day's really a blur."

"Can you remember anything specific that she said about herself? Where she lives? What she does for a living? If she was visiting Belfast?"

"Oh, she was visiting Belfast."

"Did she tell you why?"

"I don't really remember."

"How long were you two talking for in the park?"

"Got no watch, couldn't tell you."

"Could you maybe guess?"

"Half hour, maybe? It was a while."

"Was there anyone else in the park who saw you two talking?"

"Oh yeah, loads of people."

"Can you describe anyone in particular?"

"Wasn't really paying attention."

"No one you remember at all?"

"No, I was really just paying attention to her."

*

Slowly, a new routine forms for her. A bare almost-schedule that seems to prop up her empty existence.

Every Thursday is her useless session with The Haven in Camberwell. Every Tuesday afternoon, she rides the bus out to Wandsworth, to see the private counsellor her boss is paying for. Maybe ventures a few steps into the open park next door, then rides the bus back to Vauxhall.

In between, she feeds herself out of some sense of duty, stares out the window, lies on the couch.

Then there's piano.

She starts playing piano again. For weeks it had sat there, forgotten, the digital piano she'd so proudly bought in January with £400 that she felt justified spending. But one weekday afternoon when her flatmates are at work, she opens the lid, powers it on, sits down, and plays.

One note, then another. A chord she hasn't played in over ten years.

And the music starts to trickle out. It never left her.

Classical cadences, blues scales, and that book which came with the piano: *50 of Piano's Greatest Hits*. Inside are all the familiar pieces she's played growing up. Bach minuets and Mozart rondos and Beethoven sonatas. Some are rusty, but with a little practice, she can play them like her thirteen-year-old self again. Only with more control this time.

Leafing further through the book, she finds the music for Clair de Lune by Debussy. She'd never learnt it as a child, but now she has all the time in the world. And it's not as difficult as she'd feared. Note by note, she pieces together the sharps and flats that crowd the staff lines. Listens to how one chord resolves into the next.

Then she moves onto the second movement of Beethoven's Pathetique Sonata. She'd heard it so many times before and

240

remembers the concert pianist who played it in that church hall in North Jersey, how the notes spilled out so earnest and poignant. If she could just learn to play that, then her life won't be a complete waste.

A few days later, she has learned the first page and a half of the movement.

See, progress.

And she doesn't feel like such a pathetic loser anymore, bereft of the life she once led. Because whatever happens, she still has this, she still has this.

*

"So you two are talking for twenty, say thirty minutes. Then what happens?"

Now here's where you use your imagination. You've thought this one through. Worked a charm on McLuhan. Now tell it to the peelers.

"Well, we were just chatting and walking the whole time."

"Up the Glen, toward the halting site?"

"Yeah, walking up the Glen, to where she wanted to go. And I'd said I lived in the area. So she asked if I could walk with her, be her guide, like."

"So she asked you? Or you offered?"

"It was kind of both."

Morrison does this grumpy mouth twist, to show that's not good enough.

"Maybe she asked. Yeah. She was making like she didn't know the area. I did, she wanted some company."

"She said that to you?"

"Well, she asked if I could walk with her then, yeah."

"Right, and when did this happen? Where in the park were you?"

"It was, uh…" Jaysus, this peeler's loads of questions. "It weren't too far from where you pass under the road there."

"You mean the Glen Road?"

"Yeah, the Glen Road. You pass under the road, and then

on the other side, there weren't so many other people. So that's where she started to really, you know, smile and say stuff like me joining her for the walk."

"So what were you thinking then?"

"Just that like, yeah, this beour's keen on me."

"What do you mean by that?"

"Oh, that she might, you know, fancy a shag or something. Why else would she ask me to join her?"

"But you didn't at that point, talk about sex or anything?"

"No, no, we was just talking."

"So from then on, what happened?"

"Uh, we kept on talking. She weren't sure how to cross the stream there, so I showed her how."

"And did anyone see you at this point, from the moment you two passed under the Glen Road?"

Think think think. Was there anyone? "I don't really remember. Maybe one person, then no one else."

"Can you describe what that one person was like?"

"Naw naw. Like I said, I was mainly just chatting with her."

"Can you remember if this other person was male or female?"

Probably not a woman, else he would of noticed. But he shakes his head no.

Morrison nods and takes a break to write some more down. McLuhan clears his throat.

"So after you showed her how to cross the stream, where did you go from there?"

"So's then, we agreed that we'd walk together."

"For how long?"

"We didn't say for how long, but I could tell she wanted to go with me somewhere."

"How could you tell that?"

"Smiling and flirting, all them things girls do."

"When you say flirting, what do you mean by that?"

"Just uh…" And picture it, picture her. What would she say? What would she do?

242

"Well, she put her hand on me… on me shoulder. Kinda rested her body against mine and laughed for a bit."

"Did she? And when did she do this?"

"Just after I helped her across the stream. Just sort of a thank you, because I helped her."

"And what else?"

"And she… she took off her socks and shoes to show me her legs when she was crossing the stream. She didn't have to. I told her how to cross it on the stones, just hopping across, but she stripped down to show me her legs."

"How much did she strip down?"

"Just her shoes and socks. But, like, she wasn't hiding her legs or nothing. She wanted me to see them."

"And did she put her socks and shoes back on?"

"Yeah, after crossing. But that's when she leaned on me, like."

Morrison pauses, brow all wrinkly. The other peeler shakes his hand out from all that writing. "Then what?"

"So's by then, we were walking together, like. And I helped her up the slope."

"You showed her the way?"

"Oh, yeah yeah. She was really grateful. She wouldn't of been able to get up the slope without me. But I showed her."

*

Her friend Caroline had called after hearing what happened.

"Are you at home now?" Caroline had asked, with a strange urgency. "I'm coming over. I have to come over."

And ninety minutes later, Caroline is in her lounge. The two of them on the couch, drinking mugs of herbal tea.

"I'm just processing," Caroline says. "I'm so sorry this had to happen to you."

She shrugs. "Well, there isn't anything I can do about it now."

"It's just…" Caroline starts, then pauses, looks out the window at the river. "Well, you know, it happened to me, too."

She looks up, surprised, but Caroline is turned away from her. She's known Caroline for three years and this has never come up.

"When did this happen?" Some protective instinct rears up in her, a muted rage.

"I was young. I mean, I was nineteen, I was interning in DC for the summer. There were a bunch of us living near each other, who all interned for the same congressman. You know how DC is just a hive of young college students each summer."

She offers a small smile. Seems like another lifetime, to be an eager intern during your college summers.

"There was this one guy, we hung out a lot. It was strictly platonic between us. Or at least, I was never interested in him in that way. And then one night, we were hanging out, smoking some weed, and I wasn't very sober. I don't know how it happened. One minute we were laughing and smoking in my bedroom, and the next, he's pinning me down on my bed.

"And I just remember thinking afterward, 'I didn't agree to that.' But later, I convinced myself I had, just to make it normal somehow. Even though I had a boyfriend back in California."

Caroline's still gazing at the Thames, the late afternoon light falling across her high cheekbones.

"But just to make the rest of the summer livable somehow, I told myself me and this guy were dating. Because we had to work together everyday. We were part of this social group that hung out all the time."

Caroline's green eyes are full of shame.

She looks back at Caroline, the same way all her friends must look at her when she tells them *her* story. The eyes wide in shock. The mixture of sympathy and anger. Caroline continues, no longer hesitating.

"And he kept coming over and having sex with me all summer, and I just let it happen. I never tried to stop it. I don't know why, maybe I didn't want to cause a stir, as ridiculous as that sounds…"

Caroline trails off, her story over, and suddenly she looks

much less assured. Caroline Sanderson – the bright, beautiful third daughter in a Midwestern family of patrician blondes. Her father and grandfather powerful businessmen, her male cousins rising politicians. She wonders if this family legacy made it more difficult for Caroline to admit the truth of what had happened to her.

"And the worst was, at the end of the summer, he went to kiss me goodbye, he said, 'Oh, we should keep in touch, you never know what might happen.' And I..."

Caroline's face crumples, her voice catches in her throat.

"And I told him never to try and contact me again. How *dare* he try to keep in touch?" Disgust punctuates her voice, and she can imagine Caroline jabbing an angry finger at the unnamed guy, all those years ago. That veneer of impeccable manners momentarily cracked.

"I didn't tell anyone about it at all," Caroline continues, her voice calmer now. "I just kept it to myself. I kept seeing that same boyfriend, though I felt like I'd cheated on him. And then, two years later, it all came out. I just got so horribly depressed, I wanted to end it all, and... so, I started seeing a therapist."

"And what did the therapist say?"

"She was good, real good. She told me it wasn't my fault. I hadn't cheated on Derek, but I would need to tell him, if I wanted to start to feel better."

"And did you?" She herself feels the twist of queasiness at the thought of telling a boyfriend.

Caroline nods, and sips her tea. "And he was wonderful. Really really lovely and supportive. But I guess I just needed some time away to really heal, once I was willing to address what had happened. So the timing wasn't right for us. He's married now, to a girl who's perfect for him."

"Is that why you moved here to the UK?"

"Maybe. I had to get away. I didn't want anything to do with DC or Capitol Hill after that. The worst was, my dad and uncle were really disappointed that I didn't want to continue with politics. They were so excited about me working in DC, wanted to pull out all the stops for me to have a career there."

"And what did you tell them?"

"Just that after interning, I realized it wasn't for me." They both watch the Thames turning grey in the afternoon.

The sadness and regret is palpable in Caroline's face. "But I guess that's just the way things go sometimes."

The shape of our lives. How they can be molded by people you hardly know. And never want to know ever afterward.

Caroline turns away quickly, and starts to sob.

"I'm so sorry. I meant to come here to comfort you, and now look at me..."

She looks on with a shared pain, but she herself has no more tears to shed.

Since Belfast, she has cried herself dry.

*

"Okay, so when you got to the top of the slope, what happened?"

"Well then, it was grand, like. Beautiful view and just the two of us."

"What do you mean by that?"

"She was out of breath from the climb, like. We both were. So we were leaning on each other to catch our breaths. She was laughing at me, and all. So I could tell I was in, like."

"What do you mean by 'in'?"

"Just that, you know, she wanted me."

"'She wanted you.' As in she wanted to do something with you?"

Jaysus, these fucking peelers.

"Yeah yeah, she wanted to shift and then some."

"What do you mean by that?"

"You know, like, kissing and stuff."

Morrison sighs. "Look, Johnny, you need to be more specific here in terms of what you did with this woman. Was it just kissing?"

"Well, at first, yeah. Just some kissing. But she was really going for it."

"Who started the kissing? Was it her or you?"

"It was both. We both wanted it."

"What do you mean when you say she was 'really going for it'?"

"Like, shoving her tongue down me throat and all, letting me do the same to her."

"And were you two standing at this point? Right where you'd come up the slope?"

"Yeah, that's where we started kissing."

"And was it just kissing?"

"Well, just like hands groping and all."

"Whose hands?"

"Both of us."

He shoots a look at Uncle Rory, who's maybe just staring at the wall, pretending he ain't there.

"So where were your hands when you were kissing?"

"At first, we was just kissing. But then when she got more into it, we got a bit closer. So her hands were, like, on me back and pulling me close to her. And I had mine on her back and then on her bum. And then moving up to her... her tits, like."

"So your hands touched her bum and her breasts while you were kissing?"

"That's right."

"And she let you do that?"

"Yeah yeah. She didn't say nothing that it was a problem. She let me touch her there."

"And where was she touching you during this time?"

He's almost getting hard, with this new version of his. It's as good as true, right? What lad wouldn't get horned up, shifting a woman like that, right in the middle of the woods, no one else around?

"She was touching me on me back and neck. And then her hands slid lower down me back and grabbed me bum."

"Okay."

"And then... and then, she reached for me prick."

247

"She touched you in the genital area?"

"Yeah, just on the outside of me jeans. Just for a moment. But that's when I knew she wanted me like, right there."

"So then what happened?"

"Well, then she broke off. We stopped kissing."

"Why was that?"

"'Cause she wanted to lead me on this chase, like. So we're shifting and all, and then she breaks away and starts sort of running down the path, looking back at me and laughing. Wanting me to chase her down."

"How do you know she wanted you to chase her down?"

"'Cause of how she was looking at me. Looking back and laughing and all 'come and get me'."

"Right, did she ever say this at any point? 'Come and get me.'"

Yeah, why not? Have her say this.

"Yeah, I think she did. 'Come and get me.' That's what she said."

*

Sleep becomes untrustworthy. It won't welcome her back into its warm embrace. It toys with her, pretends to reach out, then flings her away.

When she does dream, it is always in the last five minutes before waking up: manic, vivid dreams that seem more real than her dull, grey life now.

Once, she dreams she is trying to hide inside a bedroom, at some college party, but there is a mob of braying, boastful jocks rattling away at the locked door. Football players and frat boys who will gang rape her, once they get inside the room.

All she can do is hide and pretend she isn't there, even though they know she's inside, they're trying to break down the door. But there's no escape. No window, no weapon inside the room. It's only a matter of time before they get through.

When she wakes up, the sunlight is streaming through the curtains by her bed. Her heart is still pounding from the dream, dreading the inevitable. The room is bright, her flatmates are at work, and she is all alone inside the flat.

*

"So what did you take this to mean, when she said: 'Come and get me'?"

Look at the peeler like he's an eejit. "Just yeah, she wanted me to come get her and fuck her right then and there."

"Did she at any point, specifically say she wanted to have sex?"

He snorts. "Naw naw, beours don't say it like that. They just kinda giggle and smile and that means they want it."

Morrison looks at McLuhan, but solicitor man don't give nothing back. Morrison writes something down.

"So, how were you feeling around then?"

"Horned-up, you know what I mean? Like here was this beour, sexy and all forward, and she'd made it clear she wanted to, you know, do the business right then and there."

"So you wanted to have sex with her?"

"Yeah yeah, of course."

"And how long did this... this chase go on for?"

"Not very long. I mean, the path goes for a bit, then it gets to the halting site. So it was before then."

"Before you got to the halting site?"

"Yeah yeah, I wanted to reach her by then so we could you know, do our thing, while we still were in the woods."

"And why is that?"

"Well, for a bit of privacy. I mean, you don't want to do it right in the open, where people can see you."

"And you weren't worried about it being uncomfortable? To have sex right in the middle of the forest?"

"Listen, she was well up for it. That was the whole point. She wanted it raw and nasty."

"Did she say this to you?"

"Well, there weren't no need to say it. When I chased her down, I spun her back, like, and we started kissing again.

249

And then she started ripping me clothes off. So if she's that keen, I'm not going to be that picky about where, know what I mean?"

"And by this point, you weren't too far from the halting site. So it didn't occur to you to invite her back to your caravan to have sex?"

"Oh well, the caravan's a proper mess anyways. So the forest, you know, the view and the trees, it was more romantic."

"Romantic?"

"Yeah, romantic."

Morrison purses his lips funny.

"Besides, us pavees can't be bringing random girls back to the caravan, not where I live with Michael and Da. I'm still young, like. They wouldn't be too happy with it."

"Right, so you wanted the privacy of the... woods. And you said she was ripping your clothes off you. Which articles of clothing?"

Christ, you lot are a bore.

"She went right for me jeans, pulling them off. Putting her hands down the front, clearly wanted to have a go."

"Right, and how did that make you feel?"

"Well, I was dead keen by that point, too, you know? Had me hard-on and all, so yeah, whatever she wanted, I was up for too."

"And what did she want?"

"That beour wanted everything. Every position she could imagine, and some I don't even know about, 'cause I'm still young, like. But we did it all."

"And how did you know she wanted this?"

"'Cause she asked for this position and then that one and all these other ones. Couldn't get enough."

"And what else did she say?"

What else... what else. She said something, that woman. In the middle of everything, in the middle of the trees and the dirt and all that thrusting. He remembers now.

"She said, 'I bet you can go all night.' That's what she said."

Morrison perks up, like he's heard it before. Something different in his eyes, then he hides it away.

"Did she say that?"

"Yeah, I'm sure of that. 'I bet you can go all night.'"

Grin a little grin to yourself. Dead on, with that one.

*

In June, she is called into the Southwark Police Station to identify her attacker. He's not there in person, of course. But there's something called a video ID parade, which Detective Morrison explained. There had been a partial DNA match between the genetic evidence they'd found on her in the forensic exam, and an individual in the police records. Perhaps a relative, they'd said, his older brother. If she can identify her perpetrator in the ID parade, that'll help to tick all the boxes. It's not crucial, of course. But it would strengthen their case a lot.

Her friend Monica accompanies her to the police station; their interaction is strained. Monica doesn't know what to say, and they sit wordlessly in the waiting room while the anxiety builds up inside her. The tears have returned and they slide silently from her eyes. She wipes them away, trying to pretend they're not there.

"Do you want something to drink?" the receptionist asks. She requests a Diet Coke, and she sips at the can, as she continues to twist the fringe on her grey scarf.

Morrison had said the boy was part of a certain community in Ireland. An Irish Traveller. They don't look any different from the rest of the Irish, but they live differently and they're treated differently. Sometimes they stand out, he'd said. She wonders what this means, wonders if he'll stand out to her on the screen today. But your rapist is your rapist. Doesn't matter where he's from, he's unmistakable.

Eventually, she's asked to step inside a room on her own.

A kindly spoken policeman with a hook nose, reads from a script.

251

"You're going to see on screen a series of faces, one of which is the individual who is alleged to have assaulted you…"

She will be shown each face twice, in sequence. At the end, she is to identify which one she believes is her assailant. Is everything clear?

She nods. Faces the small TV screen, as the policeman cues up the DVD.

Nausea rises inside her gut. Surely, she will vomit if she sees him. She can already feel the muscles of her throat ready to rebel.

It's just video footage of his face. They filmed it weeks ago. He's not physically here.

"Are you ready?" the policeman asks, and she nods.

The footage is amateur; it would almost be comical in another context. One face appears, a boy around the age of fourteen, staring straight into the camera. It's clearly not him, but the boy keeps staring, as if looking right at her. Freckled face, but his hair is too light.

Five seconds, and then a '2' appears on screen. And then another face. This one is all wrong. Both the hair and the eyes are too dark.

A flash of fear runs through her: what if I can't recognize him?

This newfound doubt, compounded with the original nausea, doubles the surging in her stomach. Sweat starts to collect on her palms, and she presses them against the cool of the Coke can for relief. She nervously dents and un-dents the metal. Pop in pop out, pop in pop out.

Number Three appears, then Number Four.

But when Number Five shows up there's an indisputable flash of recognition. Those ice-blue eyes, more fierce than the others. The other boys are just play-acting, teenagers the police hired to sit in for the ID parade. But this kid… he's the real thing.

She instinctively looks away. Despite her relief at identifying him so easily, she doesn't want to see him anymore. But the parade runs through ten more faces, then repeats them. On the second showing, she forces herself to stare at his face the entire time it's on screen. Something hardens inside her. That implacable fury, compacted into a cold, hard stone.

This is him. This is the kid who raped you. Now send him to jail.

The policeman switches the TV off and turns to her. "Now, would you be able to identify which of these individuals was the one you alleged to have assaulted you on the 12th of April this year?"

She clears her throat, and says in a hoarse, low voice, with no hesitation: "It's Number Five."

She squeezes the Coke can a little harder, and feels the metal crumple slightly under her fingers.

Later, she sits in the Starbucks next door with Monica, and sips on a soy cappuccino. "How was it?" Monica had asked. And she just said it was fine. Weird and awful, but in the end, fine.

During the awkward silence, she scrolls mindlessly through her new phone for messages. Her good friend Jen has emailed from Malawi, where she's on a mission with her boyfriend, having taken a six-month sabbatical.

We're engaged! Jen writes. *Daniel proposed the night we visited Victoria Falls. Earlier that day we'd flown on a microlight and it was amazing to be so high above the jungle...*

As she types back her congratulations, she knows she is meant to be happy for them, and she is, on a rational, surface level. But below that surface, a part of her sinks deeper with this news. A sense of separation from her closest friends. That their existence continues moving forward on a blessed plane, while hers is stalled in muck and hopelessness far below.

"Do you want another coffee?" Monica asks.

She shakes her head. "No, I should get home. I have Julia's hen party tonight."

"Viv, will you be okay?"

She shrugs. "Yeah, I guess so."

But on the bus ride home, she's shaking. She can't get her hands to stop trembling and she tries sitting on them, to hide them from the other passengers. What is wrong with her? The ID parade is over. She identified him. She saw his face and she survived. Is it the hen party? The knowledge that she has to gear up again, face the world, pretend to be cheerful and happy for her friends, while her own life is falling apart?

She tells herself that she can do this. It's just a few hours of socializing.

No, a voice says back. I can't do this.

Back in the flat, she crumples over the Ikea table in the lounge and starts sobbing.

There's a black dress she needs to get into. Heels to wear. Make-up to put on, to somehow salvage her face after this latest breakdown.

But not yet. She's not ready. Right now, all she seems able to do is cry.

*

"Did you ejaculate Mr Sweeney?"

Shite. Here's a tough one. Wanna say you did, but they'd have checked, wouldn't they? Have tests for that kinda shit.

"Uh, naw naw, I didn't."

"You didn't ejaculate?"

Yes, officer, just rub it in.

"Yeah, for some reason, I didn't. I dunno. Think I was freaked by doing it right there in the middle of the woods and all. Like I say, I'm still young at all this."

"But just a few minutes earlier, you were fine with having sex in the woods."

"Well, that was 'cause she was so keen. But as we got on, all these different positions, I got a little worried, like. In case someone would come by and see us. So I didn't enjoy it so much then."

"And the woman? How was she during all of this?"

"She seemed to enjoy it. Y'know, kept asking for more." He flashes a grin at Morrison. Morrison just looks at him.

"So when you got worried, what did you do?"

"I suggested we stop, maybe go home or go somewhere else."

"And what did she say?"

"She didn't say nothing. So's I guess she was okay stopping."

"And then what happened?"

"Uh, we talked for a bit after."

"Did you stay right there? Or did you then accompany the woman on the walk, like she'd asked?"

"Oh well, she didn't really want me to walk all that way with her. That was just her way of, y'know... asking for a fuck."

"Right. And, how do you know this?"

"Well, after we had the sex, she said she wanted to keep on walking on her own."

"And how did you feel about this?"

"Well, it was fine by me. I mean, I got to have sex with her."

"And you weren't interested in anything more with her?"

He looks at the peeler. What's he mean by that? "No, I mean, the sex was grand. And then I was on me way."

"So did you make plans to meet up again or exchange phone numbers or anything like that?"

"No."

"So what did you talk about then, after you'd had intercourse with Ms Tan?"

"Just this and that. Me going over to Armagh and to Dublin."

"Did she say anything about herself?"

"No. Don't think so. Can't remember much. See, I'm not very good with words and conversations and all that."

Morrison's looking at him like he don't believe him.

"Wait, I do remember one thing she said."

"Oh yeah, and what's that?"

"She said, 'Don't worry, I won't tell anyone about this.' It was funny, like, but yeah, that's what she said." There, that ought to shut them up.

Morrison pauses, writes something down. Fixes an eyeful straight at him.

"And what do you think she meant by that?"

"Just what she said. She weren't going to tell no one."

"But what would prompt her to say that?"

"Well, I guess maybe posh American woman like that don't want it getting out that this is what she does for kicks. Shagging young boys in parks, you know."

"What was your reaction when she told you that?"

"Hey, even better. I didn't want me da or the others finding out about me and this woman." He glances at Uncle Rory next to him. Hasn't said a word. Just staring at the table.

"But they *have* found out."

He nods. "Guess so. They know now."

"So how do you feel *now* about what she said back then?"

"Well, just…" He trails off, he's been over this again and again. This sore point against the woman. Why did she say that? And then it rips through, all that clawing. Straight into the open.

She was always going to tell someone about it.

That bitch had it planned all along. Lie right through her teeth to him and then run off and call the peelers first thing. She had it in for me from the start.

Morrison is still looking at him, like he's trying to read his face. So fucking calm down, act natural.

He clears his throat.

"Johnny? What were you going to say?"

"Oh nothing, just that… sorry, what'd you ask?"

"How do you feel about what she said, about not telling anyone what you two did?"

"Just kinda disappointed. I thought we had a thing, you know. Now she's gone and told everyone."

"You thought it was going to be something secret, between you and her?"

"Yeah, but guess she changed her mind."

"Why do you think she did?"

256

"Maybe she was embarrassed after, about what she done with me. Maybe one of her friends found out?"

Morrison nods, frowns as usual, and says nothing.

"'Cause really, she was just after the sex."

*

"What's going to happen to him?" Jen asks her one day, when she's back from her sabbatical in Africa, the engagement ring glinting on her finger.

All her friends ask her this. They all despise him in equal measure, this unknown smudge of a person whose name they don't even know. To them, he may as well be a comic-book villain.

But she knows his name now. A few months after the arrest, Detective Morrison had sent her a letter in the mail, with a few sentences printed out on the PSNI letterhead. Her alleged perpetrator is now in remand, but his name must remain confidential due to his young age. His name is John Michael Sweeney.

The name itself means nothing to her, as non-descript as any other male Irish name. But she distinctly remembers it was *not* the name he told her, neither before the assault, nor after, when she was sitting by the trail.

"Is he in jail now?" another friend asks.

Sentiment comes in various forms: *I hope he rots in there for the rest of his life. I hope he's been raped ten times over in jail.* Although the latter tends to come from her male friends.

She shrugs. She's almost indifferent to his fate. On one hand, her pervading sense of justice demands that he get his just rewards. On the other hand, it's not worth the energy to feel so much outrage against the boy. Energy is still at a premium for her. Anger is too destructive, too exhausting.

So she lets her friends bear that outrage, lets the justice system run its course.

"But will he stay in jail until the trial?" they ask.

The word 'trial' sets off another wave of nausea. "It depends," she answers. "He may keep on reapplying for bail, but the police don't think that'll be granted."

"And when will the trial be?"

She shrugs again. She doesn't even want to think about it. "Sometime early next year. That's all they know right now."

She has no idea how she's going to make it through until then. All that nothingness, between now and that inevitable date.

But this is her life now. The only thing she has to look forward to is the one thing she dreads the most.

*

"One other thing, Johnny. Ms Tan did have quite a lot of bruises and scrapes on her body. Do you know anything about this?"

"Oh yeah." Grin here, like you're remembering. "Yeah, well, like I says, she liked it rough. It was, uh, it was not really gentle sex or anything like that."

"So you're saying all her bruises came from the intercourse?"

"Yeah, yeah. Like I said, it was right on the ground, stones and all, and she wanted all these different positions."

Look the peeler in the eye, like you mean it. Your story's just as good as hers.

"Can you remember any specific things you might have done which would have resulted in a bruise on her body?"

"I can't... I can't remember any one thing, like. It was all very wild."

Morrison clears his throat again.

"Right then, Johnny. I think we're finished here for now."

*

She is in Brighton, the morning of her 30th birthday that October. She'd been invited to spend the weekend with Jen and her fiancé, Daniel, and the night before, they'd had curry and a few bottles of wine. On occasion, she can still play the part of the old Vivian, get tipsy with friends and pretend to enjoy it. But the charade is draining, and leaves her exhausted for days afterward.

This morning, Jen and Daniel are at work. So she has decided to wander through Brighton on her own, before catching the train back to London.

After meandering through empty streets, under the lonesome calls of drifting seagulls, she finds herself at the Esplanade, where families and couples stroll, enjoying the view of the glittering sea. The huge structure of Brighton Pier stretches boldly into the ocean.

She finds herself in awe of its fearless straight lines, promising amusement rides far out above the water.

She steps onto the pier and cautiously treads the wooden planks, glimpsing the cold water crashing far below. On a Monday afternoon, in the off-season, there are still enough people on the pier for it to shudder with their footsteps. Children squeal and chase each other and she catches the aroma of cotton candy and popcorn sold nearby. Suddenly, she is reminded of a summer when she was eight, and her family took a rare vacation to Wildwood in South Jersey. In the evenings they'd walked onto the five piers that jutted from the boardwalk, each with their own rides. A carousel and bumper cars. A giant towering Ferris wheel. A rollercoaster that shook the pier every time it raced past with its screaming cargo. And she was amazed at the great, massive construction of the piers, which allowed rollercoasters and Ferris wheels to churn away on top, while under those wooden planks, the ocean still moved. Tides moving in and out.

Now, on Brighton Pier, all she can feel is the fear and the anxiety, as she stares at the frigid green sea snapping and seething at the foot of the pier, where fishing nets have snagged on rusted bars of ancient metal.

Around her, families take in the bright sunlight, oblivious to the rough surge of cold water below. She suppresses the familiar urge to vomit. This far out, the ocean must be deep and deadly, and yet, only a slim wooden board separates her from those angry waters.

All she needs to do is slip through the railing and let go. She'd go numb within seconds of hitting the water. And then all this misery and loneliness would be gone forever.

Cold water. Then nothing.

She grips the railing to steady herself. Not today, not on her birthday. Her breath shortens with panic, and she knows for her own safety, she needs to get back to land as soon as possible. What are all these people doing out here, laughing, when any moment the pier could collapse? What is *she* doing out here, with these kinds of thoughts haunting her mind?

Slowly, she works her way back to shore, clutching the railing the entire time. Once she steps back onto land, she is able to breathe easier. She is no longer eight years old and innocent, staring up at the flash of colors in awe and wonderment. We get older, we turn 30. We understand fear.

Hours later, she is on a London-bound train, and fields stretch away in the darkening light. For a few minutes, she watches in awe as the setting sun bursts fiery and red through the evening clouds. But the late autumn sky hangs low, promising more cold and snow in the coming months.

It starts to rain. The downpour pelts against the window as the sky quickly turns grey, then dark with nighttime. She is tired, she just wants to get to her own flat, turn on the heater. Then she notices a missed call on her phone.

On voicemail, Detective Morrison is mumbling something about her availability in the coming months. He mentions the first week of March. Does that mean the trial will be then? Until now, it has been an abstract concept, but now, to fix a date marks it as something concrete. Suddenly, the anxiety and the helplessness flood her again, and there on that train shuddering through the evening rain, she starts to cry.

She hides it from the other passengers, puts her face in her hands and sobs quietly. None of this is fair – this loneliness, this constant dread, the cold and the impending trial. She wants, just once, to escape the pain and isolation. To feel some sense of hope.

The train hurtles on towards Gatwick, then East Croydon, then Clapham Junction. She tells herself, soon enough she will be home. A couch to fall asleep on, a duvet to hide under. And she looks out the window into the rainy night.

PART
FOUR

Belfast smells like shit from the moment you step off the plane, she thinks. She is atop the staircase at Belfast International Airport, looking at low green fields, and the sharp stench of cow manure hits her nostrils.

Behind her, Jen touches her on the elbow.

"Are you okay?"

She nods and closes her eyes for a brief second. Early March and she's back. To where she never wanted to return.

She breathes in the smell of shit, accepting it for what it is. Then opens her eyes, picks up her hand luggage, and starts down the stairs.

*

"Mr John Michael Sweeney, please rise to hear the charges laid against you."

Fucking cold inside this courtroom, but then again, every court he's been in is like this. All glass panels, sitting on hard plastic, people staring away at you like it's their business.

He stands. He's used to standing before judges now. All these months, being paraded inside this dock and then that dock for another hearing. Applied for bail, was told he was too 'dangerous'. McLuhan calls this 'part of the process'. Get handcuffed, marched down a hall, put behind another glass panel. At first, he couldn't hardly get what these judges were saying, but now he's catching on. Like another language, really. The judge and the solicitors – the ones with the wigs – speak like this, and everyone else has to listen to their rubbish.

All them other times, there haven't been many other people. But now, this morning, the room is packed, every row is full. Who the fuck are these people? Some people got notebooks and pens, some older couples, even some girls.

It's been ages since he's seen a proper beour. Earlier, he was eyeing them young girls, the backs of their heads, the long hair flowing down. Almost felt himself go hard, but not in this fucking courtroom.

McLuhan warned him there might be a fair few people at court today. Journalists, that kind of thing. But this packed? He's practically famous.

He sees Da hunched over. Michael's next to him. Gerry's vanished since the day he got arrested, but Uncle Rory's there, Kevo, and fuck that, Donal, too, the big tall lunk. Not too bad a showing, eh?

So now the clerk is asking him to stand.

"John Michael Sweeney, you are hereby charged with three counts."

McLuhan explained it this morning. "You see, the complainant, the woman you met, she did show up this morning."

McLuhan had been saying for weeks that there was a chance she wouldn't. Too scared or too much trouble for her to fly all this way back to Belfast.

So if she don't show, well then, the case collapses. No complainant, no rape case. And happy days for him. He can practically walk straight out of the box a free man.

"Do you think she's the kind to show?" Da asked the other day. Hoped she'd stay at home in her nice posh house, in London or America or wherever.

But deep down, he sorta knew she wasn't the kind to balk. Not that crafty bitch, with her fucking lies. That bitch was out for his blood.

"On the count of vaginal rape, how do you plead?"

He looks ahead, straight into the air.

"Not guilty."

In his mind, McLuhan's preaching again: "So Johnny,

I must remind you that pleading guilty now will earn you a much lighter sentence than if you move ahead with the trial and are found guilty at the end. Do you understand?"

Yeah yeah. You think I'm guilty, old man. Me and all us other Travellers.

"On the count of anal rape, how do you plead?"

"Not guilty."

He remembers shouting: 'I wanna fuck you up the ass!' She wanted it, too.

"On the count of battery, how do you plead?"

This one's easy.

"Not guilty."

You didn't have to lamp her, 'cause she wanted it all along. Them bruises, came from just plain, rough sex is all.

"The defendant may sit down."

Sit down, look down. Don't make no eye contact with no one. He knows all them eyes in the courtroom are looking at him. Judging him and hating him. That gypo bastard. Lock him away forever.

Only one pair of eyes he's scared of, though he don't want to admit it.

Them eyes ain't here right now.

*

She sits uncomfortably, drawn into herself, in the room reserved for the complainant. That's what she's officially labeled at the trial: the complainant. Not the victim. The one who complains. It's been a long time since she's worn business clothes like these: grey pencil skirt, deep purple blouse, black patent leather heels. Everything seems to bite into her: the waist of the skirt, the leather edge of the shoes.

Her bra feels tighter than usual, making it difficult to breathe.

In this windowless room, she looks down at the copy of *The Guardian*, which she brought with her. But there's no point in trying to concentrate. Her mind keeps wandering off, drifting inevitably to whatever is happening just down the hallway, behind another indistinguishable door.

"Are you all right, sweetie? Is there anything I can get you?" Jen asks her this, sitting quietly next to her.

"I'm all right," she says, shaking her head. Jen doesn't turn away yet, keeps looking at her. "Okay, I'll have some green tea." Erika sits across from her and she can see the sideways glances, checking up on her every now and then. Jen gets up and crosses over to the kettle.

Last night, before the shops closed, they found a Tesco in the city center and bought a few necessities for the week: soy milk, box of green tea, painkillers. Melissa has sent a lavender-scented candle in a jar, which she has brought to soften this dull, characterless room.

"Also, are there any matches? I might want to light that candle."

Jen nods, and goes to speak to the Victim Support volunteer, a gentle, balding middle-aged man named Peter.

She turns back, looks down at the Lifestyle section of the *Guardian*.

12 Top Tips for Smooth Skin! Equal Pay: Is It Still Years Away?

She grimaces and flips the newspaper over.

That hard rock of anxiety, which she has been carrying deep inside herself these months, has now expanded. It weighs down her every movement.

She thinks of geological processes. Minerals slowly petrifying wood over centuries. Sap speckled with dying insects, hardening into amber. This is what has become of her. The anxiety has pickled her.

Deep down, her heart still beats. She wonders how long a fly continues to live after it's been caught in sap. How long before life expires, before its heart beats its final beat.

She feels an affinity with that fly, about to breathe its last.

She can hardly move, and yet, all she wants to do is break free. Run down the halls, out of the building into the fresh, biting air. Say fuck you to the whole criminal justice system, to the barristers in their robes, to the little shit of a boy who started all this.

Be done with it all. Move onto the next phase of her life.

But she knows the only way she can really say fuck you to the boy, is to stay here and testify.

So sit and wait, let the anxiety smother you, render you lifeless. That appears to be the only way out.

*

Sitting inside this box is killing him, and it's hardly been an hour, according to that clock with the big numbers. He's wearing a buttoned white shirt that Da got him, the fancy grey trousers. Waiting and waiting.

But now lookee here... something is happening. The jury is shuffling in from a door in the corner, settling down in two rows.

They all shoot shifty looks at him. He sketches each of them, one by one. Twelve of them, all buffers, of course. They'll never get no Travellers coming to jury.

There's seven women, five men. Two youngish women, one sorta pretty. Two grannies, three somewhere in the middle. The grannies are gray, hunched over, one wearing specs, both miserable. The young women look scared, every time they glance over this way. One man is young, wearing a tracksuit and chains around his neck. He'll understand the score. Another man's bald and looks meek, and two men with gray hair. One skinny in a fancy shirt, the other one tough-looking in a jumper. Then there's a Paki. Can't tell how he'll vote.

So there's the jury, gonna decide what'll happen to me.

Can't say he's feeling rays of love streaming from this lot.

McLuhan said this might go over a week. He don't think he can last that long. Almost would rather be back inside, where everyone minds their own business. Here, it's like they can't wait to pin this crime on the knacker boy. Make an example of him.

Well, he'll show them. He's not going down without a fight. Not this Sweeney.

*

"Vivian," Detective Morrison says to her. "The prosecutors just wanted to have a word with you."

She looks up, from where she'd been staring into space, and sees the barristers billow in. William O'Leary is tall, silver-haired and imposing, while Geraldine Simmons has her brunette hair in a bob and seems a bit more approachable, warmer.

"Good morning, good morning." They smile to the room, like minor celebrities.

"Good morning, Vivian," they announce, all gleaming confidence and positivity, their Northern Irish accents polished by education and elocution. "How are you feeling today?"

They shake hands. This is the first time she's met them in person. Two weeks ago, after months of asking Detective Morrison, she was finally set up on a video conference call with the prosecutors, where they answered the questions that had been building up inside her for months. Yes, it would be open to the press. Yes, it was possible for her to testify behind a screen, but they advised against it.

"These are my friends, who came with me from London." Vivian introduces Jen and Erika. The prosecutors smile their hellos.

Small talk about finding the courthouse, the flight, the hotel. She can't imagine they actually care.

They start explaining what's happening.

"The defendant has pleaded not guilty to all three charges: that's vaginal rape, anal rape and battery."

The words fall out of their mouths so matter-of-fact, as if recalling the daily specials. How surreal to hear it spoken about in such emotionless terms.

"We were hoping he would might plead guilty at the last moment, because you *have* actually shown up."

She nods. She had been shocked to consider that some rape victims wouldn't show up to the trial. But this morning, she is starting to understand why.

"But obviously," O'Leary says, "he continues to plead not guilty, so he doesn't want to play that game."

Simmons explains the jury is being sworn in, and then O'Leary will do the opening speech. And after lunch, she, Vivian, will be brought in to give evidence, as the chief witness for the prosecution.

"It'll be quite straightforward," O'Leary says. "Of course we'll see you again before you take the stand. But just answer the questions I ask you, and be as truthful and informative as you can be. It's quite simple."

Simple?

Never before has one word been so underestimated.

So this is actually happening. She imagines herself stepping into that courtroom – the room that waits for her behind a closed door. Where everyone will be looking at her: the rape victim. Everyone. Including him.

"As we discussed before," O'Leary continues. "We will not be using special measures, so you'll be in plain view of everyone in the courtroom, and I think that will reflect very positively on you."

She is taken aback, but she knows what they mean. The rape victim who sits in plain view, telling her story, is the rape victim who has nothing to hide. "You'll be great," Simmons is saying to her. "Just be yourself. Try not to be too nervous. We'll be right there with you."

But you want me to cry.

The prosecutors haven't said this, of course, but that's the implicit hope. That she will break down on the stand, in front of everyone. The stress will be too much, having to see the boy will be too much, and only then – with the tears and the sobbing – will the jury and the public really see how traumatized she is. The ultimate sympathy vote.

And isn't this what everyone wants to see in a courtroom? Isn't that why the public has come, why the journalists are scribbling away? The lurid appeal of the rape case. The tearful rape victim, the remorseless rapist. The shocking details of what happened between their bodies.

She sinks her thumbnail into the fleshy side of her index finger, willing it to hurt, wanting to feel something, some pain.

"So do you have any questions for us, Vivian?"

"Yes," some part of her says, surprisingly able to locate her voice. She asks if Jen and Erika can sit through the first part of the trial since she herself can't be there, and Detective Morrison says he will find seats for them.

"Does that mean there are a lot of people in the public gallery? How full is the courtroom?"

Simmons hesitates. "Given the high profile of the case..."

"Are there many journalists inside?"

"I wouldn't worry about it," O'Leary says. "Journalists or not, just answer the questions as best you can, and try to pretend no one's there."

She wants to laugh at how ridiculous that last comment is.

*

Judge – Judge Haslam they said his name was – is eyeing him something harsh, and them jury hanging on to every word he says, like they're the ones it's life or death for. Judge is going on about their duty, how they need to listen closely, take on board every detail, determine what they believe is the truth beyond a reasonable doubt. He musta practiced this speech loads. Sitting there year after year. This man is ancient, all wrinkly skin and white hair under that stupid wig. Case after case, telling jury after jury the same thing. Who wants that for a job? He'd die of boredom.

Now the judge is finished and your man, the tall grey one that McLuhan warned about, he's getting up.

This one's out to get you, that's his job. So anything comes out of this man's mouth is shite. Fancy-sounding, but still shite.

"Ladies and gentlemen of the jury," he says. "I'm here to tell you about something shocking and cruel that happened one afternoon last April, right in West Belfast. It's perhaps an event you remember from the papers at the time, precisely because it was so shocking. But I am asking if you could try and ignore what you may have heard earlier, and only focus on what is being presented to you as evidence over the next few days."

Jaysus, we have to listen to this guy drone on for days?

"What you are about to hear is all the more shocking because the prosecution argue the crime was caused by *that* young boy, sitting right there in the dock. The defendant, John Michael Sweeney."

Of course, all eyes cracking onto me now, like they never saw me before.

But McLuhan told him it'd be like this. Everything going against him until he gets the chance to cross-examine the woman.

He don't want to admit it, but his heart's starting to beat a load faster.

"Now the injured party in this case is a young lady whom you will have the chance to meet later on today. She is American, her name is Vivian Tan, and she lives and works in London. At the time of the offence, she was twenty-nine. Her situation is sadly very ironic, because she had been invited to Belfast as a visitor, to participate in a prestigious event celebrating the tenth anniversary of the Good Friday agreement. She had been invited to celebrate peace in Northern Ireland, yet her own visit ended in violence. You see, years before, Vivian had been selected as a very elite group of promising young Americans called the George Mitchell Scholars, who were awarded fellowships to study in Ireland. The scholarship was designed to foster a better understanding between Ireland and the United States…"

Well, this is news. Didn't know this about the woman. Mighty impressive, but McLuhan never said nothing about this.

Da and the lads are exchanging glances, looking over his way.

But so what? She's a fancy-arse. Posh people can want it raw, too. In the mud, bruises and all. He's saying this to himself, but all the time, his heart is galloping away and he wants to just vanish. Anywhere but this clear little box for everyone to stare at.

*

"Is he good, the barrister?" she asks Jen and Erika, when they're back in the room with her.

"He's getting the job done. Making it clear to the jury how difficult it is for you to come back here to testify."

Something about that stretches her even more taut. Step right up, ladies and gentlemen, and witness the brave little rape victim.

"And him? Is he there?"

But of course, she knows he is.

"He's very young," Erika says. "It's terrifying that a kid that age can do something like that. I mean, my own daughter is older than him."

"So is it difficult for people to believe that he'd commit a crime like this?"

She gets the sense that her friends are sifting through their words carefully. "I wouldn't say he's making the most positive impression," Jen explains. "But then again, I think everyone's waiting to hear what you'll say, and then what he'll say."

She nods. Message understood. Well, when it comes to speaking in public, having a Harvard education and a career in media may give her the edge. She at least has an objective confidence about that.

Wordlessly, Jen reaches an arm out and encircles her shoulders.

"Don't worry, you'll do just fine." Erika smiles and squeezes her hand.

Everyone keeps saying that. She's not so sure.

"How about we take you out for lunch?" Erika suggests.

But the nausea hasn't subsided and she doesn't want to go outside. Who knows who might be out there? Journalists, people from the public gallery, maybe even his relatives? People staring, nudging the person next to them, mouthing 'That's the rape victim.'

No, she'd prefer to stay secluded in this little room, with the lavender candle burning and the window she can look out. Hidden from all the world, for now. Invisible.

*

Lunch. Some microwaved pasta shite that he eats off a cardboard tray, while sitting in another fucking cramped cell. Guards don't smile at him. Shoot him a grim look, peel the plastic off the food and slide it over.

And like any right eejit, he burns his tongue on the food. Now trying to blow air into his mouth as he chews the steaming pasta and them guards are looking at him, like he deserved it.

After he's done eating, nothing to do except sit and stare at these walls.

"You stay strong, Johnny." That's what Da said, muttering through the slot in the glass panel of the dock, right after the judge had left the room.

Rory and Donal nodded too, though didn't say much.

And Michael... Michael waited till the others were ahead, then leaned his head against the glass. "Don't let what them bastards say get to you. You know what happened. You wait, and then you tell 'em."

This rings in his head now. The empty, tiny cell.

You wait and then you tell 'em.

*

"Now ladies and gentlemen of the jury, I've summarised the outline of the crime, but shortly you will hear from Ms Tan herself what actually transpired on the afternoon of the alleged attack. I must warn you, the details are harrowing and quite unpleasant. But when she speaks, you'll understand how it came to be that a professional, well-educated young lady like her found herself to be subject to a rape this violent and unexpected."

O'Leary stops to swig some water. Look at them eejits, everyone hanging onto him like every word out of his mouth is the gospel truth. Even Da and Michael are hooked. Thank Christ me mam ain't here. Fuck knows what she thinks of all this.

He looks down, swallows, still nursing the burnt tongue. Wants to block out your man, but there's no way to get away from the stream of words.

"...So please do give your utmost attention to Ms Tan when she speaks. It is up to you to decide if she is telling the truth or not, but do consider the great and uncomfortable lengths she has gone to be able to be here today. And consider if a woman would really put herself through all that, come back to a city which clearly holds much pain and distress for her, if it weren't a genuine criminal act against her."

Look at this, already labeling him a criminal on the very first day.

"The Crown would like to call our first witness, Miss Vivian Tan."

*

Detective Morrison walks her down the corridor, all modern gleaming surfaces with an expansive window showcasing a view of Belfast Harbor and the hills beyond, green and gray below lowering clouds.

Click click click, her heels echo against the tiles and it feels like someone else, walking in her shoes, treading that path to Courtroom Eight.

She's vaguely aware of a few people loitering around in the hall, maybe there for other cases, but staring at her. She pretends not to see them.

"You all right there?" Morrison asks, just before they're about to enter the room.

She pauses for a moment and looks at him. She's tempted to say she can't do this. She wishes she were somewhere safe and very distant.

Instead, she takes a deep breath and nods. "Yeah. As good as I'll ever be."

"You'll be fine," Detective Morrison says, his grey-blue eyes looking straight into hers, a light touch on her elbow. "I've seen loads of victims in my time. And if anyone can do this, you can."

And somehow, this unexpected kindness almost sets her off into tears. But she steels herself, clenches her right hand into a fist, pushes away that mounting nausea. She's been waiting for this moment, ever since last April.

"Ready?" the usher asks.

"Yeah." She nods, trying her best to be brisk and business-like.

The usher pushes the door open and she follows him in. She's aware of the room bristling with energy, faces turning towards her, but for now, she looks straight ahead, focuses on the witness stand.

She does not look around. She does not look for him. Without having to see his face, she knows he is there in the room, staring at her.

*

Everyone in the room all turning to the door.

It opens, old man clerk comes out, and then there she is. The woman. Don't matter what name she goes by now, or what fancy job and learning she's had. That's her. The same long dark hair, the dark eyes. Slim tiny frame, but still that sorta no-nonsense feel to her, focused and fucking self-important.

That's her. Only everything else is different. She's dressed all fancy and sleek, posh women's shoes that clack away. You'd see her type on some TV show about American lawyers, but not wandering on her own in the Glen.

The sight of her makes him want to look away. That's her all right.

Lump of pasta in his stomach swells up into his throat, ready to make him sick. He sees Michael's eyebrows jerk up. Like he's surprised. At what? That she's this posh? This grown-up? This kind of a beour?

Everyone else is staring at her. All watching her get in the box, say her oath.

Your Paki one in the jury looks from her and over to him, catching his eye by accident.

Yeah yeah, he knows what they're thinking. Them two. That pretty posh woman and that boy. Is that possible? The two of them? In the woods?

And he can tell from their faces, there's not a chance.

*

Her face is set, her mouth drawn. What kind of expression should she have? How do they expect a rape victim to look when she enters the courtroom? Terrified? Vengeful? Somewhere in between?

There is a sea of people and faces and eyes, most of them strangers, all of them staring at her, but she is comforted to know that at least Erika and Jen are there in their midst. And Detective Morrison.

She is aware of a sheen of glassy wall in the center of the room, and behind it, a figure. But she does not look. She knows who it is, and that is enough.

She is a given a Bible to take the oath on, and asked to repeat after the clerk: "I swear that the evidence I shall give to this court shall be the truth, the whole truth, and nothing but the truth."

She sits down. Her feet, trapped as they are in their heels, are relieved to find the floor to rest on. She had been careful not to tie the knot in her purple blouse too tightly, but it still chafes at her neck.

O'Leary gets up and she looks into his face, searches for

278

some familiarity beneath the ridiculous wig and the haughty demeanor.

"Would you please state your name to the court?"

"My name is Vivian Michelle Tan."

For months, she has imagined opening her mouth and no words coming out. Her voice gone entirely, just a rush of breath and a wheezing emptiness. Now she's relieved to hear her voice, low and familiar. But it's almost as if it's not her own. It speaks of its own accord from some mechanical part of her mind.

"And where do you reside, Ms Tan?"

"I live in London, England."

O'Leary takes her through her age, her occupation at the time of the incident, and she answers easily enough.

"And, of course, we've all noticed your accent. You're not from London originally, are you?"

"No, I'm originally from America. But I moved to London seven years ago. To work there."

"Very good." O'Leary takes his time and looks around at the jury, nodding as if to say, see, perfectly respectable woman here.

"And if you could be so kind as to tell the jury, why were you in Belfast on the 12th of April last year?"

She pauses for a moment, draws in a breath.

She looks at the judge, for the first time. When she meets his eye, there's the briefest look of surprise from him – that she should be looking at him this directly. Then his gaze softens slightly.

"I'd been invited to attend this event..."

She describes the conference, not in great detail. The tenth anniversary of the peace process... She'd been invited as a George Mitchell Scholar...

"And how did you become selected for this fellowship?"

"There's an application process," she begins.

Do I mention Harvard? Will that make me sound cocky? She decides to go ahead. It is the truth, after all.

"You apply, and finalists get invited for an interview. I

279

applied in my final year at Harvard, where I had done my undergrad."

"Is that Harvard University in the United States?"

"Yes."

"And what did you study when you were there?"

"Celtic Folklore and Mythology. So, Irish and Scottish folklore mainly."

She expects giggles or some kind of reaction from that answer, the kind she's had all her life. But thankfully hears nothing. Then again, she feels as if she's caught in a hermetically sealed jar, a curious specimen for everyone to stare at, and any sound from outside is muffled.

"And what did you study when you were a Mitchell Scholar in Ireland?"

There's a mumble of words from the judge. "Mr O'Leary, if we could move to the incident at hand?"

"Yes, of course, Your Honour. I just wanted to establish the context for Ms Tan's familiarity with Ireland and her reasons for being in Belfast at the time of the incident."

She remembers what O'Leary told her earlier. She has to try and look at the jury from time to time.

She takes the opportunity to scan those twelve faces sitting opposite her, watching her attentively. She's surprised to see a South Asian man. And more women than men. That's a good thing, right?

Slow down, speak loud and clear, make eye contact. Only, don't appear too poised for a rape victim.

"Ms Tan, I'm now going to start asking you some questions about the day of the incident. I know this will be difficult for you, but please, take all the time in the world, and answer as truthfully as you can and with as much detail as you can. Is that all right?"

Of course, none of this is all right.

But she nods. "Yes," she says and looks at O'Leary.

Let it begin.

*

What's this shite about Harvard? Place he heard of, once or twice before. She went there? And the fancy event with all them politicians and the peace process? He don't really understand what they're saying, but what the fuck was a woman like that doing in a park on her own?

That's what he tells himself. She's not always this smooth, polished woman. He's seen her covered in mud and bruises on the ground, her tits out.

It's like you want to rip off that fancy blouse, so's they can see what's really underneath. Expose her. Do it all over again to her, in court. Make that fucking bitch pay.

Now she's talking about the park. Her low American voice talking about the walk up the Glen. The people she passed. And then him.

"I immediately thought he just looked strange because of what he was wearing. It wasn't like what you'd wear if you were going for a walk in the park, more like what you'd wear to go out at night."

She describes his white jumper, his jeans, his shoes. Jaysus, that bitch has a good memory. They asked him and he couldn't remember much about what she was wearing. Except that bra he ripped.

"There seemed to be something strange about him. Like he was a little disoriented, or just out of it."

Oh, fuck off. Who is she to say I was out of it?

"I couldn't quite get a handle on him. He wasn't really giving a straight answer to anything, and even when we were talking, he'd keep on changing his story."

She talks about walking under the road, then having to call her friend. Then her trying to cross the stream. So weird hearing it from her mouth. And so different. Fucking creeps him out, how calm she seems to be on the stand, explaining all this.

"At this point, what were you thinking in regards to the boy?"

"At first, I thought he was strange and I suppose, annoying."

He balls his hands into fists.

"But, by this point, I guess I was getting a little scared. I didn't know why he was still hanging around me."

Stupid bitch. Serves you right for wandering around that park on your own. You and your fancy schooling and your book you were looking at. How much did that help you?

*

She's been keeping it under control until now. Sentences are coming out easily, even though she has to keep the panic at bay. O'Leary is feeding her questions one by one, laying out a lifeline for her to follow, hand over hand, heading into the murk. So far so good.

"When you got to the top of the slope, what did you see?"

She closes her eyes for a minute and imagines herself in that moment again: catching her breath, the spreading view of Belfast in the shifting sunlight, the false sense of escape.

"You didn't see the defendant?"

"No, I didn't see him. I thought I'd lost him, and for that reason, I was relieved."

"Why were you relieved?"

"I thought… I wasn't sure what he wanted from me, but I felt uncomfortable having him around. So I was relieved he was gone."

"You just wanted to get on with your walk, did you?"

"Yes, that's correct."

There's a pause. She draws in a breath, aware of what's coming up.

"So, please Ms Tan, tell us what happened next."

"So, I…" She sees the path in her mind and her voice falters. The jury notices this. She notices the jury noticing this.

Her breath shortens, her throat swells.

O'Leary is nodding at her, not entirely sympathetic, more like a vaguely tolerant uncle. Let's get on with it, shall we?

The trees overhead. The edge of the ravine.

"So, I thought for a moment, that he was gone. And because the view was so nice, and I was on my own with just the trail ahead of me, for the first time that afternoon, I was able to really enjoy myself. I thought I had finally gotten free of the boy and the city, and I could just hike."

"And then?"

"Well, then I was walking, taking in the surroundings. Kind of excited about it all. But then I looked down the slope and I saw him."

"You saw the defendant?"

"I saw his white jumper. It was unmistakable, it was so bright against the trees. He was down below me on the slope, but it was like he was trying to hide while climbing up towards me."

She remembers the fear from that moment, and it grips her anew. Her vision blurs, and unseen by anyone else, she grips the padded seat of her chair to root herself.

"And what did you think when you saw him?"

"That was when it hit me. I thought, this kid is definitely following me."

"And what did you do?"

"I wanted to get away from him as fast as possible. So I just started running…"

She describes the run to the open ground, and how when she got there, she saw just an abandoned wasteland with nowhere to go. She describes him coming out of trees, and her confronting him, tired of his tricks.

"So you explained to him one more time how to get to Andersonstown?"

"Yes, I did. Even though by then, I guessed it was just a ploy."

"What do you mean by a ploy?"

"Well, if he was really lost and trying to get to Andersonstown, he would have gone in that direction ages ago. So I suspected he was after something else, which made me scared, and I wanted to, I guess, confront him about it."

"And how did you do this?"

"So after I gave him directions, I said, 'Listen I already told you how to get to Andersonstown. What do you want?'"

"How did you feel about saying that?"

"I was scared, of course. But I was tired of whatever game he was playing. I wanted to know what the score really was."

She's conscious of using these slang Americanisms... *the score... whatever game...* Doesn't know how receptive the Belfast jury will be.

"So what did he say?"

Pause. Remember to breathe. Up until now, it's just been her walk in the park, followed by this strange boy, but nothing horrific. You say these next words and everything changes.

The nausea of that afternoon reclaims her in a flood. To say those words, his words, will be to begin the descent anew. This time, with an audience.

She steadies herself. Tell them. Force them to come with you on this journey.

"He said, 'Do you like to have sex outdoors?'"

She cannot bring herself to look at the jury now. The shame is too great.

*

'Do you like to have sex outdoors?'

He forgot about that. He'd asked her, when he couldn't keep playing the lost card anymore. When he'd run out of ideas, and it was now or never.

He asked her, and she said no, all fucking self-important like she is now. And that's when he got angry.

*

The struggle, the weird stand-off under the sun, on the field that afternoon.

"And then what happened?"

"And then, I don't know, I must have either slipped or fallen or he pushed me down. I'm not sure. The next thing I know, I hit the ground."

"So you were on the ground?"

284

"Yes, I had fallen, almost sitting down, or lying back but my backpack was between me and the ground... and he was over me... and he... and he..."

Stop to breathe. There's a rushing sound in her ears, and her heart is hammering uncontrollably.

Everyone's staring at her. They always have been, but now it's as if the intensity of their staring has increased – jury, judge, public gallery, figure behind the glassy wall. All focused on her.

She finds her voice again.

"And he was shouting things like 'Shut the fuck up, bitch. You say anything, I'll slit your throat, I'll bash your head in.' He picked up a rock and he was threatening to hit me."

It seems so surreal to be channeling his anger somehow, investing that kind of energy into his words when she speaks them.

"And what else did he do?"

"Well, I was struggling to get away from there, I was trying to get up from the ground, but he was physically stopping me from doing that. He... he punched me in the head, and that hurt a lot. He took two fingers from my left hand and bent them back. And he... he..."

Here she has to stop. She struggles again to get the words out, they become garbled in a sob, caught in the back of her throat. She can feel the tears welling up in her eyes, and she wills them away. How humiliating it would be to break down in front of the jury.

And then, she remembers, this is what they *want* to see. The crying rape victim.

So she goes there. She stops holding back.

"And then he started choking me. His hands were wrapped around my throat and I couldn't breathe."

The tears have begun to spill over, streaming down her face, but she doesn't care. Let them see how miserable you become when you are raped.

In therapy, this is always the moment in the narrative when she breaks down. For weeks in a row, she's had to come in and tell the story of the attack over and over again to Doctor Greene. Go home, listen closely to the tape of her telling it, and find 'the point of greatest distress' for her. What part of the story makes you the most upset?

The part when he's choking me.

And why is that upsetting?

Because I thought I was going to die.

Well, you didn't die. You still have your life.

That's right. I still have my life.

This is her life, right now, every second of it suffused with misery and shame, sitting in this courtroom for everyone to see.

And because I have my life, I'm going to put this kid in jail, where he belongs.

"Ms Tan." The judge is saying this now. "Ms Tan, are you all right?"

She looks up at him and doesn't know what to say.

"Shall we take a ten-minute break?"

"No," she manages to say, her voice thick and low.

"Are you sure?"

"I'm sure."

"It's not a problem, we can easily…"

"No. No break. I want to finish this."

*

Oh boo hoo, don't we all feel sorry for the poor posh girl crying her eyes out now in the box. See how the whole room eats it up. But that's women – always end up in tears when they don't get their way.

Girl shoulda known better. Beour like that shouldn't go walking on her own, certainly not near where the likes of me hang out.

But even Da and Michael are caught up in what she's saying.

Once, Da breaks away from looking at the woman, shoots an eye over in his direction.

It's not an angry look, but it's not nice neither. It's a look that says 'What the fuck were you even thinking?'

*

Now the worst part. Once she's broken down, they move onto the actual rape.

"What happened after you decided to relent, so to speak?"

"I didn't want him to lick me... down there... because I suspected that once he got my underwear down, he'd want to do more than just that."

She can sense the courtroom squirming in embarrassment.

"So... I... tried to bargain with him instead. I offered to give him a blow job. I thought that if I could at least get him off with a blow job, then he'd have gotten what he wanted, and the danger would be gone."

"When you say 'get him off'...?" O'Leary moves in to dissect further.

"I mean, get him to come. To orgasm."

O'Leary nods.

She tries to take a deep breath, to keep the queasiness at a manageable level. How much longer will she have to stay up here? She imagines hours. Take your time, make them listen to every single last humiliating detail. Make them feel the shame you feel.

"And then what happened?"

She describes her unsuccessful blow job. In her mind, she is reminded of the sour jab of his cock in her mouth. That cock, that boy sitting behind that wall of glass, only meters from her. The thought of this is enough to bring the bile to her mouth, but she forces it down.

"And after this, what happened?"

O'Leary's questions are relentless.

The first position the boy wanted, the next one, the next one. His ridiculous schoolboy demands.

The catalogue of sexual positions is embarrassing for everyone in the room, but O'Leary dissects them with clinical precision. She knows he is just doing his job. Still, a part of her begins to resent him intensely for subjecting her to this kind of ruthless indignity.

"So just to reiterate, there was oral, vaginal, and anal penetration during the assault?"

"And how many different sexual positions would you say he subjected you to?"

She has counted this out multiple times in the past few months, even drawn stick-figure diagrams to remind herself what they were. But now she finds herself silently counting on her fingers, holding her hands out of sight from anyone else.

"At least five. Maybe six."

"Other than demanding these various positions, did the defendant say anything to you during the assault?"

"At one point, he said…" She trails off, reluctant to reveal this ultimate disgrace, but knows it will help her case. "At one point, he said, 'Nice tight Asian pussy.'"

Perhaps she feels a collective, silent shudder around the courtroom. A quiver of combined disgust and pity. Or perhaps these mainly white faces just stare on at her, implacable, the racial insult hardly registering for them.

"And how were you feeling throughout this whole sequence of events?"

"Scared, of course. I was just doing whatever I could to survive. So that meant trying to appease him. Let him have whatever he wants and he won't hurt you so much."

She realizes she will have to talk about her own underhanded tricks, the demeanor she took on to convince him she was on board. The pretense of being complicit, when really she was not. This could be a sticking point for the jury. Here's where she's not an innocent, helpless rape victim, but a woman consciously crafting a plan, acting deceptive in order to live.

"I felt like I had to flatter him. If this kid was trying to act out whatever twisted fantasies he had, then playing into those fantasies might make it seem less like I was resisting."

O'Leary nods. "And you felt like you had to do this?"

"Yes, I felt like it was my best chance for survival. To keep him appeased sexually would keep him away from physical violence."

She's not sure if the jury are buying this, but it's the truth.

"So at one point I said... I said something like, 'I bet you could go all night.'"

She notices a change in the jury then. No innocent rape victim says something like that – only someone more brazen and knowing.

But O'Leary and Simmons said to tell them as much as she could remember. The more details the better.

Still, she wonders if that was a mistake.

*

He sits up through all of this, forehead against the glass, and the guard has to keep reminding him to sit back.

He can't really remember every single thing the woman is saying. Is she making it up?

Don't matter either way. What matters is if them jury believe her. Right now looks like they're finding some things hard to believe. Like when she said 'I'll bet you can go all night to him.' Them women didn't look happy.

Oh, she said that all right. He remembers.

And when she says it was five, six different positions, the men raised their eyebrows.

Probably better than you ever get from your wives back home, eh?

Oh no, this weren't no ordinary roll in the hay.

*

O'Leary takes her through the aftermath. The strange, pathetic conversation the boy had with her after the rape. How she got out of there, calling Barbara on the phone, waiting for the police to arrive.

She is exhausted, but O'Leary has someone produce the

clothes she was wearing on that day, and lay them out on a desk. Exhibits TM 8-13. Her blue hiking shirt. Her black bra, torn. Her underwear, smeared with mud. She wants to be sick, just looking at them. They seem like garments long ago peeled from a dead person. But she nods, yes, she wore those on April 12th last year.

O'Leary plies her with more needling, hair-splitting questions. Again, what kind of bodily harm did he inflict upon you? And you did state explicitly that you did *not* want to have sexual intercourse with him, correct?

"Yes, several times. When he asked about having sex outdoors, before he became violent. Then later, I was trying to get away, screaming for help. And again, when I suggested the blow job instead."

There, how's that, O'Leary?

There is a slight twinkle in O'Leary's eye. As if to say, 'Good job'.

"I believe I have no further questions for the time being, Your Honour."

O'Leary bows towards the judge, and he sits down, his tall, robed form folding behind the desk.

There is silence in the courtroom.

"Well," Judge Haslam says. "Thank you very much, Ms Tan. I know this is not easy for you, and I gather you must be quite exhausted after that long session. We certainly appreciate what you've done, coming all this way to give evidence."

Unexpectedly, these few words cause her to well up again.

The Judge seems slightly taken aback at the sight of fresh tears, but he continues, in a gentle, paternal voice.

"Now, as you know, this is not over. The defence still needs their turn to ask you their questions. But what I suggest is that we finish for today. You go home, get plenty of rest, and we'll start with you first thing in the morning, if that's all right?"

She nods, and wipes away a tear from her cheek.

"Okay, Your Honour."

And those three words sound so out-of-place, she adds, as if to correct herself: "Yes."

After the jury leave, and the judge too, then he can relax. Da and Michael come up to the glass.

"Don't be worrying about her," Michael says. "Your man will tear her apart tomorrow."

Later, Da and him, McLuhan and his barrister, Quilligan, talk in one of them tiny private rooms. Is there anything else he should be asking her about tomorrow? Any details she left out?

But the problem is, her memory's better than his. It's just a blur to him – trees and mud and shouting and pussy. She even brung up when she said, 'I bet you can go all night.' She even said that.

McLuhan takes off his specs, rubs his eyes.

"As you have chosen to plead not guilty, I need to remind you that your version of the events must be rock-solid in your mind. You need to know exactly how your story differs from hers."

"It's the same as what I said before. You need me to tell you again?"

Quilligan shakes his head. "No, no. But just think, in the same way that I'm going to try and undermine her version of events tomorrow, they're going to try and do the same to you when you're giving evidence. You understand?"

He nods, and McLuhan looks between him and Da.

"So you be prepared for that. Know your version of the events inside and out."

He smiles, small and secret.

*

She goes straight back to the hotel and gets into bed. Barbara, called as a witness for the trial, has arrived from DC, and wants to take her for dinner in a few hours. Jen and Erika have gone down to the hotel bar, to make phone calls, drink cocktails, try to forget the stress of the courtroom.

But for her, that is impossible. The thought of all that public chatter and clinking in the bar. No, she needs to be inside, under covers, away from people.

She draws the curtains shut, lights some scented candles, flicks on the TV, surfs aimlessly through channels, and flicks it off. Lies back on the bed. Her mind is empty, devoid of thoughts.

She is tempted to run a hot bath, but looks at the messages on her phone first.

Her sister, Serena:

How did it go on the first day? Thinking of you. Let me know if you want to talk. xxx

And Stefan:

Did they jail the bastard yet? Wish I were there to smash his face in, but please do it instead through your eloquent testimony. Lots of love, call if you need anything.

And Caroline, whom she hasn't seen in months:

Thinking of you on this difficult first day. Hope it went well x

She'll reply to these texts in a bit, she doesn't have the energy just now.

Baskets and bouquets of flowers line the floor and shelves of the room. She's seen most of these last night, but a few more arrived this morning when they were at court.

An elegant bouquet of purple tulips and white lilies from Melissa. She prises open the tiny envelope and card. *Dear Vivian, I am in awe of how strong you are. Just know I am with you in spirit and wishing you the very best. Hope to see you soon.*

She opens other cards.

Vivian, I can't imagine what you are going through, but I am with you every step of the way. Lots of strength and support and love.

Hey Viv, if anyone beats up on my girl, they're going to get it from me. Sorry I can't be there, hope the courts do it for us xx

Each of these messages, in their own way, is a revelation.

She always knew she had these friends, but to have it spelled out so clearly, in objects and words, is more than she can bear, in her weakened state.

For what seems to be the fifteenth time that day, she breaks down. Didn't think it was possible to shed any more tears, but here they come, familiar, like spring melt finding its way down well-worn stream beds. These tears start silent, but here, in the privacy of the hotel room, surrounded by flowers and tasteful wallpaper and soft cushions, she has all the freedom in the world to sob as loud and as hard as she wants.

And so she does. Great, heaving shudders that well up from her body. She sits on the carpet, against the side of the bed, and curls over, letting the tears flow.

The baskets of flowers, the silent television, the closed curtains all bear silent witness. In twenty-four hours, she thinks, it'll all be over. I'll be done giving evidence.

But even then, she knows, it won't really be over. That will only happen days or weeks from now, when she'll have to confront the worst moment of all: the verdict.

*

In jail, that night, he don't talk much.

After rattling on back in the armoured car, handcuffed, his knees crushed up inside, he's just glad to be back where no one's staring at him no more. He's just one of the other lads.

He lies in bed, staring up at the ceiling. Thinking what he would do to that woman if he could get his hands on her now. Squeeze that throat and slam her head straight into the concrete wall, over and over, all bloody, 'til she stops all her crying. That would show her.

But he can't reach her now. She's all dressed up in her fancy clothes, and tomorrow he'll have to watch her crying all over again to the jury, as he's stuck in that glass box. Might as well be in another world.

*

"Good morning, Ms Tan," Judge Haslam says to her. He seems brighter today, on Day Two and she's glad of this, almost wants to smile herself. And then, she realizes how inappropriate it would be for her to smile, on this day, the morning of her cross-examination.

She nods, a courteous look at the judge.

"I hope you've rested well over the evening, and thank you very much for being back with us on this second day."

He reminds her ever so slightly of a staid morning talk show host, absurdly wigged, welcoming her back on stage. A witness stand instead of comfy sofas, but otherwise, the audience is still there, in rapt attention, waiting to be entertained.

She wonders if she gave them a good enough show yesterday. Today will be harder.

Today she is wearing a blue-grey knit sweater dress, falling to her calves, with knee-high black boots underneath. She realizes no one will see her shoes when she's on the stand, so the torture of high heels is unnecessary. She feels more solid in these boots. They are militant, ready for battle. And on this second morning, so is she.

The figure behind the glass remains just that, a blur. She still has not looked at it directly or assigned it a face. To do so would only distract her from the task at hand.

The jury have an air of studied concentration about them. She hasn't won them over yet. Or even if she has, that could all be undone this morning.

And then, Quilligan QC. The boy's defence barrister sits in front of McLuhan. He is an average-sized man, without the height of O'Leary, but with more girth. His balding head sprouts grey curls from under the white of the barrister's wig. He has wire-rimmed glasses and for a moment, their gazes meet by accident.

So this is the man. The one who has been appointed to tear her story apart.

She wonders who would ever take on this job, who would willingly do this for a living. Surely no one with a conscience.

Hold your ground. Don't let your hatred for him show.

Quilligan QC stands up, clears his throat, recenters his gaze towards her. It is cold and clinical, and she returns a look that she hopes is similarly devoid of emotion.

"Now then, Ms Tan." His voice is calm, almost condescending. A sly smile works across his face. "Let's begin."

*

Day Two in the courts, and, Jaysus, you could swear there's more people watching than before. All goggling for a look at her, then swiveling back to look at him.

Yeah, gape and goggle all you want.

Today that woman's gonna get her story ripped into shreds by your man Quilligan. No idea what he'll be like. Fancy that – your fate being decided by an absolute stranger wearing a stupid wig.

But either way, grab the popcorn, should be a good show.

"Ms Tan," Quilligan starts. "I was wondering if you could tell us a bit more about yourself, your background prior to the events of April 12th. More specifically, about your experience traveling on your own. Could you tell us how often you do this? Go traveling on your own?"

"Quite a lot, I guess."

"How many trips a year do you take?"

She thinks for a moment. "Business or leisure trips?"

"Both, please."

"I'd say, in total, eight to ten trips a year?"

"On your own?"

"Many of them on my own. Some for work, some as a vacation. As a holiday."

"And how long have you been doing this? Traveling on your own?"

"Since I was eighteen, I guess."

"And remind us of how old you are now?"

"I'm thirty."

"So for twelve years, you've been traveling on your own. Eight to ten trips a year—"

She cuts in. "Well, it wasn't always eight to ten trips a year. That's only happened more recently."

"Right, okay. But surely, you're very *experienced* at traveling on your own, correct?"

"I suppose."

"Mm-hmm." Quilligan looks at the jury. "And this business of hill-walking, of hiking as you say. This is also something you do a lot?"

"Not at lot, but I've done a few hikes on my own."

Quilligan sure is taking his time. Better make that a large popcorn. This might be all day.

*

Why is he asking me about my hiking and traveling? What's he getting at?

She's answering the questions cautiously, but behind her composed façade, her mind is racing through the possibilities.

"Where have you done some of these walks on your own, Ms Tan?"

"In Germany, in France, other parts of Ireland, in Wales."

Calm down. He's only asking you about your travels…

Yes, but he's doing this somehow to undermine my story.

She fixes Quilligan with a stare. Tries not to think ahead. Just answer the questions as they come.

"And may I ask why do you enjoy walking on your own? Weren't you ever scared that something might happen to you?"

"Well, I am now, after what's happened in Belfast. But until then, I'd always liked being outdoors on my own. There was something… refreshing about it."

"And is there something refreshing about traveling on your own?"

"Yes, I like learning about new places and cultures, meeting new people."

Quilligan picks up on this.

"Ah, meeting new people. And... as a young woman traveling on your own... do you often meet men?"

"I wouldn't say I often meet men any more than I meet women."

"But you do meet men when you travel on your own, correct?"

"It's impossible not to. They make up 50% of the human race."

There's a slight ripple across the courtroom, the crowd finding some humor in her comment.

O'Leary and Simmons shoot her a cautioning look, and she gets it immediately.

No one likes a sarcastic rape victim.

Quilligan plays along, rephrasing his questions. "What I meant was, have you ever met men while you were traveling on your own, and had a romantic encounter with them?"

She's tempted to ask him to define 'romantic encounter', but she doesn't want to appear too difficult.

"It has happened occasionally, yes."

"So would you say you derive a certain thrill from romantic encounters with men you meet while traveling on your own?"

She doesn't like this question, or its implications. If she were entirely honest, she would say yes now. But she knows that would be damaging to her story. So she words her answer carefully.

"That's not why I go. I travel on my own to immerse myself in a place and a culture, not to meet men."

Quilligan breathes a patronizing sigh. "Ms Tan, that wasn't the question. When you meet men, while traveling on your own, do you derive a certain thrill from it? Yes or no."

"Not really," she lies. "I suppose there could be a thrill, but it happens quite rarely."

"But there is a thrill. There is a thrill," Quilligan gloats, as if to press a minor victory.

But I don't have sex with these men right away, she wants to say.

"So you would say that, theoretically, if you were out

297

traveling on your own, and you met a man that you were physically attracted to, you would have no objection to engaging in a romantic encounter with him?"

Her eyes widen upon hearing this, and she sees Simmons perk up as well.

"Forgive me for saying this, but can you ask me theoretical questions like that? I don't see what this has to do with the rape."

"Well, this has everything to do with your alleged rape, Ms Tan—"

But the judge cuts him off. "Please only ask her the necessary, factual questions relevant to the incident at hand, Counsel."

Quilligan clears his throat and starts again. "So you admit to deriving a certain thrill from romantic encounters with men you meet while traveling on your own. And prior to meeting the defendant, you had in fact engaged in these kinds of romantic encounters, correct?"

Time to make things clear. "In all my years of travelling on my own, I have never simply met a man and had sex within hours of meeting him. I've met men where there is a romantic energy, I've perhaps kissed them, but I've never sought to engage in actual sexual intercourse with them right away." Even from her first backpacking trip in Germany, and in all her traveling since, that has always been the truth.

"Ms Tan, I was merely looking for a yes or no answer."

She levels an unapologetic look at the barrister.

"So to take us back to the day at hand. Here you are, ready to go on a hike. As you've described it, you've had a busy few days, lots of dinners and cocktail parties, and on Saturday morning, again, as you've described it, you're looking for some way to escape it all. Correct?"

"Yes, that is correct."

"And you're looking to really let loose, be a bit reckless, and what better way than to go hiking in a park you've never been to before in your life? The thrill of the unknown, so to speak. So here you are, looking to let off a little steam, surrounded only by strangers, you're saying hello to people you pass, you're very open. Is that correct?"

"I was saying hello to people I passed because it seemed like everyone else was being quite friendly—"

"Yes or no, Ms Tan. You were being quite friendly to the people you met?"

"Yes, I suppose. I said hello to them."

"And who should cross your path but this young man, who seemed very interested in getting to know you better. Correct?"

"He did cross my path, if that's your question."

"And according to you, *he* asked you for directions. And you were very willing to help him. Is that correct?"

"I tried to help him best I could—"

"Yes or no, Ms Tan."

"Well, no. I wasn't *very* willing to help him, I just tried to help him because he asked me for directions. Like anyone else would."

She's aware that defensive note has crept into her voice again.

"Ms Tan, I suggest differently. I suggest that you were very willing to speak to this young man who crossed your path. In fact you were feeling a bit reckless, you wanted to let off some steam from the very busy few days you'd had. In fact, you welcomed the chance to meet this young man and see where it might go, correct?"

"No, I just wanted to go on my hike."

"Ah, that might have been your *initial* plan for the day, but things changed. I suggest, Ms Tan, that you have a bit of a wild streak. Underneath that very polished, very professional, accomplished demeanor, you just want to let loose. You sometimes just want to find a nice young man and see where things go with him, with no obligations and no strings attached."

She hates him then. She gives Quilligan a spiteful stare, wishing he'd drop dead and stop speaking. In a sense, yes, she *would* like to explore the world, meet a nice young man, and see what happens.

But Mr Quilligan, you're forgetting the defendant was not a nice young man.

Only, he never gives her a chance to say that to the jury.

*

A lot of fucking words they've been spewing up there. Quilligan bashing away, the woman trying to answer back. She's feisty, this one. He remembers that now from the day. The way she looked at him direct and spoke in that low voice, no messing around.

She's like that now. Even though she's wearing the nice dress, sitting there all smooth. The rest of the crowd are leaning in, listening. Everyone likes a good fight. They seem surprised that she wants to fight back like this. Not sure what they were expecting, from a shy little Chinky.

Funny, but he don't know if her speaking up like this is doing her any favours with the crowd. So that's a good thing for him. Keep speaking up, and they won't like you no more, bitch.

Some things you don't learn so well at your fancy schools.

*

Quilligan can go burn in hell. But she reminds herself showing anger is unseemly for a rape victim. She tries to stay calm. Her emotions are so volatile right now, she could go in any direction.

"So you've been speaking to Mr Sweeney for ten, twenty minutes now, as you've been going on your walk. At any point, if you didn't want to continue talking to him, you could have done something, correct?"

"Well, I didn't want to appear rude."

"Rude, Ms Tan? If you were really worried for your safety, you don't strike me as the kind of woman who's afraid of appearing rude."

She looks at him coldly. "At that time, I wasn't worried for my safety, because he was just talking to me—"

Quilligan cuts her off again. "I suggest, Ms Tan, that at no point did you actually want to stop interacting with this young man, because you were quite interested in seeing how things developed."

"No, that's incorrect. I tried to make that phone call as an excuse."

"Tried, but failed. You called one friend, and you claim you didn't have enough of a signal. But you could have tried again, or walked to try and get a signal, correct?"

"I could have, but I wanted to continue on the hike—"

"Yes or no, Ms Tan. You could have tried a bit harder to make that phone call, yes?"

"Yes, I guess I could have, if I wanted to, but—"

"In fact, if you really wanted, at that very moment after trying to make your phone call, Mr Sweeney wasn't next to you, you were standing right next to the Glen Road, you could have just stopped your walk. If you were fearing for your safety, you could have walked down to where there were plenty of cars and gone back into town. No one was pressuring you to stay in that abandoned park, so why did you continue on the walk?"

She's asked herself that question every day for the past ten months. But to hear it put to her in court like this, from the sniveling mouth of the defence barrister, in argument against her innocence, is the cruelest twisting of the truth.

She knows that to flash out in anger would appear negative, so she speaks slowly. "I continued on this walk because that's what I had set out to do. I'd specifically packed my hiking shoes and my guidebook on this trip because I wanted to hike that walk which was described in the guidebook. And I wasn't about to stop walking just because some annoying kid was trying to talk to me. It never occurred to me that a boy that young would be capable of such a crime." She turns her eyes to the jury. "Yes, I could have stopped walking, and in hindsight, of course I wish I did. But unfortunately, I continued on my hike, and now I'm here, giving evidence against my rapist."

That ought to put Quilligan in his place.

Quilligan merely raises his eyebrows and looks at the jury. "Well, that's what the lady says." His voice is wry and patronizing, and she wants to bash him over the head with one of his thick legal books.

He clears his throat. "Now, Ms Tan. Thank you for explaining *so clearly* why you did not stop walking, even though you had already been talking to the defendant for twenty minutes. I'd like to skip ahead to the second time Mr Sweeney approached you, which was when you were about to cross the stream."

It goes on. The same arguments, the same questions lobbed and directed at her from a slightly different angle. When he showed up a second time, at the stream, why didn't she leave? She explains it was just the two of them, no one else around, and wherever she went, he could have easily followed. She did make it clear to him she wanted to walk on her own.

"Very clever of you to say that, Ms Tan. But I suggest you were leading this young lad on. You mentioned you saw him looking at your legs. But it was *you* who decided to remove your shoes and socks to cross the stream, even though he had pointed out another way to cross it using the stepping-stones. You deliberately wanted to show him your legs. You *knew* he was a young lad who was interested in you, you *wanted* to see how much farther you could take this."

There's a collective murmur around the courtroom. She doesn't know if the audience are reacting for or against this suggestion, but she shakes her head slowly, her stare trained on Quilligan.

"That's the most ludicrous thing I've ever heard in my life. As I've already explained, I removed my shoes and socks because I didn't want to run the risk of them getting wet. The last thing I wanted in the world was to lead this boy on. Just to reiterate, I do *not* have any interest in boys half my age."

Quilligan smiles snidely at this.

"Ms Tan, you seem to be very astute at defending your honour in a public forum such as this. I'm trying to pierce into the heart of what your intentions *really* were on that afternoon. Here's an innocent-looking young lad, with all the curiosity of a teenage boy. Surely, you must have been aware of the possibilities at hand. The two of you alone in a forest. An attractive, well-traveled woman like yourself-"

"Those possibilities were the farthest thing from my mind. I only wanted to go on that walk. On my own."

Judge Haslam leans forward. "Again, Mr Quilligan, you need to phrase your case in the form of questions to the young lady."

The young lady. An attractive, well-traveled woman. The sorts of superficial labels that are always being pasted on her.

"I think, Ms Tan," Quilligan intones. "I think you are very good at presenting a certain smooth, accomplished exterior. Perhaps something you learned at Harvard or at these high-profile public events that you frequent. But underneath it all, you have a reckless desire for escape, for a thrill, shall we say. Travelling to new places on your own, meeting new men, even young boys. And when one of these encounters does *not* go according to plan, as it did with young Mr Sweeney, it was all too easy for you to blow the whistle and accuse the lad of assaulting you."

He nods a self-satisfied grin at her, and she realizes that any way she reacts – irate or assertive or articulate – he'll be able to make her appear at fault. There's almost no point in fighting. But still she tries.

She leans into the microphone.

"Is there a question in there, Mr Quilligan? Because you couldn't be farther from the truth."

The cross-examination toils on. When he gets to the rape, the actual rape, she starts to breathe shallow again. Her heartbeat tripping at a faster tempo, her head starting to spin. She digs her nails into her palms to steady herself, while Quilligan seems to delight in her discomfort, drawing out his questions slowly and asking her yet again about the crude facts of what the boy made her do.

"So that's five or six positions you've mentioned," he

sneers. "Surely quite a lot. At no point during this did you try to fight back?"

But she's already explained it. She'd realized how violent he could be. It would be safer to let him have what he wanted.

"I don't get it." Quilligan shakes his head in mock ignorance. "According to you, you *allowed* this boy to have sexual intercourse with you in these multiple positions. He didn't have a gun, there's no evidence he had a knife. At this point, he wasn't hitting you anymore or being specifically violent. Why did you let him do that? You decided to *let him* have intercourse with you in so many different positions? You had in fact *consented*? You claim you feared for your life, but in this moment, what exactly was he doing to threaten you? I suggest, you were actually enjoying the sex, because it was you who had initiated it. 'I bet you can go all night'... Who really says that while they're being raped?"

Quilligan's remarks rain down on her. Try as she might to explain her way out of his sneering comments, he turns it this way, then the other. Out of disgust, she just wants to shut up, stonewall him. But she does her best to reply.

"Mr Quilligan, I'm going to say this one more time. I sustained a lot of injuries during the attack. I was afraid I would sustain more serious ones if I didn't go along with what the defendant wanted."

"I just fail to understand how a professional woman like yourself, independent, well-traveled, would allow this much younger boy to have sex with her in five, six different positions, if it weren't without some consent on her part."

BECAUSE I FEARED FOR MY LIFE she wants to shout, but instead, she stays seated.

"I'm sorry you don't understand that, Mr Quilligan. But maybe you've never been in a position where you genuinely thought you were going to die."

Judge Haslam cuts in. "Once again, this is not meant to be a debate between the complainant and the defense counsel. Mr Quilligan, do you have any further *questions* for Ms Tan?"

And of course he does. After the rape, after they'd put their clothes back on, why did she stick around? Why didn't she leave when she had the first chance?

"Because I didn't want to turn my back on the defendant. I was scared what he would try to do."

No, because she wanted to continue talking to the boy, to make sure things were cool, things were normal. She wasn't scared at all by that point.

No, I wanted him to think things were normal so he wouldn't suspect I might report him.

A lot of double-crossing there, Ms Tan. Being rather deceptive to the boy, just as you are being to us.

I was just trying to survive.

Just as you're creating the best situation for us to believe you were a victim of a rape, and not actually a woman fully in control.

She's shaking her head, staring straight at the barrister.

"You're entirely wrong. Your suggestions are insulting and nothing but false."

Some of the jury are shaking their heads, too, but she doesn't know if it's because they agree with her, or because they think she's lying. This entire cross-examination is like some torturous farce allowed to run on for too long. How much longer will she have to put up with these questions?

Because for every accusation, every insinuation, something pierces her protective hide, wriggles its way under her skin and festers like a parasite.

Quilligan asks her about the following day, her flight back to London. A film premiere? She went to a glamorous party with celebrities the day after her alleged rape? He's even produced a photo of her on the red carpet, the one from the publicist's reel that evening. Judge Haslam rules out using the photo as evidence, but it's too late – Quilligan's already described it. Ms Tan is smiling, she's wearing a fancy gown, she has a handsome date. She hardly looks like the victim of a traumatic assault that took place a day before.

She seethes upon hearing this. They have no idea how

difficult it was for her to attend that event. But she's given no chance to explain.

"Ms Tan, I suggest you knew exactly what you were doing when you spoke to the defendant in the park that day. It was *you* who initiated the sexual activity with the young Mr Sweeney, and when things got a bit out of hand – when he got a bit too enthusiastic and those bruises and injuries began to appear – that's when you started to regret this encounter you had initiated. He never yelled at you or held you against your will, and as we will see when Mr Sweeney takes the stand, it was him who was following your lead in this sexual encounter."

She looks at him sadly and says: "That is entirely incorrect."

"We shall see about that, Ms Tan," Quilligan replies. He turns to Judge Haslam. "I have no further questions, Your Honour."

Quilligan sits, and there's a palpable sense of relief in the room. She looks around at the jury, the public gallery, the journalists, and she slowly realizes she hates them all for coming to watch this, like it's some form of gladiatorial combat.

It's entertainment for them.

But I'm the one who has to live it.

Lunch. She sits in the complainant's room, the lavender candle burning and quietly spoons potato-and-leek soup into her mouth.

Barbara, Erika, and Jen are hovering around her.

"How'd I do?" she asks, almost devoid of emotion.

Kind hands on her shoulders, stroking her hair.

You did great.

Amazing.

I am so so sorry you have to go through this.

But somehow, even their kind words hardly pierce the surface, when Quilligan's inane suggestions managed to.

O'Leary and Simmons step into the room, billow over to her in their robes.

"You've done well. He was nastier than I thought he'd be, but you've done very well to discredit him firmly, while still carrying yourself in a respectable manner."

A respectable manner.

"I should have cried, shouldn't I?"

Simmons says some platitude: there's no should have, you react in the way that seems natural to you.

Only there is nothing natural about this entire situation, she wants to say.

O'Leary clears his throat and starts to explain the next steps.

"Now after lunch, I'm just going to ask you a few more questions, just to re-establish your story a bit after the cross-examination. And then you should be free to go for the time being."

But she knows she won't really be free, not while this trial's still going, and maybe not ever.

One of these days, she tells herself, she'll be able to walk into a field on her own. An open field under the broad sky in the middle of the day. She'll be able to lie down on her back, feel the grass beneath her, the sun on her face, close her eyes, and she will feel completely content. And she will feel no danger.

Only then, will she really be free.

They file back into Courtroom Eight, O'Leary working to repair some of the damage Quilligan has done.

Perhaps it's part of the show, but he looks at her carefully, solicitously now, weighing his words, and placing each question down, like a hand of cards laid one by one on a tabletop, a shared knowledge that each card she overturns will be one in her favor.

"Ms Tan. Just to return to some things Mr Quilligan was implying, in all your years of traveling, have you ever met a much younger man and engaged in sexual relations with him?"

"No, I've never done that."

"And once he became violent, how did you decide to enact your main thought, of trying to survive the assault? And that's why you did certain things and said certain things during the assault, right?"

She answers these easily enough, her confidence and sense of dignity slowly being restored.

"And how have you felt since the assault last April?"

"Pretty awful. I've been diagnosed with post-traumatic stress disorder. I have flashbacks and agoraphobia. I'm anxious and nauseous all the time. I feel like I'm a shell of the person I used to be. And I don't know if I can ever really go back to being who I was before the assault."

O'Leary lets her last statement sit there, a somber bell-ring filling the air. He turns to the jury and looks at them.

"Thank you, Ms Tan. No further questions, Your Honour."

Relief and a surreal giddiness roll over her, but she keeps this below the surface, sweeps her eyes around the room, over the jury. She searches for traces of sympathy. Maybe, perhaps, in the younger woman, the middle-aged mother, the Indian man. Or maybe she's imagining it.

Barbara, Erika and Jen beam proud smiles at her, and so does Detective Morrison.

Emboldened by this, she looks further. Notices a couple of hardened-looking men sitting in the public gallery near the dock. Maybe the boy's dad or brothers.

And then she looks straight at the glass panel.

He is sitting there, looking down, that ginger-brown hair she recognizes in a flash, the pale white skin.

She assesses him coolly. He's in a box. With security around him. He can't do anything to her. There's a roomful of people between them, law enforcement, the press, a judge and several barristers.

Same two people. A different arena.

And then he looks up. Straight at her.

She shudders for a moment, but doesn't flinch outwardly. She doesn't look away. She looks straight back, what she hopes is a cold, remorseless stare. Her eyes piercing into his familiar ice-blue ones. She doesn't care if the rest of the courtroom see this exchange.

*

Weren't expecting her to glare straight at him like that. What's gotten into this bitch?

Almost looks like she's gonna kill him.

As if a softie like her could do something like that. But still, he don't like it.

Quilligan wasn't able to trip her up, not really.

So she sailed on through, smooth, and now at the end of it all, gives him that look.

Ah, fuck her, and fuck all of them in the courtroom. He'll get his chance. He'll show them all.

*

The streets of Belfast look the same, once she steps out of the courthouse. Same grey skies and grey buildings, same unsmiling people on the sidewalks.

Jen is walking with her, back to the hotel, and probably wondering why she's so quiet. But the day's proceedings have gouged her clean of coherent thoughts. She just wants to lie in bed in the dark, an inert being, devoid of emotion or life.

Tomorrow, she knows O'Leary will continue his show: more witnesses for the prosecution. Barbara, Detective Morrison, Doctor Phelan, even some of the people who saw her and the boy in the park. As the complainant, she can't sit in the courtroom, for fear her presence might influence what the witnesses would say. Even though the defendant is allowed to be present through it all. But Jen and Barbara will be there, her ears and eyes.

At least the worst of it is over, that much she knows.

She looks out to the hills on the horizon, the ones that

309

fringe the other side of the harbor. The clouds hang low, flattened and bleak, above those hills.

And she thinks, if this were a film, and this were one of those moments in a film there'd be a little chink of light in those clouds right now. Shining through to tell her everything will be all right, tomorrow is another day, all those wonderful things they tell you in the movies.

As Jen walks alongside her, she keeps her eyes trained on those clouds, waiting for that chink of light to break through.

But it never does.

Later that evening, out of the blue, her mom calls. She's lying on her bed in the hotel room, drowsing with the lights turned low, when her phone goes off. Unusual, for her mom to call her cell phone long-distance.

She reminds her mom that she's in Belfast on a business trip, just some meetings to prepare for a TV series they might shoot in Northern Ireland. She'll be here next week, too, for further meetings. The lies lodge in her throat.

"What's the weather like over there?"

"Kind of the same as London, maybe a bit colder. Grey, rainy, you know, Ireland." At least that wasn't a lie.

"But it's safe in Belfast?" Mom asks. "I always think of all that fighting that used to go on there."

"Oh yeah, it's safe," she says, and the ridiculous irony of that statement catches her. "Most of that political fighting died down years ago," she adds. "Remember, I came over here for that conference to celebrate the peace process, last year."

Why did she even say that? Such a morbid delight in her own ironies.

They chat some more. Mom, relaying details of her life in Southern California.

"You know, we got a new class at the senior center. This thing called zumba. Do you know it?"

Yes, she's heard of zumba.

"I had the worst dream two nights ago," Mom says.

Something pricks at the back of her neck. "Why? What was it about?"

"I dreamt I was in my old childhood home in Taipei, sleeping in the bed I used to share with my grandmother when I was a little girl."

She sinks further into the hotel bed's duvet. An uncomfortable feeling is creeping into her, at the sound of her mom's words.

"…But this time, my grandmother wasn't there. I woke up in my dream, all on my own. And this man came into the room… and he… he assaulted me."

"He what?"

"He assaulted me, it was horrible."

She sits up. She knows her mom wouldn't use the word 'rape', but she can read between the lines. Somehow that image – of a fictional, dream-rape – is enough to chill her. That her mom would have to experience that kind of terror, even in a dream.

"Did you know the man in your dream? Was it anyone you recognized?"

"No, no one I recognized. But it was horrible, I still can't forget it. Now why would I have a dream like that?"

In that moment, she is tempted like never before to tell her mom the truth. To tell her what happened.

But she can't bring herself to say those words. Imagine the devastation they would cause. Her mom's already this traumatized by a dream. What would the truth do to her?

She forces herself to harden her voice.

"I don't know," she lies. "I'm sorry you had to have that dream. But at least it was only that… a dream."

*

In prison, that weekend. It's like an escape. From all that staring, the tiny glass box, the microwaved shite pasta he burns his tongue on every day.

311

Hey, Sweeney, like a celebrity in court, are ya?
You speak yet?
What kind of pussy they got on display there?

He ignores all that. A week ago, he was looking forward to court. A change of scene from inside, you know.

But now he'd rather be here, safe in his cell, not going nowhere.

*

Tuesday of the second week, Quilligan tells him, he'll be up on the witness stand. So be ready. Know your story.

That fucking story, he knows it back to front and front to back, recited it in his head for months now.

So now is his chance to show all them buffers.

The woman's been gone since that day Quilligan tried to tear her apart, but he's been warned she might be back.

"Don't you worry about her," McLuhan said. "Just focus on yourself. How you present yourself. Look at the barristers and the judge when you answer their questions. Don't keep looking down or away, that makes people suspicious."

'Course, they're already suspicious.

Puts on a bit of a show. One of them nice shirts he's been wearing for court. Hates buttoning them, putting on the stiff shoes. But when he looks in the mirror, has to admit he's like a different person. Hair combed over to the side. He could almost walk into a pub, order a pint, start chatting with the buffers.

Now that he's here, fancy clothes and all, he don't think he's ever seen this many people looking at him before. Everyone just goggle-eyed. See here, a real, live gypo rapist.

Heart starts hammering and he tells himself to calm down, be quiet, not that big a deal.

But the judge ain't smiling, and neither are them barristers nor anyone in the room.

He's looking over in the gallery for Da and Michael. At

312

least two friendly faces in the crowd, eh? Da gives him a nod and Michael a wink.

But then, just a few seats over from them, one row closer, he sees her.

The woman. She's in her TV lawyer clothes again, sitting next to them other women who seem foreign and posh. Her mouth is set. She looks straight at him, no hesitating. The way she did when she left the room last week.

Jaysus, that woman gets on his nerves. He shifts his glance away. Pretend she ain't there.

Quilligan is clearing his throat, asking him a question.

"Could you please state your full name to the jury?"

This one's easy.

He opens his mouth. "John Michael Sweeney."

That's him, it is.

*

This kid, looking so out of place in his button-down shirt and trousers. The image jars for her. In her mind, he should always be wearing that bright white jumper and the jeans. Here, his attempt to look grown-up, mature in court just seems pathetic.

She still can't comprehend. *I was raped by that? How did I let that happen?*

But to dwell on that further would only make her sick.

She can sense Jen twitching and glancing over. *Are you okay?* That same question, so common these days no one needs to actually say it.

She nods back at Jen. *I'm fine.*

She flicks her eyes back to the boy, forcing herself to combat the disgust.

At least, I told the truth. What's he going to come up with?

*

"Tell me, step by step, what happened on the afternoon of April 12th."

He wants to get this over with, get away from that woman staring at him – your one who knows what actually happened. But Da and Michael told him not to rush through this part.

So he spins it, answering Quilligan's questions one by one. But all the times he practiced in his cell, he weren't prepared for the whole world staring.

Still, say what you practiced.

"I noticed she was a good-looking woman, but it was her who came to me first. Said she was lost and needed directions. I could tell by the way she was acting, she was interested in, y'know… getting to know me better. She took off her socks and shoes so she could show me her legs. She didn't have to, but she wanted me to see them. I knew what that meant…"

All comes out in one go, don't it.

Whole thing would be a lot easier if that woman weren't in the front row, giving him that smug eyeful. But her stare hardly moves, and even when he's not looking, he knows she's still there, glaring away.

*

She never imagined she could get this angry, simply listening to another person. But she can't stand up and scream. Instead, she has to remain calm and controlled, while the rage mounts inside of her.

He's taken every single little fact and detail, and warped them so they point away from his guilt, towards her as the initiator. She can feel her breathing grow heavy and she sinks her nails into the palm of her hand, forming dark half-moons in her skin.

And then she realizes how ridiculously unfair this whole system is. She was the one who was walking along on her own, when he did this to her. And then she has to wait almost a year to sit in front of a room full of strangers, tell them the humiliating truth, stand up to a sleaze-bag barrister trying to paint her as a villain-seductress and then listen to the boy make up this trash about her?

314

Is this what we have to subject ourselves to, in order to get justice?

She can feel the tears blurring the edges of her vision, and the more she thinks about it the deeper she stabs into her skin.

The tears spill over.

I can cry all I want. Because these tears speak the truth.

*

For fuck's sake, that woman started crying again. She's worse than Mam.

He suddenly sees Mam, standing in that peeler's station in Kilkenny, crying her eyes out about Michael. Women. That's all they do.

She's doing it so they'll feel sorry for her, and look at them – all them jury throwing glances over at her, but that ain't fair. This is my turn! My story now. Look at me, you fuckers.

The weird thing is, that woman is still staring at him the whole time. Not looking down, all embarrassed. Just keeps glaring straight at him, with her tears pouring down.

He looks away.

Stay on Quilligan.

"Just to reiterate, Mr Sweeney. At any point, did you use violence on the woman before you engaged in sexual contact with her?"

"No, I didn't."

"And at any point did she indicate that she was scared of you? Or didn't want to engage in sexual contact?"

"No, she didn't. She was inviting me, like. She was friendly the whole time."

"So you were surprised when you found out the police were looking for you?"

"Yeah. She obviously wanted sex, so I was real surprised, because I didn't do nothing wrong."

"Thank you very much, Mr Sweeney. Now I don't have

315

any further questions for the time being, but I'm sure my learned friend Mr O'Leary does, if you could just stay there on the stand."

Now this part, he ain't looking forward to.

O'Leary clears his throat.

Now them tough questions are gonna come. He feels a line of sweat run down the side of his face. Look him straight in the eye.

You ain't scared of his questions.

"Mr Sweeney, you described how prior to the day you met Ms Tan, the night before, you were with your friends and you'd had some marijuana, correct?"

"Yes, I did."

"Is this a common thing, you taking marijuana with your friends, and other forms of drugs?"

The trial's about rape, but them jury don't like drug-takers no matter what. So just lie on this one.

"We just do it once in a while."

"And as well, would you mind telling the jury, how often do you, for fun, meet new women and engage in sexual conduct with them?"

"Um... that's once in a while, too."

"And just to clarify, by this I mean, new women whom you've never met before in your life. So in the past, once in a while, you have met women, struck up a nice conversation with them, and within hours or even minutes, engaged in sexual conduct with them?"

"Yes, I have."

A mumble around the room, but don't pay no attention to them. They can laugh all they want.

"Can you estimate for me how many times in the past you've done this, prior to you meeting Ms Tan?"

What seems okay here? He has no idea.

"Maybe four or five?"

"Four or five." O'Leary nods. "So here you are, fifteen years of age—"

Quilligan stands up now. "Your Honour, I'm not sure if this is relevant to the case at hand."

O'Leary don't skip a beat. "Your Honour, defence counsel were allowed to ask Ms Tan about her previous behavior while traveling on her own, so I think it's only fair I can ask similar questions of the defendant."

Your old judge is okay with is.

He cracks his knuckles under the chair.

"These four or five women you'd met before and engaged in sexual conduct with... Where had you met them?"

Now this is gonna take some spinning. But just go on and say something.

"Well, it was all different places. Nightclubs, parties."

"Had you ever met any of them in a park outdoors, during the day?"

Shite, what to say here?

"Uh, no. I hadn't."

"So this was unusual, this situation with Ms Tan. Correct?"

"Yeah, it was different from what I done before."

"Very well. And you knew right away that Ms Tan was older than you, too. Had these previous four or five women also been significantly older than you?"

Keep spinning...

"Yes, most of them, yeah. A little older."

"And these previous instances, with these other older women, had it been the same? Had it been them initiating it, or yourself?"

"Well, kinda both. I might start chatting to them, see how they are, and then one thing leads to another, you know."

"But who would suggest the sexual contact, you or them?"

"Sometimes them, sometimes me."

Quilligan coughs or something.

"And these other women, you didn't keep in touch with them afterward?"

"Naw naw, it weren't like that. It was just, y'know, a bit of fun for the while."

O'Leary nods. "Fun," he says and looks around. "I take it you didn't remember any of their names afterward?"

Oh, he can remember names. Sarah was the first one, that skinny thing walking home from her friend's party outside Dublin. But he ain't telling them those names.

"No."

Quilligan speaks up again. "Your Honour, I don't think this is—"

"Very well, very well," O'Leary says, his hands up. "I'll move on. Let's take your word for it. By the young age of fifteen, you already have sexual experience with four or five older women, who remain unidentified. So when it came to meeting Ms Tan, did it seem like a situation you were already familiar with? Meeting an older lady, seeing where it would lead?"

"Yeah, I s'pose so. Never done it in a park before, though."

"So were you scared about having sexual relations with a woman you'd never met before in a park, in the middle of the day?"

"Mm, a little scared we'd get caught."

O'Leary laughs. "Oh, that's a nice touch, Mr Sweeney. Well, in reality, it was not consensual sex, Ms Tan had not initiated it. You were forcing yourself on her and of course you were scared you'd get caught because you knew you were committing a crime. You were, in fact, *raping* her. Isn't that correct?"

"Ain't true."

"We have thirty-nine separate injuries on Ms Tan to corroborate her claim. Members of the jury, I am holding up Exhibit TM-3, Doctor Phelan's report, which I believe you can find in the book in front of you."

"Well, she liked it raw."

"Mr Sweeney, I don't know if you realise how ridiculous you sound. Here you are, claiming Ms Tan 'liked it raw' as you say. That she wanted to have sex with you, a boy half her age, outdoors, in the mud, on the ground, in the middle of the day, and she didn't mind all the bruises and injuries you inflicted on her, because that was all part of the sex. Is that correct?"

"Yeah, it is."

"Mr Sweeney, this is absolute rubbish. You've heard what Ms Tan has to say. How can you possibly expect us to believe this when witnesses have testified how traumatised she was after the incident, when photographs prove how many injuries she received, when her account of the event has been entirely consistent and reasonable throughout the entire legal process—"

"She ain't telling the truth."

"Allow me to ask a question first, Mr Sweeney."

That same hard tone, the same way all them peelers and teachers ever spoke to him. He clenches his jaw.

"Please explain what you mean when you say Ms Tan 'liked it raw'? How do you know she actually wanted it? Clearly, if you're as experienced as you claim to be, you can enlighten us and describe what signs indicate that a woman is interested in having sex with *you*."

"You want me to tell you?"

"Yes, more specifically. Tell us what Ms Tan did to give you the impression that she actually wanted to have sexual relations with you."

O'Leary's making fun of him. He'd headbutt the fucker in a flash, if there weren't everyone else around.

"Well, she came on to me. She was laughing and smiling, like."

"Mr Sweeney, a woman can laugh and smile, that doesn't necessarily mean she wants to have sexual intercourse."

"That was just at the beginning. Then…"

Come on, you fucking did this at the peelers the first time. Say all that same stuff again.

But his mind's going blank, with all them buffers staring at him, and your man railing away, and her just sitting in the front row, streaming tears down her face, and fixing him the look of death.

"It's all in what I told the police before."

"Yes, we know that some of it's in your police statement, but I'm asking you now, in front of the jury, while you're under oath, to repeat some of that and if possible, provide more detail. Could you please describe to us, what Ms Tan specifically did or said, to give you the impression she wanted to have sex with you."

He wants to be sick. But he looks over at Michael, who nods.

It's her word against mine.

"Like I said, she started by laughing and smiling at me a lot. She was the one who asked me for directions. And when a woman speaks to you first, you know she's keen. Then she kept talking to me. Then, we were getting to a part of the Glen with no people around, and she didn't mind being there with just me. Any other woman who didn't want to be with me coulda just left."

He goes on: she showed him her legs, she asked him to walk with her.

"That's interesting, because Ms Tan says the exact opposite. She says *you* asked *her,* if you could accompany her on her walk. And she told you she just wanted to be on her own."

"Well, I'm telling the truth, I am."

"And then what else? There's still a big difference between wanting to go on a walk with you and wanting to have sex with you."

Jaysus, around and around with your man. Same kinda questions the peelers asked him, but O'Leary dresses them up with fancy words, like he's presenting some comedy act to the jury.

"Did she specifically say, 'I want to have sex with you?'"

"No, but come on, women don't say that. They just tell you with what they do. So she kept kissing me, starting to feel me, take me clothes off."

With the peelers, he was even starting to enjoy this part himself. But here, with all them staring at him, it's not much fun. He keeps talking, though.

"I think I even said 'What you mean, right here? In these woods?'"

"Mr. Sweeney, just to clarify. You specifically asked her, 'What you mean, right here? In these woods?'"

"Yeah."

"And what did she say?"

"She didn't say much, just smiled at me and kissed me some more and kept on going."

O'Leary nods. "Now, that's interesting. Because it's not in your police statement."

Shite. Got a little carried away there.

"I can't remember everything all the time."

"Mr Sweeney, you did not provide this key detail to Detective Morrison that day. Why didn't you?"

"Well, like I said, I didn't remember this bit at the time. I was high on drugs when this happened with her, I don't remember everything."

"You can't remember. That's very convenient for you."

O'Leary stops, looks down at his papers. Starts asking about them removing their clothes. Honestly, who remembers this shite in real life? When you're having sex, no one seems bothered by who took what off and when.

"So's... Yeah, we're standing up, kissing, feeling each other, all that. Then I say, 'Are you sure, right here?' And she don't say nothing, but 'cause she's still kissing me and taking my clothes off, I know she wants to."

"And how do feel about all this, at that moment? What are you thinking?"

"Just well, scared we might get caught, but yeah, if this beour's game. Then happy days, y'know?"

Quilligan shoots him a warning look. Maybe he went too far saying that.

Now O'Leary wants to know how they ended up on the ground. In the pornos, your housewife would take the plumber by the hand, lead him into the lounge, and then just lie back on the sofa and pull him over. So that. That's what she done. She pulled him down to her.

"So you're saying, she went from standing, and then she just reclined back? Onto the muddy ground right there?"

"Yeah, I guess."

"And once she pulled you toward her, how was your body in relation to her?"

"So's then I'm lying on top of her."

"How were you lying on top of her? Facing away from her or toward her?"

Christ, has your man even had sex before?

"Facing her, of course. So's we could kiss some more."

"And then?"

"And then we just took off the rest of our clothes and just... started."

"You say you 'took off the rest of your clothes'? So you took off *all* of them?"

"Well, not all of them. Just some of them."

"Can you describe how much is 'just some'? Were you completely naked at any point? Did you remove your socks and shoes?"

"Aw, Jaysus, I can't remember this stuff!" he shouts this out at your man, boiling. "I was high, I was caught up in it. I weren't really paying attention to how much clothes we was wearing!"

Fuck, he shouldn't of shouted like that. Quilligan's looking at him, shocked. Them jury too.

Your man's almost having a laugh. "Right so, evidently you can't remember *any* details about the removal of clothing. Let me walk you through it: did your shirt get removed at any point?"

"I don't think so, no."

"Earlier you said she started to take off your clothes, but this didn't mean your shirt?"

"No, no. She had her hands down me trousers, like."

"So she wasn't actually removing your clothes from your body, at this point? Not when you were both standing up, kissing?"

"No."

"So, just to clarify for the jury, that's a change from what you said before. Before, you said she was removing your clothes when you were both standing up, kissing. Now you say that didn't happen until you were down on the ground."

Yeah, fuck you, old man. So you got me.

"But at no point did she remove your shirt, the white jumper which she and the other witnesses described?"

"No, guess she didn't."

"During this sexual activity, can you tell me, were your trousers ever removed?"

"Yeah."

"And what other articles of your clothing were removed?"

"Me pants." Obviously.

"And who removed these articles of clothing?"

"Both of us. She'd had her hand down me trousers from the start. Then we're down on the ground, she's feeling me and kissing me, she's starting to take me trousers off, and I help her."

"So who removed your undergarments?"

"Both of us, we both took that off."

"And your socks and shoes?"

"Listen, I can't quite remember about the socks and shoes. I had other things on my mind, y'know?"

"Well, try and think. Can you remember if your bare feet ever touched the ground?"

He's about to burst, when Quilligan speaks up.

"Your Honour, I believe my learned friend is pressuring my client to remember things he simply can't recall."

"Mr O'Leary—"

"That's fine, that's fine. Clearly Mr Sweeney can't remember these details. So your trousers are off, and your undergarments, too. Your jumper stays on and possibly, *possibly* your socks and shoes, but you can't remember. Now, how about Ms Tan. Surely, you'd be able to remember which parts of *her* body you saw naked. Can you tell me which articles of her clothing were removed?"

"Well, her knickers, for sure. And her trousers."

"And again, who removed those articles of clothing?"

"We both did."

"And above her waist? Can you remember?"

Sure can. He remembers those tits, the weird brown nipples.

"Yeah, her top came off. I think. And her bra."

"Can you tell me more about her bra?"

"It was…"

What fucking colour was it? He can remember this one.

"It was black."

"And?"

"What else you want?"

O'Leary wants a proper lamping right in his smug face, is what he wants.

"Fine, okay. I ripped her fucking bra off. Yeah, I did that, just like she said I did. Are you happy now?"

O'Leary's smiling. "No swearing, Mr Sweeney, or you'll be found guilty of contempt of court. Well, at least on that point, both you and Ms Tan agree. Tell me, Mr Sweeney, why did you rip her bra off?"

"'Cause it was getting hot just then, I was feeling it, and I just wanted to rip it off. The way it happens, y'know?"

"So it was the passion of the moment, you mean to say?"

"Yeah, yeah."

"So did she *want* you to rip her bra off? Did she say it was okay to rip her bra off?"

"No, of course, she didn't say it. I just did it. That's what happens sometimes."

Fucking O'Leary is still smiling. "Right. So… you've ripped her bra off, she doesn't seem to mind, according to you. The two of you carrying on having sexual intercourse right there, in the mud. You're half-clothed, you have your jumper still on, and she… How much clothing does she have on?"

"Listen, I can't remember exactly. But I think she had all hers off."

"So she was entirely naked?"

"Almost. Maybe. I dunno."

"But her shirt was off, because you'd ripped her bra?"

"Yes, her shirt was off."

O'Leary nods again. "Mr Sweeney, we appear to have another discrepancy here. You both agree *you* ripped her bra off, but you, Mr Sweeney, say her top, her blue hiking top, came off during your interaction with Ms Tan. But she says that despite you ripping her bra, her blue shirt actually stayed on for the duration of the assault."

"Well, how could I rip her bra off if her shirt stayed on?"

Explain that one.

"Well, we have photographs from the forensic exam, before Miss Tan changed out of her clothes."

He turns to the jury. "I refer you to Exhibit TM-5, photos of Ms Tan in the Rape Crime Unit care centre of the PSNI, shortly after the incident."

And the fucker actually hands him a photograph, while all them in the jury shuffle through their papers.

The photo. There's the woman, looking pretty minging and banged up, to be honest. Standing, staring straight ahead. Down to her knickers and bare feet. She's still wearing her black bra, which is ripped right down the middle, hung together by a thread, but still covering up her weird brown nipples.

"So? She coulda just put her shirt back on afterward."

"She could have, you're right. But during the exam, it seems that all the scratches and dirt marks on Ms Tan's body were from the torso down, on the lower half of her body. Her shoulders and upper arms and upper chest remained clean and virtually unscratched. Which indicates that her shirt stayed on during the assault. To the jury, I refer you again to the detailed report from the forensic doctor, Exhibit TM-3, where Doctor Phelan has listed one by one, each of the scratches, bruises, and injuries on Ms Tan's body."

He just looks at O'Leary, quiet.

"If you claim that she was lying back and that all these different positions were being used and that your intercourse got a little 'raw' as you say then surely, if her shirt were off, she would have picked up some dirt or some scratches on her upper back and shoulders, just like she had on the bottom half of her body. Correct?"

"I dunno. I'm no expert at this stuff."

"Well, I suggest that you just made that up, about her shirt coming off. Because Ms Tan's story and the evidence seem to point otherwise."

"So she's got a better memory than me, so what?"

"She's got a better memory than you because she's telling the *truth*. And you're just making it up, desperately hoping that we'll believe your pathetic lies."

Of course, always lies coming from us tinkers. He wants to kick the witness stand in, but steels his leg. Swallows hard.

O'Leary's pleased with himself, that he is. Your man takes his time, looking to the judge and the jury, then back to him. Jaysus, he can't wait to get off this stand.

"Just a few more questions, Mr Sweeney. You've explained repeatedly that you were under the influence of drugs, so that may have impaired your memory, correct?"

"Yes."

"Is there any chance it may have impaired your judgment? That because you were under the influence, you may have misinterpreted Ms Tan's behaviour?"

He don't quite get that question. Can't your man just ask it straight?

"What do you mean?"

"I'm asking if there's any chance the drugs led you to believe Ms Tan *wanted* to have sex with you, when she actually didn't. Were you 100 percent sure she wanted to have sex with you, according to the signs and the behavior she exhibited towards you, as you claim?"

That didn't help much. He gets the sense this is an important question, sort of. That if he answered one way, he could say it's the drugs and not really him. But all that fancy solicitor talk is confusing him.

"We're waiting on your answer, Mr Sweeney."

That O'Leary all smug again. And then he don't fucking care anymore, all these fancy-talkers, throwing these impossible questions at him, so many words in the way.

"No," he spits out. "Listen, I'm not stupid. Maybe I didn't get my learning in no school but I know when a woman wants it, and she wanted it."

A slow smile spreads across O'Leary's face, who glances at the jury like it's something important. When he speaks, his voice is all big and grand, like.

"Well, Mr Sweeney, it seems to me and all of us here, that Miss Tan did not want it. So maybe your learning's a little incorrect." He pauses, then looks to the judge. "No further questions, Your Honour."

*

Her friends are on Vivian-watch. At least that's what she terms it: this kid-glove handling of her, making sure she's never alone in the courthouse. Already, she's felt the urge to vomit several times this week, and rushed down the gleaming halls to the women's room.

The cool tile of the bathroom floor, and Jen or Barbara's voice, from the other side of the stall door. "Are you okay? Let me know if you need anything." The pitying looks of the other women who pass her in the bathroom.

That physical nausea is humiliating enough. But counteracting that, there's the anger. This distinct desire to snap the boy's neck in two. It's a new feeling, somehow energizing. Something she's hardly felt in all these months of numbness and withdrawal. In all her conversations with friends since the attack, they have been the ones to speak of pummeling the boy, locking him up for good. She herself had moved to a place beyond anger: the grey, flat lake, where nothing moves and waves do not ripple. She's lived on that lake for eleven months.

Now, she's found ground again. The anger is back. And it's not just anger at the boy. The entire system is at fault.

On the first day of the defence's case, she studied what must have been the boy's family. A middle-aged man, dark-haired and stoop-shouldered. Probably the father. He was there nearly all the time. And a young man, not dissimilar in looks to the boy, a few years older. Pale skin, blue eyes and brown hair – darker than the boy's. A gold-looking chain gleamed around his white neck, and he had a cocky, shifty sort of air about him.

That must be the older brother, she thought. Wasn't there a brother's DNA in the police system, a partial match to the DNA they found on her?

She's seen the way he interacts with the boy, giving him occasional winks and nods of approval. The way he slyly checks out the women in the room and appraises the jury.

Once, the father caught her looking at him. He held her gaze for a moment longer than she expected, then looked away. She kept on staring. She doesn't know what she saw in his gaze, maybe an apology, maybe guilt, maybe hatred. She's never seen it again, because he's made sure not to look in her direction.

From the older brother, she's never gotten anything. He pretends she's not there.

She sometimes wonders if her constant, glowering presence is helping the case or hindering it. Prosecution had explained that most victims only show up to give evidence, and then to hear the verdict. Some don't even show up for that.

Perhaps she's being too serious. But what do they expect her to be? She is not that cowering Chinese girl they reported on the radio.

No, she's relentless. The same way she would pursue a trail, back when she hiked on her own. That refusal to be distracted or discouraged by an uphill climb, a vanished path.

That's what she is now. Relentless. Seeking one thing and one thing only.

"Would all parties related to the case of Crown vs Sweeney, please come to Courtroom Eight?"

She hears it over the tannoy, and that unbearable queasiness surges in the pit of her stomach.

She's sitting in the witness room, where she's been trying to absorb a book of Thomas Hardy's poetry, hoping his quiet images of rural tranquility can block out the stress of the trial. But her mind has inevitably wandered to what those twelve jury members are discussing.

She shuts the book.

"Well, looks like they've made a decision," Detective Morrison says in a try-jolly voice, and stands.

Unbidden, Jen and Barbara come to her side, guiding her forward with supportive arms. In days past, she might think this was pathetic, an overdependence on others to even take a step. But here, at this moment, she knows there is no way she could make it into that courtroom without her friends around her.

"Good luck," Peter, the Victim Support volunteer, says as they pass him. He offers a nervous smile.

"Thanks," she says in a quiet voice.

They reach the threshold of the witness room, and she closes her eyes for a moment, feeling her heartbeat throb in her throat.

In all these months, she's never thought about how she'd react if he was found not guilty.

Because to her, that never seemed like a possibility.

*

He's sitting in his cramped cell, when he hears that voice on the system.

"Would all parties related to the case of Crown vs. Sweeney, please come to Courtroom Eight?"

About fucking time. He's been hearing them announcements all morning, and all day yesterday. For this case, that case, but never his own.

He knows he bollixed the cross-examination. That sly O'Leary had it in for him, and couldn't wait to trip him up with all them fancy questions.

Thing is, it'd be a lot easier to answer the questions if

they just asked them normal, like. The police were better, spoke simple. But these fucking barristers, and the judge. Does your head in trying to catch what they're saying. So many fucking words. All these people speaking some other language you can't understand. Yet they're the ones deciding your fate.

So when he hears that voice announcing Courtroom Eight, he's never been this nervous before in his life. Not when stealing bags from the buffers and trying to run off. All that he could get, it was real. You see a bag, you take it. You get caught or don't.

But here, this trial. You sit in a room, hear a bunch of people with wigs mumbling away, answer some fancy questions, at the end of it all, they decide if you're going to prison for years and years, or if you get to walk free.

Just like that. Your whole fucking life decided in moments. By complete strangers.

The door clatters, as a peeler unlocks it, steps in.

"Looks like it's your moment."

This guard's not too old. Around the same age as Michael. Blue eyes, blond hair, like he belongs on some advert for milk. He wonders if he could make a go of it, kick his stomach in, knee him in the face, and then just run down the hall, get the fuck out of there.

But he knows five other guards would be on top of him in a flash. And even then, the door at the end's bolted, there's the security man at the front.

Not worth it.

No fucking way out of this one.

*

There's a slight flurry of commotion when she enters. The public gallery is packed, not a spare seat in the house.

The usher smiles at her, a broader grin than usual, as if to acknowledge that today is different from all the others that have come before.

The same three seats in the front row have been reserved for her. She can sense everyone turning and watching as she makes her way forward.

The air in the room is close, stilted. No one speaks.

She passes the dock without looking at the boy. She passes his father and brother without looking at them. In her seat, she keeps gazing forward, and only when Jen winces, does she look down. She realizes she's been squeezing Jen's hand until her fingertips have turned red.

'Sorry,' she mouths, and relaxes her grip, but continues holding it.

Barbara takes her other hand and she remembers what she said to her all those months ago, when she lay with her legs in the stirrups in the forensic exam, dreading the inevitable thrust of the speculum: *You squeeze as hard as you need to.*

How many more times does she need to be flayed alive in this process? Every single step of seeking justice involves exposing herself, more and more. Until there is nothing left of her. And yet, everyone watches on, wanting to see how she'll react.

"All rise," the somber-faced clerk announces, and everyone rustles to their feet as Judge Haslam walks in.

Even the judge acts more formal this morning. He surveys the courtroom, the public gallery, his eyes wandering to the dock and then to her, and finally to the barristers. O'Leary and Simmons look at him, Quilligan and the defence counsel on the other side. Four white wigs, sitting awkwardly on these unmoving heads.

"Are we ready to let the jury in?" he asks the clerk. The usher opens the door.

The jury file in. They have been in deliberation for hours now – at least 3 hours yesterday, and another hour or so today. That can't be good news.

The jury find their seats, sit down obediently.

Judge Haslam leans into his microphone with a benevolent half-smile. "Now, ladies and gentlemen of the jury, I need to remind you that the verdict in this case needs to be a unanimous one. Mr Foreman, can you confirm that your decision has been unanimous?"

The foreman, the second-oldest looking man on the jury, the one with the graying temples nods.

"Then let's proceed."

The clerk speaks: "Will the defendant, John Michael Sweeney, please stand?"

There's a ripple in the courtroom as everyone turns around to see the boy stand up. Jen and Barbara turn, too. But she keeps looking straight ahead.

It strikes her as surreal and a little ironic, that he is behind her again, the same way he trailed her that afternoon. *Him* following *her* up the Glen, up the slope, to that place where the forest meets the field.

Keep looking ahead. Don't look back.

"Will the foreman please stand?"

He stands, assumes that male, reporting-for-duty stance, his arms a V in front, right hand grasping his left wrist. She wonders if he's ex-military. And if that's a good thing or a bad thing.

"Will you please confine yourself to answering my first question simply, yes or no."

The foreman nods.

"Members of the jury, have you reached a verdict upon which you are all agreed in respect to this indictment?"

"Yes."

She shifts her gaze from the foreman, stares into the middle distance, at the blank wood panel below where the judge sits. At this moment of truth, she can't bear to look at anyone. Just the wood.

"On Count 1 of this indictment, rape by vaginal penetration, do you find the defendant John Michael Sweeney guilty or not guilty?"

At the same time, Jen and Barbara squeeze her hands.

*

He don't think he can stand, when the clerk asks him to.

He wants to run and hide, or duck under the seat. But there's nowhere to go, and the clerk, the judge, the jury, them security guards inside with him, they're all waiting for him to get up. The whole fucking lot of them, giving him an eyeful.

Get up, you gobshite.

He can tell that's what Da's thinking, just outside the box. The same fucking line he'd mumble after giving him a good lamping.

Legs feel like fucking water. He wants to piss, shit, and puke all at the same time.

Get up, you gobshite.

Then he sees the back of the woman's head. She ain't turned around, for whatever reason. No creepy glares from her this time. So he pins his eyes on her glossy black hair, almost like pushing against it to get up.

Don't turn around, don't turn around. If you just stay like that, not looking at me, I can stand.

He gets to his feet, looks ahead.

"On Count 1 of this indictment, rape by vaginal penetration, do you find the defendant John Michael Sweeney guilty or not guilty?"

The foreman doesn't hesitate a moment, answers in a loud voice.

"We find the defendant guilty."

The other words hardly reach him. Anything else your man says is blocked out. Like he's underwater and the rest of the world's above, and everything's out of reach.

The judge is saying something and most everyone looking at him, and Da is looking down at his feet, like he's ashamed or something.

Guilty.

Guilty guilty guilty.

Now some people in the room are smiling, whispering like, yeah that tinker boy deserved it, but the judge is still talking.

"Sit down," one of them security guards mutters to him.

He does.

But then another second and everyone's standing up because the judge is leaving.

But stand up or sit down, it don't matter, because he's still thrashing around underwater, trying to gasp for air, but knowing that he'll never get to the top now.

*

The moment she hears it, she closes her eyes.

Relief floods through her, returning after a year of drought, to wash away the anxiety and the nausea and the fear.

She hears the other counts, anal rape and battery, and she hears that word repeated twice again: guilty.

Jen and Barbara are crushing her in a hug now, murmuring congratulations. Tears trickle down Jen's face and gleam in Barbara's eyes. And even though she feels the tears welling up again, she forces herself not to cry. Not yet. Not now.

Detective Morrison is turning to her with a giant grin on his face – is she imagining it, or do his eyes look moist, too? And Simmons is smiling at her, and even O'Leary, too. Smiling and nodding.

Judge Haslam is still talking.

"Mr Sweeney, you will be requested for sentencing in the next few weeks. In the meantime, you will remain in remand, and transferred to the appropriate facility. I hope in the years moving forward, you will be able to look back on this crime and learn to rehabilitate your behavior during your sentence."

He turns to her. His tone changes, almost apologetic.

"Ms Tan, I thank you for your time and your cooperation in getting this crime convicted. You've been a most remarkable complainant – a most remarkable victim, should I say – and I hope this verdict is the beginning of a positive process of healing for you, after such a grievous assault to your person. While I can't imagine this experience in court has been a pleasant one for you, it has been vital for the proper functioning of our criminal justice system. And on behalf of all of us in the court system and the Department of Justice, I hope this verdict serves as *some* compensation for the horrible injustice that was done to you while visiting Belfast last year."

She nods back at the judge, knowing it's likely the last time she'll ever see this man.

She wants to thank him, but it's not her turn to speak. Because now the judge is finished. And this case is over.

*

"Serves you right." Some fucking punter says this to him as he walks past. The other ones muttering, giving him dirty looks.

Some reporters look like they want to ask him something, but Da shoos them away. They're all going after her, anyway.

That woman. Of course, people only care about her.

She won, that bitch won, and he has how many years ahead of him in jail?

"Sorry how it went." Michael is shaking his head. "It weren't fair, how they treated you from the start. Maybe we can appeal."

"Easy for you to say. What's the longest you've ever been inside? Six months?"

Da looks at him, serious and grim, but not like he's gonna lamp him.

"I'm sorry, Johnny," he finally says. "Bad luck today."

Bad luck? Whose fucking idea was it to give me up to the police in the first place? If it weren't for Da, he'd of gotten away. Over the border to Dublin, and he'd be down there perfectly free, living like normal. Or maybe somewhere even farther – France or Spain or somewhere warm. Mallorca.

"We'll come see you in prison soon," Da says. "Soon as we can. Try and bring your mam too."

But the worst is just then. It's not Da or Michael, mumbling their shite at him, it's her. The woman. From the corner of his eye, he can sketch her turning around. And before he can help it, he looks over.

She's looking straight at him. Only for a second. No one else catches this. But there's a gleam in her eyes. Something intense. A year ago, maybe, or at a pub, he'd find that gleam sexy, some sorta invitation from across the room.

But now it's telling him something different. *See that?* she's saying. *I just fucked you over.*

*

One final look at him and she's done. He's finished, out of her life. She'll never have to worry about that boy again.

But she knows what awaits her once she exits the courtroom. Already a few journalists have crowded round and she told them she'd speak to them outside.

Deep breath. It's time to face the press.

Outside the courtroom, it's not like in the movies, with a crowd of reporters shoving their microphones in her face. These are print journalists, they're respectful, they come up to her, almost one by one. They're mostly young-looking women, who scribble away on notepads, hold out slim audio recorders.

Ms Tan, obviously we will retain your anonymity from the media...

Ms Tan, how do you feel about the verdict?

How long do you think he should go to prison for?

What's the first thing you're going to do now?

Will this help you to move on?

It strikes her, how bland and surface her answers are. "Obviously, I'm pleased that he's been found guilty on all three counts... it's been an agonizing process for me... I'm just glad it's all over."

What can she say that doesn't sound clichéd in some way? How can any articulate statement possibly convey what she's just been through? Not just the trial itself, but the loneliness, the fear, her diminished sense of self? Even now, with this verdict, she suspects her life won't magically bounce back.

But she doesn't say this. These journalists aren't after depth. They just want a quote for their deadlines that evening. She answers their questions dutifully, even though the exhaustion is starting to get to her.

She turns to go, flanked by Jen and Barbara, but a journalist shouts out one final question.

"Ms Tan, do you think you'll ever come back to Belfast, after something like this?"

She hadn't anticipated that one.

"It's… tough to say. I haven't really thought that far ahead."

A murmur of appreciative laughter, but they're still standing there, expecting something more.

"If he'd been found not guilty, it would have been a definite no. But now, well, at least there's hope I might come back."

She smiles, a wry little smile, and the journalist gives her a nod, before she turns away, her boots echoing down the hall.

PART
FIVE

She does not hear the man the first time he speaks.

She is facing the brilliant blue of the Mediterranean, her back to the rest of the world, and the wind and the surf drown out his words.

She turns, catching the end of his sentence, realizing he must be speaking to her in Croatian. He is roughly her age, standing a decent distance behind her, and strikingly handsome. Dark hair, blue eyes, strong jawline. But clearly addressing her, because there is no one else around.

He speaks again, this time in accented English.

"Hello, are you okay?"

"Oh, um..."

"Sorry, I did not mean to scare you."

He holds his arm out, a half-gesture of apology.

"It's okay, I was just admiring the view." The sea is behind her, turquoise waves crashing against the rock face below them.

"My friends and I were just wondering, we saw you here on your own, and... will you join us for a drink?"

"Your friends?"

Surprised by this invitation, she looks around, but can see no one else on this escarpment overlooking the sea. It is mid-afternoon, too early for locals to watch the sunset from this seaside pathway. The Mediterranean sun drenches the surrounding cliffs in a focused light.

"Oh, you cannot see them, but we are just over there. It is hidden, we have a clubhouse, you see."

The man gestures to his right, further along the path, and apprehension immediately prickles the back of her neck.

"Come, you can see for yourself."

He takes a few steps in that direction. Keeping her

distance, she takes a few steps too, reassures herself that she can bolt at any moment, if she needs to. She glances again behind her – wide open spaces, no one else around.

Three days ago, she was in Belfast, at the sentencing hearing of the boy. Six weeks since the trial and she found herself sitting in court one final time, mere meters from him in the dock, watching as another judge passed down a sentence of ten years in prison.

A day later, she was surfing online and decided to book a flight. One-way to Split, returning from Dubrovnik six days later. It would be her first time traveling to a new country on her own, since the attack. But it seemed right.

He's been sentenced to ten years. You've done your job. Now you can start to relax.

Escape London with its interminable grey skies, the apartment windows that continually showcase the world while keeping her glassed in. The tired faces of strangers, this city where people avoid eye contact, day in and day out.

So this morning she flew to Split, one of the oldest cities in Croatia. Hadn't even booked any accommodation in advance. But stepping off the bus from the airport, the Mediterranean sun shone bright, and old men and women crowded round the tourists, holding up signs for private rooms available to rent. Within fifteen minutes, an old man was showing her a bedroom in his second-floor apartment, where he and his wife lived. She bargained him down to 350 kuna for two nights, and just like that, she had the keys in her pocket and was free to wander the city's ruins.

It was coming back to her, this ability to travel. A sense of her old self. The forgotten thrill of new cities, waiting to be discovered.

Tomorrow she will visit Trogir, and the next day catch a ferry to Dubrovnik. From there, maybe she can take a day trip to Bosnia or Montenegro.

Now, she hesitates as she watches this handsome Croatian man clambering along a path that skirts the rock face, turning to see if she will follow him.

A male stranger approaches you when you are all alone. He seems friendly. How do you react?

It's like a question on an aptitude exam, a question she knew was coming but had no idea how to prepare for. For over a year, she's avoided answering it. She's been sequestered at home, cautious, untrusting. Not the Vivian who would jump on a plane, armed with only a light backpack and a guidebook, excited by the unknown.

Today, she decides to follow the man, remaining a safe distance behind. The path leads around a rocky headland, the Mediterranean crashing a few meters below.

Beyond the headland, the path opens onto a flat, patio-like shelf, the rock walls protecting it like a grotto. Here the man stands, in front of a table laden with food, and five other men sit in chairs around it. They are a variety of ages, most of them middle-aged and grey-haired.

They grin and wave hello to her.

"See, from here, we saw you standing on your own." He points to where she had been watching the ocean before, though their location now is hidden. "We thought we could offer you a drink or something to eat."

The men nod and she looks at the table. Home-cooked dishes of meat and fish, grilled vegetables, what looks like pasta. Another man emerges from a doorway in the rock face and he's carrying a glass and a bottle of wine.

"Please," the first man says. "He is Drago, and this is wine his cousin makes."

Glasses of wine are poured out, including one for her.

"*Zivjeli*," she says in Croatian, holding her glass up, and the men are impressed.

"*Zivjeli*," they answer back. *Cheers. Life is beautiful.* She takes a tentative sip.

"This is fish we caught this morning. Please try some." Another man gestures to a dish on the table. "And this rabbit, it is a local dish here in Dalmatia."

"This is your clubhouse?" she asks, hardly believing the feast in front of her. She looks around at the cliff walls that shelter them, the view onto the sparkling sea. "This is incredible."

The men grin, proud. The first one, who clearly speaks the best English, explains. "We come here every Sunday afternoon, to get away from our families, and we fish and we cook and eat. It's very nice."

"Please, you are a visitor, we want you to try some of our local food."

They have made a chair available for her and are setting out a plate and cutlery. Something is taut within her, the familiar tension she has carried for over a year now. But perhaps it is starting to ease in the heat and the light of the sun.

"You have time to join us?" The first man asks her this.

"Sorry, I am Tomo," he says introducing himself, his hand on his chest. She notices he is wearing a wedding band. This puts her somewhat at ease.

"My name's Vivian." She smiles slightly and looks at the other men nodding. She sits down then, the metal of the chair grating against the rock, and the Mediterranean sun is warm on her back.

*

"Johnny boy, there's someone to see you."

That screw, Elliott, says this through the window to him and he sits up on his bed, where he'd been lying, fucking bored out of his mind, for the past hour.

"Yeah?"

Hopefully Michael or Kevo, probably Da. He rolls his eyes. Here we go again.

But the screw's grinning at him, different from normal. "You're lucky. This one's a girl, not too bad neither."

A girl? He don't know no girls. Maybe Nora Callahan from next door...

"She got a kid with her?"

"Naw, too young for that. Though maybe not for you lot."

Then again, seems Nora started hating him the moment she heard what he done to that woman. In a couple of years, the only girls he's seen are the ones visiting other lads here.

"Surprised, eh? Us, too. Can't imagine why any girl would want to see a sick perv like you."

He grimaces at Elliott. Always hated this one anyway.

The screw laughs, as he unlocks his cell door. "After you, rapist."

When he comes into the visiting room, he don't recognise her. Curly brown hair, her face turned down. Skinny, a nice coat with a belt.

He steps in front of the little table, coughs. Still don't know who the fuck this is.

"Johnny!" she says, looking up. Gets to her feet, a wide grin on her face that fades to a small, shy smile when he don't react.

Freckled face, blue eyes like his own.

"Claire? What you doing up here?" Realises he's smiling. Just to see a new person, someone he don't have to play no games with.

Her voice is so different. Almost like a woman. "I come up here to see you, Johnny. Huh, you've changed. So much taller now!"

"Same as you."

"Well, it's been a long time." That's for sure. Last time he saw her, she was nine? Ten?

"How old you now, Claire?"

"Fifteen." She grins. And he can't believe it, but his own sister's turning into a beour. Someone the lads would try to shift at a bar.

"You're seventeen now, right, Johnny?"

He nods. Miserable seventeenth birthday he had, here in jail. Michael and Da and the lads brought a cake, they ate it in a room with one of them screws watching. Couldn't have no proper drink nor nothing. Slipped him some yokes and porn mags, as a present, but later, the other lads here stole the mags, so he couldn't even look at them when he was rolling.

"You come up to Belfast on your own?" he asks.

"You mad? Mam wouldn't let me, all on me own. I come up with me friend Josie and her auntie Pauline. Just for a few days, you know. Belfast's really different now."

"Yeah, I guess." The fuck would he know.

They chat away. Weird as fuck talking to his sister grown up. Can't believe this is the same brat who wouldn't stop crying, always whinging when he and Michael went off together and left her at home with the babby. She uses big words. Sounds like she's been learnt at a school or something.

"How's Bridget? And Sean?"

"They're grand. A lot bigger than when you saw them. Bridget's eleven. Sean is nine."

He can't imagine either of them two being able to say a normal word even. Always crawling around in nappies.

"And uh… Mam? How's she?"

He sees the catch in Claire's look.

He don't want to really hear the answer. Tried not to think about Mam most of these years, how she'd react to the news about him. She never did come and visit.

Claire's shifting her eyes around. "Mam's, uh… she sends her love. Working hard, the three of us to look after."

"Working? You mean, outside?"

He jerks at the thought of this.

"Yeah, she works at a creche, minding other women's kids. It's good work, pays decent and all. And Bridget and Sean can be there, too."

"How long she been doing that for? Minding buffer kids?"

"Oh, a few years now."

He wonders if Da knew about any of that. "You seeing Da or Michael at all when you're here?"

Claire stops short, like she don't know what to say. "Yeah, I might."

"You might? Come up all the way to Belfast, you might not even seen your own da?"

Claire frowns at him, almost like she's gonna speak up. "He's not the easiest to get ahold of, y'know? Neither him nor Michael. Don't answer their phones half the time."

"Yeah, that's for sure."

"Besides..."

The drink, the lampings. Not exactly fond memories she has of Da, most likely.

"I come up here to see you. At least you don't move around so much these days. Kinda stuck in one place, hey?"

"Aw, fuck off!" He smirks and she laughs, her teeth gleaming and nose crinkling up. He don't think he's ever seen Claire laugh like that.

He finds himself laughing, too. First time in he don't know how long.

Claire asks him more questions, wants to know what it's like inside.

Lots of buffers, but even them other pavees don't always want to go with him. Some don't like the Sweeneys, they'll lay in wait to spring on him. He don't tell her this though.

And does he have other friends?

"Mmm, some."

Word got out what he was in for. That famous rape. Of the Chinky American woman. After that, no one wanted to be near him. Or they'd lamp him a good one when they got the chance, or tried something even worse, but the screws keep a good eyeful, at least.

"What kind of stuff they make you do in here?"

He shrugs. "Boring shite. Laundry and chores and all that. There's a workshop where you can make things in wood or metal, if you're lucky. They're making me do some schooling."

"Schooling? You?" Claire looks like she wants to laugh again. "Like, maths and reading and writing?"

"Yeah."

"*You* can read?" She laughs. "I gotta tell Mam that. Go on, tell me what you can read."

He shrugs. "I don't know, just some kiddie books for now."

"Like what? You read Harry Potter?"

347

He backs off. "Naw, that stuff's for babies."

"Oh, it's too easy for you, is it?"

"Naw, it's…" Actually, he can't manage Harry Potter yet. "I'm not reading no books about wizards and shite."

"So what d'ya like to read?"

"Some comic books and stuff." Comic books and porn. Wouldn't be able to last through prison without them two.

Claire nods, looks at him sly from the corner of her eyes.

"Sounds like *you* been schooling," he says. "What, Mam got you going to school everyday?"

"Yeah, for years now. Monday to Friday."

He shudders. "Fucking awful, that must be."

"No, I like it."

Now it's his turn to laugh. "Sure you do."

"I do! The homework's a pain sometimes. But I like it. Now I can read the letters that come in the post for Mam. I'm gonna try and get me Leaving Cert."

"Leaving Cert! No way, you're joking."

Claire giggles again. "Am not, it's only a few more years."

"I don't believe it." And he shakes his head at Claire, but still grins. "So this school, is it for buffers or Travellers?"

"Mainly Travellers. There's some buffers, too. They ain't too bad. Not with so many of us around."

He's shaking his head. "Mam working, you getting a Leaving Cert, school just for Travellers. What the fuck's happening down in Dublin?"

"It's good." Claire shrugs. "We've a nice new house we're living in."

"Bigger than before?"

"Yeah. And a better area to live. And Leaving Cert would be great, but anyways, they'll be wanting me to get married soon."

"Why, you've a fella?"

Now this is too much. The thought of his little sister with some greasy chancer.

"No, I don't." She blushes. "No one yet. But you know all them aunties and uncles are starting on it, making comments about finding a nice boy... Annoying, really." She rolls her eyes.

They're quiet for a moment. Claire looks around her, at the other lads meeting with their mams and wives at their little tables, everyone chattering.

"You have trouble finding the place?" he asks.

"Naw, Josie's auntie drove me here. She's, uh... she's actually waiting outside for me..."

"Oh, so's..."

"So I should get going."

"Oh right, yeah." He's surprised she's staying for so short. Almost wishes she could stay longer. But he don't know what to say.

"Well, uh, you have the address here, so's you can write me if you want."

"Can you read a letter if I send it?" Claire asks.

"I can try," he grins. "Got a lot of fucking time in here to learn."

"All right, we'll see. I won't put no tough words in the letter or nothing. Start you off easy."

"Hey now!" He stands as she gets up, his little sister all grown, talking back like this. It's weird, but good.

Something crosses her face. "Johnny, what was it like?"

For a second, he almost feels that clawing again. That old friend that comes back when he's at his worst. "What?"

"The, um, the trial?"

"Oh that." He shrugs. "Bunch of shite, really. A load of questions I didn't understand. Everyone staring at me the whole time. I hated it."

"Was it tough?"

No one's really ever asked him that before. Da and Michael with their shrugging and muttering. Some of the counsellors in here asked him, too, but didn't really care what he said.

"It, uh... it weren't easy. I didn't get what they were saying half the time."

Claire looks like she wants to ask another question, but he's relieved when she don't.

"Oh, I forgot, we made some cake for you, but they says I can't bring it in. So here's, um…"

Claire's fiddling with her necklace now, she's wearing a glittery heart-shaped locket, opening it up, digging something out. A small colorful bit of paper, cut into a heart to fit the locket. She holds it out on the tip of her finger. It's a photo of her, Mam, and must be Bridget and Sean. They're smiling in the sun, arms round each other.

"That's us, you see?"

He frowns, 'cause he don't want no tears or nothing to come out. But somehow, the back of his throat is swelling. No space in that tiny heart for him or Michael or Da, it's too crammed already. He don't dare try to speak.

"Here, you can have it, Johnny. I can print out another at school."

He shakes his head but Claire keeps at it.

"I'll give it to the guard to give to you. It's yours to keep. Honest."

He looks at her from across the table, but his throat is still too thick for words.

Walking back to his cell, that colourful bit of paper tucked into his pocket, and that screw Elliott slides up to him, sneering.

"Got a girlfriend now, gypo?"

"She's me sister." He says this straight, almost protective.

"Yeah? Even better. I'd fuck her. Good and hard. Bet she'd like that, being your sister and all."

He don't say nothing. Just glares at Elliott and walks on.

*

"So this is our final session here at the Maudsley." Doctor Greene is saying this, smiling. The psychologist's blonde hair is in a pert ponytail, and outside the window, London is mellowing into a fine, tawny September. It's nearly a year and a half after the assault.

"We normally use this time to recap all the progress you've made in the previous fourteen sessions, as well as think of some next steps for how you envision your recovery moving ahead. Does that sound all right, Vivian?"

It sounds a bit frightening, in fact. These appointments with Doctor Greene have been a lifeline for her in the past year. When everything else in her life seemed cast adrift on that endless grey lake, her friends unsure of how to treat her, her job no longer feasible, she always knew Doctor Greene could offer some assurance, a practical understanding of this strange, directionless place she found herself in, and a possible way forward. She wishes she could see Doctor Greene more often, but the NHS has only allocated fifteen sessions of Cognitive Behaviour Therapy for her.

"So, how are you feeling these days?"

"Better." She looks around for the postcard of the lone palm tree on Doctor Greene's cork board, is relieved to see it again, this time surrounded by photos of her cats.

"I mean, a lot of those PTSD symptoms are gone... I don't have agoraphobia anymore. The panic attacks are gone, too. But I'm still really..." She pauses. "I'm just really down a lot of the time. I feel like I'm stuck."

Doctor Greene nods. "Well, let's think of how to get you un-stuck. Remember when I kept on asking you to tell the story of your attack? Over and over again?"

Of course she remembers. Week in, week out, having to recite the play-by-play of her assault, with as much detail as possible. Recording it on an audio tape, listening to it repeatedly, finding 'the point of greatest distress'. And through it all, feeling nauseous, wanting to just curl up into a ball in her bed and forget anything like this had ever happened.

"And remember the way we used cognitive behaviour therapy to counter the worst emotions you felt at that moment?"

The point in the narrative where I'm being choked...

"What were you feeling at that moment?"

The memory of not being able to breathe, the boy's fingers digging into her throat.

"I felt like I was going to die."

"And what would be so bad about dying?"

They've gone through this before, but reciting it is like some reassuring litany, a familiar call-and-response between a pastor and her one-person congregation.

"That I wouldn't live."

"And what would it mean to not live?"

"That I... wouldn't be able to travel to all the places in the world that I'd still like to see."

"And what else?"

"That I'd never get to have the kind of career I'd like to have."

"And what else?"

"That I'd never get to fall in love."

"And what else?"

"That I'd never get a chance to have a family, or children of my own..."

The doctor nods. "But you didn't die. You're still alive. So you can *still* do all those things you want to do. You can still travel, work again, have a career, meet someone, maybe have a family."

Doctor Greene is telling her this, as if they are abstract truths, but they seem far from the concreteness of her own reality now.

The psychologist moves to the whiteboard in her cramped office and starts to write on it in blue marker. *Travel. Career. Relationship. Family.*

The words are stacked vertically on top of each other, along the left side of the board. To the right of them, the board is still blank, a white space waiting to be filled.

She shudders to see her life goals spelled out so starkly, as if they were a grade-school lesson to be memorized.

"So I want you to think... what steps can you take. Even really small baby steps to start reclaiming these things which you can still have?"

To think like that seems too difficult, too single-minded. The old Vivian could have done it, flashing ahead with a solution in seconds. But now she sits daunted by these huge questions, these possibilities from a previous life. She forces back tears, the familiar feeling of uselessness.

"I don't... I don't know where to start."

Doctor Greene pushes on. "Travel. What can you do to start traveling again? Or maybe you've already started?"

There was the Croatia trip. It went a lot easier than expected. She had conversations with men and nothing happened to her. She was fine.

"So... do you think you could travel again?"

"I'd like to."

They talk about booking another trip, maybe one with a friend. Cheap flights within Europe are easy to find. It could just be a weekend away... For a brief moment, she feels that old sense of excitement flaming up again, a gleam of light from a door that cracks open somewhere. But then the familiar fear returns, and the door snaps shut. She is back in darkness, but she has been reminded.

"And career?"

This one is harder. She's never returned to that office in Old Street, aware of how much energy her job as a producer requires and how little of that she has now. Last year, she cut herself loose from Erika's company and this year, the company's been bought out. Roles have been consolidated, workloads possibly increased and she knew she wasn't up for the fight. All that striving, trying to prove to the world that she is full of ideas and initiative. The truth is, she isn't. Not right now.

She shrugs at the doctor. "My old job isn't there anymore, and I suppose in theory I'd like to work again in film, but I don't know when I'll be ready. And I have no idea how I'd go about getting a job."

"Are you desperate for money?"

"I'm on Incapacity Benefit, which helps." But it's not enough to cover the high cost of living in London, even when she's at her most frugal. For the moment, she's draining her way through her life savings.

"There's also some government compensation I should be

getting from the assault, but I've been told that'll take years to process."

She can't ask her parents for money. They still don't know about the attack, and asking them for money is something she would never consider. And besides, it's not so much about the cashflow, it's more about feeling useful, productive, good at something. Not like a traumatized wreck with no purpose in this world.

"So as one of your steps, would you say, start applying for jobs?"

More forms to fill out.

"I guess, but…"

All the effort of completing job applications; all the joy of being rejected. Besides, she knows that's not how jobs in the arts work. Nothing is advertised, everything is word-of-mouth. Out of the office for over a year and she feels like a complete outsider.

She explains this to Doctor Greene.

"Maybe just start thinking about the kind of job you'd like to have?"

But why tease yourself with delusions of something that can never happen? She can't go back to being the old Vivian, living and breathing for her exciting career. That much she knows.

Doctor Greene writes *Start thinking about types of jobs* on the whiteboard.

"And finally, relationship." She taps the whiteboard with the marker. "I'm going to fold the topic of family into this, as they're kind of related. How do you feel about the prospect of dating again?"

She groans, a kind of hopeless, wordless sulk.

"I don't feel great about it."

"So why do you feel that way?"

"I don't want to go on dates."

"And why not?"

She sighs, struggling to think of how she can put her thoughts into words.

"I know that boy was so far off the scale, he doesn't fit in the same category as most men. But... this whole thing about sex, guys wanting it. I just, I don't know. I don't want to have to negotiate all that again."

"You don't have to address sex right away. I mean, you could just start by having coffee with someone."

Yes, but it'll still always be there. The prospect of sex. That unspoken thing which undercuts every interaction with straight men. Even if you're just having coffee.

Doctor Greene continues, "Think of it this way, if you do want to have a relationship some day, you *will* have to go on a date with at least one person in the future, right?"

There's no arguing with that logic. She laughs. "Guess so."

"So, just think about it. Go to a singles' night with some friends. You don't have to expect anything from it, but just be in that space, and see how you feel."

She nods. The prospect still fills her with a certain nausea, but she can try.

On the board, next to *Relationship*, Doctor Greene writes *Singles' night with friends?*

She puts the marker down and the two of them look at the board.

"Do you think you could consider trying some of these steps in the next week?"

It seems so cut and dried. A three-step instruction manual to rebuilding her life. Part of her thinks, what's the point in planning? You can plan all you want, but you can't ever predict when a complete stranger is going to barge into your life and destroy your entire world within minutes. But the other part of her — the optimist, the achiever, maybe a ghost of the old Vivian — sees the words on the whiteboard and thinks that she can do it.

Still, she remains torn, apprehensive.

Doctor Greene looks at her warmly. "I know it seems tough, but you should be proud of all the progress you've made in the past year. You've worked really hard. You've kept pushing yourself to go out of your comfort zone, you just need to push yourself a little farther and you'll get there."

*

For years, it's been the same. These... these interventions. Sitting in a room with a counsellor. Then in a group with some other lads and a counsellor. Talking and talking.

'Cause talking solves everything, right?

We want you to start thinking about what brought you here in the first place.

We want you to understand your part in it all. How that kind of behavior impacted on another person.

We want to make sure you're making progress, Johnny.

Progress is this cartoon staircase on a poster hanging above their heads. And the coloured steps going up: Acceptance. Regret. Understanding. Changing. Renewal.

It's all shite but he gets why he has to go. It's about starting new. That's what he'd like to do. As long as that means getting the fuck out of here.

At first he hated it.

He tells the story, the version he tells everyone here. Good thing they don't ask for too much detail. Just they had sex outside, she left, and then the whole town's screaming about the rape.

The others got stories of their own, which he hears in time. All about girls, too. Paddy, it was this girl he was seeing, on and off. They got drunk, they got in a fight, he got angry, he wanted to show her. Then, next thing he knows, he's getting arrested two days later. She still had the bruises.

Dan, it was a younger girl, thirteen or fourteen. She was a friend of his niece. She was smiling at him, all giggly. Pretty girl for her age. He knew she wanted it, he just had to get her into a room on her own. She didn't seem to complain much, through all the times he done it with her. And he's the one getting arrested.

Paul is quiet, like. He says it was different women he'd

meet at bars. They were better after you put something in their drink. They wouldn't remember when they woke up, and he always put all their clothes back on, leave them on the couch so they wouldn't suspect nothing when they woke up. Except one or two, he weren't that careful with. And now he's here.

None of them want to be here. Everyone fucking hates this class, but they keep at it. Wanting them all to keep talking about this, about that, about women.

Them two that run the class, they're nice about it, at least. But it's clear no one's going anywhere, not up that cartoon staircase on some shite poster on the wall, not at all, if they're not gonna talk.

"Do you ever think about how the woman felt, after what you'd done to her?" your counsellor man Sam asks him this, and the others are looking at him.

"Like, what d'ya mean?"

"Imagine you're her. Put yourself in her shoes. You're visiting Belfast, going on a walk through this park, beautiful Saturday afternoon, just want to be on your own and enjoy the outdoors. And you come across a young boy, like yourself."

"But if I'm her, then I'm not a young boy no more."

Paddy and Dan snort. He had to point that out, just to get a laugh.

"Very clever, Johnny. You know what I mean."

"Naw, don't think I do."

"Johnny, this is the most crucial part of the intervention. I know it's tough and you may not want to think about it this way, but I want you to try real hard. Close your eyes, try to imagine you're her."

He grumbles, but does it. Pictures that spring afternoon again, sun and shade in the Glen. Only he's not rolling on a yoke this time.

Sam talks him through it. Musta taken notes on his story, because he knows it pretty well.

"What do you feel when this boy yells at you to shut up, tells you he wants to have sex with you, hits you?"

357

"Well, I'd lamp him something serious."

"No, but you're not yourself in this, Johnny. You're her. You've never punched anyone in your life before."

Can't imagine that. How do you not punch back?

"That don't make sense. Whoever I was, I'd lamp him some."

"Imagine you've never thrown a punch in your life. You've lived a very different life. You're on your own in a city you don't know well, and this boy's threatening you like this, demanding you have sex with him. You're very scared."

But he won't go there. He shrugs. "I wouldn't be scared."

Sam sighs, don't look happy. Nor is he. Just wants to get out of here, away from these fucking questions.

"Let's try it another way. You meet someone, who comes up to you, asks for directions. You trust this person, he doesn't seem dangerous..."

"I wouldn't trust no one!" he shouts. "That was her problem. She shouldna done that. Coming up near us, trying to go on that walk on her own. She was fucking asking for it."

"No, Johnny, no." Sam says this sharp and looks at him angry. He's dropped the nice act. "You can't say that. You can't assume someone's asking for it. Not someone you don't know at all. You have no right to interfere in someone else's life like that."

Oh, and like all them others have a right to interfere in mine?

But he don't say this. Just glares at Sam.

"She didn't provoke you. She didn't threaten you, she wasn't mean to you. What gives you the right to do something like that to her? She was very clear she didn't want it."

"So this is about rights, is it?"

"This is about respecting other people. Other people who have done you no harm."

"All them others... do they respect me?" He laughs. "I don't fucking think so. They hate me the minute they see me. No-good tinker boy, that's what they think."

"That's not true, Johnny." Sam shakes his head. "We don't think that of you. We're here trying to help you."

Sam looks around to the other lads. "Aren't we all here to help Johnny, the same way we're here to help all of you?"

Paddy, Dan, and Paul, the three of them look at him, open their mouths, not sure what to say.

"Yeah, of course," Paul says, and Paddy and Dan nod, too.

"Yeah."

"That's right."

But it's all just shite.

"Aw, fuck your help!" He swats at the air. "I don't need none of it."

"Johnny, we can't go through this world living entirely on our own," Sam says. "We need other people's help sometimes."

"Oh, for fuck's sake, you lot know nothing."

Sam almost looks hurt. "Johnny, I've been doing this for years now…"

"Well, go do it on the other lads. How comes no one makes me da go through all this? Or Michael? Why's it have to be me? Or any them others, sometimes done worse things and got away with it?"

"It'll come to them in time. It will. Trust me on this, Johnny."

But that he definitely don't trust.

He shakes his head and stares at Sam. Won't take part no more in this load of ridiculous shite. He gets up and walks away, though he has to stop where the room ends because there's screws on the other side of the window, staring in at him.

These people are blind, like. Think everything's fair, everything's gonna work out, that the people who deserve what they got will get it. And if you work hard and are nice to others and all that shite, then life will be good to you. All cheery and nice and pointing to that staircase over and over.

What the fuck.

What do they know.

"Johnny, how's your writing skills coming along? Davey tells me you're good. Smart. You can write good sentences now."

"Guess I'm all right."

There's some others in his class. Harry and Ciaran, real fucking dumb nuts. At least he's not one of them.

"Well, how's about we do something different today? None of this talking."

No shite talking. That's a start.

"What you got?"

Sam sits down at the desk next to him. Sitting in the chair backwards, so he's straddling, his legs on either side, and leaning in close.

He pulls back. Sam better not be trying it on with him. Too many bent chancers have pulled that shite on him here.

"How about instead of talking today, you try writing a letter."

What, should he be shouting for joy? He keeps staring at Sam.

"Just have a go, might not work out. But this letter's going to be addressed to someone in particular."

"What kinda letter?"

"Don't worry, it's not actually going to be posted out. But I want you to think about writing a letter to the woman you met in the park. The woman you did this to, what led you to coming here."

Jaysus, what the fuck. "Why you want me to do that?"

"Like I said, it's not something she's going to see, unless you want to send it to her. But write a letter and tell her how you feel about what happened."

"What's the point of writing it if she ain't actually going to see it?"

Sam sighs. "Johnny, this is a way for you to express your feelings about what you've done. If you feel angry, then write that. If you feel guilty, then write that, too."

"Still don't see the point."

"Tell you what, if you write it, that's a big achievement, both for your schooling and for you. Davey and I will make sure you get some enhancements. Maybe you can use them to buy a new video game or even a DVD player in your cell."

He thinks about that. Been getting bored of playing the same games, after all.

"And she's not going to read it?"

"No, the only people reading it will be me, Davey, and your officer, Conor."

That's three people too many, but fuck it, what does he care? Everything's the same inside this shite place anyway.

He nods. "Yeah, all right."

"Very good, Johnny. That's great. I'll get you some pencil and paper then."

Sam gets up and claps him on the shoulder. He flinches and hunches over. Writing letters to the woman. What's next, baking a cake for her?

Dear Woman,

But Sam stops him right there.

"No, Johnny, write her actual name. Do you remember it?"

"Yeah."

"Well, call her by her actual name."

He's still holding the pencil above the paper, fingers not moving.

"What's her name, Johnny?"

"It's something like... it's Vivian."

'Course he knows that name. Weird name. Never knew anyone else with it, kinda old-timey and British. Who the fuck names their kid Vivian these days?

"Do you know how to spell it?"

"V..."

Sam's looking at him, that hopeful wide-eyed look these types get when talking to him.

"Viv, so, V... I... V..."

Sam's nodding. "Great, you got it."

"Vivi-an... V-I-V... Viv-ee-un... E?"

Sam shakes his head. "It's like the boy's name 'Ian'... Viv-Ian."

"V-I-V... I-A-N?"

A wide grin from Sam. "Perfect. That's it! Now write it out."

Don't want to admit it, but a flip of pride he's figured out that name.

Pencil on paper, and he writes out the big letters.

Dear VIVIAN,

Here's him, feeling proud for spelling out the name of the woman. Oh Christ, the shite Michael would say about this. The highlight of his fucking week here in prison.

But Michael don't need to know. None of them need to know. Just three of them gonna read this letter. He thinks, and taps the pencil against the desk.

Dear VIVIAN,

I am writing this be coz they say I shud. What do I hav to say to you?

I probly shud not have dun that to you. I am here inside prison becoz of it now. I have been here 3 almost 4 yrs now. I dont like it here, but its ok I guess. I want to be out side.

That day I did that to you. I was hi. On drugs. I thout you looked good, like some girls I have saw in the pornos sometim. That got me thinking. I also thout like you wanted to know me. Not many peple want to know me. But you spoke to me were nice, and so I wanted to do it.

I probly shud not have hit you, but I am good at that. At hiting. That is how I get things sometim. Sometimes they say I do things like I am a monster, but it just happens.

I dont know were you are now but its probly better then me in prison. I guess I hop you are ok. They say you are very hurt by what I dun to you. I guess I am sorry then. To be in side here. And I cant wait to get out.

I saw how you looked at me in cort. And you probly hate me. But you won and now Im here. So Im sorry it happend.

Bye,
Johnny

He remembers now, sitting by the trail, after the deed, both of them covered in mud. He'd said sorry to the woman. It just kinda came out. But yeah, he's sorry now. Four years inside will make you sorry.

He folds the paper in half, hands it to Sam. Who looks at him, unfolds it, gets up to read it a few desks over.

His head fucking hurts from all that thinking and writing.

Fuck the staircase.

*

His hearing is coming up. Michael's been giving him advice for months now. What he should say at the hearing this time around, now that he's up for probation.

"You know what they want to hear. If you don't say some things, they'll never let you out."

So yeah, all the usual: *I feel sorry for my victim now, I feel bad, I know what I done wrong…*

I realise the error of my ways.

He laughs at that one. Who the fuck speaks like that?

They'd never believe him if he said that.

So he's been practicing. Pacing up and down his cell at night, mouthing them words. *I been inside for five years now and I wish hadn't come to prison. But I had to. 'Cause otherwise, I would of kept on doing those things – fighting and doing drugs and lashing out at people, just 'cause I didn't know them.*

"Don't make it sound like you been practicing," Michael warned him. "You gotta sound like you really mean it."

And does he mean it?

Well, yeah. He wishes to hell he hadn't done that and

ended up here. He wouldn't of picked such a smart beour, he wouldn't of let her get away. Now, if he stepped into that same park, met that same girl, or another like her... Would he? Hard to say. At least he knows what it's like to get caught now.

So when that fucker Elliott come to unlock him this morning, he'd put on the white shirt, the one makes him look grown up. He's allowed to dress nice for this meeting. Conor came right up to the cell, too. Smiled at him, shook his hand, serious, man to man.

"I know you can wow them today, Johnny. I know you got it in you."

He took one more look at the card Claire sent him, lying on his bed. Big sunny card with cartoon trees and a cottage on a hill.

Good luck, Johnny – from all of us. We know you will do good and we will see you soon. Lots of love.

It was signed by all of them: Claire, Bridget, Sean, and, scrawled at the end (in Claire's handwriting), Mam.

And last week, he even spoke to Mam over the phone. Weird call. Not much said. She sounded real different, brighter somehow.

"Johnny, I will be so proud of you when you get out."

His own fucking mam said that. First time he heard her voice in years.

"You should come down here to Dublin, stay with us. You'd like it. Get away from Belfast for a bit. Lots of good things for Travellers happening down here."

So he's thinking that, as he goes down the hall with Conor and Elliott.

Come down here to Dublin. Get away from Belfast.

Conor is muttering some things as they walk along, but he's hardly hearing them.

"Don't forget to mention all the work you've done in the intervention programme. What Sam said about your progress. Of course, I'll say it, too, but it's even better if you talk about it yourself."

But even Da, even fucking Da had something to say about this hearing.

"Try not to fuck this up."

That was his advice.

"We'll sort something out for you nice, when you get out. Found a house you could live in, maybe with Michael or Kevo. Owned by another Traveller, he'll rent it to us."

He thinks of that. Not living in a caravan. No more wind rattling the walls and tromping out in the cold to hook up the generator. And no view of Belfast, all spread out with the hills below him and the waterfall and hardly no one else to bother him.

Instead, living in a house. Four walls, stairs, with buffer families all around. Everyone into your business. He's not so sure.

And here they are now, at the end of the walk. A blank door that Conor knocks on, before turning to him and winking. Conor's like a puppy, that excited. Rubbing his hands and eager to please. Gestures for him to go first, and in through the doorway now, with Conor yapping and Elliott silent behind.

Inside the room, a long table with three people behind it. All old, all serious.

"John Michael Sweeney, is it?" A man he don't know says this.

"Yes, that's right." Standing still, looking them in the eye, like Conor told him to.

There's papers in front of them on the table. Stacks of files, and the same file opened up before each of them.

"Please, Mr Sweeney, have a seat."

*

Four years after the assault and she is hiking on her own in Oman. In a valley. In the dark. She hadn't quite planned it this way, but sooner or later, she knew she'd have to start hiking again. That familiar urge had lain dormant for so many years, hemmed in by a cloud of fear, and finally, in a foreign country where she couldn't even remotely understand the language, she told herself she would attempt her first solo hike in years.

It had happened almost imperceptibly, the chain of small decisions which led her to this valley on her own at the age of thirty-three. She had wanted simply to get away from London, the job rejections, all her friends moving on in their adult lives while she stagnated. After years of unemployment, she received a temporary job offer to work on a film festival in Dubai. So now, after working that festival, she's escaped Dubai's glitzy, artificial towers by coming to Oman. Here in Mutrah, a seaside town on the north coast of the Arabian Peninsula, mosques exhale the call to prayer and a range of low dry hills stretches its rugged arms down to the sea. Her guidebook has a suggested hike through those hills, an easy 2km through Wadi Ban Khalid, starting from a steep flight of stone stairs behind an outlying village.

At 5pm she had found herself at the foot of this staircase, staring up. The steps climbed the rocky hillside towards a notch in the ridge, enticing her to follow, but the ominous similarities of the situation were not lost on her. Another Saturday afternoon, another hike described in the guidebook.

She'd delayed making a decision until this late in the afternoon, and now, with the sun starting to set, she doubted there would be enough daylight to finish the hike.

Maybe just walk up to see the view from the top, she told herself.

So up the dry, rocky face of the hills, her heart pounding to catch up when she reached the crest of the ridge. To one side, the view was stunning. Muscat's series of forts gleamed white against the blue of the ocean in the late afternoon light. Down below, the traffic coursed along on the coastal road, and closer yet, she heard a baby crying in the village she just left.

She could just stay here, and go back down the staircase, but it was too late. The excitement and curiosity had gotten the better of her. What would the old Vivian have done, the one from four years ago? The old Vivian wouldn't have stopped now.

So in the waning sunlight, she crossed over the ridge, eager to push on.

Now, a mere thirty minutes later, it's practically dark. She forgot the sun set so quickly this close to the equator. And she has no idea how much further the trail will take her. On this side of the ridge, the valley is completely barren and rocky, like a primeval landscape, with the heat of the day still rising from the rocks. But there is something calming about it, an otherworldly place, far removed from everything beyond that ridge.

She is still haunted by an eighteen-month relationship in London, which has recently come to an unexpected, cruel end. In her interaction with her boyfriend, despite all the pleasantness, there had always been a gap of understanding somewhere, a void in her recent past she explained, but which he was never willing to fully grasp. And their breakup conversation had confirmed her hidden fears. 'Besides, I don't think most guys would really feel comfortable dating a rape victim,' he had said as a parting shot.

So she has taken that pain and decided to bury it. Here in Oman, through her tears, she has been following the yellow and white blazes on the rock face, which mark out the course of the path. But these have been harder to see, the more the daylight has faded. As she walks on in the empty valley, there is a gradual leaching of color from the hills. Adrenaline stirs in her, as evening sets in. She reminds herself there is nothing to fear. Until now, all her troubles have been caused by other people, and now, there are no other people around. And even if they were, they would not be able to see her in the dark.

Forget that conversation. Forget London. Just lose yourself in this landscape.

The valley merges with another and here the trail disintegrates. She stumbles among rocks and dry gravel, passes the huddled shapes of ruins in front of her. The path must be somewhere, she just can't see it yet. In a panic, she reaches for her flashlight, but already her eyes are becoming accustomed to the dark, starting to recognize forms among the black and gray. Turn on the flashlight and she'll ruin her night vision. On the eastern side of the sky, the moon has risen. Half a moon, casting enough light to distinguish tree from rock from ground. And then a new thought occurs to her, even more intriguing than the one which brought her here in the first place: what if she completed this entire hike in the dark, using only the light of the moon?

The sheer audacity of it excites her. When is the next chance she'll have to hike a trail like this on a moonlit night in Oman on her own? Possibly never. The flashlight is still there just in case. But she's going to try.

Slowly, she starts to pick out white blazes on the neighboring trees and boulders, joining one to the next. Yet the going is slow, the rocks don't offer an obvious way forward. Her heartbeat rises even faster, and she begins to feel the familiar signs of anxiety.

No, she tells herself. This is ridiculous. You're completely safe. There is no rational reason to be scared.

And yet, her heart is still hammering, and she knows in another few minutes she's going to start crying.

Get a grip. Do NOT panic.

She sits down on a boulder, fighting a wave of the old uselessness from washing over her. She is tempted to turn on the flashlight, just to reassure herself. But that would be like giving up, surrendering to the fear.

Then something breaks the silence.

A distant sound, immediately recognizable. It's the call to prayer from a mosque somewhere nearby. It floods her with relief, just to be reminded that not far from here, there are people gathering to worship. People she doesn't know, complete strangers, but still, they're other human beings. She isn't entirely alone. They're just beyond this range of hills.

So all she has to do is get to the end of this trail and she'll be fine. Follow the call to prayer. She's aware of how clichéd this scene would be, if it were to appear in a movie. A lost wanderer, falling to her knees upon hearing this sign from civilization…

Then, unexpectedly, a more pragmatic thought strikes her: if you got through the trial, you can get through this.

In all the years since, she has rarely wanted to think about those two weeks in the Belfast Courthouse, because the memories bring with them nausea and disgust. But now those memories act as a distinct reminder: I didn't survive that, just to collapse from fear in a random valley in Oman.

She gets up from the boulder, and her confidence regained, focuses on finding the next blaze.

Just concentrate on what you can see. Eventually you'll find the path.

Once or twice, she follows what appear to be blazes, only to find that they lead her up, to an uncomfortably high drop-off. She crawls back down to the valley floor, accidentally steps straight into a pool of water. But she keeps creeping along the bottom of the valley, feeling her way in the dark, for another forty, fifty minutes. The rocky hills rise higher on either side of her, and the adrenaline pumps continuously through her body. When the valley floor levels out into a wide, gravelled path, she thinks this must be the end. Surely the exit will be just around the next turn.

Only she's met with a massive wall which blocks the entire valley: a dam built to stop flash floods. Frustration grips her anew. She backtracks, almost wants to give up again, peers in the darkness for the last set of blazes. There must be another way out.

She examines the slope above her, straining to see something that could be a path, and...there. Up this hillside, there seems to be a cleared space and if she trails her eyes along it, that could be a path zigzagging upwards.

She creeps to the bottom of the slope. Crawls up using her hands and feet, scrambling to one switchback, then another, and finally she's near the top of the ridge, out of breath.

If she looks over that ridge and finds just another dark, empty valley, she doesn't think she can take it. So she hesitates for a moment in a rocky niche, preparing her for whatever lies ahead.

Just look. Don't bother delaying any longer.

And there, glowing in the blue haze of city lights, lies the town of Mutrah, the glittering waterfront along the Corniche, ringing the dark curve of the ocean. Civilization, just at the bottom of this slope and easily within reach.

She collapses with relief.

And now, she hasn't much farther to go.

She stumbles over the ridge, through a downward stretch of field. Halfway through, she realizes she's walking through a cemetery. The stone slabs of Muslim graves dot the grass around her, and she apologizes to all those souls whose graves she is treading on. But even this trace of civilization is welcome, after the empty wilderness of the place she just came from.

At the bottom of the field, she pushes through a rusty gate and looks behind her. She can see the cemetery stretching up, culminating in the jagged ridge, but nothing beyond that. No sign of the darkened valley she's just crawled through. If anything had happened to her, no one would ever know she was stranded back there. Shuddering and yet, flushed with victory, she heads into town.

Here, a dirt road soon becomes paved. Houses with lights on inside, in an open doorway, a small child swats at a cat with a broom. Two old men sit on chairs on the sidewalk, fingering *misbah* beads, and nodding at her as she walks past. If they think it's odd that she's just emerged from the back of the town, from the cemetery and the hills beyond it, they say nothing.

A block or so later, she is in the middle of town, passing a sign that indicates *Wadi Ban Khalid*. And then, she emerges back onto the Corniche, where contented tourists stroll arm in arm, locals chattering in animated groups. She can't believe how normal everything seems here, everyone going about their calm business, while half an hour ago, it felt like she was struggling for survival. The world is oblivious to what she's just gone through. And unless she tells someone, anyone, they will never know about her journey through that valley, when she felt her way through in the dark.

She glances at her watch: 6:45, right on time, according to the trail estimate. And what will she do now, for the rest of the night? She has no idea. But she's elated to be back among the living. To go from the abject terror of the dark valley, to here, surrounded by all these people. The rest of this evening is a gift. And so are all the evenings after.

EPILOGUE

"So Vivian, what did you first think when you learned that John Sweeney is now unaccounted for?"

In fact, *this* is the first time she's found out, shortly before this live radio interview. Here she is, in the middle of a business trip to Singapore, when she hears from a *journalist* that her rapist has gone missing. For some reason she cannot fully explain, she's agreed to a phone interview. So now, alone in her hotel room, she is speaking to a radio presenter in Belfast, about a person she's tried not to think about for years.

John Sweeney has violated his probation.

Her heart rate has gone up, the nausea returned, and she is annoyed that even now, over five years later, the thought of the assault still has that power over her. His actions can still exert their effect, half a world away. All that therapy, the move to another continent, immersing herself in her new career, and still her body, her instinctive reaction betrays her.

She doesn't say this to the radio presenter.

"Well, obviously I'm shocked that the authorities weren't able to keep track of him. There is a justice and law enforcement system for a reason, and if he's managed to effectively escape, then that shows the system isn't really working."

She wonders if she comes across as too rational, too intellectual.

"Yes, but how do you feel about it, knowing that your attacker is out there somewhere. Are you scared?"

"Well, I'm actually living and working several time zones away now, so I don't feel any physical threat myself. But it's not nice to think that other women and girls could be at risk, if he hasn't rehabilitated."

"Yes, but this is a fifteen-year-old boy who committed one of the worst possible crimes on *you*. Dragged you, a complete stranger, into the bushes and beat you and *raped* you. Aren't you angry?"

Yes, I'm aware of what he's done to me, she wants to tell the woman. Thank you for the reminder.

"I don't know if anger is the right emotion to have. It's quite a destructive one," she says.

"Speaking of that, it's been reported that during the rehabilitation process in prison, your attacker admitted to being a monster. What do you think? Do *you* think he's a monster?"

"Listen, I hardly know this boy. I only interacted with him for thirty minutes, so I don't think it's my place to say. Yes, he did something monstrous to me, but I'm not going to call someone I hardly know a monster."

There's a brief pause, as if the interviewer is somehow disappointed.

"But surely, Vivian, this boy is very dangerous and he's out on the streets now. The women and girls of Ireland should be fearing for their safety, shouldn't they?"

She chafes, hearing the woman call her by her name, as if they're old pals.

"Well, I'm a little hesitant to start scare-mongering like that. After all, for every rapist who does get caught and convicted, there are many others who don't. So he is certainly not the only sex offender out there."

"Vivian, you're being very generous to the boy who's done such a horrible thing to you. How have you been since the attack? Have you been able to move on?"

"It's been over five years, and yeah, I've had to work really hard to piece my life back together. I ended up moving away from Europe for a job opportunity. So I do feel like the attack is something that I've put behind me, but in some ways it'll always be part of my past."

"Well, that's great to hear, Vivian. Really encouraging. How do you feel now when you think about the incident?"

"On some level, I'll always feel sad about it. There was so much stress and anxiety tied to the event, and to the trial, that when I think about it now… it's kind of a… phantom stress that I still feel."

"And Vivian, do you think the sentence John Sweeney served was adequate? He was sentenced to ten years in prison after all, but only served five."

This had been explained to her in the past by Detective Morrison, and later various victim information schemes. Offenders rarely serve their full sentence, generally only half. That's just the way of things.

"It does seem unfair to me that the courts decided an appropriate sentence for him, but that full sentence wasn't carried out. I mean, what is the full impact that his crime will have on me? It's impossible to say, but… I don't think you can say that that's it, all my recovery has been completed in five years. Clearly, for him it isn't either, if he's run off."

"But to that point, Vivian, were you aware that just a few months ago, there were a series of community protests outside John Sweeney's home in West Belfast, when the neighborhood discovered who he was?"

More news to her. She's caught off guard on this one.

"Um, I actually wasn't aware of that."

"There was a significant community protest, over 100 people gathered outside his house in West Belfast, when they found out he was a convicted rapist. Protesting that they should have been informed beforehand. I was just wondering what are your thoughts on this? *Do* communities have a right to be informed when sex offenders are moved there?"

This is a question she's never seriously thought about before. And now she has to answer it on live radio.

"I, um… I think it's a very tricky situation. On one hand, I'd like to think that a criminal is capable of rehabilitating. And they should at least be given that chance. On the other hand, I can certainly understand why communities would want to be concerned about a convicted rapist living among them."

"But for neighborhoods to let innocent children play on

the street, right in front of where a convicted rapist could be living?"

Not all children are innocent, she thinks in annoyance. There's fifteen year olds out there who are far from it.

"Yes, I can understand a community's concern. But again, I just want to stress that for every known and convicted rapist out there, there are a great many more who remain unrecognized. So you can protest against one individual, but there are many other offenders out there who carry on with their crimes undetected. Which again is why it's very important to report any sexual assault that takes place."

"And is that your advice for victims out there who might be listening?"

"Absolutely. Don't keep it to yourself. It's very damaging emotionally to carry a burden like that around on your own. So do tell someone else, even if it's the stranger on the rape crisis hotline. And it's important to report something that does happen to you, so police can hopefully prevent that person from committing again."

She's aware it probably all sounds so rehearsed. And yet... it's true. All those other stories which trickled in, the months following her rape. They've started to accumulate, they haven't stopped.

"Well, thank you very much, Vivian, for speaking to us. It has been really good to hear from you, and we do hope that John Sweeney is apprehended soon."

"Thank you. I hope so, too."

And, like that, the interview is over. They've switched over to the next news item on their playlist and hung up. She stays where she's sitting, in the mauve upholstered armchair by the window, and she's not sure what to do next. Somewhere in Ireland, a number of strangers have tuned in, listening to her talk openly about her rape and recovery, and here, in an impersonal five-star hotel room, she has no one to talk to. She walks to the window, leans against the glass panel and looks out at the futuristic skyline, the indifferent skyscrapers above the bay.

He's out there somewhere, in a rainy, gritty part of the world. So far away, it shouldn't affect her. And yet, it has.

He's on the run. Just like her.

She picks up her phone, wondering whom she can call out of the blue like this. Her parents still don't know. Nor do her friends in Dubai. Her friends in London are probably too busy with their own lives, the last thing they need is her telling them this latest bit of strange news about a person no one wants to think about.

Don't keep it to yourself, she had said on the radio. And yet, here she is, ignoring her own advice.

What lives we lead, everyone rushing around, striving to appear successful, trying to hide the dark chapters from our past. But all those chapters gathered together could form a book, an entire library. All those other people with stories, hoping to forget the landscapes which still haunt them.

Turning her back to the Singapore skyline, she thinks of a place very different from the one outside the window. A city where you step off the plane, smell the cow shit in the air, find yourself walking past the giant behemoth of City Hall, the grid of streets that brings her to Laganside Courts, with the hills and the harbor in the distance.

There's a small park in the west of Belfast, a strip of green on either side of the narrow river, trees that overhang the stream as it winds further and further into the hills. A water bottle is lodged in the undergrowth there.

This is a place she once knew, back in another lifetime. Back when she was a different Vivian, unchanged, and then, within the course of an afternoon, irrevocably changed... and now, maybe, changed back a little bit. She thinks of two Vivians, dividing and splitting like chromosomes in a biology lesson, and then merging back into one person.

The person she is now. The person she still can be. The person she always was.

ACKNOWLEDGEMENTS

The idea for this novel occurred to me a few weeks after my own assault, but it took more than nine years of recovery and hard work for it to become a reality. This would not have been possible without the tireless support and drive of The Pontas Agency team, especially Maria Cardona and Anna Soler-Pont. Many thanks to Jessica Craig for believing in my talent.

I must thank my editors Lauren Parsons at Legend Press and Jason Pinter at Polis Books for investing their efforts and faith in *Dark Chapter*, as well as Gunilla Sondell at Norstedts and Lisanne Mathijssen at Harper Collins Holland.

I began work on *Dark Chapter* while at Goldsmiths, where Ros Barber, Rachel Seiffert, Maura Dooley, and Blake Morrison provided invaluable insight. Much gratitude to my fellow Goldsmiths students for their friendship and feedback – and to Bernardine Evaristo for encouraging me throughout the years to pursue writing seriously.

Thanks to The Literary Consultancy's Free Read Scheme, Crime Writers' Association, and SI Leeds Literary Prize for championing this novel. The Economic and Social Research Council and the Department of Media and Communications at The London School of Economics must also be thanked for enabling the final stages of my work.

Trina Vargo and Mary Lou Hartman of The US-Ireland Alliance are my real-life 'Barbara,' whose support – moral, logistical, and otherwise – has been immeasurable in the immediate and longer-term aftermath of my rape.

In Belfast, I have been blessed with many friends and advocates gained through my experience and the writing of this novel – first and foremost, Geraldine McAteer and Monica McWilliams. Stuart Griffin and the Police Service of Northern Ireland have been instrumental since Day One of my assault. For their kindness and support, I must also thank Karen Smith (née Eagleson), Dr. Patricia Beirne, Fionnuala O Connor, Victim Support Northern Ireland, Jennifer McCann, Eileen Chan-Hu, and Máiría Cahill. For helping my research, many thanks to Professor Jackie Bates-Gaston, Mairead Lavery and Simon Jenkins of the Public Prosecution Service of Northern Ireland, the Probation Board for Northern Ireland, Carol Carson, Paul Dougan, Claire Campbell, Nick Robinson, Danny and Liam Morrison, and Karen Douglas at The Rowan. Outside Belfast, my research was greatly aided by Dianne Chan, Lynne Townley, the staff at Blackfriars Crown Court, Niamh Redmond, Catherine Ghent, Tom Tuite, John McKale, Sarah Leipciger, and Dr. Nina Burrowes.

Resources and staff at An Munia Tober, Pavee Point, and The Traveller Movement helped illuminate the challenges and uniqueness of Irish Traveller culture. To this day, Traveller society remains misunderstood and misrepresented, and I do not intend for my novel (inspired as it is by my own lived experience) to portray an entire community nor to malign it.

I would not have been able to rebuild my life after my rape without the support of so many wonderful friends, for whom I unfortunately only have space to name a few: Anne Bowers, Lene Bausager, Annie Gowanloch, Catherine Hogel, Elizabeth Frascoia, Saukok Chu Tiampo, Jessica Montalvo, Arlene Dijamco Botelho, Margalit Edelman, Wiebke Pekrull, Tamara Torres McGovern, Deborah Foster. Thanks also to Dr. Jennifer Wild, the Riverside Medical Centre, and Judy Faulkner.

There are many others who contributed in small and large ways to my healing, and who continue to sustain and believe in me.

I am grateful to those who read drafts of my novel,

including Jessica Gregson, Marti Leimbach, Sharon Jackson, Siún Kearney, Kelda Crawford-McCann, Pam Drynan.

Thanks to my current flatmates Anna Kovacs, John DeWald, John Curtis, and my previous ones for being my family wherever I've lived.

But there is a larger family out there, and that includes my companions at the Clear Lines Festival, On Road Media, and the wider community of survivors and their supporters. I would not have written this novel, if not for you.

And finally, I would not be the person I am without my sister Emmeline, my Dad, and my Mom – who has always encouraged me to read, to write, and to move through this world with curiosity and compassion. Thank you for everything.

If you have been affected by this book, there are many resources out there, including:

UK: rapecrisis.org.uk or rapecrisisscotland.org.uk
or 0808 802 9999
Ireland: rapecrisishelp.ie or 1 800 778888

COME VISIT US AT
WWW.LEGENDPRESS.CO.UK

FOLLOW US
@LEGEND_PRESS